The Outlaws: Jess

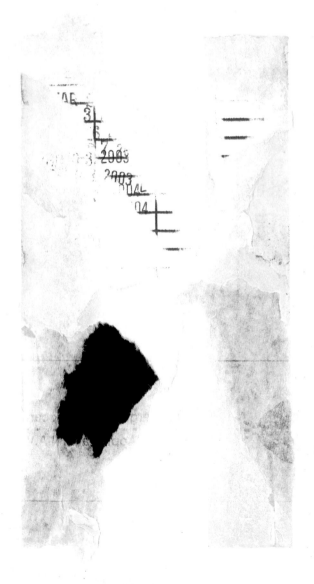

Also by Connie Mason in Large Print:

The Dragon Lord
To Love a Stranger
To Tame a Renegade
To Tempt a Rogue

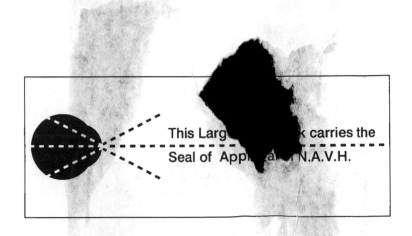

The Outlaws: Jess

Connie Mason

WHEELER
PUBLISHING

Published in 2002 by arrangement with
Leisure Books, a division of Dorchester Publishing Co., Inc.

Wheeler Large Print Softcover Series.

The text of this Large Print edition is unabridged.
Other aspects of the book may vary from the original edition.

Set in 16 pt. Plantin by Myrna S. Raven.

Printed in the United States on permanent paper.

ISBN 1-58724-354-7 (lg. print : sc : alk. paper)

The Outlaws: Jess

Chapter One

Wyoming Territory, 1868

Darkness had already fallen as Jess Gentry reined his weary horse into a stand of cottonwood trees lining the banks of the Lodgepole River. Lines of exhaustion etched his handsome features. Except during the war years, when his medical skills were needed twenty-four hours a day, he couldn't recall when he'd been this tired.

Jess dismounted, unsaddled his gelding, and tethered him to a tree, well within reach of sweet grass and water. Dimly he wondered if he dared ride into Cheyenne tomorrow and spend the last of his money on much-needed supplies. He felt fairly confident he wouldn't be recognized; it was too soon for Wanted posters to have reached Wyoming territory.

Jess stretched his weary bones and set about building a fire from dry wood and kindling he found nearby. Once the fire had caught, he rifled through his dwindling sack of supplies for the battered coffeepot he'd picked up in some nameless northwest Kansas border town. With dragging steps he walked down to the river and filled the pot with water. He produced a nearly empty sack of coffee, dumped it into the water, and set the pot on the fire to boil.

While he waited for the coffee, he found some beef jerky, a dry biscuit, and a single can of beans. He opened the beans with his knife and placed his dinner on the ground beside a battered tin plate and bent tin cup.

Almost too weary to eat, Jess leaned back against his saddle and sucked appreciatively on the freshly brewed coffee. It was just the way he liked it. Hot and murky. Strong enough to curl his toes. He closed his eyes and savored the hot liquid as it settled in his stomach like a welcome blast of heat on a cold winter day.

Unwelcome images appeared behind Jess's closed eyelids. The war. The dead. The horrible stench of mutilated flesh. Flesh he'd tried to repair. Men died. Young men with beardless faces, looking at him with hope-filled eyes. Older men with hardened visages, hoping for a miracle but too battle-scarred to expect one.

God, war is so senseless, Jess thought with a sigh. Nonetheless, he had served the Confederacy proudly, saving men who would have died without his skills. In the end, the Confederacy had been demolished, never to rise again, but Jess knew his skills would always be needed.

He was very nearly asleep when he heard

someone approaching his campsite. Abruptly sluggishness fell away, replaced by wary caution as he drew his gun and waited, his body tense and alert.

Two men rode up to the perimeter of the campsite and dismounted.

"Howdy, pilgrim," one of the men greeted. "Smelled your coffee a mile away. Mind if we join ya?"

"I only have one cup, and I'm using it," Jess hedged, none too eager to welcome the rough-looking men into his camp. Each wore a week's worth of beard and smelled of beer and stale perfume, the kind preferred by whores.

"We have our own cups," the man said.

"In that case, help yourselves," Jess replied, slapping his gun back in his holster.

"Much obliged. You from around here?"

"No, I'm from Kansas."

"Kansas, huh. Me and Lucky visited Kansas a while back. The name's Calder, Jay Calder. This here's my brother Lucky."

"You're the Calder brothers?" Jess blurted out before he could stop himself. The Calder brothers had robbed a bank in Topeka a few months ago and killed a man. But he'd heard there were three brothers, not two.

Jay poked his brother in the ribs. "What do ya know? The pilgrim's heard of us." He gave Jess an assessing glance. "You have the look of a man on the run yourself."

"You could say that," Jess said cryptically. He wasn't about to admit anything to these hardened outlaws.

"Well, well, birds of a feather," Lucky guffawed. "What's your handle, pilgrim?"

"Jess will do."

Jay retrieved two tin cups from his saddlebags, filled them with coffee, and handed one to Lucky. Then they sat cross-legged on the ground, rolled cigarettes, and smoked and drank.

"I heard there were three Calder brothers," Jess ventured.

Jay's mouth turned downward into a fierce scowl. "We buried Danny yesterday. He took a bullet during a bank robbery we pulled in Cheyenne two days ago. Thought he was gonna be okay but he bled to death before we could get him to a doctor we trusted. Damn shame. He was the baby of the family. Don't know how we're gonna explain it to Ma. Promised her we'd look after him."

They drank in silence, the Calders mourning their younger brother and Jess wondering how in the hell he was going to get out of this with his skin intact.

A gentle breeze stirred the air as the figure garbed in black crouched unseen behind a cottonwood tree. So stealthy was the mysterious figure's approach that neither Jess nor the Calders was aware of being watched. Hat pulled low over a face obscured by darkness, the watching stranger drew and cocked a pair of lethal-looking six-shooters.

While the three men were relaxed and inattentive, the intruder emerged from the darkness beyond the campsite and boldly stepped into the circle of flickering firelight with both guns drawn.

Jess and the Calders jumped to their feet, each man reaching for his gun.

"Freeze. Hands over your heads. Make one move for your guns and I'll shoot. Dead or alive, it makes no difference to me."

The voice was low, throaty, almost feral.

"A goddamn bounty hunter," Jay spat. "Where in the hell did you come from?"

"I'm here, that's all that matters. Drop your gun belts. Bringing in all three Calders at once is a bonus I hadn't counted on."

"Now hold on a minute," Jess blustered. "I'm not a Calder."

The bounty hunter's eyes slid in Jess's direction, skewering him with a contemptuous glare. "Shut up. You and your brothers killed a bank guard in Cheyenne two days ago. I don't care who did it, you're all guilty."

"But I'm not —"

"Drop your guns," the bounty hunter repeated. "Real nice and easy." When Jay was slow to act, the bounty hunter aimed a shot so precise that it nicked Jay's ear.

"Owwww!" Jay yowled, clapping a hand

over his ear. "You didn't need to go and do that."

"Then do as I say."

The voice was so coldly challenging that Jess gave an involuntary shiver. He unbuckled his gun belt and let it drop. Lucky followed suit; so did Jay. The bounty hunter walked more fully into the light, revealing a tall, slim figure clad in unrelieved black; trousers that hugged hips far too shapely to belong to a man; baggy shirt tucked into the waistband spanning a narrow waist; and black hat that concealed nearly every facial feature but for startling green eyes.

"You," the bounty hunter said, nodding at Jess. "Get your rope and tie up your brothers. Don't try anything funny if you value your life."

Jess bent to retrieve his rope from his saddle and gingerly approached Lucky, intending to tie him first. The bounty hunter was too trigger-happy for his liking and he wasn't going to do anything to rile him. Later the authorities would discover the mistake and all would be well. Unless, of course, they somehow learned that Jess Gentry was a wanted man.

Suddenly all hell broke loose. From somewhere in his clothing Lucky produced a small pistol. The bounty hunter realized the danger and got off a shot at the same time Lucky fired. Jess watched in horror as both shots hit their mark. Lucky did a slow spiral to the ground, a blossom of red spreading beneath his shoulder. The bounty hunter let out an unmanly, high-pitched scream and pitched forward.

Jay fell to his knees beside his brother at the same time as Jess ran to the bounty hunter.

"He's alive!" Jay cried. "Ya ain't gonna die like Danny, are ya, Lucky?"

"Get me to a doctor," Lucky gasped, holding his wounded shoulder. "That damn bounty hunter shot me."

"I know," Jay bit out. "I'll take care of him. We gotta get you to a doctor pronto."

He glanced over at Jess, who had turned over the bounty hunter and was feeling for a pulse. "Is the bastard dead?" Jay asked.

Jess was on the verge of lying to save the bounty hunter's life. Unfortunately, the fool chose that moment to emit a loud groan.

"He's still alive!" Jay spat. "Kill him, pilgrim. If you don't, I will."

Jay scrambled on the ground for his gun belt and drew out a gun, turning it on the bounty hunter. Jess knew he had to think fast and act faster if he hoped to save the bounty hunter's life.

"I'll do it," Jess said, reaching for his gun belt.

Jay gave Jess a hard look, then turned back to his brother. Jess stood and aimed his gun several inches wide of the bounty hunter's head. Abruptly the bounty hunter opened eyes as green as grass and stared up at him. Jess's hand faltered.

"What's keeping ya?" Jay called out. "Are ya too chicken to kill a man? Should I come there and do it myself?"

"No, take care of your brother. Press on the wound to stop the bleeding. I can do this."

"Make it fast. I ain't leaving until I know the bastard's dead."

Those unwavering green eyes were still focused on him. He saw neither fear nor pleading in their startling depths. What he recognized was acceptance, and perhaps regret.

"Close your eyes and don't move," Jess whispered, hoping the bounty hunter had the presence of mind to realize what he intended.

Holding his hand steady, he fired into the ground scant inches from the bounty hunter's head. Then he immediately dropped to his knees and smeared blood from the previous wound onto the bounty hunter's head, making it appear as if Jess's shot had been a fatal one.

"Is the bastard dead?" Jay called out.

"Can't get any deader," Jess replied.

Jay gave the bounty hunter a cursory glance. "Good. I gotta get Lucky to the doc. Why don't ya join us? We could use another gun."

"Reckon I'll have to decline," Jess replied. "Always been a loner. Go on, get your brother to a doctor before he bleeds to death."

"Yeah, you're right. If I were you, I'd high-tail it away from Cheyenne before the body is found."

The tense silence nearly got the best of Jess as he watched Jay hoist a swaying Lucky up into his saddle. By some miracle, Lucky kept his seat and the two outlaws rode off. It couldn't have been too soon to suit Jess. He turned back to the bounty hunter, praying it wasn't too late to save his life. He dropped to his knees, noting that the bounty hunter's eyes were closed.

Jess lifted the man's shoulders so he could peel off his vest. He stared in mute disbelief as the man's hat fell off, releasing a cloud of long black hair. Resisting the obvious conclusion, Jess refused to believe what his eyes were telling him.

Carefully he removed the bounty hunter's leather vest. With shaking fingers he unbuttoned the black shirt, revealing a blood-soaked camisole trimmed in dainty lace. He stared in disbelief and no little amount of dismay.

What in the hell? A woman!

Never in his life had Jess encountered anything so ridiculously absurd. Women belonged at home, raising children, cooking,

15

and seeing to their husband's needs, not traipsing around the countryside packing guns and chasing outlaws. The profusion of blood spreading over the woman's right breast turned Jess's thoughts to more important matters. It wasn't for him to judge another human being; his mission in life was to heal people.

Focused now on saving a life, Jess retrieved his black medical bag, which never left his sight, and returned to the wounded woman. He used his scalpel to cut away the bloodied shift, concentrating on the gaping wound instead of the most perfect pair of breasts Jess had ever seen. Milky white mounds topped with pert, rosy nipples.

Reaching once more into his bag, Jess uncorked a bottle of carbolic acid and poured it over his hands. Then he probed the wound with his finger. The woman moaned and opened her eyes.

"Don't . . . touch . . . me . . ." Her voice was filled with pain.

"I'm not going to hurt you. The bullet has to come out. I have some laudanum in my bag that should help dull the pain."

"Don't . . . touch . . . me . . ." she repeated through clenched teeth.

"Look, lady," he explained gently, "either I remove the bullet or you die. Those are your only options, and there's no time to waste. You've lost a lot of blood."

Vivid, pain-filled green eyes bored into him. "Your brothers . . ."

"They aren't my brothers and they're gone." He reached into his bag for the laudanum. "Are you going to cooperate or do I have to pour this down your throat?"

She pressed her lips together and gave him a belligerent glare.

Jess sighed. He was so damn weary; he shouldn't have to deal with this. Uncapping the laudanum, he held it to the woman's lips. When she refused to drink, he pinched her nostrils until her mouth opened; then he poured a generous dose down her throat.

She shuddered, gagged, and swallowed. Satisfied, Jess sat back on his haunches and laid out his instruments on a white cloth he'd brought from the depths of his bag. Then he poured carbolic acid over the lot. By the time he'd built up the fire to provide sufficient light for the surgery and turned back to his patient, she had fallen under the spell of the laudanum.

"Good," Jess said to himself as he reached for the scalpel. He didn't want to hurt her any more than he had to.

Jess studied the wound before probing for the bullet. The bullet had entered two inches below her shoulder, just above her right breast, narrowly missing the lung. His concentration was so intense that beads of sweat dotted his forehead and ran into his eyes. His

17

hand was steady as the scalpel bit into flesh and hit lead. Jess's relief was profound as he eased the bullet out. The rush of blood that followed worried him, and he exerted pressure until the bleeding slowed to a trickle.

When he poured carbolic acid into the wound, a scream ripped from her throat. He soothed her as best he could, gave her another dose of laudanum, and waited until she quieted to close the wound. His hands were shaking as he held a needle to the light and looped fine silk thread through the eye. But they steadied when he turned back to his patient. He had done this countless times in the past, but this was the first time he'd dug a bullet from a woman's tender flesh.

With neat, precise stitches, Jess closed the wound and bandaged it with strips of gauze. Then he sat back to inspect his work. There was a good chance the woman would live if she was strong enough to fight the fever that would soon follow.

There was little Jess could do now but make the woman comfortable. He placed his bedroll near the fire, carefully lifted her onto one blanket, and covered her with another. Then he sat beside her on the hard ground to wait and watch. Though Jess tried to remain wakeful, his weary body betrayed him and he dozed off. He awoke with a start when the woman cried out and began to thrash around.

"Zach! I hurt."

Her voice was hoarse, her face contorted. Jess was beside her instantly, bathing her face and holding his canteen to her lips.

"Here, drink."

She took a sip, gagged, then fell back into a stupor. Jess fed more kindling to the fire, then returned to his vigil beside her, pondering the unusual circumstances that might have led a beautiful woman to become a bounty hunter. And the woman *was* beautiful. Beautiful and shapely. He should have known she was a female the moment he saw those long feminine legs encased in tight trousers. And the voice. Low and throaty, too soft to belong to a male.

Damn! A female bounty hunter. What in God's good name would force a woman into so dangerous a profession? What were her parents thinking? Or her husband? Who was Zach? Obviously someone she loved. If Zach were here now, Jess would pound some sense into the man. What kind of man would allow a fragile woman to chase after vicious outlaws? The longer he thought about it, the angrier he became. She could have been killed. If he hadn't been a skilled doctor, she'd most likely be lying dead in a pool of her own blood.

Unable to keep his eyes open, Jess drifted off to sleep. He awoke to daylight, abruptly aware of luminous green eyes staring at him.

19

Meg Lincoln had been awake a good ten minutes, her thoughts in a turmoil. The man she recalled from her vague memory of last night was sitting beside her, his arms resting on his bent knees, his head bowed. He was sleeping. She could see little except his thick, sun-streaked brown hair.

She knew he was one of the Calder brothers, but found it difficult to reconcile what she knew about the outlaw brothers with this man who possessed the skills of a trained doctor. To her knowledge, none of the Calders had ever studied medicine.

Meg stifled a groan. She hurt so damn bad, tears sprang to her eyes and rolled down her cheeks. She wanted Zach. He'd always been there when she needed him.

Suddenly the man stirred, lifted his head, and stared at her. His eyes were hazel, she thought, with golden flecks in their centers. It surprised her that she would notice such details when she hurt so much. His eyes weren't the only thing she noticed. The man was handsome in a rugged sort of way. Broad forehead, a bold slash of a nose, wide mouth and full lips. None of his features were classic, but put together they seemed to work in a way most women would admire. He was a large man, sleekly muscled and thoroughly masculine.

"You're awake."

20

His voice held a trace of a Southern accent. She liked that, but shoved the startling thought aside. She had more important things to deal with.

"Why didn't you ride off with your brothers?" Her voice was little more than a croak. She wet her parched lips with the tip of her tongue but had little moisture to give.

"Would you like some water?"

She nodded weakly. He held the canteen to her lips.

"Drink slowly," he cautioned.

Meg took a sip, then another, letting the life-giving liquid soothe her throat.

"That's enough for now. How do you feel?"

"Like I've taken . . . a cannonball. You . . . didn't . . . answer my question."

"The Calders aren't my brothers. I tried to tell you that before, but you wouldn't listen. They barged into my campsite shortly before you arrived. I never saw them before in my life."

"I . . . don't believe . . . you."

"Suit yourself, lady. But why would I save your life if I was one of the Calders?"

Meg didn't know what to believe. She knew three men had robbed the bank, and that they had been positively identified as the Calder brothers. She couldn't think straight. Pain had reduced her to a mindless lump of pure agony. She'd sort it all out when she could think coherently.

"Are you in pain?"

She nodded weakly.

"I'll give you some laudanum."

He lifted her head, held the bottle to her lips, and tipped it up. This time she swallowed without offering an argument.

"What's your name?"

"Meg Lincoln."

"I'm Jess Gentry."

Jess Gentry, Meg thought as the laudanum took effect and her mind shut down. It was a lie. It had to be. The man was a Calder. She just had to figure out why he possessed medical skills and why he had chosen to save her life.

"Sleep," Jess said, brushing damp curls away from her flushed face. "You're going to need all the strength you possess to get you through this."

"Zach." The name slipped unbidden from her lips as she slid into unconsciousness.

Jess studied Meg's features while she slept. She couldn't be more than twenty-one or two, he decided. In sleep, her face was wiped free of pain. Her broad forehead was smooth and unlined above perfectly arched brows. She had high cheekbones, full, lush lips, eyes that slanted upward at the outer corners. She was a damn provocative female.

Someone ought to talk some sense into her, Jess decided. Did she have a death wish or something? Only a woman who cared little for life would take up so dangerous a profession. Looking back on her bold entrance to his campsite, he decided she must be one cool character with nerves of steel.

Rising stiffly, Jess stretched and walked down to the river to wash and refresh himself. Taking off his shirt, he splashed water over his face, shoulders, and torso. He contemplated taking a full bath but decided to wait until later. When Meg awoke she'd need nourishment. His first order of business was to bag a fat rabbit and boil it up into a rich broth. He also needed to find Meg's horse.

Jess put his shirt back on and returned to camp. Meg was still sleeping. He checked his guns, strapped on his gun belt, and disappeared into the shadows of the cottonwoods. He found Meg's mare tethered to a tree a few hundred yards from the campsite, happily munching grass. He left the mare for the time being and continued on his quest for food.

Thirty minutes and two rabbits later, he retraced his steps to Meg's horse and returned to camp with rabbits and mare in tow.

Meg slept on as Jess gutted and cleaned the rabbits and put one in the battered coffeepot to boil and staked the other over the fire to cook. Then he checked Meg for fever, pleased to find her temperature only slightly elevated, and inspected her wound for infection.

So far so good, Jess thought with relief as he sat down beside Meg. Unfortunately, things could change quickly with wounds such as Meg had sustained. He was gazing off into the distance, thinking about Rafe and Sam, when Meg awakened and spoke to him.

"Am I going to die?"

Jess's thoughts snapped back to the present and his gaze swung around to the lady bounty hunter. "Not if I can help it."

"I'm thirsty."

Jess carefully lifted her head, reached for his canteen, and held it to her lips. She drank deeply, sighed, and indicated she'd had enough.

"How are you feeling?" Jess asked, studying her pallor with a critical eye. She'd lost too much blood for his liking.

"Like I've got one foot in the grave. I still don't understand why you didn't leave with your brothers."

"I'm not a Calder," Jess replied shortly. "I told you my name last night."

Meg regarded him with confusion. "Jess Gentry. I remember, but . . ."

"Just concentrate on getting well. We'll sort everything else out later."

"I want to go home."

"You can't be moved yet. In a few days, maybe. We'll have to wait and see what develops in the next few hours."

Meg's eyes grew round. "Like what? I can still die, can't I?"

"Well, there's always the possibility of infection. I doused your wound with carbolic acid and I'm hoping it was enough to prevent infection. If not, a high fever is bound to follow. But don't worry, I'm a doctor. I know what to do to help you."

Jess saw disbelief march across Meg's features. Obviously she wasn't of a mind to take his word for anything. But he had more important things to worry about, like saving her life.

"I'm going to give you some more laudanum," Jess said, reaching for the bottle. "Rest is the best thing for you right now. When you awaken, I'll feed you some rabbit broth. You'll need it to keep up your strength."

Meg shook her head. "No. No more laudanum. I can't think when I'm drugged."

"Don't think. Just concentrate on getting well. You want to return to Zach, don't you?"

Meg sent him a startled look. "How do you know about Zach?"

"You called for him in the night. Is he your husband?"

Meg shook her head.

"Brother?" Another negative shake. "Father?"

"No."

25

Jess abruptly cut off his questioning. Clearly Zach was Meg's lover. Jess wished the man were here now so he could give him a good dressing-down. No man in his right mind would allow his woman to turn to bounty hunting for a living.

"Open your mouth, Meg," Jess said sternly. "I'll just give you enough laudanum to dull the pain."

Meg stared at him, then opened her mouth with marked reluctance. Before long she fell asleep. When she awakened several hours later, Jess patiently fed her broth and bits of rabbit meat. She fell asleep again. Jess built up the fire and settled down for the night on the bedroll he'd taken from Meg's saddle.

Her cry in the night pulled him from a deep sleep, and he sprang to her side. It didn't take a genius to recognize the irrefutable signs of infection. Meg was drenched in perspiration, thrashing from side to side, damp strands of dark hair plastered to her pale face. Her body burned with fever that would kill her if it wasn't lowered.

Disregarding propriety, he stripped off her trousers and drawers, picked her up, and carried her to the stream. Though the night was warm, the water was cool. Sitting in the water, he held her on his lap, letting the water spill over her heated flesh. He held her like that until her body felt cool to the touch. Then he carried her back to her bedroll and pulled away the bandage covering her wound.

The sickening stench of infection immediately cast him back into the last days of the war, when the wounded piled up so fast that they died before they could be treated. Those horrible days and hectic times weighed heavily upon Jess as he stared down on the unconscious woman stretched out on the ground.

I won't let you die! he silently vowed. He'd seen too many men perish, smelled the nauseating odor of death too often to give up now. Jess would defy the devil himself to save this woman. Stiffening his shoulders, he set to work to save Meg's life.

First he disinfected his hands and scalpel. His hands were steady as he cut into the infected flesh. Greenish pus spurted out, but he ignored it, pressing on the wound until the blood ran clean and red. Then he disinfected the wound with carbolic acid. He decided not to sew it up, preferring to leave it open to drain. It would leave a scar, but what was a scar compared to one's life? Lastly, he fastened a clean bandage over the wound.

As Jess washed up at the stream, he prayed that his skill had been enough to save Meg's life. No one as young and vital as Meg deserved to die.

Chapter Two

Jess worked throughout the night and into the next day to save Meg's life. He made countless trips to the river to fetch cool water to bathe her feverish body. He alternately spooned broth and water into her mouth and coaxed her to swallow a medicinal concoction to bring down the fever. He reopened the wound and squeezed out pus at least two more times.

Jess tried to retain a professional manner as he cared for Meg's personal needs, but because he was a man, because he simply couldn't help himself, he looked at her. At the sweet curve of her breasts and the long, shapely turn of her calves and sleek thighs. Not an ounce of fat rested anywhere on her taut, athletic body. Yet everything about her was softly feminine. With an effort, he forced sexual thoughts from his head and concentrated on his patient.

Three hellish days passed as Jess fought for Meg's life. On the fourth day, Jess rejoiced at the first indication that she would recover. Her fever broke, leaving her eyes clear for the first time in days. More importantly, her wound no longer oozed pus.

"I'm alive."

Her voice sounded as if she'd been chewing on gravel.

"Did you doubt it?"

"There were times . . ." Her words fell off and she grew thoughtful. "How long have I been like this?"

"Six days from the time you were shot. For a while I feared you wouldn't make it. Welcome back to the world of the living."

"I never thought I'd owe my life to an outlaw," Meg rasped.

"You don't. When you're ready to listen, I'll explain the mix-up. Right now we need to get some nourishment into you. Are you hungry?"

She shook her head. "Just thirsty."

"I can fix that." He held his canteen to her lips and she drank greedily.

"Help me to sit up," she said when she had drunk her fill.

Jess eyed her skeptically. "You're too weak."

"Lying in bed won't bring back my strength. I have to get home. Zach is surely worried sick by now."

Zach again, Jess thought. She'd called to him so many times in the past several days, he had grown thoroughly sick of the name.

"Zach shouldn't have let you leave home in the first place. What kind of man would let his woman chase after outlaws?"

Meg bristled angrily. "You don't know Zach. You have no right to criticize. Are you going to help me or do I have to do it myself?"

"Lie still," Jess said. "Moving around will only aggravate your wound. It's looking pretty good right now, but I can't guarantee a full recovery unless you follow orders. I shot a prairie chicken this morning and made some broth. After you've eaten, I'll consider your request."

Meg watched him through shuttered lids as he poured broth and bits of meat into a cup and carried it back to her.

"I won't eat unless I can sit up to do it," Meg insisted.

"You're one stubborn female," Jess growled. "Very well, I'll bring your saddle over to support your back. Try not to move around too much."

Jess brought Meg's saddle over to her bedroll and placed it behind her. Then he carefully lifted her, propping her against it.

Meg sucked in her breath, gripped in the throes of agony. But the debilitating pain wasn't the worst of it. She suddenly realized she was naked but for a bandage covering the upper part of her right breast. She grabbed for the blanket with her uninjured left hand and dragged it up to her neck.

"My clothes! Where are they?"

"I washed the blood from them the best I

could. I'll bring them to you when you're ready for them again."

"You undressed me!"

Jess raised a finely etched brow. "Do you see anyone else around? Look, Meg, I'm a doctor."

"You're a man!" Her voice held an edge of panic.

"Relax, Meg. You're my patient. I have no interest in you as a woman."

Meg was unconvinced. Experience had taught her that all men, except for Zach, who had proven his trustworthiness, were despicable animals. Zach was the kindest, gentlest man she knew. He would never hurt her, unlike most men roaming the earth.

"How do I know you're a doctor?"

"You're alive. What further proof do you need?" He spooned up a bit of meat and broth and held it to her lips. "Open."

The delicious aroma wafted up to tempt her, and her mouth opened of its own accord. Jess carefully spooned the mixture into her mouth, then another, and another, until the cup was empty.

"More?" he asked, pleased to see that her appetite had returned. She was still pale, but her lips weren't nearly as bloodless as they had been.

"That's enough for now. I want my clothes."

"Not yet."

"I have to . . ." She flushed and looked away.

"Ah," Jess said, immediately aware of her needs. "I can carry you down to the river. You can use a bath, anyway. Just don't get your wound wet."

"I can walk . . ."

"Absolutely not."

Meg turned a bright red as Jess knelt beside her, pulled the blanket away, and lifted her into his arms.

"You can't . . . this isn't . . ."

"Relax, Meg. You're my patient, remember? I see you only as someone who needs my help."

Liar! Jess thought to himself. He was profoundly aware that the bundle he held in his arms was naked female flesh. He had nursed Meg through days of illness, knew her body intimately, yet not as intimately as he would like. Try though he might, there wasn't ever a time these past days when he hadn't viewed her as a desirable woman.

He reached the river and carried her a few feet into the water. Then he lowered her to the sandy bottom and stepped away.

"Will you be all right if I leave you to fetch soap and a towel?"

"Just go," Meg said through gritted teeth.

Jess gave a curt nod and retraced his steps to the campsite. When he returned with soap and towel, Meg was still sitting where he had left her, letting the gentle current wash over her. It reminded him that he needed a bath himself, and a shave. He sat on a log and pulled off his boots.

"Did you bring the soap?" Meg asked.

He held out his hand, palm up. "It's right here. I'll bring it to you. I could use a bath myself."

He unfastened his belt and worked his trousers down his legs. Meg let out a squawk of dismay. "Can't you wait until I'm through? This is . . . indecent."

Jess gave her a hard look. "I'm sure I'm not the first naked man you've seen. Turn your head; you don't have to look."

Meg's head whipped around, but not before she got a tantalizing glimpse of strong legs lightly furred with soft brown hair. She was relieved to note that he wore drawers, and that it looked as if he meant to keep them on.

Meg kept her gaze averted as Jess waded into the river. He sat down behind her, and she felt the soap slide over her back. She stiffened. "I can do that."

"No, you can't." When he finished with her back, he handed her the soap. "Remember, don't get the bandage wet." Then he swam off into deeper water.

Meg washed as best she could. She was tiring fast and needed to lie down. Jess was right. She was still weak; she couldn't have stood on her own if her life depended upon it.

Not a moment too soon, Jess waded back to her. "Are you ready to go back?" He searched her face. "You're pale. This has been too much for you."

"I'm . . . ready," Meg said. Why did her voice have to tremble so? "Did you bring a towel? There's one in my saddlebags."

"I found it. Are you ready? Put your good arm around my neck."

Meg obeyed, wincing when her right shoulder was jostled as he lifted her out of the water. He strode to the log where he'd left the towel and sat down with her in his lap. Then he picked up the towel and used it to dry her. He worked very carefully so as not to disturb the bandage. When Jess's hands moved slowly down her torso, Meg plucked the towel from his hand.

"I can finish, thank you."

Jess gave her a lopsided grin and rose carefully, holding her in his arms. Then he retraced his steps to camp and returned her to her bedroll. She snatched the blanket up to her neck with uncommon haste.

"I suggest you try to sleep now. You've had enough exercise for your first day out of bed. I'll try to hunt up something for our dinner while you're napping."

"I'm . . . not . . . tired," Meg said, stifling a yawn. "Maybe I'll just close my eyes for a moment."

"You do that," Jess said as he walked away

to retrieve his clothing from the stream bank. When he turned back to tell her he wouldn't be long, she'd already fallen asleep.

A purple dusk was swiftly closing in when Meg awakened. A mouthwatering aroma brought a spurt of saliva to her mouth. She felt pangs of hunger for the first time since she'd been shot.

"Did you have a good nap?" Jess asked, kneeling beside her.

"Did I sleep long?"

"Long enough."

"I think I can eat something now. That's a good sign, isn't it?"

"A very good sign. I'll bring food as soon as I change your bandage."

He started to pull down the blanket and stopped abruptly when Meg placed a hand over his. "Do you have to?"

"Meg, take your hand away. I've already seen everything you've got. Your body is as familiar to me as my own."

Meg gave a soft cry and turned her head aside, unable to look him in the eye. Did he have to remind her? "Very well. Do what you must."

Jess worked swiftly, removing the old bandage and placing a new one over the wound. "You're healing nicely but you'll always bear a scar. Are you in pain? There's still some laudanum left."

"No! No laudanum. I can bear the pain."

"There," Jess said, pulling the blanket up to her chin. "All done. That wasn't so bad, was it?"

"I . . . suppose not."

"Are you ready to eat now?"

"Help me sit up."

This time she held on to the blanket as he helped her into a sitting position. When she was settled comfortably against her saddle, he returned with a battered tin plate filled with savory rabbit stew.

"I'm glad it's not broth again," Meg said, sniffing appreciatively. "Where did you get the vegetables?"

"I found the wild onions and bought the potatoes and carrots from a farmer. I happened upon a farmhouse while I was out hunting." What he didn't say was that he'd used nearly the last of his dwindling supply of money to purchase the vegetables.

Meg held the plate on her lap and clumsily spooned food into her mouth with her left hand. "It's very good."

"Do you need help?"

"No, thank you. I can manage."

And manage she did, settling back against the saddle after she'd cleaned her plate.

Jess washed the dishes in the stream and returned. He dropped down beside her and felt her forehead. It was cool to the touch.

"When can I leave?" Meg asked.

He searched her face. "Let's play it by ear.

36

I don't want you to suffer a relapse."

Meg heaved an exasperated sigh. "Why should I believe anything you say? I found you with the Calders. Three brothers robbed the bank. *Three,* not two. Your story sounds pretty far-fetched to me. How do I know you're not lying to me? Why should I believe you're Jess Gentry and not a Calder?"

"Because of the simple fact that Danny Calder is dead. Jay told me he took a bullet during the bank robbery and died from loss of blood before they could get him to a doctor."

Meg found it difficult to believe him despite his medical skills. "Where do you fit in?"

"I don't. I had no idea who they were when they stumbled upon my campsite. They weren't shy about offering their names or bragging about their exploits. I was wondering how I was going to save my skin when you appeared from out of nowhere."

"Danny Calder is dead?"

"So they said, and I have no reason to doubt them. How can you question my skill? You wouldn't have pulled through without medical help. I saw many nasty infections during the war, but yours was one of the worst."

"You were a doctor in the war?"

He nodded.

"You were a Rebel, weren't you?"

Jess gave her a lopsided smile. "It's my voice, isn't it? Rafe and Sam lost all traces of their Southern accents, but mine persists no matter how hard I try to lose it."

"Who are Rafe and Sam?"

For a moment Meg thought he wasn't going to answer; then he said, "My brothers."

"Tell me about them. Where do you hail from?"

Jess refused to meet her gaze. "I don't care to talk about them or myself right now. I'm more concerned about convincing you I'm Dr. Jess Gentry."

The intensity of his feelings, his sincerity, urged her to accept his claim. But she wasn't going to let her guard down. Doctor or not, a man was still a man. Zach was the only male she trusted.

"Very well," she said grudgingly.

"Do you want to tell me how and why you became a bounty hunter?"

Meg went still. "I don't think so."

"What about Zach? What's he to you?"

"I'm tired, Jess. Good night," she said.

Jess wisely chose not to pursue the subject. Meg's life was none of his business. Why should he care if she wanted to risk it hunting down dangerous outlaws? *Because you saved her life and you'd hate to think something like this could happen to her again,* he told himself.

"Good night, Meg."

★ ★ ★

The following day Meg awakened before Jess and gingerly eased herself to a sitting position. When she succeeded with only moderate pain, she raised herself to her knees, struggled to her feet, and headed for the nearest tree, dragging up one of the blankets to cover her nakedness.

Two steps, then two more. Her legs wobbled dangerously, and she proceeded with caution. Then suddenly she felt a strong arm steadying her and she relaxed briefly against Jess's broad chest.

"I'm fine, now, thank you."

"Why didn't you say you had to relieve yourself?"

Her chin went up. "I thought I could manage."

His arm tightened around her waist. "You're one stubborn female. Let me help you. Call out when you're finished and I'll help you back."

Meg nodded, thrilled that she'd made it this far on her own. Each step she took without help was a step closer to home and away from Jess Gentry. She didn't like the way she'd come to depend on him. There were too many things she didn't know about him. What was he doing out on the prairie alone? He didn't look like an outlaw, but being on the run from the law was the usual reason men refused to divulge the past. Jess might be a doctor, and he might have saved her life, but only a fool would trust a man who kept secrets about his past.

Meg finally got her clothing back. Jess helped her don her shirt and slide on her trousers, though it embarrassed her to have him play her maid. She kept reminding herself that Jess was a doctor, that he was accustomed to seeing unclothed women. She would have been horrified had she known that Jess's experience with treating women was limited. He had joined the war shortly after graduating from medical school, and men had made up the bulk of his patients to date.

"When do you think I can leave?" Meg asked again once she was decently clothed.

"Another day or two. How long will it us take to reach your home?"

"Us? Look, Jess, you don't need to accompany me. I can find my way home by myself. It's not far."

"You're not strong enough," Jess said with a stern shake of his head. "Listen to your doctor. I'll see you home." *And give that man of yours a good talking-to before I leave,* he thought but did not say.

The following day Jess allowed Meg to walk around a bit. Though she moved stiffly, he was satisfied with her progress. She was still pale and drawn and appeared to have lost weight, but she was so anxious to return to her Zach that he decided they could leave the following morning. He began making preparations and advised Meg of his decision.

"We're leaving!" Meg exclaimed. "Thank God. I know Zach must be frantic with worry. I rarely stay out longer than a week. If I don't have my man by then, he's probably left the area and his trail is cold."

"I hope this teaches you a lesson," Jess said with marked sarcasm. "Leave men's work to men and concentrate on something better suited to your gender. Like getting married and having children."

Meg faced him squarely, her expression belligerent. "Are you one of those men who believe women are inferior to men?"

Jess took one look at Meg's outraged features and sparkling green eyes and was aware of only one thing. He wanted to kiss her. Badly. Her pouting lips were pursed enticingly; he couldn't recall when he'd last kissed a beautiful woman. And despite her near brush with death, Meg Lincoln was beautiful, provocative, and far too tempting to resist.

Gently, so as not to hurt her injured right side, he drew her close. "Meg, I don't think that at all. I believe men should protect women, and obviously your Zach isn't doing a very good job of that. You're very beautiful, you know. You could have any man you want. Perhaps Zach isn't right for you."

She gave him a perplexed look. "Zach is . . ."

"No, I don't want to hear it. Just think about what I've said. I don't want to see you hurt again."

Her lips hovered so close to his, he could feel her sweet breath fan his cheek, see her green eyes widen with sudden awareness. Her breath hitched; he felt her body tense, and knew intuitively she experienced the same sexual attraction that made his body swell with desire.

Damn! This was no time to form an attraction to a woman, Jess thought. Meg was still weak and vulnerable and didn't need his lustful inclinations adding to her woes. But her lips! All he had to do was lean forward and . . .

The kiss was inevitable, but what happened during the kiss stunned him. The intimacy was searing, intoxicating. He expected her to draw away from him, but she shocked him when her lips softened and melted against his. He nudged her lips apart and slipped his tongue inside to explore the inner contours of her mouth. His arm slipped around her waist. A groan of pleasure reverberated from his throat as the tips of her unbound breasts brushed his chest and her loins meshed with his. He heard her whimper as he deepened the kiss.

"Meg . . . you taste . . . so damn . . . good."

His words must have awakened her defenses for she broke off the kiss and shoved him away with her good arm.

With an effort, he returned to reality, releasing her instantly. "I'm sorry," he said, backing away. "I don't know what got into me."

"You're a man," she said with scathing contempt. "It's what men do."

Meg was truly frightened. For the first time in her life she'd experienced desire, and she didn't like it. She'd lost control, something she rarely did. When Jess kissed her, a ripple of heat radiated through her body. She felt as if she were drowning in feelings, feelings that had no place in her life. To make matters worse, Jess's kiss had been no chaste kiss; it was the kiss of a man with vast experience in the ways of the flesh. He would be an expert lover who could give her things she'd only allowed herself to dream about.

What did she know about sexual hunger, or desire, or hot, insistent kisses? Very little, and she had no desire to experience those things with a man she knew nothing about.

"Is that what you think, Meg? That all men are vile creatures intent upon their own pleasure?"

"Of course. You know it's true."

"What about Zach?" he challenged.

"Zach is . . . different. He'd never hurt me."

"Some man must have hurt you badly," Jess said. "I'm sorry. You deserve better than that. Forgive me. It won't happen again."

"It had better not," Meg said.

Why did her voice have to tremble? Meg wondered as she turned away. Why did this particular man have the power to make her mindless? She had whimpered, for heaven's sake!

And another thing: She didn't like his assumption that Zach was her lover. It was none of his business. Jess was a doctor, he had saved her life, but he held no special place in her life. As soon as he returned her to Zach, he would ride off into the sunset and become a dim memory. If she remembered him at all, it would be whenever she looked at the wound on her chest.

Meg rested all that day, preparing for the ordeal of mounting a horse and riding for the first time since her injury. The wound was still painful; the merest jostle sent waves of pain radiating through her chest, her back, and down her right arm.

That evening she made her way to the river alone to bathe. Jess didn't follow and she was grateful. She didn't know how she would react if he tried to kiss her again. She was confused. Normally she couldn't stand having any man around her but Zach. After what

Arlo had put her through, she'd wanted no part of any man. Had she been wrong to lump all men in the same category? Not really, she decided. Her healthy contempt for men was what made her a good bounty hunter. That and Zach's expert training.

That night Meg and Jess ate a meal of leftovers and retired early. She knew tomorrow would be grueling but looked forward to going home.

Sleep didn't come easily for Jess. He couldn't get the kiss out of his head. He relived it over and over. Meg's lips were soft, clinging to his with sweet surrender. He wondered what had happened to make her despise men . . . and what made Zach so special.

It wasn't like Jess to take advantage of a weak woman. And that he'd done, no matter how he tried to excuse himself. Meg was his patient, for godsake! Being a doctor made his transgression even more inexcusable. But, damn, he'd wanted Meg in every way a man wants a woman. Had he been away from female company too long?

His last thought before succumbing to sleep was that he wanted to kiss Meg again.

They dismantled camp early the next morning. Jess lifted Meg into her saddle and handed her the reins. She gripped them in her left hand and slowly straightened, reeling under the pain of unaccustomed exertion.

"Are you all right?" Jess asked, his voice taut with worry.

"I . . . can manage."

"Where are we going?"

"Head for Cheyenne. I live north of the city, beyond the railroad tracks. Zach built the house on land he bought before he . . . Never mind."

"I won't pry, Meg, if that's what you're worried about. Are you ready?"

Meg nodded. Jess took the lead. "Holler out if you need to stop. If I had my way, we'd stay here until you regained your full strength."

"I'm fine," Meg said. "Weakness doesn't catch outlaws, or put food on the table. The Calders escaped, but there are other criminals out there with prices on their heads."

And I'm one of them, Jess silently ruminated. Aloud he said, "I'd hoped you'd learned your lesson. Didn't your latest narrow escape teach you anything?"

"It taught me to be more careful next time. And there will be a next time, Dr. Gentry. It's all I know."

"There must be something else you can do."

"I didn't like the choices," Meg said wryly. "You don't know Cheyenne. It's a rough town with little available for women except

. . . well, let's just say I refuse to debase myself."

"What about Zach? Can't he provide a
living for you?"

"No."

Her answer was so emphatic that Jess let it
drop. He had to see Meg's lover for himself
before passing judgment.

They rode in silence for several miles. Jess
thought Meg was doing extremely well until
he saw her slump over in the saddle. With a
curse, he rode up beside her and placed an
arm around her waist to steady her.

"I thought I told you to let me know when
you needed to stop," Jess said gruffly.

"I . . . didn't realize . . ."

"Hold on, I'm going to bring you over to
my horse."

"That's not . . ."

Her protest was ignored as Jess swung her
over to his horse and seated her before him,
gripping her firmly between his muscular
thighs. "Just try to relax," Jess said. "Will
your horse follow?"

"Daisy will follow me anywhere."

"Good. Sleep if you can."

Sleep? Meg thought wryly. How could she
sleep with Jess's arms around her and his
unique masculine scent teasing her senses?
She should hate being close to this man, de-
pending on him for her welfare, but curiously
she didn't. She felt . . . Words couldn't ex-

47

plain the strange effect Jess had on her, or express how much it frightened her to entertain those feelings.

Despite her resolve to remain alert, Meg dozed off and on during the day. They stopped briefly around noon to lunch on leftovers and relieve themselves, then continued on. Meg must have dozed off again, for she was rudely awakened by a loud, gravelly voice yelling, "What the hell did you do to my Meggie?"

"You're home, Meg," Jess whispered into her ear. "Tell your lover to put his shotgun down."

Zach's beloved face wavered before Meg as she rubbed her eyes. He was brandishing his trusty shotgun in Jess's face.

"Zach, it's all right," Meg exclaimed. "This is Dr. Jess Gentry."

"You sure about that, Meggie girl? You'd better explain before I blow the bastard to kingdom come."

"I'm sure, Zach. Put the gun down. I was shot, and Jess saved my life."

Jess's eyes narrowed as he studied Zach. Somehow he had not expected someone like this middle-aged, grizzled man with gray-streaked blond hair and beard who glared at him with obvious distrust. The face beneath Zach's untrimmed beard was deeply lined, and his nose looked as if it had been broken several times. He wore his hair long and clubbed in the back. This man was Meg's lover? Somehow Jess had expected better of Meg.

But Jess was even more surprised when Zach set down his gun and stumbled toward him and Meg. Each step Zach took seemed awkward. And then Jess realized why; he dragged his left leg behind him.

"Shot! My God! Give Meggie to me." Zach's face held a world of concern as he held out his arms.

Jess hesitated, hating to place Meg in the care of a man who might drop her.

"I can stand on my own," Meg insisted. "Put me down, Jess."

Since Jess thought that was the best course of action, he carefully lowered Meg to the ground. When she wobbled, Jess quickly dismounted to help her, but he wasn't quick enough. Zach was already beside her, placing a steadying arm around her shoulders.

Unfortunately, he gripped her too tightly and Meg cried out. "You've hurt her!" Jess all but shouted. "Be careful. She sustained a grave wound."

"Where was she shot, and who did it?" Zach growled in reply.

"Beneath her right shoulder, just above her breast. Her whole right side is tender. One of the Calder brothers did it. She still isn't well enough to travel, but she insisted upon returning home." He shoved Zach's arm from around Meg's shoulder and replaced it with his own. "Open the door and point out her room. She needs to rest."

"Now just a blasted minute! Meggie is my responsibility. I appreciate what you did for her, but I'll take over from here."

"Quit fussing, you two," Meg said in a voice that trembled from weakness. "I can do this on my . . . oh . . ." Her knees began to buckle.

Ignoring Zach's scowl, Jess scooped Meg into his arms. "Lead the way," he barked at Zach. "I need to inspect her wound. All the jostling today might have reopened it."

Zach sent Jess a hard look but didn't argue as he led the way into the house. Jess passed through a homey parlor and entered a hallway. Zach stopped at the end of the hallway and opened a door.

"This here's Meggie's room."

The room was neat and cheerful, with bright curtains at the window, a rug on the floor, and a patchwork quilt covering the bed. Jess placed Meg in the center of the bed.

"I'm all right, really," Meg insisted.

"There's blood on your shirt," Jess said grimly. "I'll get my bag."

Jess made a hasty exit. He returned a few minutes later, annoyed to find Zach hovering over Meg, holding her hand and gently stroking her face. It was obvious to Jess that Meg and Zach shared an intimate relationship. The thought of them together as lovers was not a pleasant one; in fact, it was downright disgusting.

"Move away from the bed, Zach," Jess ordered as he opened his bag and placed it on the bed. "Meg's wound needs immediate attentions."

Zach gave him a belligerent glare. "I'll do it."

One of Jess's brows rose upward. "Are you a doctor?"

Zach wasn't giving an inch. "Are you?"

"Damn right I am. Move away so I can see to my patient."

Reluctantly Zach moved aside. But when Jess started to unbutton Jess's shirt, Zach roared out a protest.

"What in the hell do you think you're doing?"

Jess gave an exasperated sigh. Meg must have noted that he was at the end of his tether, for she said, "Jess really is a competent doctor, Zach. He saved my life. It's a little late to worry about propriety."

"If you say so, Meggie," Zach grumbled. "You must be hungry. I'll go fix something nourishing to eat. You both look like you haven't had a decent meal in days."

"I'll need clean bandages," Jess called after him. "I've used up all I had."

Zach nodded and left the room. "That is one jealous man," Jess complained after Zach was gone. "How long have you two been together?"

"Five years."

Jess's hands stilled. "That's a long time. You must . . . love him a great deal."

He had her shirt off now and was carefully removing the bandage, which had become caked with blood.

"There isn't a finer man alive," Meg vowed.

"Isn't he a little old for you? A woman your age needs a vigorous lover."

Meg's eyes spat emerald fire. "You don't know a damn thing, Jess Gentry!"

Chapter Three

Jess thought he was smart enough to figure out what was going on between Meg and Zach. What he assumed had been going on for five years, in fact. Why should it matter to him whether or not Zach was a good lover? Apparently, Meg loved the man.

"My remark was uncalled for," Jess apologized. "Obviously, Zach cares for you. You did say he wasn't your father, didn't you?"

Give it up, Jess, he scolded himself.

"That's right, Zach isn't my father."

"Your uncle?"

"No."

Jess didn't press further, for Zach had returned with a handful of clean cloths.

"Will these do? I tore up a sheet."

"They're fine."

Zach's worried gaze settled on Meg. "Is everything all right? Meggie's gonna recover, ain't she?"

"There's some bleeding but it's not serious. The wound looks clean. Where can I wash my hands? I don't want to touch Meg with dirty hands."

"There's a well outside. I'll show you."

"I'll be back in a minute, Meg," Jess said. "Try to relax."

"You really are a doctor, ain't you?" Zach said, looking on as Jess scrubbed his hands.

"I said I was."

"This is rough country. One never knows. I gotta protect Meggie. I'm all she has."

Jess couldn't help lashing out at him. "Sending her out after outlaws isn't the smartest way to protect her."

"Becoming a bounty hunter was Meggie's choice, not mine."

"Why does she do it?"

"It's all she knows. She's damn good at it. I taught her myself."

"*You* taught her?"

"I wasn't always the cripple I am now," Zach said defensively. "At one time Zacharia Purdee was the best damn bounty hunter in these parts. A bullet put a swift end to my career."

Jess dried his hands on the towel Zach offered. "How did you and Meg hook up?"

"Didn't she tell you?"

"No. All she said was that you weren't a relative."

"I ain't, and that's a fact. It ain't my place to tell you about us. You'll have to ask Meggie."

Jess searched his face. "Aren't you a little old for her?"

54

Zach bristled indignantly. "I ain't as old as I look. I'm only forty-five, still man enough to take care of Meggie."

Why didn't Zach come right out and say he and Meg were lovers? Jess wondered. Why did Jess even give a damn?

"I'd best get back to Meg. I hope you make plenty of whatever it is you're planning on cooking. I'm starved."

Meg was sleeping when Jess returned. She didn't even stir when he cleaned her wound and covered it with a fresh bandage. When he finished, he sat in a chair and watched her sleep. The next thing he knew, Zach was shaking him awake.

"Grub's ready. Should I wake Meggie?"

"No, let her sleep. The ride wore her out. That bullet took a lot out of her. She's a long way from well."

"You want to eat now? I'll set Meggie's food on the back of the stove to keep warm."

Jess rose, stretched, and followed Zach to the kitchen. "You've made Meg a comfortable place here."

"Meggie deserves it. I sent back East for a cookstove, just to please her. I was flush with money then, before that blasted bullet ended my career."

"So now you think it's all right to let Meg support you," Jess said with bitter emphasis. "You sit back while she risks her life. She al-

55

most got herself killed. What about next time?"

"Don't you dare judge me, Jess Gentry. Do you think I *want* Meggie placing her life in danger for me? She's her own woman. I've never tried to tell her what to do and I ain't gonna start now. We've got an understanding. It's been that way since the day I found her."

"Do you love her?" Jess challenged.

"Damn right. That little filly means the world to me."

"Then you'd best keep her home. She seems to think she needs to provide for you. You're lame but you're not helpless. Surely there is something you can do to provide a living for the two of you."

Anger simmered in the depths of Zach's intelligent blue eyes. "You don't know a damn thing, medicine man. No one wants to hire a cripple. Besides, I've known for a long time that something ain't right inside me."

"Maybe you should let me examine you."

"Yeah, maybe," Zach said noncommittally. "Sit down, grub is ready."

Jess mulled over Zach's words as he dug into a plate of savory venison stew loaded with vegetables, and biscuits that literally melted in his mouth. He couldn't recall when anything had tasted so good.

"Reckon I'll see if Meggie is awake," Zach said. "She should have something substantial in her stomach."

"It's time for me to move on," Jess said, pushing his plate back.

Zach paused with the ladle poised over the plate he was filling for Meg. "Where you headed?"

Jess shrugged. "Nowhere in particular."

Zach searched his face, as if seeking answers. "You running from the law?"

"Ask me no questions and I'll tell you no lies."

"Suit yourself. I ain't about to delve too deeply into the past of a man who saved my Meggie. Since you ain't in no hurry to get somewhere, why not stay on here for a few days? You said yourself that Meggie ain't out of the woods yet. I'd feel a heap better if I knew a doc was nearby to tend to her."

Jess was stunned. He'd gotten the impression that Zach didn't want him around Meg. That he was jealous of another man's attention to *his Meggie*. For some unexplained reason, it irked Jess to see the older man's devotion to his young lover. They shared the kind of closeness he hoped to have one day with a special woman, should he ever be free to love and marry.

Jess had had his share of women, and upon occasion had visited whores, but none of them meant anything to him except for the release they brought him. That was why he felt such overwhelming guilt for not accepting responsibility for Delia Wingate's pregnancy.

He was a doctor. He should have protected Delia against pregnancy, but she'd seemed so knowledgeable, he assumed she had taken precautions. Besides, he knew there had been others before him; he would never know whether the child was truly his.

The guilt of making outlaws out of his brothers, however, still plagued him. He should have assumed responsibility even if the child wasn't his and taken the loan Wingate had offered. Had he done so, his brothers would be home on the farm where they belonged instead of fugitives.

"What do you say, Jess?" Zach prodded. "Will you stay on until Meg is well?"

"You sure I won't be intruding?" Jess couldn't help asking.

Zach slanted him a baffled look. "Meggie needs you; that's all that matters. She'll be out of that bed and overdoing before she's ready if someone doesn't lay down the law. She won't listen to me, and I don't have the gumption to deny her anything. Stay, Doc, for Meggie's sake."

"Very well, I'll stick around for the time being," Jess agreed somewhat reluctantly. "Meg is an exceptionally strong woman. I don't know how much longer she'll follow my advice. But if I'm going to stay, you have to promise me something first."

"What's that?"

"You have to keep Meg home after she recovers. Don't let her continue to endanger her life. She's a woman, for godsake!"

Zach bristled angrily. "Meg is more than a woman. She's a damn good bounty hunter, one who's made a name for herself in these parts. But I reckon you're right," he said more reasonably. "I worry about her constantly when she's out. I tried to earn money to support us, but no one would hire me. And decent jobs are scarce for women like Meggie. She preferred bounty hunting to the jobs she was offered in town."

"You'll just have to try harder to support Meg," Jess scolded. "For starters, you should marry her."

"Marry Meggie?" Zach said, as if the idea were abhorrent to him. "I wouldn't . . . I couldn't . . ."

"I could think of a lot of reasons why you should," Jess said, turning away in disgust. If Zach didn't want to make an honorable woman of Meg, it was none of his concern.

"Truth is," Zach confided gruffly, "I have a wife back East. We never suited one another, and she refused to accompany me out West. Since neither of us had any desire to marry anyone else, we never bothered to divorce. Had a daughter once, too."

"Does Meg know about your wife?"

"Meg knows everything there is to know about me."

"If Meg is satisfied with this arrangement,

then who am I to interfere? Where can I bed down? I noticed a barn outside. I've slept in worse places during the war."

"I never fought in the war," Zach said. "I was too busy hunting down fugitives from the law. It was a hard life, but I earned enough money to buy land and build a decent house."

He paused, suddenly lost in memories. Then he cleared his throat and said, "No need to sleep in the barn. There's a room in the attic. Nothing fancy, just a cot and washstand. You should be comfortable, though."

Jess nodded. "Sounds fine. I'll bring in my saddlebags."

"Good. You do that while I bring Meggie her dinner. You'll find the stairs to the attic right through that door," he said, indicating a door at the rear of the kitchen.

Jess found his horse in the barn where Zach had taken him earlier. Jess fed the tired animal a measure of oats, rubbed him down, and returned to the house with his saddlebags. He dropped them beside the attic door and strode down the hallway toward Meg's bedroom. The door was open and he paused in the doorway, frowning when he saw Zach carefully spooning food into Meg's mouth.

Meg looked up and saw him.

"I should check Meg's bandage one last time for blood," Jess said as he approached the bed.

"Soon as she's done eating, Doc."

Meg pushed the plate aside. "I've had enough."

"No, you ain't, honey. You gotta get your strength back, don't she, Doc?"

"Zach is right, Meg," Jess concurred. "How do you feel?"

"I slept most of the afternoon but I'm still tired. And I hurt. But I suppose that's normal. I'll be on my feet in a day or two."

"Like hell," Jess argued. "I should have listened to my better judgment and insisted that you stay put for another day or two before attempting the journey home. The ride wore you out. Maybe even set you back some. You're not getting out of that bed until I say so."

Meg's chin tilted stubbornly. "After you're gone, I can do as I damn well please."

"I forgot to tell you, Meggie girl," Zach explained. "I asked Jess to stay on a few days, until you're feeling better. Since he ain't headed anywhere in particular, he agreed. You're to do as he says, hear? I ain't taking no more chances with your life."

"What does that mean?" Meg challenged.

"It means your bounty-hunting days are over," he said sternly. "I don't want to lose you, honey."

"You won't lose me, Zach," Meg said, touching his face.

Jess didn't know how much longer he

could watch the tender display between Meg and her lover. For some unexplained reason, he wanted it to be his face Meg was caressing.

"If you've finished eating, I'll check your bandage before I turn in," Jess said, interrupting the poignant moment.

"I'll take the dishes to the kitchen and clean up," Zach said, relinquishing his place to Jess. "I'll come back when the doc's finished."

"There won't be any need for you to return," Jess said. "I'm going to give Meg laudanum for the pain. She should sleep the night through."

Zach sent Jess an unwavering look. "Nevertheless, I'm gonna be right here beside her all night."

Did Zach intend to lie in the bed with her? Jess wondered, picturing Zach in bed with Meg and not liking it one damn bit.

"Try not to jostle her," Jess said sourly. "She's still in considerable pain."

"I ain't gonna hurt her," Zach retorted. "You don't have to warn me. Just see that you practice what you preach." With a last look at Meg, he picked up the dirty dish and shuffled out the door, closing it softly behind him.

Meg searched Jess's face. She couldn't imagine why he hadn't already left for parts unknown. "Why did you agree to stay?"

Jess shrugged. "You're my patient. I want to make sure you're completely healed before I leave. Besides, as Zach said, I've no place in particular to go."

He lowered the blanket and opened her shirt so he could inspect the bandage he'd changed earlier. "Looks good so far." He pulled the blanket down further. "You're still dressed. Do you have a nightgown? You'd be much more comfortable without those tight trousers."

"There's a nightgown in the chest at the foot of the bed. Bring it to me and I'll put it on."

Jess found the nightgown and shook it out. "I'll help you. You can't possibly manage on your own."

Meg groaned inwardly. Though Jess had seen every inch of her, she was suddenly uncomfortable with the thought of him looking at her. The idea of those incredible hazel eyes moving over her flesh made her feel . . . not exactly uncomfortable but . . . tingly all over

"Just give me the gown, and I'll do it myself," Meg bit out.

Jess searched her face. "Oh, I understand. You'd rather have Zach help you."

Meg gritted her teeth. What an impossible man! Whatever had given him the idea that Zach was her lover instead of the father she had adopted as her own? Her own father had given her away, without a thought to her welfare.

"No," she said, slowly and precisely. "I'd rather do it myself."

Jess handed her the nightgown and stood aside, arms crossed over his broad chest. "Very well. You're welcome to try."

Meg grabbed the gown with her left hand. "Turn your back."

Jess complied.

Meg's movements were clumsy as she tugged at her shirt with her left hand. She managed to shrug out of it without help, but when she attempted to pull her camisole over her head, pain stole her breath away and she whimpered.

"Are you ready to accept my help now?" Jess asked.

Meg glanced up. He had turned around and was watching her, compassion etched in every line of his face.

"I can't stand to see someone suffer."

Meg nodded, overwhelmed by waves of stabbing pain.

"I'll try not to hurt you." Carefully he raised her into a sitting position and worked her camisole strap down her left arm. He did the same with the right strap, lowering the garment until it was bunched around her waist. Immediately Meg's hands flew up to cover her breasts.

Jess slanted her an amused glance.

"They're beautiful, you know."

"You're not supposed to notice."

"I'm a doctor, not a dead man. Lift your hips," he ordered hoarsely as he unfastened the waistband of her trousers.

Meg raised her hips and Jess slid her trousers down her hips, over her legs, and off, tossing them onto a chair. His expression was unreadable as he removed her bloomers and camisole.

Did Jess pause a moment longer than necessary, stare at her with more heat than a doctor should display? Meg wondered, feeling her cheeks flame.

"Now for the nightgown," Jess said. "I'll ease it over your head first, and then you can work your left arm into the sleeve. If it hurts too much to move your right arm, we can leave it."

Meg had never known such gentleness from any man save Zach. She felt no pain, at least not from her injury, as Jess slipped her nightgown over her head and helped her ease her left arm inside the sleeve.

"Shall we try the right arm or leave it as it is?" Jess asked.

"I'd feel more comfortable with both arms inside the sleeves. The nightgown buttons down the front, almost to the waist, so you'll be able to treat my wound without removing my nightgown."

"All right. Ready?"

65

Meg sucked in a steadying breath and held it as Jess carefully eased her right arm into the sleeve. By the time he finished, tears were rolling down her cheeks.

"Oh, God, Meg, I'm sorry," Jess said, wiping away her tears with the callused pads of his thumbs.

"It's all right, Jess. I'll survive." She gave him a watery smile. "This will teach me to be more careful next time."

Jess went still, his expression fierce. "There won't be a next time."

Meg returned his scowl. "Who's going to stop me? Bounty hunting is my profession."

"Zach might have something to say about that. He loves you. I think you love him, too."

"Of course I love Zach," Meg exclaimed, indignant. "But that has nothing to do with anything. I'm my own woman. I've learned to make my own decisions. Life is never easy, Jess, as you probably know. It's even harder for a woman."

"Not if a woman has a husband. Or in your case, a protector."

"You're so damn sure of yourself, aren't you?"

Jess heaved a weary sigh. "Meg, I didn't save your life so you can go out and lose it a month from now. I had a talk with Zach. He agrees with me."

"You've had a busy day," Meg said sourly.

"You're right. I'm exhausted. I'm going to give you some laudanum to help you sleep. Zach will be here soon." He gave her a hard look. "And Meg, don't attempt any strenuous exercise until I say it's all right. I'm sure you know what I mean."

"Strenuous . . ." His meaning finally became clear to her, and she sent him a contemptuous look. "Don't worry, *Doctor*, I'll try to control myself." She turned away.

Jess captured her face between his hands, forcing her to look into his eyes. "Meg, I know how it is between you and Zach, I'm not blind. As a doctor, I care what happens to you."

"Of course," Meg answered dryly. "As a doctor."

Meg was startled when those golden flecks in his eyes glowed with emotion. "If I weren't a doctor, if I were just a man you had encountered by chance, I'd do this."

Meg watched in utter fascination as Jess's lips hovered scant inches above hers. His cheeks bore a day's growth of beard, and lines of exhaustion rimmed his eyes, but his lips . . . ah, his lips looked so soft and inviting that she felt herself being drawn irresistibly into his kiss. He let out a long, slow breath moments before his mouth closed over hers. A tiny moan slipped past her throat. The sound seemed to spur him on, and he deepened the kiss. His tongue was in her mouth, and his hand . . . his hand was on her left breast, surprisingly gentle, shockingly arousing.

His fingers found her nipple through the material of her nightgown. Meg felt heat spiral downward from where he touched to her belly, and lower, oh God, yes, much lower. His hand followed the flaming path to the place between her legs that suddenly felt wet and swollen. She thought Jess must be feeling the same things she was, for he groaned her name into her mouth. Then abruptly he broke off the kiss and stared at her. There was an utterly bewildered look on her face.

"That's what I would do if I weren't a doctor," Jess whispered hoarsely. "Knowing that you and Zach are lovers wouldn't stop me, either. You're quite a woman, Meg Lincoln. You deserve better than Zach, but that's only my opinion. Think about that kiss and how it would feel to be loved by a young, vigorous man."

He poured a measure of laudanum into a glass and handed it to her. "Good night, Meg."

Unconsciously Meg drained the glass before she realized what she had done. Jess watched her drink, then strode from the room. Meg watched him leave, wondering why he had kissed her with such passion. Jess Gentry presented a challenge she didn't need.

Conceited ass, Meg thought, disgruntled. What made Jess think she would regard him at all? She knew about men. They were all the same. They took and took and then they used. She should know. She'd fallen victim to that kind of man once. Not that she would place Jess in the same category as Arlo. There was no comparison between the two. And that was where the danger lay. It would be easy to trust Jess; so easy to . . . care for him. But she was afraid. Once bitten, twice shy. Besides, men with secret pasts were better left alone.

Zach arrived a few minutes later. "Is Jess gone?"

Meg sent him an irritable look. "Do you see him anywhere?"

Zach pulled the chair close to the bed and sat down. "What's wrong, honey? You like the doc, don't you?"

"He saved my life. I'll always be grateful to him, but that doesn't mean he can dictate my life."

"It's for your own good, Meggie girl. This latest incident made me realize how vulnerable you are. You could have died. Even if I wanted to go with you, I . . . I'm not up to it."

She touched his beloved face. He was so dear to her. "You've been looking peaked lately. Is anything wrong? Maybe you should have Jess take a look at you."

"Maybe," Zach said, refusing to meet her gaze. Abruptly he changed the subject. "Jess ain't like Arlo."

Meg slanted him a curious glance. "How do you know? I don't trust any man who's secretive about his past. Jess is hiding something."

"So are you, Meggie girl. You and Jess are alike in that respect. I've been studying him since he arrived, and I believe he's a good man. He certainly is a conscientious doctor."

Meg's suspicion was aroused. What was Zach brewing in the back of his fertile brain? "What are you implying?"

Zach sent her an innocent stare. "Nothing, honey. Just keep an open mind where Jess Gentry is concerned."

"Then you must keep an open mind about my profession. I have no intention of giving up bounty hunting. It provides us with a good living. Not all jobs are as dangerous as the one involving the Calder brothers. I just happened to stumble upon them and couldn't resist the chance to capture all three brothers at once."

"You could have died, Meggie."

"But I didn't. Go to bed, Zach. You look exhausted." She yawned hugely. "Jess gave me laudanum. I'll be asleep soon."

"I'll just sit here until you fall asleep."

Zach sat back, hands laced together, watching Meg drift off. She could have been the daughter he'd lost many, many years ago, he mused. She had come into his life months before he'd taken that blasted bullet, and had since become a vital part of his existence.

Zach's mind shifted back in time, to the day he'd found Meg on the prairie; a bruised and battered woman hardly more than a child. No one would recognize her today as that pitiful wreck he'd brought home and nursed back to health.

He'd taught Meg to become the independent woman she was today. For years he'd been preparing her, perhaps needlessly, to defend herself against Arlo, should he turn up again. She could shoot straight, wield a knife when she had to, and track outlaws. She'd soaked up everything he'd taught her and became so proficient at what she did, he'd grown complacent over the years, ignoring the danger she faced whenever she set off on her own.

But no more, by God. The poor state of his own health and Jess's providential appearance in their lives had set him to thinking about Meggie's future. Smiling, he picked up Meg's limp hand and threaded his fingers with hers. He had plans afoot, plans he intended to set into motion very soon. He knew his Meggie. She wasn't as immune to the handsome doc as she pretended to be.

Furthermore, he had peeked inside the room while Jess was alone with Meg. What he'd seen didn't surprise him. Jess was kissing Meggie, and she wasn't complaining. He'd watched for a moment, then returned to the kitchen to plot and plan. He fell asleep with a smile on his face and his fingers still clasping Meg's.

Jess awakened during the darkest part of the night and decided to look in on Meg. He pulled on his trousers and padded barefoot from the attic to Meg's room. Flickering lamplight created a warm, intimate atmosphere inside the room. Meg appeared to be sleeping soundly. So was Zach. His head was lowered upon his chest and his hand was entwined with Meg's. Jess stared at the lovers with an anger he shouldn't have felt.

Why should it bother him that Meg and Zach were lovers? Meg was nothing to him but a patient. There was no place for jealousy in their relationship. He chided himself anew for kissing her; it had been uncalled for. But he couldn't have stopped himself if he'd wanted to. Those sweet, lush lips just begged to be kissed. For some damn reason, he wanted to show Meg that kissing a tired old man was far different and much less enjoyable than kissing a vigorous young one.

Suddenly Zach lifted his head and looked toward the door, where Jess stood poised in the shadows. Zach disengaged his hand from Meg's and walked over to Jess. The older man placed his finger against his lips and walked into the hallway, motioning for Jess to follow.

"Everything is fine," Zach said, indicating Meg with a nod of his head. "She's sleeping soundly."

The dim light made Zach's pallor appear more pronounced. "You should go to bed yourself. Not Meg's bed," Jess stressed. "She needs undisturbed rest."

Zach sent him a puzzled look. Jess assumed he was deliberately pretending to misunderstand. "Surely there's another bedroom in this house where you can sleep." He couldn't be plainer than that.

"Of course."

"Then use it. You look drained. Perhaps I should examine you tomorrow. Have you seen a doctor recently?"

"That ain't necessary. I know what's happening. Excuse me, I'm going back to Meggie. I don't want to leave her alone."

"Go to bed. I'll sit with Meg."

Jess got the impression that Zach was pleased with the offer.

"I think I'll take you up on that, Doc. I am a mite weary."

Jess watched him limp away, a sudden jolt of compassion diminishing the jealousy the man's presence in Meg's life provoked. Jess approached Meg's bed and lowered himself into the chair. Meg's small, delicate hand was splayed out over the covers. It appeared fragile and somehow needy. Without conscious thought, Jess reached out and gently enfolded her fingers in his.

Jess dozed off, holding her warm hand snugly. A short time later Meg's thrashing around in bed awakened him. He swore softly, fearing she would reopen the wound, which had just begun to heal. He was on the verge of awakening her when her eyes opened wide and she reached for him.

"Don't let him find me," she sobbed, obviously still under the influence of laudanum.

Jess had no idea whom Meg was talking about but decided the best course of action was to humor her. "Don't worry. No one will hurt you as long as I'm here."

Her wild thrashing continued. Unable to make her understand that she might hurt herself, Jess lay down beside her and gently placed his arms around her. She quieted immediately, snuggling against his bare chest. Jess kissed the top of her head and felt her relax. When he was certain she had drifted off again, he closed his eyes and let sleep claim him.

Chapter Four

The lamp had sputtered out and daylight was streaming through the window when Jess awakened. Meg was still sleeping soundly within the circle of his arms. Carefully he unwound himself from her soft, warm body and rolled off the bed so as not to disturb her. He glanced down at her one last time before quietly departing.

Jess walked into the kitchen, surprised to find Zach busy at the stove. He gave Jess a knowing grin.

"How's Meggie?"

"She was a bit restless last night. She's still sleeping; I overslept myself."

"You can wash up at the pump outside. There's a mirror hanging on the back porch if you want to shave. I'll have breakfast dished up by the time you're finished."

"I'll fetch my shaving gear and shirt from the attic. The shirt could use a good washing."

Zach eyed Jess's bare chest. "You can borrow one of my shirts, if you want. Don't bother washing your own. Just bring it and anything else that needs laundering down and I'll do them later. Put everything in the basket on the back porch."

"You don't have to wash my clothes, Zach."

"It's the least I can do for the man who saved my Meggie's life. I can't pay you in cash, so you'll just have to accept my services, such as they are. Go wash up. Do you like flapjacks?"

Jess eyed him curiously. "If I didn't know better, I'd think you were trying to butter me up."

"Maybe I am," Zach said with a chuckle.

Jess returned to the kitchen a short time later; water dripped from his hair and he was cleanly shaven. He spied a plaid shirt hanging over the back of a chair and pulled it on. Zach set a plate piled high with flapjacks on the table.

"Sit down and dig in, Doc," Zach invited, pouring him a cup of steaming coffee.

Jess didn't need a second invitation. He was starved, despite having eaten a substantial supper the night before.

"How about some bacon and eggs to go along with those flapjacks?"

"Sounds good," Jess mumbled around a mouthful of food.

Zach dished up Jess's bacon and eggs and sat down to join him. "You say Meggie was a mite restless last night?"

"Yeah, she was, but she calmed down after I . . ." He flushed and lowered his gaze. Then he stuffed his mouth with eggs and mumbled something unintelligible.

Zach slid back his chair. "Reckon I'll take her some water and towels so she can wash up and clean her teeth. Sit here and finish your breakfast."

Zach rose, stumbled over the chair leg, clutched his chest, and turned deathly pale. Jess was beside him instantly, easing him into a chair.

"Are you all right?"

"Just let me catch my breath. I get these spells now and again. I'll be all right in a minute."

"I'll get my bag."

"Not now, Doc, I'm better already. It always passes."

"How often do you have these *spells?*"

"Now and again," Zach hedged.

"What happened?"

Both men turned toward the doorway at the sound of Meg's voice. Jess spit out a curse when he saw her leaning against the doorjamb, cradling her right arm, her long white nightgown clinging to her supple curves. He surged forward and slipped a supporting arm around her waist.

"What in God's name are you doing out of bed? Don't you ever follow orders?"

"Now you see what I've been up against all

these years," Zach muttered.

"It goes against my nature to lie in bed all day," Meg said in a trembling voice that convinced Jess she was pushing her strength to the limits.

Without giving her a chance to protest, he swept her from her feet and carried her back to bed. "Lie still. You're not ready to test your strength yet. I'll fetch water and towels and bathe you myself, if need be."

"I can manage," Meg protested. "How long are you going to keep me tied to this bed?"

His gaze traveled the length of her and back. He missed nothing, not her paleness nor the purple shadows beneath her eyes. "Until you're ready to leave it."

"What did I interrupt in the kitchen?" Meg asked. "There's something wrong with Zach, isn't there? I've suspected it for some time, but he'd never admit anything to me."

"I won't know until I examine him, but he keeps putting me off. I suggest you concentrate on getting well before worrying about Zach. Are you hungry?"

"Not really."

"You're going to eat. I'll fetch soap and water, then your food. If you don't eat enough to satisfy me, I'll feed you myself."

"Despot," Meg muttered. "I'm not a child."

"Then prove it. Someone has to set rules

around here. Obviously, you have Zach wound around your little finger. While I'm here, you'll do as I say regarding your health. Is that clear?"

Meg's eyes blazed defiance. "You're my doctor, Jess Gentry; not God."

"That's right. I'm your doctor, and you'll do as I say."

Tyrant, Meg thought sourly as Jess stalked from the room. Why didn't he understand she couldn't wallow in bed like a slacker? There was no money left; she needed to work. Winter was coming, and they had to lay in supplies for those bleak months. Sometimes weeks passed before weather permitted her to use her skills as a bounty hunter. She never knew when a storm would blow in, so she rarely ventured far from home during the winter.

Meg's greatest fear was Zach's declining health. She was astute enough to know he was ill, though he tried to hide it from her. What if he needed expensive medicine to keep him alive? The money just wasn't there for an emergency. She had to make the most of what was left of the summer and fall to earn enough money to see them through the winter.

Meg was still ruminating on Zach's fragile state of health when Jess returned with a basin of water, soap, and towels.

Jess set the basin down on the nightstand.

"Do you need help?"

"No, thank you." She flushed and looked away. "There's a chamber pot under the bed. Would you please pull it out for me?"

Jess brought out the chamber pot. "Are you sure you . . ."

"Very sure," Meg said through clenched teeth. "Please leave. I can manage just fine on my own."

Jess gave her a crooked smile and held up his hands. "I know when I'm not needed. I'll return later with your breakfast."

Meg waited until Jess closed the door before sliding out of bed, using the chamber pot, and pushing it back out of sight when she was finished. So far so good, she thought as she plunged a cloth into the basin of water and plied it with soap. Just being able to do these personal things for herself was gratifying. She was weak, true, but not helpless. She washed quickly, then cleaned her teeth, anxious to finish before Jess returned.

Jess.

She must have been dreaming last night when she felt him in bed beside her, holding her, chasing away her fears. Even in her dreams his arms had been comforting. She didn't remember her dreams often, but when she did, they were always the same. She knew Arlo couldn't hurt her anymore, but some part of her inner self still feared him and what he could do to her. Imagining

Jess's presence beside her had been enough to chase away the dark fears plaguing her.

Meg frowned. She didn't like the way she'd become dependent on Jess in the short time she'd known him. She supposed it wasn't unusual, however, for patients to feel that way about their doctors.

"What's that frown all about?" Jess said as he stepped through the door with a tray balanced in his hands. "Are you in pain again?"

"No more than usual. And don't try to feed me laudanum. It makes my mind fuzzy."

Jess set the tray on the bed. "No need to worry. The laudanum's gone."

"There's a drug emporium in Cheyenne if you wish to replenish your supply for future use before you leave town."

Jess slanted her a wry grin. "Unfortunately, I'm fresh out of money." He raised the tray to her lap and handed her the fork.

"Can you eat left-handed?"

"The pain in my right shoulder is somewhat diminished. I think I can manage with my right hand."

"Go ahead and try," Jess said, watching her closely as she lifted the fork and speared a wedge of flapjack.

Meg managed to get the food into her mouth without undue pain and flashed him a smile. *I told you,* her eyes seemed to say.

Instead of leaving, Jess settled down in the chair. "I'm thinking of hanging up my shingle in Cheyenne."

Meg couldn't have been more stunned. "You are? What made you decide that?"

Jess shrugged. "It's as good a place as any. I've heard the town is growing. Men are pouring in daily, bringing their families with them. There's a need for doctors here."

Meg mulled over Jess's words. She had liked it better when she'd believed he would ride off into the sunset one day. She didn't cotton to the idea of a man becoming important to her. Zach didn't count, because he was a father figure and presented no danger to her independence. But Jess was different. Jess was a potent, thoroughly masculine man who made her heart pound whenever she looked at him.

He was also dictatorial, tyrannical, and much too handsome for her peace of mind. There was something mysterious about Jess Gentry. He was hiding something, she was sure of it. Furthermore, if Jess lived in Cheyenne, she'd be constantly reminded that there was a man capable of arousing her passions.

Meg continued to improve. Jess allowed her to move around a bit more each day, and Meg began to exercise in her room without his knowledge. Her right arm was still weak but was gaining strength, and her wound only hurt when she stretched. The day she dressed and walked outside for the first time, she found Jess mending a porch railing.

Meg's mouth went dry. His chest was bare, his skin glistening with sweat. Taut muscles rippled beneath the smooth surface of his skin. She swallowed convulsively. Jess might not be the most attractive man in the world, but he could be rated right up there in the top ten percent. A shiver of awareness slid down her spine. The very air around him seemed to radiate energy.

Her heart skipped a beat when he turned toward her and smiled.

"I'm glad to see you looking so well." His gaze slid down her body, then back to her face. "You're wearing a dress. It's most becoming."

"I don't always wear trousers. Only when I'm . . . working. I feel very well, thanks to you. I'm back to where I was before I was shot. Where's Zach?"

"He rode into town to look for work."

"What? He knows he's not up to doing physical labor. We were doing fine until you came along."

Jess put down the hammer and glared at her. "Don't you mean until you got yourself wounded?"

"I . . . oh, never mind. Have you examined Zach yet?"

"I'm going to have to lasso him to get him to sit still for an examination."

Meg sat down on the porch steps. "I can't lose him, Jess."

Jess eased down beside her. It galled him like hell to listen to Meg bemoan her lover's illness.

"I'll do my best," Jess said. "Zach has led a hard life. He didn't take care of himself in his early years. I'm not a miracle worker. I don't even know for sure what's wrong with him."

"But you will find out, won't you?"

"I can try."

"That's all I ask."

"Meg, I know Zach can't marry you now, but he can obtain a divorce to make it possible."

Meg gave him a horrified look. "I could never marry Zach."

"Funny, Zach said the same thing about you. What is it with you two? Do you enjoy flouting society with your love affair?"

Meg closed her eyes and breathed deeply. She had to count to ten before she could speak coherently. "If I want to flout society, that's my business. You're nothing to me. Not my conscience, my father, nor a male relative."

Anger hardened Jess's features. "I may be nothing to you, but you can't deny the way you responded to my kisses. You kissed me back, damn it! Your body turned to flame in my arms. Can you say the same about Zach's kisses?"

"I . . . no. You don't understand how it is between me and Zach."

"Why don't you tell me."

"Because you're so damn judgmental, you probably wouldn't believe me. What about your own life, Jess Gentry? Is it so exemplary that you can pass judgment on others?"

Jess hissed out a breath, as if she'd struck him a mortal blow. "My own life is nothing to brag about. I've made some bad decisions along the way. But we both know standards are different for men and women. Do people know you're living out here with Zach, without benefit of marriage?"

Her chin went up. "I don't care what people think. The only time I go into town is to check the Wanted posters. The sheriff has been most accommodating in sharing them with me."

Jess searched her face. "Don't you want what other young women want? A husband, a home, children?"

"I have a home. As for children, they would only get in the way of my profession. And I don't need a husband telling me what to do. Tell me, do you have a wife waiting for you somewhere?"

"No wife."

"Fiancée?"

"No."

"Parents?"

"No parents."

"Just brothers," Meg probed.

"The best. I'd do anything for Rafe and Sam."

But he hadn't, had he? He'd let his brothers become outlaws because he hadn't had the gumption to admit that he might possibly be the father of Delia Wingate's unborn child. As a result, her irate father had accused the Gentry brothers of robbing his bank. God, it hurt to think about his cowardly act. During the war he'd risked his life countless times, remaining behind enemy lines to save wounded soldiers. But faced with a loveless marriage, he'd turned tail and run.

"Tell me about Rafe and Sam," Meg prodded.

Jess's mind turned inward, picturing his brothers as he'd last seen them. Frantic. Angry. Eager to escape the posse.

"Rafe is a year older than I. Sam a year younger. We're exceptionally close for brothers."

"Where are they now?"

"I wish I knew. We split up a few weeks ago. We lost the family farm and . . . well, Rafe rode west and Sam south. We made plans to meet in Denver a year from the day we split."

"Why did you split up? Was there nothing you could do to save the farm?"

Jess's expression hardened. "There was one

thing we could have done, but it was unacceptable." His eyes turned bleak, and he looked away. "I could have . . . but I didn't. It's too late now. The damage has already been done."

Meg searched his face. What she saw puzzled her. A mixture of guilt and remorse dulled his expressive eyes. "I don't understand."

"No, I don't suppose you do. The fault is mine alone to bear." He gave her a brittle smile. "Enough of my problems. I think we can safely say you can resume light exercise. Riding is permitted, but only if you don't overdo."

Meg felt like jumping up and cheering. Instead, she said demurely, "Thank you, Doctor."

"I mean it, Meg. No strenuous exercise for another couple of weeks."

"I'm fine, Jess, really."

"Let me be the judge of that."

Exasperated, Meg sighed and gazed off into the distance. "Oh, look, there's Zach."

Jess watched Zach approach with growing alarm. The closer he came, the more aware Jess became that something was wrong. Zach's shoulders were slumped, his face was ashen. He sat his horse awkwardly, barely able to keep his seat. Jess rushed forward to help him dismount. Zach's lame leg caught in the stirrups, and he would have fallen if Jess had not steadied him.

"Thanks, Doc," Zach said.

Meg ran over to join them, her expression stark with concern. "Are you all right, Zach? You shouldn't have gone off without telling me. I would have gone with you."

"No, you wouldn't have," Jess said sternly.

"I'm fine, Meggie girl. Didn't have much luck in town, though. Jobs were scarce for a cripple. The ones available were beyond my capability, and those I could do were already filled." He turned away in disgust. "I feel so damn useless. I'm half a man, with one foot in the grave and the other on a banana peel."

"Don't say that!" Meg cried fiercely. She turned to Jess, her eyes pleading. "Can't you give him something to make him better?"

"Not until I now what's wrong with him. I need to examine him."

"Then do it!" Meg demanded.

"What about it, Zach? Will you let me examine you? I'll be leaving in a day or two; now is as good a time as any."

Zach looked from Meg to Jess, as if trying to make up his mind. Then he nodded slowly. "Very well. You two have worn me down. Might as well get it over with."

"I'll wash up and fetch my bag," Jess said. "I'd prefer to do the examination in private."

"My bedroom, then," Zach said. "I'll wait for you there."

Jess's brows rose in surprise. He'd always assumed that Zach and Meg shared the same bedroom.

Zach limped away. Meg followed him as Jess went off to scrub his hands. When he entered Zach's room with his medical bag a short time later, Meg was there, fussing over him. She was reluctant to leave, but Jess was adamant. As soon as the door closed behind her, Jess opened his bag and removed his stethoscope.

"No need for that, Doc. I know what's wrong," Zach said. "I only agreed to this for Meggie's sake."

"Why don't you tell me your symptoms?"

"It's my heart. It just ain't right. Hasn't been for a long time."

"Let me be the judge of that. Have you experienced pain?"

Zach gave him a wry smile. "You could say that. Sometimes it's so bad I can't catch my breath. I try not to let on for Meggie's sake, but I know my days are numbered, Doc."

Jess wasn't about to make a diagnosis without evidence to back up Zach's complaints. He placed the stethoscope over Zach's heart. He listened, frowned, and listened some more. He moved the stethoscope to Zach's back, still frowning.

He put the stethoscope away and tested Zach's responses. Then he looked into his eyes, his ears, and his mouth. The examination was as thorough as Jess knew how to make it. When he finished, he sat back and stared at Zach.

Zach returned his perusal. "I was right, wasn't I, Doc? It's my heart, ain't it? I've lived a hard life. Drank too much, smoked and caroused like there was no tomorrow during my early years. Now I'm paying for it. I don't care for myself; it's Meggie I'm worried about."

"I'm not going to lie to you, Zach. You have angina, or progressive heart failure. There is medicine that will ease your pain but no cure."

There was acceptance in Zach's eyes. "I ain't proud of my life. There are things I would do over if I had the chance. But meeting and caring for Meggie ain't one of them. I'll always be grateful for the time I had with her."

Jess didn't want to hear about Zach's relationship with Meg. "I'll give you some pills. Take them whenever you feel the pain come on. When they're gone, you can buy more from a druggist. It's a common enough remedy."

"How long do I have?"

"Only God knows that. My advice is to make the most of the time you have left. Try not to overdo, and rest when you feel tired."

"Don't tell Meggie, Doc. I don't want her

worrying about me."

"I doubt you can keep it from her. Meg's an astute woman. She's smart, strong, and independent. She has a right to know."

"She's all of those things and more," Zach admitted, bursting with pride. "She wasn't always like that. You should have seen her when . . ." He paused, giving Jess a sheepish look. "Forgive my rambling."

"Tell me about Meg," Jess said. "I know so little about her."

Zach shook his head. "Ask Meg. It's not my place." He sent Jess a hard look. "You care for Meggie, don't you?"

Jess shrugged. "Of course. I care about all my patients."

"I don't mean those kinds of feelings. I'm talking about feelings a man has for a woman."

"Look, Zach, you've nothing to be jealous about. Meg loves you."

"Hell, Doc, you don't need to tell me that. I've been watching you two since you arrived. Meggie is attracted to you. You're exactly the kind of man she needs. She'd make you a good wife."

Jess's mouth fell open. "You want me to marry Meg?"

"You could do a helluva lot worse. I know she's a mite strong-minded, but ain't that better than having a wife who's afraid of her own shadow?"

"You want me to marry Meg?" Jess repeated harshly.

"Well, hell, Jess, I know for a fact there's more passion in her little finger than most women have in their whole body."

"I'll bet you do," Jess said sarcastically. No matter how ill Zach was, it just wasn't right for him to offer his lover's hand in marriage to another man.

"I'd rest a whole lot easier in my grave if I knew Meggie was being taken care of after I'm gone."

"Why marriage?" Jess challenged. "Why not offer her to me as my mistress?"

Zach stiffened, and his eyes narrowed with outrage. "Why would I do a thing like that? I want only the best for Meggie. Nothing but marriage will do for her. You're a damn fool to think she'd become your mistress after I'm gone."

"I don't think anything at all," Jess said, pretending a calm he didn't feel.

Jess was ready to blow. Only Zach's precarious state of health prevented him from doing so. How could Zach speak so casually about the woman he loved, a woman who loved him? This whole impossible conversation was beyond his understanding. There was only one answer he could give.

"Sorry, Zach. Taking a wife at this time isn't feasible. You'd be doing both yourself and Meg a favor if you divorced your wife

and married Meg before your health deterio-
rates."

Zach sent him a puzzled look. "That
wouldn't be right. Meg needs a young man,
one who can do right by her."

"You should have realized that a long time
ago," Jess chided in a voice ripe with disapproval. "I won't change my mind, Zach. A
wife is the last thing I need right now."

"Why?" His eyes narrowed. "Meg thinks
you're running from the law. Is she right?
You don't look like an outlaw, but life has
taught me not to judge a book by its cover.
Are you a wanted man, Jess?"

Jess's gaze slid away. "A man's privacy
should be respected. Suffice it to say, taking
a wife isn't in my plans at the present time. I
suggest you quit trying to foist her off on the
first young man who meets your require-
ments and marry her yourself."

"Damn young fool," Zach muttered beneath his breath.

Jess pretended not to hear. "I'll leave this
bottle of pills with you. Take them whenever
the pain comes on. You can live a long time
if you take care of yourself. Keep that in
mind."

Jess's angry steps carried him from Zach's
room. The man was too ill to lay into, but
that was exactly what Jess felt like doing.
This whole situation was abhorrent to him.
He couldn't understand how Zach could ca-

sually hand his mistress over to another man, demanding marriage, no less. Who did Zach think he was, Meg's father?

Jess stormed into the kitchen, disgruntled to find Meg waiting for him, her expression anxious. "What's wrong with him, Jess? He's going to be all right, isn't he?"

"It's Zach's place to tell you," Jess said shortly. He turned away.

"Dammit, Jess, Zach won't tell me anything. But I have to know. If something serious is wrong with him, I want to be able to help him."

"There's nothing you can do," Jess said, his expression softening. "Don't worry; he's not in any immediate danger."

Meg's features hardened. "Tell me, Jess. I can take it."

Jess shook his head. "Have you never heard of patient confidentiality? Zach asked me to keep my diagnosis private. Were you his wife or daughter, it would be a different matter. But as his lover, you have no rights."

Meg's rage and frustration were palpable.

"Is that your last word, Dr. Gentry? How dare you play God like this? I deserve to know what's wrong with Zach."

Jess knew he should walk away before his temper got the best of him. Unfortunately, he waited a moment too long. "Your lover just asked me to marry you. He says he can no longer take care of you like he should. Now who's playing God?"

Two bright spots flamed on Meg's cheeks. Jess could tell he'd shocked her. He should have kept his mouth shut, but he was still incensed over Zach's outrageous suggestion. When he decided to marry, it wouldn't be because a dying man wanted to make sure his mistress was in good hands after his demise. Not only was the suggestion embarrassing, it was downright insulting to both him and Meg.

"I can't believe Zach would do such a thing," Meg choked out. "He knows better than anyone that I don't want a husband. I'm perfectly happy seeing to Zach's needs."

"Zach shouldn't be . . . exerting himself. He can't be a real . . . lover to you anymore," Jess said, choosing his words carefully. "You're a young woman. Can you settle for that?"

Meg's chin rose pugnaciously. "You don't know a damn thing, Jess Gentry. If you don't know by now that Zach and I are . . . Oh, what's the use? I don't care what you think."

Jess grasped Meg's wrist and pulled her against him. "You're a challenge, Meg Lincoln, and I like challenges. There's an innocence about you that I can't quite figure out. On the other hand, you can be a tempting seductress. I've tasted your mouth, felt it cling to mine, begging for my kisses. Like now. Those pouty lips are irresistible. Did you know your eyes glow when you're angry? You're an enigma, Meg Lincoln. It would take a lifetime to learn all your secrets."

"Let me go."

"Was it your idea to marry me, Meg?"

"You're dreaming."

"Maybe you put the idea in Zach's head."

"You're mad. So is Zach for suggesting such an outrageous thing. I wouldn't have you if you were the last man on earth."

"Don't worry. I'd refuse."

"Fine."

Still he held her. She felt so damn good, he couldn't let her go. He wanted to kiss her. No, he *had* to kiss her. *Needed* to kiss her. He did, full upon the mouth, his lips slanting over hers until her mouth opened beneath his. His tongue slipped inside. He moaned softly into her mouth. She tasted sweeter than he remembered.

He kissed her until her lips softened beneath his, until her body melted against him, until he felt her tremble. His hands roamed down her back, to her curvy hips, pulling them against his hardening loins, making her aware of his arousal. He had no idea why, but he wanted her to feel him, to know how a potent man would react to a desirable young woman. Meg could deny it till doomsday, but she wasn't as opposed to him as she'd like him to believe.

A chuckle rumbled in his chest when he

heard her moan his name. Meg had said she wouldn't have him if he were the last man on earth. He had just made a liar of her. He was experienced enough to know when a woman wanted a man.

Chapter Five

The kiss took on a life of its own. Jess couldn't seem to stop kissing Meg. She tasted delicious, her lips lush and full beneath his. He slanted his mouth over hers, gathering her completely into his arms, aware of how very fragile she was beneath her veneer of prickly independence. He felt his loins harden and brought her closer against him. Had he dared, he would have cleared the table of dishes, pushed her down on the hard surface, and thrust himself into her. He wanted to ride her hard, ride her until they were both sated.

Long minutes passed before Jess realized the sound thrumming in his ears wasn't the pounding of his heart. Someone behind him was clearing his throat. With marked reluctance, Jess broke off the kiss and backed away.

"Am I interrupting?" Zach asked, pinning Jess with a hard, probing gaze.

"Your timing couldn't have been better," Jess said, grateful for the intrusion. Another minute and he would have taken Meg on the kitchen table, and propriety be damned. Zach's appearance had saved him from making a fool of himself.

He glanced at Meg. Speech seemed to have deserted her. She was staring at him, her eyes wide, the fingers of one hand splayed over her lips.

"Have you changed your mind about what we talked about?" Zach asked, glancing from Meg to Jess.

Meg suddenly found her voice. "No, he hasn't. I don't know what possessed you to even suggest such a thing, Zach Purdee. Men!" she said, her voice ripe with disgust.

"I could have sworn you were kissing Jess when I walked into the kitchen just now," Zach said.

"Most certainly not! Jess was kissing me. There's a difference."

Suddenly Jess felt as if his world was skittering out of control. And all because of a female bounty hunter who hadn't the sense to stay home and be a woman. He couldn't recall when a woman had set him on his ear the way Meg Lincoln did. She was unique and special, a woman who followed her own rules. He had to forget her. If he knew what was good for him, he would walk away and never look back.

He was a wanted man. Meg already had a lover. He didn't need a woman in his life right now. She didn't want anyone but Zach.

There were countless reasons why he and Meg should steer clear of one another, every one of them valid.

"I'll be leaving within the hour," Jess announced. "I've done all I can here. Meg is nearly back to normal, and I've given Zach my professional opinion of his condition and the medication I had on hand to treat it."

"You're leaving?" Zach didn't seem at all pleased, and that puzzled Jess.

"I think it's best."

"Where will you go?"

"Somehow I'm going to scrape up enough money to open an office in town."

"I'd like to help, Doc, but me and Meggie are a little short ourselves."

"I'll manage," Jess said. "Take care of yourself. You, too, Meg. I'll stop by in a few days to see how you're doing."

"No need," Meg said. "I'm perfectly fine, and quite capable of taking care of Zach."

"Aw, Meggie, I don't need no one to take care of me. There's a heap of life left in me yet."

"Well, then, I reckon I'll say good-bye," Jess said. "It will only take me a few minutes to gather my things."

Zach stuck out his hand. "I hate to see you go. It's been a real pleasure, Doc. Come back any time. Me and Meggie will be glad to see you, won't we, Meggie?"

"The man who saved my life will always be

welcome here," Meg said.

"Think over my proposal, Doc. It's still open."

"Zach!" Meg rounded on him. "I know what you did, and I'm not pleased. We'll discuss this later, when we're alone."

Jess made a hasty exit while Meg and Zach were bickering. He could understand Zach's need to provide for his lover after his demise, but to offer her to the first likely man to come along was reprehensible. Besides, Zach still had many good years left if he took care of himself.

No one was on hand when Jess rode away. It was better that way, he thought. He couldn't look at Meg without remembering that last kiss and how it had affected him. Damn, he wondered if Rafe and Sam were more knowledgeable about women than he was. Rafe was resourceful; he wouldn't let himself become romantically involved, Jess decided. It was Sam he worried about. Impulsive Sam would probably fall head over heels for a dozen women and discard each one by the time they met in Denver next year.

Jess rode down Cheyenne's main street, his body tense as he searched the fences and posts for Wanted posters on the Gentry brothers. The streets were a seething mass of men and women from all walks of life. Gamblers, railroad workers, farmers, ranchers, shifty-eyed criminal types, whores looking for a quick two bits, and a few decently dressed women and children.

Jess dismounted in front of the Whistle Stop saloon and tied his horse to the hitching post. It had been far too long since he'd tasted a beer or felt a shot of whiskey slide down his throat. The way he felt now, he could drink the saloon dry. Drowning himself in alcohol seemed a pleasant way to forget how damn good Meg felt in his arms, how she had melted against him and opened up to his kiss. God, he wanted her.

Jess walked into the saloon and bellied up to the bar. Several men eyed him curiously but quickly turned away when they saw he presented no threat. Jess reached into his pocket, found a silver dollar, slapped it on the bar, and asked for whiskey. From the way he acted, no one would have guessed it was the last dollar he owned. The bartender placed a glass and a bottle in front of him. Jess nodded his thanks, picked up the glass and bottle, and wandered over to a table.

The whiskey slid down his throat smooth and warm. Two tables away, five men were engaged in a poker game. Jess stretched his long legs in front of him, sipped his whiskey, and watched the players. Jess had always handled himself well at poker. He couldn't count the times he and his brothers had ridden into

Dodge when they needed money and won enough at the tables to satisfy their immediate needs. He didn't like to brag, but he was better at it than Rafe, though not quite as good as Sam, who took to the game like a duck to water.

The stakes grew larger and the men became more reckless with their betting. Jess concentrated on each man's face, watching attentively as he played the game. After a few hands, he discovered he could correctly read each player's hand by watching his expression. A plan began to form in his mind. He had nowhere to go, no money, and virtually no hope of practicing medicine without money to set up an office. He was desperate enough to try anything, and that poker game looked damn inviting.

Jess reached into his vest pocket and withdrew the solid gold pocket watch that had once belonged to his father. There had been time to do little more than stuff a memento or two in their pockets when he and his brothers had fled from their farm with the posse on their heels. Rafe had taken their mother's wedding ring, Sam had selected their father's gold cuff links, and he had chosen the watch.

Jess dangled the watch by its gold fob. Could he do it? Should he lose, he'd have nothing: no watch, no money. Just his medical bag and the few instruments it contained. Was the possible gain worth the risk? Maybe he should find a job and save money to open his practice.

That could take forever and he didn't have forever.

Jess wasn't even aware he had risen from his chair and approached the poker table until he was standing beside it.

"Can anyone join in?"

Five pairs of eyes regarded him with interest.

"You got money?" a rough man with a week's growth of beard asked.

"I've got this," Jess said, dangling the watch by its gold chain.

A man nattily dressed in fancy duds held out his hand. "Let's see it."

Jess handed over the watch to the man, who had all the markings of a professional gambler.

"Aw, let the man sit in, Fisk," a distinguished-looking man wearing a dark suit said. "We need some new blood."

Fisk inspected the watch carefully. "Belong to your pa, did it?" he asked Jess.

Jess nodded. "It's solid gold."

"You must be desperate for a game if you'd risk an heirloom," Fisk said, turning the watch over in his hands. "It's gold, all right. What do you say, boys, shall we deal the tenderfoot in?"

When no one objected, Jess pulled up a chair.

"Five card stud," Fisk said, dealing out the cards.

Jess fanned his cards close to his chest. He kept his expression carefully blank. Luck was with him. He held a pair of kings. The betting became heated. Jess watched the gambler closely for cheating. His intense scrutiny was rewarded when he caught Fisk dealing himself a card from the bottom. Jess slapped his hand down on the deck.

"From the top, please," he growled.

The bearded man leaped to his feet. "You been cheatin', Fisk?"

"Sit down, Brewster. The tenderfoot don't know what he's talking about."

"Calm down, gentlemen," the well-dressed man said. "Let's give Fisk the benefit of the doubt this time. But we'll all be watching you, Fisk, so if you've a mind to cheat, don't. We should thank . . . what did you say your name was, mister?"

"Jess. Jess Gentry."

"I'm Earl Wyland. I, for one, am grateful for the warning."

"It's Dr. Gentry."

"A medical doctor?" a young cowhand asked. "I'm Pace Lynch."

"I'm Chet Conner," a sad-eyed man in a wrinkled suit said.

"And I'm Burl Brewster." This from the bearded man.

"Howdy," Jess said. "Yes, I'm a medical

doctor. I'm thinking of opening a practice in town. Remember me when you need a doctor."

Fisk sent Jess a murderous glare. "Are we gonna play poker or sit here and chitchat?"

"Get on with the game," Jess said. "Deal from the top this time."

The game continued. Jess discarded three cards and was dealt an ace, a deuce, and another king to go along with his pair. The bidding continued. At the final lay down, Jess held the winning hand. He scooped up his winnings and placed his watch back in his pocket. His luck held out. He won two out of the next four hands. He owed his success to reading expressions and knowing when to stay and when to fold.

Sad-eyed Chet Conner said little during the play. He bet with a reckless abandon that bothered Jess. The man appeared to be sober, but Jess could tell his heart wasn't in gambling. He lost consistently and appeared not to care.

The game progressed. Gold coins and paper bills piled up in front of Jess. A few hours later, Jess became aware of the passage of time and of his incredible good fortune, and he didn't want to push fate. The nighttime crowd began drifting into the saloon, some gravitating toward the poker table to watch the play. Saloon girls sashayed through the crowd, urging men to buy them drinks and making appointments for later.

When the deal came around to Jess again, he placed the cards face down on the table and announced his decision to call it a night.

"You can't quit now, Gentry," Fisk charged as Jess rose and stretched. "Give us a chance to win our money back."

"Another time," Jess declared. "It's getting late. I still have to find a place to stay for the night."

"I'm through, too," Conner said. "Cleaned out."

Fisk rose as if to challenge Jess.

"Accept your losses and let it go at that, Fisk," Wyland advised. "We all lost tonight. And we're all aware of your cheating now, thanks to the doc here. I suggest you keep your nose clean from now on."

Fisk slanted Jess another lethal look and stalked away.

"Nice meeting you all," Jess said, eager now to clear out with his winnings. They would be put to good use.

"Are you really going to hang up your shingle in town?" Conner asked.

"Just as soon as I find a place to rent within my means," Jess said. "Until I won tonight, I didn't have a nickel to call my own." He tipped his hand. "I owe you all my thanks, gentlemen."

"Dr. Gentry, might I have a word with you?" Conner asked.

Jess was surprised to find the meek Mr. Conner following him. "Of course. How may I help you? Are you ill?" Jess took a closer look at the man, thinking he might be consumptive.

"No, not sick. At least not in the way you mean. My wife of thirty years just passed away and I'm taking her back to Philadelphia for burial. It was her wish to be buried beside our only child, who died before we left Philadelphia."

Jess led Conner to a table and invited him to sit down. Conner took a seat and stared at his hands. Jess waited for Conner to state his business.

"You need to rent a place to practice medicine."

"That's right," Jess said, wondering where the conversation was going.

"I own a house on the main street that might suit your purposes. Would you care to look at it? I'm departing on the train tomorrow. I intended to leave the house empty until I return, but that doesn't make sense. Renting it will help both of us. Frankly, I could use the money, Dr. Gentry."

Jess tried to contain his excitement, but it was difficult. Practicing medicine again was his fondest wish. "You were gambling rather recklessly tonight, Mr. Conner."

"I know. Since Elsie died, I haven't been myself. I came out here with a nice little nest egg. I built the house and opened a dry goods store. I guess I'm not much of a businessman, for my store failed quickly.

"I took a job in a bank. Bank clerks don't make much money, and I rarely gambled until today, but something snapped inside me when I lost my wife. All my dreams were gone, just like Elsie. I didn't regain my wits until you accused Fisk of cheating. Suddenly I realized how foolish I had been. I need money to see me to Philadelphia and pay for Elsie's funeral."

"How long do you intend to be gone, Mr. Conner?"

Conner shook his head, his grief palpable. "I don't know. Perhaps I won't return at all. I have a brother in Philadelphia. He's offered me a job in his hardware store. I just might take it."

Jess's eyes lit up. "Would you be willing to give me, say, a six-month lease?"

Conner blinked. "I'm sure something can be worked out that will please both of us."

"When can I see the house? If it suits my needs, I would be interested in renting."

Jess followed Conner out the door. "It's not far," Conner said. "We can walk, but bring your horse, if you'd like."

Jess decided to take his horse and led the animal down the street. They passed the bank, the mercantile, the sheriff's office, two saloons, a barbershop, grocery store, blacksmith, bathhouse, and not one but two daily newspapers.

"All this building happened since the first tents went up in eighteen sixty-seven, just over a year ago," Conner explained. "I arrived with the early settlers. Elsie and I lived in a tent until our house and store were built. Almost overnight, four thousand residents swelled the town, and an army supply depot was built nearby to protect the railroad workers. Despite the army presence, a sheriff, and town government, Cheyenne is still a lawless town. Most people refer to it as 'hell on wheels.' "

"Is there a doctor in town?"

"There is, but he's worthless," Conner spat, surprising Jess with his sudden ferocity. "The man is always drunk. Had he been worth his salt, my Elsie might be alive today. That's one of the reasons for my offer. You seem to be a responsible young man, one a body could trust with loved ones."

Conner stopped before a neat little cottage at the end of the business district, far enough away from the saloons to escape the noise and rowdiness.

Jess smiled as he looked over the clapboard cottage with a critical eye. The two-story white house sat on a large, shady lot surrounded by a fence. Jess swung open the gate, making a mental note to fix the squeaky hinges. Conner dug a key from his pocket and unlocked the door.

"Go right in, Doctor. I'll light a lamp so you can take a look around and see if it will suit your purposes."

Jess stepped inside. Conner struck a match to a lamp and led Jess through a rather large parlor that would serve nicely as a waiting room. Off to the side was another, smaller room. Beyond was a kitchen. Conner opened the door to a pantry, and Jess was pleased to note that it held a full complement of dishes, utensils, and cooking pots. There was even a shiny black cookstove.

"The stove was Elsie's pride and joy," Conner said wistfully. "Everything is just the way she left it. Would you like to see the upstairs?"

Jess nodded and followed Conner up a closed staircase to the second floor. There wasn't much to see. Two fairly large bedrooms with the usual complement of furniture. Colorful quilts covered the beds, and cheerful curtains hung at the windows. Everything was clean and neat as a pin.

"One of Elsie's friends came in to clean after Elsie —" Conner's voice cracked. "The outhouse is in the back, well away from the house, and we have our own well. There's even a lean-to for your horse. What do you think, Doc?" Conner asked as he led the way back downstairs. "Will it do?"

"Quite well," Jess said, excitement thrumming through him. "The anteroom off the parlor will make an excellent examining room and private office. One of the upstairs bedrooms can be used for seriously ill patients. Indeed, your house will suit my purposes extremely well. How much rent are you asking?"

Conner grew thoughtful. "Before tonight and that blasted poker game, I hadn't even considered renting. Let's see," he said, tapping his chin. "Would twenty dollars a month be too much? It's hard to find a decent place these days. You couldn't do any better. A six-month lease sounds reasonable to me. And if it's possible, I'd like the first six months' rent in advance. I wouldn't ordinarily ask such a thing, but I'm desperate for money, and collecting it monthly would be nearly impossible with me so far away."

Jess had won 600 dollars tonight, and a good share of that money was Conner's. If luck was with him, he'd have six months, maybe longer, before anyone suspected he was a wanted man. He could conceivably live here forever if business was good and his past didn't catch up with him.

"I think that's a reasonable request, Conner. Can I move in tonight?"

Conner nodded. "I intended to spend the night at the station with Elsie's coffin anyway."

Jess counted out 120 dollars from his

poker winnings and handed it to Conner.

"I'll write out a lease so there will be no question about the legality of our deal," Conner said, moving to the small desk in one corner of the parlor.

He set the lamp down, found what he needed in the desk, and wrote out a document giving Jess a six-month lease on his house, making the notation that the rent had been paid in advance. Then he handed it to Jess and they shook hands.

"Should I decide to sell, I'll let you know. Your six months' rent can go toward the sale price, if that's all right with you."

"Sounds fair," Jess said, pleased with the deal. "Good luck to you, Mr. Conner."

"And to you, Doctor."

Conner took one last look around the pleasant parlor, then quietly departed. Jess felt sorry for the man, but meeting him tonight had been a stroke of luck. In fact, his luck tonight had been phenomenal on all accounts.

Jess led his horse around to the lean-to, unsaddled him, and rubbed him down. He made a mental note to stop by the feed store tomorrow when he purchased food for the larder. He also needed to replenish his medicinal supplies, and order what he couldn't find. He supposed a cot would do for an examining table for the time being, until he found something suitable.

Jess had 480 dollars left from his winnings, and that had to pay for food and supplies and hold him over until money started coming in. He hoped patients would arrive soon after he hung out his shingle. Perhaps a few handbills would be a good idea, he thought as he returned to the house and chose one of the bedrooms for his own.

Jess undressed, doused the lamp, and went to bed. Of all the incredible things that had happened today, one stuck out in his mind: holding Meg in his arms and kissing her. He knew she had enjoyed his kisses. She wouldn't have kissed him back or melted in his arms if she'd been repulsed or angry. How could she profess to love Zach and still respond passionately to his kisses? The longer he thought about it, the more that relationship puzzled him.

Meg was different from any woman he'd ever known. She was brave, passionate, independent, and thoroughly exasperating. She resisted taking orders and refused to comply with any but her own edicts. For her sake, he hoped Zach could convince her to leave bounty hunting to men who were cut out for that kind of work.

Jess awoke early the following morning, ready to begin drumming up business. He strolled down the street and ate breakfast at the Railroad Cafe. Then he visited the nearest newspaper office and ordered a dozen handbills advertising his services.

Jess was delighted to find an apothecary down one of the side streets and was able to find everything he needed for his office, from bandages to laudanum. He made sure the druggist knew he would be ready to receive patients in a day or two.

At the grocery store he introduced himself as the new doctor in town, bought a variety of provisions, and arranged to have them delivered to his house. He felt strongly that word of mouth would work almost as well as handbills in advertising his services. His next stop was the bathhouse, then the barbershop, where he had a shave and haircut, making friends with the customers and inviting them to seek his services when illness struck.

One place Jess steered clear of was the sheriff's office. It was his fervent wish that the local law would never learn that he was a wanted man. Jess's final stop before returning home was at the cabinetmaker, where he order a shingle to hang over his door. The sign was to read *Jess Gentry, M.D.* The cabinetmaker promised to have it finished the following day.

Jess spent the rest of the day stowing away his provisions and setting up his office. The first patient arrived unexpectedly shortly after dark, before he was fully prepared to treat anyone. The patient was a child who couldn't have been more than three years old. He lay whimpering and feverish in his father's arms.

"Are you open for business, Doc?" the man asked. "I'm Ben Dunn, and this here is little Bobby. He's terrible sick, Doc. Mr. Coleman over at the apothecary told me you were the new doctor in town. Can't find old Doc Holloway."

"Bring him in, Mr. Dunn," Jess said, ushering the man into his office.

Jess took the child from his father's arms and laid him down on the cot. He conducted a thorough examination before offering a diagnosis.

"It appears that Bobby has the mumps, Mr. Dunn. It usually runs its course in the young, but I can give him something to ease his symptoms. Does he have brothers and sisters?"

"Not yet, Doc."

"Keep him away from other children until the swelling subsides. Have you and the missus had the mumps?"

Dunn scratched his thatch of dust-colored hair. "Don't rightly know. Is it dangerous?"

"It can be in adults. Keep checking yourselves for swellings beneath the ears and in the groin area. If you or your wife experience fever or any of the symptoms I just mentioned, see me immediately. Mumps is especially hard on adult men.

"If Bobby's fever rises, rub him down with

116

alcohol or cold water. Give him plenty of liquids and keep him quiet. You should see an improvement in a few days."

"Thanks, Doc. Me and Bobby's ma sure were worried. This is our first, and we don't want nothing to happen to him. How much do I owe you?"

"Can you pay?"

Dunn's chest puffed out. "I have steady work. I can pay."

"Very well. Is one dollar too much?"

Dunn dug in his pocket and pulled out a silver dollar. "It's not too much, Doc. Much obliged. It's about time Cheyenne had a doctor the citizens can depend upon. My wife will be over one day soon to welcome you to town."

Jess stared at the silver dollar long after Dunn and his son had departed. It was the first dollar he'd earned at his profession, unless he counted his meager army pay. He'd joined the army right out of medical school, before he'd hung up his shingle. And when he'd tried to practice in Dodge City, the citizens shunned him because he'd fought for the Rebel cause. It felt damn good to earn money after all those dry years, even if it was only a dollar.

Business picked up daily. Jess was so busy administering to the sick, he could only spare brief moments to think about Meg and wonder how she was doing. Jess's reputation grew until everyone in Cheyenne had either heard about or personally met young Dr. Jess Gentry. His waiting room was usually filled with patients needing his services, and he was summoned often to make emergency house calls.

Within two weeks, Jess had delivered a baby, sewn up dozens of wounds, both minor and serious, and treated various illnesses. He'd also captured the attention of several unmarried ladies who considered the handsome bachelor fair game. Invitations began to pour in. He accepted some, turned down others, but found no woman who could compare favorably to feisty, unconventional Meg.

The first morning Jess found no patients in his waiting room, he decided to visit the apothecary to replenish his supply of medicines. He had just finished his business and was returning to the office when he saw Zach coming out of the Railroad Cafe across the street with a woman on his arm. Thinking it was Meg and eager to see how she was faring, he hailed Zach and hurried across the street.

"Doc!" Zach greeted. "I was planning to visit you today. There's someone I want you to meet. Jess, this is Widow Dowling."

Widow Dowling offered her hand. "My friends call me Mary. I've heard a lot about you, Dr. Gentry. All of it good."

Jess must have made an appropriate reply but he was too dumbfounded to remember. What in the hell was going on here? Where was Meg? What was Zach doing squiring around another woman? Zach even looked different with his hair all slicked down and his beard trimmed.

"May I have a word with you in private, Zach?" Jess said, his voice ripe with disapproval.

"Sure thing, Doc. You'll excuse me a minute, won't you, Mary?"

"Of course, Zach," Mary graciously allowed. "I wanted to step into the dry goods store a moment anyway."

"What in the hell is going on, Zach?" Jess demanded to know. "Where's Meg? Does she know what you're about?"

"Hell, Jess, a man's gotta socialize once in a while. Those pills you gave me worked wonders. I feel like a new man. Maybe my heart isn't as bad as I thought it was."

"I'm glad, but what about Meg?"

"Meg's doing just fine, Doc. Back to her old self again. I'm doing my best to convince her to give up bounty hunting."

"You have to do better than that."

"I'm trying, Doc. Got some good news to tell you. I got me a job. One that doesn't tax my leg or my heart. Mr. Henley down at the hardware store needs a clerk. It's a far cry from what I'm used to, but Meg and me need money powerful bad."

Jess sent a dark look at the woman who had just disappeared into the dry goods store. "What's that woman to you?"

Zach sent him a puzzled look. "Mary? We've been friends a long time. Hell, Doc, a widow has needs just like anyone else."

Gorge rose up in Jess's throat. How could Zach do this to Meg?

"Come out to the house sometime, Doc," Zach invited. "I know you've built up a busy practice in town, but that's no reason to make yourself scarce. Meg misses you. She hasn't said anything, but I can tell. She needs to be around young people. Have you thought any more about what we discussed?"

"I'm in no position to marry anyone," Jess asserted. "I can't believe you'd even suggest such a thing, Zach. Don't you have feelings for Meg?"

Zach frowned. "You ain't making sense, Doc. You know how I feel about Meg."

From the corner of his eye, Jess saw Mary returning and bit back his caustic remark.

"Looks like Mary is done shopping," Zach said. "We'll talk later, Doc. Why don't you go out and visit Meg? Tell her not to keep supper for me tonight."

Jess stood with his mouth hanging open as Zach and Mary strolled off arm in arm.

Chapter Six

Jess whirled on his heel and strode away. Rage blinded him to everything but the grinding need to see Meg, to learn if she was aware of Zach's betrayal, and if she was badly hurt by it. Jess reached home in record time. He didn't bother checking to see if he had patients waiting, but went straight to the lean-to and saddled his horse. Meg needed to know about the man she claimed to love, he decided, spurring his horse down the road. Jess had come to like Zach, but this time the older man had gone too far.

Jess galloped his horse all the way to Meg's house. He knew he'd ridden his poor mount hard, but he was mad, damn mad. At Zach for betraying Meg, and at Meg for letting it happen. Did she have no pride? No sense at all?

He dismounted, tossed his reins over the porch railing, and charged up the steps. He stormed into the house without bothering to knock.

"Meg!"

No answer.

"Dammit, Meg, answer me."

Meg came hurrying out of the kitchen, wiping her hands on the apron she wore around her middle. She looked beautifully disheveled and flushed.

"Jess? Whatever is wrong?" Suddenly her face turned white. "It isn't Zach, is it? He's been doing so well lately."

"You're damn right it's Zach, only it's not what you think. Do you know who he's with?"

She sent him a puzzled look. "No, but I can guess. He's with Mary."

Jess sent her a pitying look. "Doesn't that make you angry?"

"Why should it? Zach is a grown man. He's free to do as he pleases. So am I."

He grasped her shoulders and gave her an angry shake. "The man doesn't deserve your love."

"Don't ever say that! Zach saved my life."

"So you said. And you repaid him by becoming his lover. He doesn't deserve you, Meg."

"Zach is not now nor has he ever been my lover," Meg bit out. "You're dense as a doorknob, Jess Gentry!"

Jess stared at her. Her color was high, and her incredible green eyes glittered like brilliant emeralds. He could tell she was angry, and he wanted to kiss the pout off her lush lips.

"You're denying that you and Zach are lovers?" he hissed.

"Haven't I always denied it?" Meg charged. "You're the one who keeps persisting. Let me go."

He pulled her against him. "Zach said to tell you not to keep supper for him. Though he didn't come out and say it, he'll probably spend the night with the attractive Widow Dowling."

"Zach and Mary have been friends for years. Before I came into his life. Let me go," she repeated.

Jess couldn't explain why he didn't accept Meg's word and let things go at that. But a devil inside him wouldn't let the subject rest. He was like a dog with a bone, digging beneath her denial for the truth.

"If Zach can take another lover, why not you?"

Meg gave him a startled look. "You're not offering yourself, are you?"

"Why not? Lord knows I've tried to treat you as a patient, but I'm not made of stone. I know your body intimately, Meg. I bathed you, took care of your needs. Every time I touched you I forced myself to think of you as someone in need of my services, not as a beautiful woman with a body that would tempt a saint. I'm not too proud to admit that I want you, Meg Lincoln, and Zach be damned. Just thinking about you and me together makes me hard as stone."

Meg realized Jess was going to kiss her, and she wanted to turn and run. She didn't.

"You liked my kisses once, Meg."

"You just thought I did."

His gaze settled on her lips. He stared at them for the space of a heartbeat before his mouth came down hard on hers. Her protest became a mewling sound, one that Meg scarcely realized had come from her own throat. His kiss was hot and intense, a searing mingling of tongues and unrestrained longing.

Jess broke off the kiss, the golden flecks in his eyes glowing like precious amber as he searched her face. "You want me," he crowed.

Meg expelled a shuddering breath. "No! I don't . . ."

"Don't deny it, Meg. You want me as badly as I want you." He grasped her hand and placed it on his erection. "See what you do to me?"

He grinned knowingly when she snatched her hand away. Then he kissed her again. He touched her breast, not with a doctor's impersonal touch, but with that of a lover. Meg felt a coiling fear begin in her stomach and spiral upward. She'd known no man except Arlo, and he'd been brutal. In all the years since, she'd sworn that no man would ever get close enough to hurt her again. Yet here she was, acting like a wanton in Jess's arms.

"Jess, I don't want . . ."

"Yes, you do." His disarming smile turned into a thoughtful frown. "You're not afraid of me, are you? Is Zach a brutal lover? Is that why you're so skittish? I promise you, Meg, I will give you nothing but pleasure. I'd never hurt you. You believe me, don't you?"

Meg thought about it a moment and decided that if she could believe any man, it would be Jess. If only he wasn't such an ass about her and Zach. She didn't believe Jess would knowingly hurt her, but he was a man. Arlo had been full of promises, too, but he'd hurt her terribly and would have continued to do so if she hadn't had the gumption to do something about it.

"I believe you wouldn't hurt me, Jess, but that doesn't change things."

"Are you denying you want me? Or are you worried about betraying Zach?"

Meg flushed and looked away. Never had she experienced the kind of unfulfilled longing that Jess's kisses aroused in her. She'd had so little experience with men that those feelings frightened her.

"I'm not sure what I want, Jess. And for your information, since Zach and I aren't lovers, I wouldn't be betraying him."

Apparently, Jess perceived her answer as permission to proceed, for he swept her off her feet and into his arms.

Her voice rose on a note of panic. "What are you doing?"

"Taking you someplace where we can both have what we want. You're contrary as all get out, Meg, but that only makes you more desirable in my eyes."

He strode to her room and shoved open the door with his shoulder. Then he let her slide slowly down his body. She felt his arousal, and fear shuddered through her. She couldn't let him do this.

He kissed her again, and Meg's wits flew out the window. A moment later her foggy brain registered a new feeling, one that made the breath catch in her throat. His hands, his large capable hands, were everywhere, touching, caressing, arousing. When he cupped her between her legs, panic rose thick and hard inside her, and she pushed against his chest.

"Stop! This is going too fast. I'm not sure this is . . ."

Jess's hands fell to his sides. "You're right. I'm too damn eager and I should know better. We'll do this your way, love. Slow and easy."

"That's not what I mean."

"I know what you mean," he said as he tangled his hand in her hair, easing her head back.

Meg shuddered as he kissed the tender flesh beneath her ear, the wildly thudding pulse at the base of her throat. She murmured something incoherent and clung to him. He found her breasts, kneading them gently through the material of her bodice. Her fingers dug into his shoulders, and she stifled a moan.

He plucked impatiently at the offending garment. "This will have to go."

He released the buttons holding the bodice together and stripped it down her arms, taking her chemise with it. Meg's hands flew up to shield her breasts. Jess pulled her hands down to her sides.

She held her breath as he studied the puckered scar above her right breast, touching it gently with his fingertip. Was it so ugly?

"The scar detracts not at all from your breasts. This isn't the first time I've seen them, you know. You're beautiful. I want to tell you all the things I've been thinking since the first time I undressed you. Your body is perfect. Strong, athletic, yet soft and feminine and alluring." He rubbed her nipples with his thumbs. "I want to touch you all over."

Meg stared into the torrid depths of his glittering eyes and felt her heart pounding violently against her chest. She wanted him. The unexpected truth came to her in a blinding flash when she looked into his eyes and recognized hunger, the same kind of hunger she was experiencing.

How could it be? Hunger was the last

thing she wanted to feel for a man. She feared the ravening desire that Jess had aroused in her. Feared what Jess would do to her. She'd thought Arlo was a kind man until her wedding night, when he'd torn into her like a rapacious beast, laughing at her pitiful cries of pain.

He'd told her she should get used to it, for he intended to use her youth and innocence to help him step up in the world, stressing that not all men were gentle lovers like himself. She'd nearly laughed in his face. She thought he'd merely been trying to frighten her into submission, until he offered her as collateral in a poker game. That night her innocence had been shattered for all time.

Her thoughts were still focused inward when she suddenly became aware that Jess had pushed her dress and chemise down past her hips, taking her drawers with them. They fell in a puddle around her feet and he lifted her out of them. His face was stark with need, his muscles tense as he tumbled her onto the bed and stared down at her. Meg's first inclination was to pull the covers over her nakedness, but the look on Jess's face told her it would do her no good. He was determined to have her.

His gaze held her suspended as he slowly began to undress. She wanted to look away but was unable to move or direct her gaze elsewhere. His shirt hit the floor. She stared at his chest and shoulders. Rippling tendons and long muscles jerked in response to her intense perusal. Meg thought him magnificent, and she hadn't even seen all of him.

When Jess whipped off his belt and opened his trousers, Meg's fear returned. A small cry of alarm slipped past her lips when she saw his eyelids drift half closed, concealing the intense gleam of his eyes. Her heartbeat skittered. With fear? Anticipation? Probably a mixture of both. Could he tell how frightened she was?

Jess's trousers and drawers dropped to the floor and he stepped out of them. Meg tried not to stare, but it was impossible not to. It was full daylight; sunshine streamed through the window. Every impressive detail of Jess's hard body was blatantly displayed. There was no fat anywhere on his magnificent form. Her gaze flitted down his broad chest, over a washboard stomach, slim hips, and muscular legs, then returned again to that rigid muscle standing upright between his thighs.

He was huge. His fully aroused sex rose regally against his stomach, its purple head moist and throbbing. Meg gulped back a scream. To a woman who'd only known pain from her brief sexual encounters, it was an alarming sight.

Jess was thoroughly puzzled by Meg's apparent fright. Did she think he would hurt her? He couldn't imagine Zach engaging in rough sex, but nothing was impossible. He eased down on the bed beside Meg and took her into his arms.

"Fear has no place in this bed, love. I promised you pleasure and you shall have it."

"Pleasure? Is that possible?"

Meg's question startled Jess. "You've never experienced pleasure from lovemaking with . . . anyone?"

Meg shook her head. "I don't believe it exists. Please, Jess, can't you see this is a mistake?"

A thought suddenly occurred to Jess. What if Meg had been telling the truth about Zach? Maybe they weren't lovers.

"Are you a virgin, Meg?"

Meg looked unflinchingly into his eyes and shook her head. "I'm not a virgin."

A sense of disappointment tugged at Jess. He'd been willing to give her the benefit of the doubt about Zach, but her words had dashed that hope. How many others had there been before Zach? Why hadn't any of her previous lovers given her pleasure?

"I'm going to give you pleasure, Meg, never doubt it. Forget your other lovers; they don't count. Concentrate on me. I'm going to make your body sing."

He bracketed her face in his hands and took her mouth. When his tongue filled her mouth, she forget her fear. Blood pounded through her veins so hard she imagined she could hear it. He brought her beneath him, trapping her. Then he gave her his passion, his fire, the sweet memorable taste of him.

It was frightening. It was heady and intoxicating.

She squirmed beneath him, and heard him groan. The sound returned her scattered wits, and she pushed against his chest.

"I don't want this, Jess."

"We both want this," Jess panted into her ear. "Don't worry about Zach. He's probably enjoying himself with his lady friend."

He filled his hands with her breasts, kneading their fullness, teasing her nipples with his long, talented fingers. His weight shifted and his hand slipped down between their bodies, his fingers finding a sensitive spot that caused her to jerk in response. Her head fell back, and a soft mewling sound came from her throat.

Jess rose up on his elbow and smiled down at her. "See, I told you there'd be pleasure."

Before she could draw a calming breath, he molded his mouth to hers, forcing her lips open, invading her with his tongue. She felt his finger pierce her from below, then move in imitation of his tongue. She felt overwhelmed, possessed. She could think of nothing except the moist heat of his mouth and the wicked pressure of his finger.

Then his mouth left hers with an abruptness that startled her. Her entire body felt shaken, her lips swollen and bruised. Her blood rushed through her veins, pounding against her temples and that place where Jess's finger tantalized her. Was this passion? Or was it simple pleasure making her body melt into a boneless lump? Was there a difference?

She splayed her hands against his chest, trying to put some distance between them so she could think.

Jess must have read her mind. "No, love, don't think. Just feel. Experience all the wonderful emotions and feelings; let your body respond. Lovemaking can be powerfully rewarding if you let it."

"It can also be painful and degrading," Meg whispered shakily.

"Not with me."

Meg wanted to believe him. More than anything, she wanted to forget the painful coupling Arlo had forced on her. She wanted beautiful dreams to fill her nights instead of the frightening ones that usually plagued her. Could Jess's lovemaking be the miracle she'd been praying for? Until Jess, she'd never encountered a man with whom she'd wanted to explore her sensual nature.

"Stop thinking, Meg," Jess chided, as if aware of her thoughts.

He pressed his finger deeper inside her.

She gasped and arched against him. "You don't play fair."

A chuckle rumbled in his chest. "Neither do you. Why do you pretend you're not enjoying what I'm doing to you? Your face is flushed with excitement and your body is taut as a bowstring. You're hot and damp and slick as sweet cream. I'll bet you taste delicious."

His words appalled Meg. But what he did next left her gasping with shock. He took her with his mouth. At first she hadn't known what he intended as his mouth slid downward, between her breasts, over her quivering stomach, lower, to where his fingers were producing all those wonderful sensations.

Her head tilted back. A soundless cry vibrated in her throat. Tension pulled her legs rigid. She nearly jumped off the bed as a trembling ecstasy built inside her. Then the rough pad of his tongue moved over her, inside her, soothing the slick, swollen flesh that suddenly felt feverish and taut.

Meg buried her face in the pillow to stifle the moans of pleasure building in her throat. She'd never known the sensations she was experiencing were even possible.

Fiery ripples began deep in her belly, at the very center of her being, and spread in ever widening waves until they consumed her utterly. Her body stiffened, held captive in an exquisite state of violent emotional upheaval.

Then everything seemed to culminate in a blinding flash of raw sensation. And she melted.

"Now it's my turn," Jess said, raising himself above her. "I need to be inside you."

Slowly he sank down on her body. He kissed her open mouth, exulting in her soft, panting breaths. He moved his arm beneath her, lifting her buttocks toward him as he penetrated her with a single deep thrust. He heard her cry out but was too far gone in lust to give meaning to it. There was no maidenhead to impede him, but she was so damn tight she might as well have been untouched. She surrounded him so snugly he could feel vibrations when she took a deep breath.

He nearly lost it when she moved her body to better accommodate him. "Don't move," he said through clenched teeth.

She inhaled slowly. A curse ripped from Jess's throat. "Damn! It's too late."

He began to move. He sank into her and felt her quiver. He withdrew and sank into her again, savoring the slick, scalding heat of her. He held her steady and planted himself as far as he could go, nudging her legs wider.

"You're so damn tight," he groaned into her ear. "Like a velvet glove made just for me."

Jess felt as if he had never possessed a woman as completely as he now possessed

Meg. All the women who had gone before her were nothing. The intense pleasure searing his mind and body was coming from the woman beneath him, from the slick heat of her tight sheath. Suddenly he was desperate, frenzied, like a volcano about to explode. Tucking her buttocks more firmly against his hips, he moved forcefully inside her, thrusting deeply, powerfully.

"I can't wait, love. Hurry," he grated hoarsely against her lips. "Come with me."

Meg lifted her hips to meet his strokes, stunned by the powerful sensations racing through her. Pleasure, relentless, fervent, held her in its grip. She was close to frantic now, and then he released her in one powerful stroke that sent her soaring to oblivion. On the edge of her awareness she heard Jess cry out her name, felt him collapse against her.

Long moments later, Meg opened her eyes and looked up into Jess's glittering gaze. A look of confusion wrinkled his brow.

"What is it?" Meg asked.

He pulled out of her and rolled over on his back. "You're a puzzle, Meg Lincoln. I can't quite figure you out."

"What do you mean?"

Jess turned on his side and raised himself up on one elbow. He lifted his hand to idly draw a finger down her throat to the swell of her breast, then over her belly.

"When I first started making love to you,

you acted like a scared rabbit. As if you feared I would hurt you. Why is that, Meg? Who was the brutal lover in your life? Is it Zach?"

"No!" Meg denied hotly.

Jess's voice hardened. "Keep Zach out of your bed from now on. Maybe what you feel for Zach isn't love. Could it be pity?"

"Zach wouldn't stand for my pity," Meg scoffed.

Jess's finger paused in the soft thatch between her legs. "What now, Meg? Where do we go from here?"

"What we did just now changes nothing."

Jess went still. "It changes everything. I don't want you living here with Zach any longer."

Meg surged upright, her expression fierce. "You have no right to tell me what to do. This is my home. Zach needs me. He's not a well man."

"He looked fine to me today."

"Zach finally admitted to me that he has a bad heart. The medicine you gave him helps, but we both know his condition will worsen."

Jess didn't know why he was making demands on Meg when he had no right to demand anything of her. He was a wanted man. The law could catch up to him today, tomorrow, or never. He could offer her nothing except an uncertain future. Meg was a bounty hunter; how could he expect her to feel anything but revulsion when she learned he was a wanted man?

"I can rent a room for you at the boardinghouse," Jess offered. "I'm making enough money to pay for your keep."

"What will I be, your whore? The townspeople already hold me in contempt for choosing a profession not suited to my sex. No, thanks. I'll stay here where I belong."

"Dammit, Meg, my life is complicated right now. I can't give you anything beyond what I just offered. I want us to be together. I don't want you to stay here with Zach."

"If you think I want an offer of marriage from you, you're dead wrong," Meg said stiffly. "Marriage is not in my future. I'm perfectly happy the way I am, with what I'm doing."

Jess arose abruptly and began pulling on his clothing. "Does placing your life in danger make you happy?"

Meg nodded emphatically. "Why not? It pays well and puts food on the table."

Jess buttoned his shirt and slammed on his hat. "I won't have it, Meg. You're not going chasing after criminals again, and that's final."

Meg lifted her chin. "You and who else is going to stop me?"

"I'll have another talk with Zach. If your lover can't stop you, I will."

Meg reared up out of bed, apparently unconcerned about her nudity as she faced Jess squarely, hands on hips, jaw jutting pugnaciously.

"Zach is the father I wanted all my life but never had until he found me half dead on the prairie and nursed me back to health. He was a rough, hard-living bounty hunter when we first met, but he showed me a softness no one else had ever seen. I became the daughter he lost years ago. When he took the bullet that ended his career, I decided to become what he had been. I owe him my life."

Perhaps for the first time, Jess honestly considered what Meg had been telling him for weeks. Could it be true? Her explanation seemed logical enough, but the fact remained that Meg hadn't been a virgin.

"You weren't a virgin," Jess reminded her. "Who was the man in your life if not Zach?" His eyes narrowed. "Or were there more than one? Why were you alone on the prairie? What happened to you?"

"My past is my own business," Meg said. "You have no right to judge me."

"I wasn't judging you. I'm merely curious. Lord knows I'm no saint."

"Maybe someday I'll tell you, after you tell me your secret. Are you wanted by the law, Jess?"

Jess's gaze settled on her breasts, and he felt himself grow hard and thicken. He directed his gaze elsewhere so he could think.

Making love to Meg had definitely complicated matters. What was he going to do about her? Should he tell her about himself?

Meg had finally convinced him that her relationship with Zach was purely platonic, but what about his own feelings for her?

Jess hadn't had a woman in a very long time, and he didn't want to confuse lust with deeper emotions until he'd had time to sort them out. Especially since he wasn't presently free to nurture emotional ties.

"Jess, are you gong to answer my question?"

"I have no secrets," Jess lied. "None that I care to divulge."

Meg yanked the sheet from the bed and pulled it around her. "You'd better leave, Jess. Please don't come back. A relationship between us will only complicate matters. I don't want marriage, and neither do you. Satisfy yourself with whores, for I'm not about to become one. My life is here with Zach."

"Promise me one thing."

"I know what you're going to ask, and the answer is no."

He grasped her shoulders and gave her a rough shake. "Dammit, Meg, I care about you. It doesn't matter what you are or what you've been; chasing danger is not what I want for you."

"What *do* you want for me, Jess?"

Jess flushed and looked away. He wanted her to keep herself safe for him. He didn't know how he would do it, but he was determined to prove he wasn't an outlaw, even if he had to return to Dodge and face down Mr. Wingate. But he couldn't tell Meg that. Not yet.

"I want you near, where I can keep an eye on you. Soon, perhaps after I've taken care of . . . certain matters, we can talk further about our . . . feelings. About the future."

"I don't really think there is a future for us, Jess. I'm not going to give up bounty hunting. I enjoy my independence. I've learned the hard way that men can change overnight. They aren't what they seem. They'll turn on you when you least expect it."

Meg's words stunned Jess. "Did I hurt you, Meg? Was I cruel or brutal? Didn't I give you the pleasure I promised? Who hurt you? What man made you distrustful of males?"

"You didn't hurt me. Perhaps you're that exceptional man like Zach, who wouldn't hurt a woman. I don't know you well enough to judge. You did give me pleasure, the kind I never experienced before. As to who hurt me . . ." She shook her head. "I'm not ready to talk about that with anyone."

"Very well. Keep your secrets, but don't expect me to keep my distance. Not after what we just shared. And don't make the mistake of thinking I'll let you risk your life again. Zach is in agreement with me. One brush with death should be enough to persuade you to give up the dangerous life you were leading. If I have to tie you down to keep you from chasing after criminals, I'll do it."

Meg's eyes blazed defiance. "Don't threaten me, Jess. I'll do as I please, and you can't stop me."

"What if I've just given you a baby?"

Meg blanched. "You didn't . . ."

"I might have."

Only then did Jess realize why he hadn't taken precautions. He was a doctor; he knew how to prevent pregnancy. If he made Meg pregnant, he'd have to marry her. Was that what he'd wanted all along? For fate, or God, to take a hand in his life? Did he care for Meg enough to marry her despite all the problems he had to overcome?

He didn't know. The only thing of which he was certain was that he wouldn't hesitate to marry her should she become pregnant with his child.

Would Meg marry *him?* That question was far more difficult to answer. Baby or not, she'd probably reject his offer and live her life according to her own dictates. It was obvious that Meg didn't trust men. Had little use for them, in fact. He'd give the man who'd hurt her a good thrashing if he knew his name and where to find him.

"This conversation is ridiculous," Meg said. "It's highly unlikely that this one encounter will result in pregnancy. And since I don't intend for it to happen again, we have nothing to worry about."

Jess gave her a tolerant smile but said nothing, since their thoughts on the subject were poles apart.

"I reckon that's my cue to leave," Jess said. "My office is probably full of patients awaiting my return. But before I go . . ."

Grasping one end of the trailing sheet covering Meg, Jess reeled her into her arms, like a fish on a hook. "Kiss me good-bye, love."

"You've had all the kisses you're going to get from me. Neither of us needs the complication of a relationship right now."

"You're right about that, Meg," he admitted. He kissed her anyway. A long, lingering kiss that made her blood thicken and her heart pound. Then he released her. "This isn't finished between us by a long shot. You wanted me as badly as I wanted you. It will happen again, take my word for it."

Meg watched Jess leave with a heavy heart. She was so confused. She'd let Jess make love to her, and that was a miracle in itself, considering how she felt about men in general. But, oh, how he'd made her body sing, her soul soar. She could very easily become addicted to Jess Gentry. She wouldn't have known lovemaking could be enjoyable if Jess had not shown her.

But she knew better than to let emotion rule her life. Both she and Jess harbored secrets neither was willing to reveal. And Jess's determination to change her into the woman he thought she should be didn't sit well with her.

Forgetting Jess Gentry was her best bet, Meg decided as she began to dress. What she needed to do now was resume her life as it had been before she met Jess. A visit to the sheriff's office was in order. Perhaps he had a new batch of Wanted posters with new faces, new outlaws for her to bring to justice.

Chapter Seven

Meg had no intention of visiting Jess when she made the trip into Cheyenne two days later. Her emotions were still too raw to see him again.

Pushing thoughts of Jess from her mind, Meg drew rein in front of the sheriff's office and dismounted. She had important business to conduct today and couldn't afford to let her mind wander.

The sheriff looked up from the document he was perusing and smiled at Meg as she entered the office and closed the door behind her.

"Howdy, Miss Lincoln. I reckon I know why you're here."

"Hello, Sheriff Bufford. Anything new come in lately?"

"Got a new batch of posters in yesterday. Haven't had a chance to look at them yet. I heard your last venture nearly cost you your life. Why don't you retire and let someone else go haring off after outlaws?"

"Not you, too, Sheriff," Meg exclaimed. "You're not going to side with those people who think I should stay home and take up sewing, are you?"

"You've got plenty of guts, Meg, and lots of savvy, but sometimes it takes more than guts and savvy to bring in a dangerous outlaw. How does Purdee feel about your profession after your recent brush with death?"

Meg flushed, recalling the argument she'd had with Zach on the same subject. He wasn't aware that her trip to town today involved a stop at the sheriff's office. He'd assumed she'd wanted to see Jess and had encouraged the visit.

"Zach isn't crazy about the idea of me riding out again, but he'll come around when he learns I have no intention of giving up bounty hunting."

"It's your life, Meg," Bufford said as he removed a stack of Wanted posters from a drawer and slapped them down on the desk. "See if there's something here you're interested in. Take your time. I'm off to make arrangements to escort a prisoner to Denver."

He rose, picked up his hat, and shoved it on his head. "Oh, by the way, I have something that might interest you. Ever hear of a man named Duke Fremont?"

Meg shook her head.

"Fremont is a slick cardsharp and ladies' man who raped and brutally beat a young girl in Denver after she'd spurned his attentions. The poor girl died, but not before she'd identified her assailant.

"I just learned that Fremont is in the area. He must be desperate for money, because he broke into Jake Royce's house, robbed him of all the cash he had on hand, and raped his daughter."

"What's he doing in Cheyenne?" Meg asked.

"Looking for easy pickings, I reckon. Cheyenne has earned itself quite a reputation."

"What makes you think he's still around?"

"He was spotted yesterday skulking around the vacant Floyd place. I rode out there when I heard, but found nothing, though I did see indications that someone had been out there. I'm going to form a posse and track him down as soon as I deliver my prisoner. My gut says he's still in the area."

"Give me a shot at him first, Sheriff," Meg pleaded. "Zach and I need the money. There's a reward out on him, isn't there?"

"Got word from Denver yesterday. The dead girl's parents are offering five hundred dollars for his capture, dead or alive."

Meg's eyes narrowed as she calculated how long 500 dollars would last her and Zach.

"Perhaps I'll look through the posters anyway, before I decide to go after Fremont. There might be something more attractive here."

"Suit yourself. You can let me know what you decide when I return."

Meg sat down behind the desk and picked up the posters, studying each one carefully. Most of the outlaws weren't worth pursuing, either because the rewards weren't hefty enough or they were last seen in parts too distant from Cheyenne to make pursuit practical.

She had reached the bottom of the pile when a face she knew seemed to leap out at her. With shaking hands, she picked up the poster bearing badly drawn images of three men. The headline on the poster proclaimed them the Gentry brothers, Rafe, Jess, and Sam, fugitives from the law. They had robbed a bank in Dodge City, Kansas. They were armed and dangerous, the poster warned. A reward of 500 dollars each was offered for their apprehension.

Though the image was not clear, Meg easily recognized Jess, the man who had taught her that lovemaking needn't be painful.

Jess.

An outlaw.

Hadn't she always known Jess harbored a secret? Hadn't she always suspected something like this? But seeing it in writing was more damning than anything she could have imagined. Thank God the sheriff hadn't seen the poster. Jess, a bank robber? It just didn't fit. Jess was a skilled doctor who went out of his way to save lives. She took a furtive look around, intending to stuff the poster into her pocket, when the sheriff returned, making it impossible to conceal the drawing.

"Have you decided on anyone?" Bufford asked.

"I . . . oh, I believe so."

"Can I have a look?" Bufford said, craning his neck for a look at the poster Meg held in her hand.

"I . . . decided to go after Fremont," Meg said, quickly shuffling the posters together so that the one picturing the Gentry brothers ended up on the bottom. With any luck, Bufford would forget about the posters.

Bufford shrugged. "Suit yourself, though I think you're biting off more than you can chew with this one. Now, if this were five years ago, and Purdee was going with you, I'd have no qualms. But you're a woman, Meg. I can't say as I blame your detractors for thinking you shouldn't be engaged in this kind of work."

Meg bristled angrily. "Just because I'm a woman doesn't make me any less capable to do the job. Look at my record. I've brought in more dangerous outlaws than any bounty hunter in these parts except for Zach. Being a woman works in my favor, as I've proven many times in the past."

"It's your life," Bufford said without enthusiasm. "But I'll only back off until I return from Denver. I'm taking the train today and

148

will return day after tomorrow. If you don't have Fremont by then, I'll take over."

"It's a deal," Meg said, rising. She picked up the Wanted posters. "I'll just put these away for you before I leave." She opened the drawer and shoved them inside, well to the back.

"One day I'll take them out and have a look," Bufford said. "But if none of them interested you, I reckon they won't interest me."

Meg left the sheriff's office in a daze. Just one word from her and she could have collected the reward for Jess. She never even considered it. She'd feel a whole lot better, however, if she'd been able to destroy the poster before anyone else saw it. She glanced down the street toward Jess's office, wondering if she should tell him that she knew he was an outlaw.

Yes, she decided, but not now. Perhaps after she returned with Fremont. The sheriff didn't seem to be in any hurry to look at the posters, and she had a job to do first. If she told Jess now, he would probably guess she'd been looking at Wanted posters. Then he'd try to stop her from going after Fremont. An argument would likely ensue, and Jess would enlist Zach's help to stop her.

No, she decided, she had to keep this to herself for the time being. She needed to think about the poster and try to figure out how Jess had earned the title of outlaw.

A continual flow of patients kept Jess busy during the following days. So busy he hadn't had time to return to the house to see Meg, but he thought often about what had taken place in her bed. He tried to convince himself that he should forget it had ever happened. But he seriously doubted he could do that. He'd relived it over and over in his mind, until every incredible moment of their loving was indelibly etched in his memory.

And what a memory it was! No woman had ever made him feel the way Meg had. Despite her prickly disposition, her independent streak, her recklessness, he doubted there was a woman alive to match her. Meg appealed to him on every level. She might be a bit rash and headstrong, but taming her would be half the fun of having her in his life. *If* he were free to pursue her.

Today was just like any other busy day in the life of Dr. Jess Gentry. The usual assortment of patients were lined up in his waiting room with the usual complaints. But the moment Jess had opened his eyes this morning, he'd experienced a twinge of anxiety. He'd had the feeling many times in the past, especially during the war when danger threatened. Anticipation made him edgy, draining him emotionally as he began the day.

Jess had just seen the last patient of the

day and he was tired. Bone tired and irritable. A meal and a bath were in order, he thought as he locked the front door and wandered into his office. He was straightening his instruments when he heard a racket at the front door. Heaving a weary sigh, Jess walked resolutely to the door, hoping the emergency wasn't a serious one.

Jess's breath caught in his throat and blood pounded through his veins when he found Zach standing on the doorstep, clutching his chest, his eyes wild.

"Zach! What happened? Are you ill?"

Jess helped Zach inside, easing him down on the cot in his examining room. But Zach would have none of Jess's pampering.

"I'm fine, Doc," he said, brushing aside Jess's concern. "A little pain ain't gonna kill me. Just let me catch my breath."

Jess took a bottle of pills from his medicine cabinet and handed one to Zach. "Here. Dissolve this under your tongue."

Jess chafed impatiently as he waited for the pill to take effect. What dire emergency could have brought Zach racing hell for leather to his office? he wondered. All he could think about was Meg. Something had happened to her; he could feel it in his bones.

"Can you talk now, Zach? Are you still in pain?"

"I'm fine, Doc, thanks. It's Meggie."

"She's not ill, is she? I'll get my bag and

go out there immediately."

"Hang on, Doc, it ain't what you think. She's gone. I didn't know she intended to leave until she walked out the door with her saddlebags."

"Gone where?"

"After Duke Fremont. She told me she'd visited the sheriff's office yesterday and learned that Fremont was seen in the area. He's wanted for rape and murder. I tried to talk her out of it, but she wouldn't listen. I stopped off at the sheriff's office before I came here, but Bufford wasn't there. The deputy said Bufford was escorting a prisoner to Denver.

"Fremont is dangerous, Jess. I'm so damn worried about Meggie that I considered going after her myself, but my body ain't what it used to be. There was a time . . ." His voice faltered. Jess was shocked to see tears in his eyes.

Jess reached for the gun belt hanging over the back of the chair and buckled it on, his face grim with determination. "I'll find her, Zach. Do you have any idea where she might be headed?"

"The deputy told me Fremont was spotted out by the old Floyd place west of town. I reckon you can start looking there." He glared at Jess. "None of this would have happened if you'd taken my advice and married Meggie."

"I can't marry anyone right now. Besides, I thought you and Meg . . ."

Zach gave a bark of laughter. "I know. Meggie told me you thought we were lovers. I don't know how you came by that stupid notion. I love Meggie like a daughter and she loves me like a father. Look at me, Doc. What do you see? A crippled, washed-up bounty hunter who lived hard and played even harder. A miracle happened when I found Meggie. I stopped drinking and carousing because Meggie needed me. If anything happened to her I would die."

"Nothing is going to happen to her," Jess vowed. "I'll bring her back safely, and when I do, you'd best chain her to the stove if you want to keep her home."

"She'd be better off married to you."

"We'll talk about this later," Jess said as he plucked his hat from the rack and slammed it on his head. "If I'm not back in two days, tell the deputy to form a posse. Why in blazes did the sheriff agree to let Meg go after Fremont alone?"

"Deputy Taylor told me that she asked Sheriff Bufford to give her the first shot at Fremont. Meggie can be pretty damn convincing. The sheriff didn't stand a chance against her. Anyway, he gave Meggie two days to bring Fremont in. If she doesn't return by then, Bufford is gonna form a posse. Meggie is damn good at what she does, Jess.

153

I know it and the sheriff knows it."

"Well, I don't know it," Jess said through clenched teeth. "I'd hoped she'd learned her lesson after the Calder fiasco. Spend the night on the cot in my office, Zach. I'll bring Meg here when I find her."

A trace of daylight remained when Meg spied the Floyd place in the distance. It stood in the midst of a grassy plain, with no visible cover for miles except for a deep gully cutting a swath through the tall grass. Meg reined her mare into the gully and dismounted, securing the reins to the ground with a rock. Then she sat down and waited for darkness. When the last vestiges of daylight disappeared, Meg checked her guns, wound a rope around her waist, and crept on her belly through the grass toward the house.

The place looked deserted, and Meg feared Fremont had already fled. If that proved to be the case, she'd spend the night in the house and start tracking him tomorrow. But until she found out for sure that Fremont was gone, she had to remain alert. She couldn't afford to become careless again.

Jess was going to be furious when he learned what she had done, she reflected. Not that it was any of his business. Just because she'd made love with him didn't mean he owned her.

She had almost reached the house when

she saw a brief flicker of light in one of the upstairs rooms. It had disappeared so quickly she might have imagined it, but she trusted her eyesight. Had Fremont lit a cigarette? The flicker of a match could account for what she had seen.

Meg reached the front porch. A quick glance showed a broken railing and caved-in front steps. The front door hung open on broken hinges. Meg smiled to herself as she went up the steps. Fremont had made it easy for her by not barricading the door. Was he that sure of himself?

Meg stepped through the door. The house was bereft of furnishings, and she could see stars through open spaces in the roof. The stairs loomed ahead of her. Did they squeak? Would they hold her weight? She eased her gun from her holster and placed a foot on the first step. Nothing. So far so good, she thought with relief. She'd been in similar situations many times in the past, and relying on surprise had always worked for her. It didn't matter whether she brought Fremont in dead or alive; he deserved his just rewards for raping two innocent women.

The moment she'd learned Fremont was a rapist, Meg knew she had to bring him to justice. A shudder passed through her. What Arlo had done to her was still a painful memory, one that would remain with her forever.

Her foot landed on another step. A loud creak rent the stillness. Meg froze. Had Fremont heard? Obviously not, for he hadn't come charging out to investigate. Just in case, she cocked her weapon and curled her finger around the trigger. She'd never had to kill a man before, but she wouldn't hesitate if she had no other choice.

Meg climbed two more steps, pausing after each one to listen. The waiting silence was deafening. Darkness closed in around her, and her heart began pounding so hard she feared Fremont could hear it from where he had hidden himself. The next step was missing. She drew in a steadying breath and stretched her leg up to bypass it.

Finally she reached the top, pausing on the landing to get her bearings. There were two doors, both slightly ajar. Meg blessed the full moon. Tonight it was her ally, for once she pushed a door fully open, moonlight pouring through the broken windows would illuminate both the room and Fremont.

Cautiously she moved toward the first door and placed her hand on the knob. She held her breath as she pushed the door wide and stepped inside. Only a very slight squeak gave away her presence. She exhaled sharply when the room proved to be empty.

Meg turned around and slowly moved toward the other room. A floorboard creaked beneath her foot. She inhaled and let her breath out slowly when Fremont's head didn't pop out of the room. Slowly she eased back the door and squeezed through the narrow opening. Crouching low, she swung her gun in a wide arc, holding it steady with both hands.

The room was empty! Had she been mistaken? Had the light she'd seen been a figment of her imagination?

Suddenly the door slammed against her, knocking her off balance. A man stepped out from behind it.

"I've been waiting for you," said a smooth-as-silk voice just before his fist connected with her jaw. Then everything went black.

Meg awakened slowly. Her jaw was on fire and her head felt as if it had been split open. A lantern flared somewhere on the other side of her closed eyelids. A booted toe nudged her none too gently in the ribs.

"Wake up."

Meg groaned. She'd done it again. Luck was surely against her.

A face floated into view. It wasn't a bad face as faces went, except for the cruel glint in the cold, colorless eyes and the harsh lines around the flattened lips and bared teeth.

"I've heard about you," Fremont sneered. "You're Meg Lincoln, that crazy lady bounty hunter."

"How did you . . ."

The words died in her throat when she saw his pale eyes slide down her body. She glanced down at herself, gasping in dismay when she saw that he had unbuttoned part of her shirt and untied the strings of her camisole, exposing the tops of her breasts. But that wasn't all. He had tied her arms behind her with her own rope.

"Bastard!" she hissed. "What gave me away? How did you know I was here?"

"That creaking floorboard. I never even heard you climb the stairs. I hid behind the door and waited for you. Of course, I didn't know you were a female. Not until I clipped you on the jaw and your hat fell off. I knew immediately all that beautiful black hair had to belong to a woman. You must be either mad or desperate to get into this kind of work."

Meg gave him a defiant glare. "What are you going to do now? I'm not the only bounty hunter after your hide. Sooner or later you'll be brought to justice."

"We'll see," Fremont gloated. "But in the meantime I have plans for you, pretty lady. Indeed I do."

He stared at her long legs encased in tight trousers and rubbed his chin. "Those britches you're wearing might present a problem, but nothing I can't handle. I'll cut them off if I have to. For a whore, you're a damn toothsome little piece, Meg Lincoln. A

158

woman who takes up a man's profession can't be respectable. How many men have you spread your legs for?"

A red haze formed behind Meg's eyes. "Raping me will only add another nail to your coffin."

He gave her an oily smile. "Women usually *give* me what I want. Why should you be any different? If you're good, I might let you live."

"What about that poor girl in Denver? She didn't live."

"She should have cooperated and given me what I wanted."

He dropped to his knees beside her and fondled her breasts. "That's the best pair of tits I've seen in a long time. Don't fight me and I'll make this good for you. Most women like what I do to them. Please me and you'll live to brag about what a good lover I am."

He unbuckled her gun belt and fumbled with the fastenings on her trousers. Meg bucked wildly. This couldn't be happening. Everything she'd suffered as Arlo's victim came back to haunt her. If Fremont raped her, he might as well kill her, for she'd never be the same.

Fremont caught her thrashing legs and sat on them as he worked her trousers over her hips and down her legs. When they were down around her ankles, he yanked off her boots and pulled the trousers all the way off, tossing them aside. With a flick of his wrist, he pulled her shirt apart and ripped her camisole down the center. Then he sat back on his haunches, his eyes glittering as he stared at her.

"You really are something, lady."

He unbuttoned his fly and prepared to climb on top of her. Meg drew back her legs and kicked him in the chest. He landed on his rump, his expression murderous.

He reared up and slapped her. "Try that again and you'll regret it."

Though aware that no one within miles could hear her, Meg opened her mouth and screamed.

"Stop that, bitch!" Fremont roared. "No one is killing you . . . yet."

Meg didn't stop screaming until he placed a hand over her mouth. She looked up into his twisted features and saw death — her death — in the colorless depths of his eyes. With renewed effort she fought him, kicking and spitting like a wild woman. If she was going to be raped, she wasn't going to make it easy for him.

Darkness had slowed Jess's progress as he followed Zach's directions to the old Floyd place. He knew he was near when he heard an ear-splitting scream cut through the stillness of the night.

Meg! He spurred his horse until horse and

man were flying over the dangerous terrain. The house suddenly came into view, a decrepit hulk, forlorn and sinister, squatting beneath the full moon. A light shining from a broken window guided him like a beacon. He rode up to the house and sawed on the reins. He was off his horse before it stopped prancing. He leaped over the broken steps, drew and cocked his pistol, and pushed through the door. He heard Meg scream again and took the stairs two at a time.

He followed the light to the open doorway and barged inside. What he saw froze the blood in his veins. Fremont, or the man he supposed was Fremont, was kneeling over Meg. One hand was fondling her breast and the other was clamped over her mouth. His wet, glistening sex protruded obscenely from his open fly as Meg bucked wildly beneath him. Cursing him every which way to Sunday, Jess roared in outrage when he saw that Meg's hands were tied behind her and her body was naked from the waist down.

Fremont whipped around but he didn't have a chance. Jess brought the butt of his gun down hard on Fremont's skull. Fremont moaned once and collapsed. Jess grasped his collar and tossed him aside like a bundle of rags.

Had Fremont hurt Meg? Had he arrived too late? He dropped to his knees and gathered her in his arms, crooning softly in her ear. She remained limp and unresponsive.

"Meg. Speak to me. Are you all right? Did the bastard hurt you?"

No response was forthcoming.

"Meg, answer me."

He breathed a sigh of relief when recognition registered in her eyes.

"Jess?"

"Yes, love."

"Fremont . . . he . . ."

"He's out like a light. Let me get that rope off your wrists so I can use it to tie him up."

He turned her around and untied the knots, cursing fluently when he saw how tightly Fremont had bound her. "Your hands are going to hurt when blood starts flowing to them again."

Meg moaned as Jess massaged the numbness in her hands. "Fremont . . . he . . . Oh, God, it was just like Arlo all over again. I couldn't bear it."

Jess's features hardened. "You don't have to talk about it now if you don't want to. I'll help you dress after I've taken care of Fremont," he said. "Then we can talk about this. I'm a doctor. I know how to treat torn flesh and . . ." He looked away, unable to continue. Who in the hell was Arlo?

Meg merely stared at him. Jess couldn't recall when he'd ever seen her so confused, so utterly lost.

"How did you know to come after me?"

"Zach rode to town after you left and told me what you'd done. He gave me directions to the Floyd place."

Meg closed her eyes as Jess tied up Fremont. Hurtful memories assailed her. She might have been Arlo's wife, but what he had done to her was closer to rape than to normal relations between husband and wife.

Jess returned with the lantern, and Meg opened her eyes. "I dragged the bastard into the corridor," Jess said. He tried to nudge her legs apart, but Meg resisted. "Relax, love. I need to see how badly he hurt you."

Meg shook her head. "He didn't. You arrived in time. He clipped me on the jaw and slapped me, but that's all."

Jess turned her face to the light. Meg saw his jaw tauten and knew the bruise marring her chin couldn't be pretty.

"I ought to kill the bastard," he hissed.

"I'm fine, really. Hand me my clothes."

Jess fetched her trousers and boots. Meg let him help her pull them on.

"We should wait till morning to take Fremont back to town," Jess said.

Meg shook her head in furious denial. "No! If we leave now, we can reach town by morning."

"Are you capable of riding? That bruise looks pretty nasty, and you've been badly shaken."

"I'm fine. I want Fremont behind bars,

163

where he won't hurt another woman."

"Very well. I'll drag him downstairs and find his horse. By the way, I didn't see your horse."

"I tethered my mare out of sight in a gully."

Jess started to leave, then spun around and grasped Meg's shoulders.

"Damn you! I ought to turn you over my knee. I was so damn scared when Zach said you'd gone after Fremont. When I walked in here and saw that bastard on top of you, I nearly had a heart attack."

Then, his anger vented, he pulled her against him, tilted her chin, and kissed her. Hard. With a passion she felt clear down to her toes. Then he was gone, leaving her reeling.

Her hands were shaking as she strapped on her guns and pushed her hair under her hat. She waited a moment to pull herself together, then started down the stairs after Jess.

Meg felt a keen jolt of satisfaction when she saw Fremont lying across his saddle, belly down, his hands and feet secured with a rope running beneath the horse's belly.

"I found Fremont's horse out back," Jess said. "I hope he enjoys riding back to town on his belly."

Meg made a wide berth around Fremont's horse. "He's awfully quiet."

Jess sent her a smug smile. "I gagged him.

I took exception to what came spewing out of his foul mouth."

Jess mounted and reached out a hand. "Put your foot in the stirrup and I'll give you a lift up."

Meg gave him her hand and he pulled her up. She settled behind him, resting her cheek against his back as her arms encircled his waist. Meg stifled a moan. The heat emanating from his hard body scorched her. The bold masculine scent of him, the feel of his hard muscular body against hers, produced unruly emotions in her. With difficulty she pushed those feelings aside. Until she learned more about Jess and his past, she couldn't allow her heart to become involved.

They retrieved Meg's horse from where she had left it, and Jess helped her mount. Then they started back to town.

Chapter Eight

Meg was drooping in the saddle hours later when they reined in at the sheriff's office. Deputy Taylor was just opening the office for the day and appeared more than a little surprised by his unexpected visitors.

He tipped his hat. "Mornin', Miz Lincoln. Doc Gentry." He stared at the bound and gagged man lying face down across the saddle of his horse and thumbed his hat to the back of his head. "I see you brought in a prisoner. Is that who I think it is?"

"It's Fremont," Meg said, dismounting. "He's all yours, Deputy."

"Well, I'll be. You did it again, Miz Lincoln. He's a bad one, all right. Did he give you any trouble?"

She and Jess exchanged glances. "A little, but I don't want to get into that right now."

Taylor stared pointedly at Meg's bruised face and merely nodded. "I'm expecting Sheriff Bufford on the evening train. He'll be mighty glad to see Fremont behind bars. Come back in a week, I'm sure the reward money will be here by then."

Taylor untied the ropes binding Fremont, dragged him off his horse, and prodded him into the jailhouse. Fremont sent a murderous glare at Meg and Jess before he stumbled through the door.

"I should go home and let Zach know I'm all right," Meg said, exhaustion slurring her words.

"Zach is waiting at my office," Jess said. "You're not going anywhere in your condition. Tomorrow is Sunday. Since I don't expect any patients, you can use the spare bedroom. I need to keep an eye on you for a day or two."

"I don't need looking after," Meg argued.

"Maybe not," Jess said, unconvinced. "However, I intend to examine you before you leave."

"Really, Jess," Meg said as she raised her foot into the stirrup. But she must have been weaker than she'd thought, for she couldn't quite pull herself into the saddle.

Jess was beside her instantly. He lifted her into the saddle and walked her horse down the street to his office. Zach rushed out the door to meet them.

"Thanks be, you're back!"

"Open the door, Zach," Jess said as he lifted Meg from her mare.

Zach hastened to do Jess's bidding. "What's wrong with Meggie? Did you get Fremont?"

"Put me down, Jess. I don't know what got into me," Meg said. "I'm not a weakling."

"You're the strongest woman I know. You've just been through a harrowing ordeal, however, and are understandably distraught. You've also gone the entire night without sleep. No more arguments. You need a good night's rest before I'll allow you to leave."

"Will someone tell me what in the hell happened?" Zach all but shouted. "Is Meggie hurt?"

"I'm not hurt," Meg insisted.

Apparently Zach got a good look at her face, for he turned the air blue with his curses. "Did Fremont do that? Where is he? I'll kill the bastard!"

"He's in jail where he belongs," Jess said. "Meg hasn't slept in twenty-four hours. I'm taking her upstairs and putting her to bed. Take care of the horses, will you, Zach? Come back when you're finished and I'll tell you all about it."

After a last glance at Meg, Zach hurried off.

"Really, Jess, I can walk," Meg persisted.

Jess ignored her as he carried her up the stairs and into the spare bedroom. He sat her at the edge of the bed and pulled off her boots.

"What you need right now is sleep. I'm going to tuck you in, then go down and talk to Zach. If you're not sleeping by the time I

168

return, I'll dose you with laudanum."

Jess unbuttoned the remaining buttons on her shirt, the ones that Fremont hadn't torn off, and pulled her shirt free. Her camisole was all but destroyed, and he quickly removed it, sucking in an angry breath when he saw the livid bruises marring the creamy flesh of her breasts. He muttered something obscene and turned his attention to her trousers.

"I can finish undressing myself," Meg insisted. "I'm not helpless."

"Very well," Jess said gruffly. If he discovered any more bruises on Meg's flesh, he feared he wouldn't be responsible for his actions. Fremont deserved a good thrashing, and the way Jess felt now, he'd fight the deputy to get to the bastard if he had to.

"I'll be up later to check on you."

"Jess," Meg called after him. "Don't tell Zach that Fremont tried to . . . tried to . . ."

Jess's mouth tautened. "Get some sleep." Without another word, he strode out the door.

Zach was waiting for him in the parlor. "How is she? How badly did Fremont hurt her?"

"She's bruised and exhausted, which is understandable. I'll know more when I examine her tomorrow. Sleep is what she needs right now."

"Do you know what happened?"

"Meg didn't say much, but I suspect Fremont got the drop on her, knocked her out, and tied her up. I got there while he was . . ." His words fell off as he recalled Meg's request.

"While he was what?" demanded Zach. "You might as well tell me all of it, Doc. Did he rape her?"

"Meg said he didn't. I won't know for sure until I examine her. It's entirely possible, given the scene I interrupted when I arrived."

A string of obscenities spewed from Zach's mouth, and his fierce expression gave Jess a brief glimpse of the hard man Zach had once been. "I'll kill him! I don't care if he is behind bars. I'll kill him."

Jess nodded sagely. "I know exactly how you feel."

"No, you don't, Doc. And neither of us knows what went through Meggie's mind when the bastard was attacking her. You can't possibly understand, because she hasn't told you what happened to her when she was a young girl."

Jess went still. "Why don't you tell me?"

Zach shook his head. "I can't. Meggie will tell you if she wants you to know. I know for damn sure that this latest fiasco spells the end of Meggie's career. God knows I never meant to put her in danger. I taught her everything I know. She learned to shoot, ride, and track a man. And she was damn good at it.

"At first the lessons were meant to take her mind off her problems, and to give her confidence. Then everything changed. Meggie became serious about bounty hunting, and no amount of persuasion could change her mind. I began to relax when she brought in her first outlaw without mishap. After that, there was no stopping her. The Calders were her first mistake. Fremont was her second. Her third could be fatal. I know it and she knows it."

"I hope you're right," Jess said with feeling. "Go on home and get some rest, Zach. I'll bring Meg home tomorrow."

"I could wait around, Doc."

"I expect Meg to sleep the clock around. I could use some sleep myself. Don't worry, I'll take good care of her."

"If you're sure," Zach said with marked reluctance.

"Very sure. I'm going up to check on Meg now; then I'm going to find my own bed."

Jess locked the door after Zach and started up the stairs. He hadn't been lying. He was so bone weary he couldn't think straight, but he wanted see Meg first. Cautiously he opened the door to the spare bedroom and peered inside. Meg was lying in bed atop the rumpled coverlet. She was still wearing her gun belt, trousers, and boots. Jess smiled and shook his head. Apparently she'd been too tired to remove them by herself.

Jess tiptoed to the bed and carefully removed her boots. Meg didn't even stir. Her gun belt went next. Jess tossed it onto a nearby chair. Then he unfastened her trousers and pulled them off along with her drawers.

An angry gasp exploded from his lips when he saw purple bruises marring the tender flesh of her inner thighs. He heard her whimper in her sleep, and his gaze shot up to her face. Even in sleep her expression was troubled, as if she were suffering untold anguish. It nearly ripped him apart. What terrible secret was Meg hiding? Who had hurt her?

Meg moved restlessly in her sleep. Another moan slipped past her lips, and Jess could bear it no longer. He quickly shed his clothing and climbed into bed beside her, tugging the bedcovers up over both of them. Then he took her into his arms and crooned softly, "No one is going to hurt you, love. Rest easy. I won't let anyone harm you."

It must have worked, for Meg sighed, snuggled against his chest, and immediately calmed. Moments later, Jess joined her in sleep.

Purple shadows flirted with daylight when Meg awakened. Her mouth was dry, her body ached, and she was starving. She also had to use the privy. Slowly she became aware of a warm presence beside her and an unaccustomed pressure around her waist. She went very still, suddenly aware that she wasn't in her own bed. Turning her head, she was stunned to see Jess's big body curled around her, his arms hugging her middle.

It took but a moment for her to remember everything that had happened during the past twenty-four hours. Her last recollection was of Jess carrying her into his spare bedroom. What happened after that was a blank in her mind.

Her squirming around must have awakened Jess, for he opened his eyes and smiled at her. "How do you feel?"

"Like I've been thrown from my horse." Gingerly she touched her jaw and winced.

"Fremont was pretty rough with you." He surged out of bed. "Lie still. I'll fetch water and towels so you can clean up. After that, a thorough examination. Then breakfast."

Meg rose up on her elbow. "Jess, I don't think . . ."

"I'm the doctor here, remember?"

"I have to . . ."

"The chamber pot is under the bed," he said crisply, as if reading her mind.

"I'm not an invalid. A few bruises aren't going to kill me."

"Nevertheless, humor me."

Her answer died in her throat when he paused beside the bed, hands on hips, daring her to protest. He was nude, every magnificent inch of him. Everything about this man was pleasing to look at. He might be a doctor, but the width and breadth of his strong body proved he was no stranger to physical exercise.

Her gaze followed a tantalizing path down his muscular chest and taut stomach. Her breath hitched and her eyes widened when she saw his sex rising from a nest of dark hair at the juncture of his thighs. Flushing, she returned her gaze to his face.

"Sorry about that," Jess said, sounding not at all apologetic. "You have but to look at me and I get hard." He turned away and pulled on his clothes. "I'll be back," he said as he hurried out the door.

While Jess was gone, Meg used the chamber pot and studied herself in the narrow mirror hanging over the dresser. Her face looked terrible. The bruise on her jaw spread upward in a purple smudge across her right cheek. Her other cheek bore the imprint of Fremont's hand. So did her breasts. She couldn't see beyond that in the mirror, but she supposed she bore more bruises on her thighs.

Meg knew her days of bounty hunting were over. Her close call with Fremont had all but destroyed her confidence. She'd always been so sure of herself, so confident of her ability, that she'd never considered failure. After she brought in the first outlaw, the others became easier. Until the Calders. Until Jess had walked into her life.

Her inspection finished, Meg pulled the sheet around her and sat on the edge of the bed to wait for Jess. He returned a short time later, freshly shaved and wearing clean clothing. He set the basin of water and towels he carried on the nightstand.

"You can wash up while I go fetch my medical bag."

Meg made good use of the water and towels during Jess's absence. By the time he returned, she was back in bed with the sheet pulled up to her neck.

Jess wore a businesslike expression as he set his black bag on the bed and took Meg's pulse.

"There's really no need for this, Jess," Meg said. "I'm fine."

"Let me be the judge of that."

"Where's Zach?"

"I sent him home. I told him I'd bring you home myself tomorrow."

"What time is it?"

"Seven-thirty. We slept nearly the whole day through. I'll bet you're hungry."

"Starved."

"When I finish up here, I'll see what I can find in the pantry."

He peered closely at her face, his fingertips gentle upon her tender flesh. Then he pulled the sheet down to her waist, clucking his tongue as he examined the bruises on her breasts. His fingers felt warm and slightly arousing as they slid over her. She sighed softly and tried to think of other things as he accidentally brushed her nipples with his knuckles.

His hands left her breasts and traveled over each rib, searching for fractures. He seemed satisfied with what he found, for his grim expression eased. When he shoved the sheet down to her ankles, Meg shuddered and went still.

"I'm going to ask you one more time, Meg, and I want the truth. Did Fremont rape you?"

"My answer is still the same. No, he didn't. These bruises will heal in a few days and I'll be just like new. Can I get up now?"

Meg's breath hitched as Jess parted her thighs and touched the livid bruises he found there. "I should have killed him," he muttered darkly. His hazel eyes glowed with restrained ardor as he lowered his head and laved each purple bruise with his tongue.

Meg arched into his caress. "Jess!"

His mouth moved upward along her thigh. She knew what he intended and girded herself against the exquisite pleasure of his intimate kiss.

Jess took a deep wild taste of her and knew he would never get enough of her. He heard her whisper his name, felt a tremor go through her and her legs stiffen. Spreading her thighs wide, he parted the tender petals of her inner flesh, teasing the sensitive nubbin at the entrance of her sex with his tongue. He heard her breath quicken and let his own out in a groaning sigh. She tasted sweeter than ambrosia; he couldn't get enough.

Suddenly he felt her body go rigid. She let out a sobbing cry and clutched his shoulders so hard he was sure she had scratched them through his shirt. When her last shudder stilled, Jess removed his mouth and tore off his clothing. Then he covered her with his body. Her arms went around him, as if she feared he would leave.

"Jess."

His name was a soft, heated whisper on her lips, her breath warm upon his face. He drew her nipple into his mouth and suckled her gently. He heard her gasp. Her hands tightened in his hair, holding him against her as his mouth laved and teased her nipples.

"Open for me, love," he whispered hoarsely. "It's been so long . . . so damn long."

Nudging her knees apart, he settled between them and kissed her full on the lips; a kiss of possession, of hungry passion, as he slowly filled her with himself.

Meg held him tight and let the pleasure build, let it carry her beyond herself. Each sensation battered her senses, overloaded her mind. His hard body, heavy on her, his chest hard, hair-roughened, rasping against the soft flesh of her breasts and sensitive nipples. She was aware of the flexing of his spine, the rhythmic fusing of their bodies as he anchored her hips in his big hands and drove into her. Excitement, hot, unquenchable, erotic, swelled and built.

She felt him deep inside her, becoming an integral part of her, her softness gripping his hardness, taking all of him and needing more. His kiss deepened, and she tasted his passion on her tongue.

With a shuddering moan, Meg felt her bones melting, felt her senses soar. She was floating, taking all he had to give, her eager body begging for more.

He gave her more, filling her body and her senses with heady delight. She gasped, moaned, and arched, fearing she would break on the torturous rack of sensual excitement. But she didn't break; instead she shattered. Ecstasy filled her. Whatever she needed, he gave. Mouth to mouth, breast to breast, softness gripping hardness.

Jess drove himself into her, savoring every torrid inch that hugged him so tightly, pausing a moment to feel her throb around him. He withdrew, only to thrust deeply again, and yet again, pushing her higher until her head was thrashing blindly from side to side. He knew when the end was near, for he felt the keen edge of her tension ready to explode. Then he released her. She went rigid, screaming his name.

Raising himself on his elbows above her, he paused to watch her. He'd never seen anything or anyone more beautiful than Meg in the throes of ecstasy. Gloriously wanton, recklessly abandoned, wild in her need. Her volatile climax triggered his own. He thrust deeply, once, again, gave a shout of triumph, and spilled his seed deep inside her. Then slowly he relaxed atop her, lowering his weight on her briefly before he rolled to one side, still holding her in his arms.

"I didn't hurt you, did I?" Jess asked anxiously. She made him so damn hot he'd lost control. "You've bruises all over your body. I'd never forgive myself if I added to them."

"You didn't hurt me," Meg said. Her eyes grew misty. "I never knew making love could be so wonderful. I was too frightened the first time we made love to enjoy it as much as I did today."

Jess grasped her hand and brought it to his lips. "You're not frightened now, are you?"

"Of you? Never."

He shifted her in his arms until they were facing one another. He needed to ask Meg something, but didn't know how to broach the subject. Finally he just blurted out, "Who is Arlo?"

Meg went still. He could tell by her stunned expression that he had surprised her.

"How do you know about Arlo?"

"You mentioned his name while you were in shock after Fremont's attack."

She dropped her gaze, refusing to look at Jess or even answer.

"Meg, you can tell me," Jess cajoled. "I know there was a man or men in your life, for you weren't a virgin the first time I took you."

Meg raised her gaze to his and shook her head. "I can't."

Her hollow, vacant stare distressed him. This was something she had carried with her a long time. As a doctor he knew that getting her to talk about it would be therapeutic.

"Do you think I'd condemn you?"

"It's not that. I . . . just can't talk about it."

"Was it so horrible?"

"It was to a sixteen-year-old girl."

"What about your family? You've never mentioned them."

"Jess, please."

"Does Zach know?"

"Zach knows everything there is to know about me."

"You've carried this with you a long time, haven't you?"

He heard her suck in a deep breath. "Let's talk about you. I saw the poster, Jess."

Now it was Jess's turn to express shock. "You saw . . ."

"At the sheriff's office the day I stopped in to see if anything new had come in. You and your brothers are wanted for bank robbery. You lied to me. You *are* running from the law."

Jess scowled, his hard gaze pinning her to the mattress. "Are you going to turn me in?"

"If I wanted to, I would have done it before now."

"Has the sheriff seen the poster?"

"No. He's been too busy. My experience has been that he gives them a cursory glance when he finds the time. I shoved your poster to the back of the drawer with the others after I looked through them. Maybe he'll forget about them."

"Not the way my luck has been running," Jess muttered.

"Why did you do it?" Meg asked. "Why would an accomplished doctor rob a bank?"

Jess went still. "Do you really believe I robbed a bank?" God, how could she think that of him?

"I don't want to believe it," Meg said slowly. "What happened?"

"It's a long story. Why don't we eat first? I

don't know what's left in the pantry, but there has to be something we can throw together. I was thinking of hiring someone to cook and keep house, but now it appears that my days here are numbered."

He rose from bed and began pulling on his discarded clothing.

Meg slid out of bed and rummaged around for her clothes. "What are you going to do?"

"Looks like I've worn out my welcome here. Maybe I'll head west. To Washington or Oregon."

They finished dressing in silence. Dusk had given way to darkness, and Jess lit a lamp and led the way downstairs to the kitchen. He set the lamp on the table while they searched the pantry for food. Meg was delighted to find several eggs and some bacon wrapped in a cloth, while Jess brought forth a partial loaf of stale bread and coffee beans.

"I don't often cook for myself," Jess apologized, eyeing the pitifully small amount of food they had gathered.

"It's enough," Meg said. "You take care of the coffee and I'll fix us some bacon and eggs. That stale bread won't taste bad toasted."

Soon delicious smells wafted through the kitchen. The coffee was done about the same time Meg set a plate of bacon and eggs and a mound of toasted bread on the table. Then they dug in, forgetting for a moment the seriousness of their previous conversation. Meg waited until Jess drained the last drop of coffee from his cup before broaching the subject that was uppermost in her mind.

"You said you would tell me about the bank robbery," she reminded him.

Jess sat back and stared into his empty cup. "The Gentry brothers never robbed that bank. True, we were in the bank, but it was to ask for a loan to save our farm. The Gentrys weren't popular in town. We were Southern supporters in a place filled with Union sympathizers. As transplanted Confederates, we joined the losing side early in the war. We lost our father, but we survived.

"When Cantrell's raiders swept through Kansas, our farm was right in their path. We desperately needed money to restore our property. Unfortunately, banker Wingate didn't see things our way. He turned us down flat. We were about to leave when he shocked us with an offer. If one of us married his pregnant daughter, he'd give us our loan."

"That's despicable," Meg exclaimed. "Of course you refused."

"Of course. Obviously Wingate wasn't pleased, for we had no sooner cleared the door when he yelled 'bank robbery' at the top of his lungs. He claimed we cleaned out his office safe."

"What did you do?"

"Maybe we were wrong to run," Jess said.

"We stopped at the farm long enough to gather a few mementos. By then the posse was after us. Dodge City is a rough town with rough inhabitants. We wouldn't have had a chance if we'd stuck around to defend ourselves. We would have been strung up without a trial before the sheriff could stop it. So we split up. Rafe rode west and Sam headed south. We made plans to meet in Denver one year from the day we split up."

Meg searched Jess's face. "There's more to it than that, isn't there?"

Was he so transparent? Jess wondered. Meg couldn't possibly know about the guilt he suffered for making outlaws of his brothers.

"What do you mean?"

"I knew you were harboring a secret, and now that I know what it is, I sense that something else is bothering you."

Jess laughed, trying to make light of his guilt. "Are you a witch?"

"Maybe. Or maybe I'm astute enough to know what you're feeling."

"My brothers are outlaws because of me," Jess blurted out. "Delia Wingate's baby could be mine. I dallied with her, but I wasn't the only one. If I'd owned up to the deed, Rafe and Sam would be home on the farm now, putting the loan to good use. But I didn't want to claim a child that might not be mine. I was a coward."

"You're not looking at this logically," Meg

insisted. "You knew Delia was . . . bedding other men, so you owed her nothing. You can't blame yourself for not taking responsibility when you weren't the only man involved."

Jess shook his head. "I should have done it for my brothers. Rafe is the oldest, but I was the most responsible brother, the sensible one. The family could always depend upon me to do the right thing. Only I didn't this time."

"I'm sure your brothers don't feel that way."

"Probably not Sam; he never took responsibility for anything, not even when he was at fault. But Rafe — he might have accepted responsibility if he had been in my shoes."

"You've got to quit blaming yourself, Jess," Meg urged. "And I don't think you should leave. Not yet, anyway. Maybe Sheriff Bufford won't ever get around to looking at those posters. Besides, I wedged yours so far in the back of the drawer he might never find it."

Jess grasped her hands. "Do you want me to stay, Meg?"

"I . . . want you to stay, but I don't want you to end up in jail."

"You mean you won't turn me in for the reward?" he teased.

"That's not funny," Meg chided crossly. "I I couldn't do that."

"Then come with me. We'll leave together. I've heard Oregon is a beautiful place. Have you ever seen the Pacific Ocean?"

Jess couldn't believe he'd just asked Meg to go away with him. Was he loco? He didn't deserve a woman like Meg, and Meg deserved better than he could give her.

Meg pulled her hands from his grasp. "I can't. I can't leave Zach."

"He can come along."

Now he knew he was crazy. How could he drag a sick old man over mountains and dangerous territory?

"Zach won't leave Mary, and I won't leave him. Don't ask it of me, Jess. I owe Zach my life."

"I see," Jess said evenly. "Perhaps I should leave Cheyenne before you and I become more involved than we already are. I didn't take precautions when we made love. I'll wait around long enough to make sure you're not carrying my child, and then I'll leave."

A sob caught in Meg's throat. "I didn't mean . . . I'm sorry I hurt you, but you have to understand about me and Zach. He's not well; I'm all he has. He'd marry Mary if he could but . . ."

Jess's shoulders stiffened. "Oh, I understand. I understand very well. I'm all right to bed, but you have no intention of hooking up with an outlaw. I wanted us to marry, Meg. I didn't intend to make you my mistress."

"You want to marry me?" Meg gasped, stunned.

"That was my intention."

"I don't need marriage to be happy."

Meg realized she was afraid of marriage, of giving anyone that much control over her again. No, she wanted nothing to do with marriage.

Jess gave her a strange look. "Most women are eager to get married. Are you refusing because I'm an outlaw?"

Panic rose up inside her. She'd had all she could take of marriage. After Arlo, she'd vowed to remain unwed for the rest of her life. Even though she was fairly certain she loved Jess, she couldn't marry him.

"I've made up my mind never to marry, Jess. Your being an outlaw has nothing to do with my decision."

He gave her a heated look. "I can make you want to marry me."

"You can make me want your loving, but you can never convince me to marry you."

"Does Arlo have anything to do with your fear of marriage?"

"He has everything to do with it!" Meg said fiercely. "God, I hate him. I hate what he did to me and what I've become because of his abuse. If not for you, I would never have known the gentle side of loving. All I would have known was pain and degradation. I'll always be grateful to you for that."

Jess pounded his fist on the table. "The bastard! Tell me where to find this Arlo and I'll gladly wring his neck for hurting you." He searched her face. "What was Arlo to you?"

She shook her head. "I don't want to talk about him."

"Why is it so difficult to tell me the truth? I thought . . . dammit, Meg, I thought you cared for me, but I see now I was mistaken."

"No, you weren't mistaken. If you stay in town I'll become your mistress, but I won't leave Zach. I'll be anything you want me to be; just don't ask me to marry you."

Jess pushed to his feet and held out his hand, his features hard as granite. "Very well, if that's the way you want it. Come upstairs. I want you again. This time I'll try to remember I'm your stud and you're my mistress."

"Jess! I didn't mean it like that and you know it."

"I know nothing of the sort. Are you coming?"

Meg stared at his hand but there was really no choice.

She wanted Jess. She would always want him. Always love him.

But she had to be realistic. Jess was a wanted man whose fate rested in the sheriff's drawer.

"Are you coming, Meg? Or do I have to

toss you over my shoulder and carry you to bed?"

Meg could tell by his fierce expression that he'd do exactly as he said if she didn't go along with him peacefully. With a sad sigh of acquiescence, she placed her hand in his.

Chapter Nine

Jess's anger turned inward upon himself. He couldn't believe how foolish he'd been. He had no business proposing marriage. As long as he was a fugitive he had no future. He might always be on the run. Nevertheless, it hurt to be turned down. Knowing that Meg cared so little for him was devastating.

They had reached the top of the stairs before Jess's rage began to cool, but it hadn't subsided enough to make him change his mind. If she wanted to be his mistress, then he'd treat her like one.

Jess had reached his bedroom, had his hand on the doorknob in fact, when Meg suddenly balked.

She glared at him. "I've changed my mind."

"About what?" Jess asked coolly. "I distinctly heard you say you would be my mistress."

"Yes, but —"

"Then act like one. Don't worry, I'll be on my way soon, so you won't have to suffer my intentions too long."

"Dammit, Jess! Why are you acting like this? You don't really need a wife right now, any more than I need a husband."

"I've already come to that conclusion," Jess said harshly. "Unfortunately, I still want you."

Ignoring her squawk of protest, he swung her into his arms and carried her inside his room. Very slowly he let her slide down his body until her feet touched the floor. He heard her release a shuddering breath as he unbuttoned her shirt and pulled it down her arms. She hadn't bothered donning her torn camisole and was naked beneath her shirt.

His eyes lingered on her breasts; then his hands came up to massage them, his fingers determinedly pebbling the tips. He heard her moan when his hands cupped her bottom, dragging her more solidly against him, and he grinned.

Meg became aware that he was maneuvering her backward; soon she felt the wall pressing against her back.

"Jess, what . . ."

Jess didn't answer, so intent was he upon removing her trousers. Finally he succeeded in dragging them down around her ankles. With one arm around her waist, he lifted her and swiftly removed her boots. Then he pulled her trousers all the way off. Still holding her, he slid his hand up between her thighs, teasing her, parting the tender folds of her flesh and stroking her.

Meg gasped. She was wet, she realized, her body tense with desire. Their angry words hadn't diminished her desire for him. She could feel his hardness pressing against her, and her body caught fire. His hard mouth came down on hers, plundering fiercely, ravishing her with his tongue.

Her fingers curled into the open neck of his shirt as he continued to stroke between her legs with one hand while unfastening the buttons on his trousers with the other. Then he was lifting her, his rigid length probing, finding entrance. She gazed into his face. His expression was fiercely possessive, impossibly demanding, urgent. He kissed her hard, his hands tightening on her bottom as he began to thrust wildly inside her. He raised her legs and wrapped them around his waist, pounding into her again and again.

She felt the tension building, escalating. Her body shook; breathing became nearly impossible as she soared toward an earth-shattering release. Arms and legs curled tightly around him, she let the momentum carry her, and fell headlong into a yawning abyss of molten heat. Scant seconds later, Jess galloped to his own release.

For long minutes there was only the sound of their harsh breathing. Then slowly he eased her legs from around his waist and set her gently on her feet. He turned away and straightened his clothing. Meg watched him warily. She'd never seen Jess like this. When he turned around to face her, his face held a wealth of regret.

"Go to bed, Meg. Tomorrow I'll take you home."

Meg edged away from the wall toward the bed. "What happened just now?"

"I shouldn't have taken my anger out on you. No woman in her right mind would marry a fugitive. You deserve better. I don't get angry often. Did I hurt you?"

Meg felt an unbearable sadness. "No, but I fear I hurt you. I probably didn't explain myself well. I will never marry. I do lo . . . care for you, Jess, but I have this uncontrollable fear of marriage that has nothing to do with you."

"Someone hurt you. I've known that for a long time. No need to explain your refusal, Meg. I shouldn't have asked you to marry me while my future is uncertain. You were right to refuse. A woman would have to love a man a great deal to leave all she held dear and take up with a fugitive from the law."

"Jess, I —"

He placed a finger against her lips. "No, don't say anything you'll regret later."

She bit her lip. "Do you intend to leave right away?" God, how could she bear it?

"Perhaps not. You might be right about Bufford. Maybe you hid that Wanted poster

193

so far back in the drawer, he'll never find it. I like Cheyenne. I have a thriving practice here. I won't leave unless I'm forced to."

"I meant what I said. I'll be your lover for as long as you want me."

"I wouldn't ask that of you. Go to bed, Meg." He started to leave.

"Wait! Don't go."

He swung around to face her, his expression fierce. "Don't tempt me. We both know nothing can come of this passion we share."

Meg knew, but it made no difference. "Stay with me tonight."

The air between them crackled with charged energy. Meg could feel its powerful pull nudge them toward one another. "I need you," she whispered.

She heard him groan, saw his eyes turn murky with indecision. Then he was beside her, touching her face with a tenderness that brought tears to her eyes.

"One day I hope you'll trust me enough to tell me how Arlo hurt you, and how he turned you against marriage. I realize I'm not the right man for you, but someday a man will come along whom you'll truly love and wish to marry. Then what? Will you deny him because of what one man did to you?" His voice hardened. "Will you use Zach as an excuse to refuse him? Will you offer to become his mistress?"

Meg winced. How little Jess must think of

her. "After you leave, if you must leave, there will be no other man."

Her words seemed to take the steam out of his sails.

She pulled back the covers, holding them open in invitation. "Are you going to join me?"

Jess hesitated but a moment before he shed his clothing, snuffed out the lamp, and eased down beside her. "I don't have much will-power where you're concerned," he said, pulling her into his arms.

"Nor I where you're concerned," Meg whispered, snuggling against his chest. "Let's just take what we can while we can."

They came together again, all fire and passion, then slept deeply until late the next morning. Unfortunately, the problems they had swept aside during the night returned with daylight.

Meg washed and dressed in silence while Jess went to his own room to clean up. They met later in the kitchen.

"There's coffee left from last night and a hunk of stale bread," Jess offered.

Meg shook her head. "I'm not hungry. I'm anxious to return home and let Zach know I'm all right."

"Zach, of course," Jess said with a hint of sarcasm. "We wouldn't want Zach to worry."

"Jess, let's not part like this. You have nothing to be jealous about. I told you, Zach is like a father to me."

"I know. I've come to grips with your feelings for Zach and I understand. I have no say on what you do with your life, nor can I claim any part of it. I'm an outlaw, Meg."

Meg shook her head in vigorous denial. "Don't say that! You're *not* an outlaw. Someday you'll prove your innocence."

Jess gave a snort of disbelief. "If you say so. Come on, I'll take you home."

"I can see myself home."

"No. I promised Zach I'd see you safely home and I always keep my word."

They rode in silence. Everything that needed to be said had been said. An unspoken agreement had been reached. Neither mentioned Jess's marriage proposal nor Meg's refusal. Jess tried not to show his hurt pride, but it was difficult. He hadn't committed any crime. He was not an outlaw, and Lord knows he wasn't cut out for that kind of life.

Always on the run.

Always looking over his shoulder, wondering when the law was going to catch up with him. Jess knew things weren't going to get better. If he wanted a normal life, he'd have to return to Dodge, face Wingate, and fight the false charges made against the Gentry brothers.

It was up to him. He was the responsible

brother. He'd even marry Delia if that was what it took.

They had slowed their horses to a walk, and Meg brought her mare beside Jess's gelding.

"What are you thinking, Jess?" Meg asked.

"I was thinking that I should return to Dodge and fight those false charges. I'd even marry Delia if I thought it would help my brothers."

"You love your brothers very much, don't you?"

"We've always been close. Hotheaded Rafe, sensible Jess, and unruly Sam. That's how we were known. I was the one who tried to keep my brothers out of trouble. Now it's up to me to make things right again."

"You're not thinking straight, Jess," Meg reasoned. "Your brothers are grown men. They don't need looking after, and they probably wouldn't want you to sacrifice yourself for them."

But the longer Jess thought about it, the more convinced he became that he should return to Dodge and tell his story to the sheriff. The truth would free him . . . or would it? he wondered. Justice in Dodge City left much to be desired. And Meg's words did make sense. Neither of his brothers would want him to sacrifice himself for them. Perhaps he'd think on it a tad longer before making a decision.

The house loomed ahead and they picked up their pace. They saw Zach out by the pump, and Meg shouted his name, surging ahead to greet him. Jess hung back, not wanting to interfere. Zach and Meg shared a special relationship, and though he was jealous of it at times, he didn't want to ruin their reunion.

Meg and Zach were waiting for him when he rode into the yard. He dismounted and followed them inside the house.

"There's fresh coffee," Zach said. "Would you like some?"

"Neither of us had any breakfast this morning," Jess allowed. "Coffee sounds great."

"Sit down, both of you. I'll have breakfast on the table in a jiffy."

"No, I'm not —" Meg began.

"Don't argue, Meggie," Zach said sternly, holding a chair out for her. "Sit down. You're looking a mite pale."

"I'm fine, Zach, really. Ask Dr. Gentry if you don't believe me."

"That true, Doc?"

"Meg is fine, Zach. Those bruises will fade in a few days."

Zach nodded, though he didn't appear completely convinced. "I'll whip up a batch of flapjacks. Meggie is partial to them."

He poured coffee, then busied himself at the stove. "You know this finishes you as a bounty hunter, Meggie," Zach said without turning around. "Look how I ended up. I'm a useless cripple because I was careless one time. I won't let the same thing happen to you."

Meg stared morosely into her coffee cup. "I came to the same conclusion on my own, Zach. But what will happen to us once the reward money for Fremont runs out? We still have to eat."

"I've got a job now, Meggie, remember? Besides, five hundred dollars will last a long time if we're careful."

Jess listened to the conversation in silence. This was between Zach and Meg; he had no business horning in. But he felt like cheering Zach for putting his foot down.

"What am I going to do with myself while you're off working?" Meg argued. "You know how folks around here feel about me. I couldn't get a job even if one was available."

Zach frowned. "Do the things that keep women busy."

"Most women have husbands and children," Meg snapped.

Jess couldn't keep quiet a moment longer. "That's *your* choice, Meg," he said softly.

Zach must have picked up on something in Jess's voice, for he turned away from the stove and searched Meg's face. "What's Doc talking about, Meggie?"

Meg leaped from her chair and pushed

away from the table. "I'm going to my room to change."

"Hurry back, the flapjacks will be done soon," Zach called after her.

Jess stared at her departing back, wishing he hadn't said anything. The last thing he wanted was to upset Meg.

"What was that all about?" Zach asked gruffly. "Has something happened between you and Meggie?"

"You could say that."

"Want to tell me about it?"

"Believe it or not, I took your advice and asked Meg to marry me. I know it was wrong even to suggest such a thing when I'm a . . ." His sentence ended abruptly. Did Zach know he was wanted by the law?

". . . when you're a wanted man," Zach finished for him. "I know all about it. Meggie told me."

"I should have known."

"Did you and your brothers really rob that bank?"

Jess sent him a disgusted look. "What do you think?"

"I don't think you're an outlaw, if that's what you're wondering."

"I explained everything to Meg, and she understood."

"But she still wouldn't marry you," Zach guessed.

Jess's expression hardened. "She was right

to refuse me. I'm not free to marry. There's no future for Meg and me as long as I'm a wanted man. In fact, I'm thinking about leaving town."

"Meg doesn't want to marry," Zach confided. "It ain't you. She cares about you."

"Meg said as much, but I don't believe her. Why wouldn't a woman want to marry and have children?"

"Meggie will skin me alive for telling you this, but the reason she turned you down has nothing to do with you personally. Meggie has strong feelings for you. She wouldn't have let you . . . well, never mind that right now. Let's just say she's powerful afeared of marriage. She was only sixteen when —"

"Zach! What are you saying?"

Keen disappointment made Jess wince when he saw Meg standing in the doorway. Another moment and he would have learned Meg's secret.

"Aw, Meggie, Jess has a right to know."

"It's my place to tell Jess, but now is not the time."

Jess rose abruptly. His presence here was uncomfortable for all of them. "It's time I left. Perhaps I'll see you in town, Zach." He gave Meg a curt nod and headed out the door.

"Jess, wait!"

Her voice held a plea Jess couldn't resist. He turned to face her, his expression carefully composed. "What is it?"

"I'm sorry."

"About turning down my proposal? Don't be. I had no business asking you to marry me. Blame the moment. We were both carried away by . . ." He cast a surreptitious glance at Zach, who seemed to be hanging on to every word, and shrugged. "You know what I mean."

Meg nodded mutely.

"Keep your secrets, Meg. You don't owe me an explanation. Soon I'll be gone from your life. We both know my time in Cheyenne is limited. The danger increases each day I remain."

Jess spun on his heel and strode out the door without waiting for Meg's reply. What could she say, anyway? She knew his life wasn't his to share while he was a wanted man. And Meg had to come to grips with something that happened to her long ago before she could face her future. He sincerely hoped the right man would come along when she was ready.

Meg watched Jess ride out of her life and knew she couldn't ask him to stay for fear his past would be exposed.

"Don't let him go, Meggie," Zach urged. "You know you love him."

Meg rounded on him. "I know no such thing."

"I know you like a book, Meggie girl. You'd not let a man make love to you unless you loved him."

Meg stared at him, appalled. "How . . . how did you know?"

"It wasn't difficult. The Meggie I knew wouldn't look at a man with hunger in her eyes. I'm glad, honey. Now you know not all men are like Arlo. I'm glad it was Jess who showed you."

Meg studied her hands. "I hurt him, Zach. He thinks I turned him down because he's a wanted man. It's not that at all. That same old fear grips me whenever I think of marriage. How do I know Jess won't turn into an ogre like Arlo once we're married?"

"Your heart knows," Zach said. "Follow your heart."

"If only I could," Meg sighed. "My gut tells me Jess wasn't serious about his proposal. Like he said, it was the moment. His future is too uncertain for him to make a commitment to a wife. Jess wanted me to go to Oregon with him, but you know I won't leave you."

Zach shook his head. "As much as I appreciate your loyalty, it was wrong of you to use me as an excuse. Go to Jess. Tell him about Arlo and agree to go anywhere with him. Men like Jess don't come along every day. I'll get along just fine without you."

"It may be too late, Zach. I might have

hurt Jess too much for him to forgive me. Angry words were exchanged."

"Is there nothing I can say to change your mind?"

"No. What happened is for the best."

Zach's sad gaze followed Meg as she turned and reentered the house.

The following days were tense ones for Jess. He sat on the horns of a dilemma. His gut told him to leave Cheyenne and seek a safer haven, but his heart refused to listen. It wasn't just Meg who held him back, but the patients who needed him. Old Doc Holloway had sunk deeper and deeper into an alcoholic stupor, leaving Jess the only doctor in the thriving city who knew what he was doing.

He couldn't leave until he removed the stitches from little Kerry Wheeler's head wound. And it would be at least two weeks before the cast could come off Harry Pepper's leg. Then there was Mrs. Buxley, who needed nerve medicine to get her through a day with her eight children. And Pearl Lavine, whose weak chest was a constant worry.

Instead of packing up and moving on as he'd intended, Jess spent the following days treating his patients as if nothing were wrong. He made no effort to see Meg during that time, though his restraint cost him dearly. Meg had made it perfectly clear that she didn't want him as badly as he wanted her.

One day Miss Polly Gallagher, the grocer's daughter, was carried into the office by her father. It seemed the pretty Miss Polly had tripped over a barrel of pickles and sprained her ankle. Her worried father hovered nearby while Jess bandaged the pert miss's well-turned ankle.

"Thanks, Doc," Mr. Gallagher said as he paid Jess for his services. "Do you mind if I leave Polly with you while I hitch up the horse and buggy? Can't have her walking home on that ankle."

"That's fine," Jess said absently as he stowed away his gauze and bandages.

"You're very talented, Doctor," Polly simpered after her father left the office. "Do you mind if I speak my mind about something?"

"Say whatever is on your mind, Miss Gallagher."

Polly cleared her throat and sent him a coquettish smile. "The whole town is talking about you and that Lincoln woman," she said slyly.

Jess's head shot up. "Oh, really? What are they saying?"

"That you and that female bounty hunter have become . . . close. Rumor has it that you saved her life."

"I suppose that's true enough," Jess allowed.

"Meg Lincoln is a disgrace to womankind,"

Polly sniffed. "What she does for a living is unnatural and disgraceful. She has no reputation to speak of. Why, everyone knows she's mistress to that disreputable old cripple she's living with."

Jess hung on to his temper with difficulty. "Miss Lincoln is an extraordinary woman," he said curtly. Polly Gallagher might be pretty, but her spitefulness detracted from her attractiveness. Unfortunately, Jess knew she was only repeating the town's opinion of Meg Lincoln.

Polly held out her leg to inspect her bandaged ankle. "It's too tight," she whined.

Jess lifted her foot and examined the bandage. His eyebrows arched upward when Polly raised her skirts past her trim calf to expose a dimpled knee. He smiled grimly, aware of the game Polly was playing. A game in which he wasn't interested. He hadn't met a woman yet who could compare with Meg.

"The bandage is fine, Miss Gallagher," Jess said as he yanked her skirts down to her toes. "Rest your ankle for a few days and you'll soon be fit as a fiddle."

Polly flashed him a brilliant smile. "You have such gentle hands, Dr. Gentry. You must be lonely here all by yourself. You need a wife to take care of you."

Her hint couldn't have been more blatant.

"I have no time for a wife," Jess said bluntly. "Ah, here comes your father."

Polly spared her father an impatient glance as he walked through the door. "If you ever find yourself in need of *respectable* female company," she stressed in a coy whisper, "remember me."

"I'll try," Jess replied, wondering what Miss Polly would say if she knew he was an outlaw. She'd probably run screaming for her papa.

Zach was working in town at the hardware store now, and Jess ran into him occasionally. Though they spoke briefly whenever they met, Jess didn't once ask about Meg. Talking about her would only open wounds he wasn't prepared to deal with.

Over the course of the next few days, Jess had come to a decision. As much as he hated to leave Cheyenne and abandon his patients, he knew he had to go. After much soul searching, Jess had realized there was but one course open to him. He had to return to Dodge and prove that the Gentry brothers had been falsely charged with a crime they hadn't committed.

Jess had his saddlebags all packed and his medical bag newly stocked and was about to lock the front door for the last time when he saw Zach running down the street toward his office, waving something in his hand. Jess's heart took a serious tumble. His first thought was that something terrible had happened to Meg.

Zach was winded and unable to speak when he finally reached Jess. Jess helped him inside, easing him into a chair.

"Breathe deeply, Zach. Do you need your medicine?"

Zach shook his head. "I'll be . . . all right . . . in a . . . minute, Doc. Here, read . . . this." He thrust the paper clutched in his hand at Jess.

It was a telegram from a lawyer in Philadelphia. Jess read it through and handed it back to Zach. "I'm sorry about your wife, Zach. Do you intend to travel to Philadelphia to settle your wife's estate? According to the telegram, there's a considerable sum involved."

"I didn't know Tilly's parents had died and left her their fortune. According to Mr. Fernwood, I'm Tilly's next of kin and the money is mine. All I have to do is go to Philadelphia and claim the estate. Do you know what that means to me and Meg, Doc? We won't have to worry about money again.

"I can't wait to tell Mary. There's nothing to keep us from getting hitched now. The only problem is Meggie."

"Surely you don't think Meg will object to your marrying Mary, do you?"

"Nah, nothing like that. Meg will be glad for me. It's just that I don't want to leave her alone while I'm gone. We both know how folks in these parts feel about her. She has no one but me, Doc, and you. But you know how stubborn she can be."

"I do indeed," Jess muttered. "What are you worried about? Meg is capable of taking care of herself during your absence. How long do you intend to be gone?"

"No more than two weeks. Big cities ain't for me. Will you help me out, Doc?"

"I don't know, Zach. You couldn't have caught me at a worse time. I've decided to return to Dodge City and try to prove my innocence."

"Stay, Doc. Two weeks can't make that much difference. And I'd feel a whole lot better if Meggie had someone to rely upon during my absence."

Jess's eyes narrowed. "Why do you think Meg needs protection? Perhaps I'd be more inclined to stay if I knew the reason behind your request."

Jess watched as Zach seemed to mull over his next words. "I don't know as I have the right to tell you."

"If you want me to stay and watch over Meg, you'll have to."

"I'll tell you this much," Zach allowed. "There's a man Meg has reason to fear."

Jess's attention sharpened. "Is his name Arlo?"

Zach gave him a startled look. "Did Meggie tell you about Arlo?"

"Not really. She mentioned his name once, and when I asked about him, she turned stubborn and refused to say more. But I know he's the man who hurt her."

"I reckon I ain't talking out of turn by telling you Meggie has good reason to fear Arlo. We live every day worrying that he'll show up and make Meggie's life miserable. Meggie is a strong woman, Doc, afeared of nothing but that bastard Arlo. It happened a long time ago, but Meggie is still vulnerable when it comes to him."

"Do you think this Arlo will show up here and hurt Meg?"

Zach nodded gravely. "It's possible."

"What is Arlo to Meg?"

"I've said all I can without breaking my word to Meggie. What do you say, Doc? Will you stick around until I return? I've got an odd feeling about Arlo. Something tells me this is a bad time to leave, and my premonitions are usually right."

"So are mine," Jess said, "and my gut tells me it's time to leave Cheyenne. I'm living on borrowed luck. We both know what's going to happen when the sheriff takes those Wanted posters out of his drawer."

"I know I'm asking a lot, Doc, but I know Meggie's well-being is important to you. You two can't fool me. You care for Meggie and she cares for you."

"Perhaps, but circumstances aren't right to

do anything about it yet. That's why I'm going to Dodge. I need to get this miscarriage of justice straightened out. Meg deserves a life free from worries. I can't make that happen until I'm a free man."

"I understand, Doc, but that doesn't solve my problem. Two more weeks is all I ask. I've already bought my train ticket. I leave tomorrow."

How could he refuse? Jess wondered. If Arlo was a threat to Meg, then he had no choice but to stay and see that no harm came to her during Zach's absence. After all, the sheriff hadn't discovered the poster yet.

"What does Meg say about this? Something tells me she's not going to like it."

"She doesn't need to know. Just ride out a couple of times to see how she's doing and keep an eye out for strangers. I've never seen Arlo myself, so I can't give you an accurate description. Meggie refuses to talk about him."

"Very well, Zach. I'll stick around another couple of weeks. But it's not going to be easy watching for strangers when I don't even know what Arlo looks like."

"Slick, that's all I can tell you. He's a smooth talker, from what I gather. And he has a mean streak a mile wide."

"I'll do what I can, Zach."

Zach grabbed Jess's hand and pumped vigorously. "You've just taken a load off my mind. I've gotta go see Mary and tell her to prepare for a wedding as soon as I return. Thanks again, Doc."

"Take care of yourself, Zach," Jess said in parting. "Your heart can only take so much. Remember my advice. Take your medicine, and rest when you feel yourself tiring."

What have I gotten myself into? Jess wondered as he watched Zach limp off down the street. There was only one thing he knew for sure. If Arlo got anywhere near Meg, if he harmed one hair upon her head, he'd kill the bastard.

Chapter Ten

Several medical emergencies kept Jess busy after Zach left town. Three days passed before Jess finally found the time to check on Meg. He was preparing to lock the front door for the day when a man barged into the waiting room.

The man was flamboyantly dressed in a black suit, striped red and black vest, and string tie. His fingers were adorned with flashy rings, and a gold watch fob was draped across his trim stomach. Blood dripped from a rag clamped around his wrist.

"Can you take a look at this, Doc?" the man said, holding out his injured wrist.

"What happened?" Jess asked, ushering the man into his examining room.

"I was running a poker game down at the Whistle Stop saloon when a cowboy attacked me."

Jess slanted him a censuring glance. "That should teach you not to cheat."

The man, obviously a professional gambler, turned cold eyes on Jess. "I've killed men with less provocation."

"Listen, Mr. . . ."

"Skully."

"Listen, Mr. Skully, either you want your wound treated or you don't. It's your choice."

Skully pulled away the bloody rag and shoved his wrist under Jess's nose. "If you weren't the only doctor in town worth his salt, I wouldn't be here. I don't like your attitude."

Jess examined the wound. It wasn't deep but would require stitches. "What happened to the man who gave you this?"

"He's not dead, if that's what you're wondering. He might have been," Skully allowed, "if the sheriff hadn't been in the saloon and hauled the cowboy off to jail to cool his heels."

Jess merely grunted. It didn't take him long to decide he liked neither the gambler nor his attitude. Looking into his eyes was like looking into a crypt. They were cold and empty, utterly devoid of feeling.

"This is going to sting," Jess said as he held Skully's wrist over a basin and poured disinfectant over it.

"Holy shit!" Skully cried, jerking spasmodically. "Are you deliberately trying to hurt me, Doc?"

"Your wound needed disinfecting," Jess explained. "I'd hate to guess where that cowboy's knife had been before he cut you. This is going to need stitches," he continued.

"Just get it over with," Skully said, gritting his teeth.

Jess took his time threading the needle. He would never deliberately hurt a patient but the gambler had rubbed him the wrong way. He didn't know the man from Adam, but he still didn't like him.

Nevertheless, Jess tried not to cause excessive pain. The first stitch brought a howl from Skully. The rest went easier, however. Finally Jess set the needle aside and applied a bandage.

"You're a lucky man, Mr. Skully. The knife could have severed a tendon and then you'd never be able to deal from the bottom again."

"Just finish the damn job so I can get out of here," Skully growled.

"You're all done. Come back in a week and I'll take out the stitches."

"How much do I owe you?"

"I usually charge a dollar or the equivalent for an ordinary office visit; sewing up gamblers costs five dollars."

Skully gave Jess a lethal look and fished a five-dollar bill from his pocket. He looked ready to explode as he tossed the money at Jess's feet.

"You're pretty damn arrogant for a small-town doctor." Suddenly Skully's expression turned thoughtful. "Have we met before?"

Jess went still. He was positive he'd remember Skully if they'd met before. If he looked familiar to the gambler, that meant only one thing. *Skully had seen the Wanted poster.*

"We've never met."

Skully's cold eyes searched Jess's face. "I could have sworn I've seen your face somewhere. I've an excellent memory. One day it will come to me."

Jess sincerely hoped not. The gambler was a man he didn't want for an enemy.

Skully left shortly after that, giving Jess another thorough inspection before closing the door behind him. Jess breathed a sigh of relief. This would be a terrible time to be recognized.

Jess locked the office door and went into the kitchen to fix himself something to eat. It was too late now to visit Meg. That would have to wait until tomorrow. Tomorrow was Saturday; he would close the office early.

Jess found that he had little appetite. He was eager to see Meg and had to forcibly prevent himself from riding out there despite the darkness and late hour. Would she welcome him? Probably not. She wouldn't like the idea of Zach asking Jess to keep an eye on her. In all likelihood, she thought he'd already left Cheyenne. Did she miss him as much as he missed her?

Making love to Meg had opened him to

emotions he never knew existed. Nothing in his experience had prepared him for Meg Lincoln. He deeply regretted asking her to marry him. Not because he didn't want her, but because it was unfair to expect her to care for an outlaw. At least Meg had been wise enough to refuse. God, why did life have to be so complicated?

Were Rafe and Sam experiencing the same problems he was? Jess wondered. Had each found a special woman to love despite being pursued by the law? He prayed they were both safe, and that they would show up at the appointed time in Denver.

Meanwhile, Jess had his own problems to contend with. His days were fairly busy, but his nights, like this one, were filled with memories of Meg.

Meg was so beautiful, he thought, closing his eyes and picturing her memorable features. Hair dark as midnight, wide green eyes, lush lips, and heart-shaped face. He ached just thinking about her.

Tomorrow, Jess thought, smiling to himself. Tomorrow he would see her again, fill his eyes with her beauty . . . and try to keep his hands off of her.

Jess awoke early and opened the door to his first patient. He doled out cough syrup, bound a turned ankle, and diagnosed a pregnancy. By noon the patients had all been treated, and Jess decided to have lunch at the local cafe before heading out to Meg's place.

Jess was perusing the menu when Sheriff Bufford entered and sat down across from him.

"I'm glad I ran into you, Doc," Bufford began. "Do you mind if I join you?"

Jess's heart gave a wild leap. Had Bufford finally looked over the Wanted posters and found his picture? "Sit down, Sheriff, I'll be glad for the company. What can I do for you?"

"I know you and Meg Lincoln are" — he hesitated over the word — "close, so I thought you should know that someone has been inquiring about her."

Jess tensed, every nerve ending jangling in warning. "Who? Do you know his name?"

"It's that gambler who drifted into town yesterday. I knew he was trouble the moment I laid eyes on him. He wasn't in town two hours when a cowboy took exception to his cheating and pulled a knife on him. Fortunately, I was there to witness the confrontation. The gambler suffered only a minor wound. Too bad I couldn't prove he cheated."

"That must be the man I treated yesterday. Cold bastard, that one. Said his name was Skully."

"Yeah, Arlo Skully. Arrived on the nine-fifteen from Dodge City yesterday morning. Do you know why he would be asking about Meg Lincoln?"

Jess leaped to his feet. The chair fell to the floor with a crash. Now he knew why he hadn't liked Skully. How many men were there named Arlo? If he was the man who had hurt Meg, she could be in danger this very minute.

"Sorry, Sheriff, I just remembered something I have to do."

Bufford studied him through narrowed lids. "Do you know something I don't? I don't believe Skully is wanted for anything."

"I'll explain later," Jess said as he rushed out the door.

"If you see Meg, tell her I have her reward money," Bufford called after him.

Jess ran all the way home for his guns, making sure the chambers were loaded before strapping them around his hips. Then he saddled his horse and rode hell for leather out of town.

Meg finished her breakfast and dawdled over her coffee. She missed Zach and didn't have enough to do to keep her mind occupied. If she were truthful, she'd admit that she missed Jess as much if not more than she missed Zach. In the short time she'd known Jess, he'd gotten under her skin. He'd saved her life, and she'd always be grateful, but her feelings went deeper than that. Jess had shown her that making love with a man could be a glorious experience.

For the first time in her life she felt like a complete woman, thanks to Jess's patience. The shame of what Arlo had done to her had sloughed away, gone along with the fear of being close to a man. Vaguely she wondered if her fear of Arlo would ever be gone completely.

Meg knew a trip to town was inevitable. The reward money should have arrived by now, and she needed it to replenish her dwindling supply of provisions. She didn't look forward, however, to the gossip that would follow in her wake. She knew exactly what the townspeople thought of her. She tried not to let it bother her, but it was difficult to ignore. They considered her a whore because she had dared to engage in an unfeminine profession and had become good at it.

Would Jess still be in Cheyenne? she wondered. She was torn. On one hand she wanted him to be there, but on the other she feared for his safety. No matter how much Jess was liked, the sheriff wouldn't hesitate to put him behind bars once Jess's past caught up with him. She was almost afraid to go into town for fear she'd learn he was gone. For some reason, she liked to think Jess was nearby, though she knew she should forget him.

Meg finished her coffee and placed her breakfast dishes in the sink. She had walked into the bedroom to make her bed when she heard a rider enter the yard. The first thought that came into her head was that Jess had finally come out to visit her. She rushed to the door at the first knock and flung it open.

Uttering a cry of dismay, Meg shrank back. A moment later she came to her senses and tried to shut the door in Arlo Skully's face. He caught it with his uninjured arm and flung it open.

"What are *you* doing here?" she demanded.

"Aren't you happy to see me, *wife?*"

"I ceased being your wife a long time ago." Dear God, seeing Arlo again brought back all those terrifying memories she'd fought so hard to forget.

Arlo frowned. "What in the hell are you talking about? Of course you're my wife. I had no idea you were even alive until I heard talk about a female bounty hunter named Meg Lincoln who operated around Cheyenne. I knew it had to be you."

"Get out of my life!" Meg hissed. "You used me to repay a gambling debt. You beat me when I objected. Doesn't that bother your conscience?"

"If it makes you feel any better, I went looking for you after Tad Dunbar told me you'd escaped from his bed when he went out for a bottle of whiskey. I searched for a whole day before deciding to move on. Dunbar was breathing down my neck. He insisted I make good on the gambling debt."

"You looked for me," Meg repeated dully. "Is that supposed to make me feel better? I was sixteen years old! You took my innocence like a rutting animal, then sold me to another man to settle a gambling debt. You beat me when I defied you. You're a real bastard, Arlo Skully. Get out of my house and don't darken my door again."

"Sorry, honey, I can't do that. You're my wife. I still have the paper to prove it. You've grown into a stunning woman, Meg. I'm ready to take up where we left off. Your parents sold you to me. That gave me the right to do what I liked with your body, even sell your favors to another. I didn't intend for Dunbar to keep you. You were too good a lay for me to give you up. I'd never had a virgin before."

"Go to hell!" Meg shouted. She was literally shaking with anger. Just looking at him brought back all her old insecurities, her fears.

She remembered how Arlo had spied her walking down the street one day. He'd kept his eye on her a few days before following her home one day and speaking privately with her parents. After that, he'd come around nearly every day. At first she'd been flattered by his attention. She didn't learn what kind of man he was until her father told her he'd given her to Arlo, that the gambler had offered a sum for her he couldn't turn down.

Her parents were poor as church mice. They lived in a soddy in Nebraska along with her seven younger brothers and sisters. She really couldn't blame them for accepting money for her, but she'd never felt the same about them since. Her father thought he was doing right by her by insisting that Arlo marry her before carrying her off. She'd never forget how utterly helpless, how frightened she'd been when the preacher pronounced them man and wife. They had left immediately after the brief ceremony in Arlo's wagon.

She recalled how Arlo had pulled into a stand of trees not far from town and ruthlessly relieved her of her virginity. He'd assaulted her several times after that. And then the final degradation came when he'd offered her favors to a stranger in exchange for gambling losses.

"My, my," Arlo said, stepping into the parlor and shutting the door behind him. "That's no way for a wife to talk. You've changed from that little mouse I married."

"I have you to thank for that," Meg spat. "Did you expect me to remain the same after you beat me up and handed me over to an-other man?"

Arlo frowned. "I admit I have a vile temper. When you defied me about Dunbar, I went a little crazy. I had no other way to repay my debt without you. It was a damn tough situation to get out of. I'd lost every-thing of value I owned. I'd never had luck turn on me like that."

"Maybe you were being punished," Meg charged. "You no longer have a claim on me, Arlo Skully. I had our marriage annulled years ago."

"Annulled?" He gave a hoot of laughter. "On what grounds? I signed no papers, re-ceived no word. The annulment isn't legal."

"The grounds were desertion. The judge saw things my way and granted the annul-ment. Get out of my house."

"Your house! Ha! This house belongs to your lover. It's common knowledge that you're living in sin with that washed-up bounty hunter. Can't you do better than a cripple? You're nothing but a whore, Meg, and the whole town knows it."

"If you believe that, why do you want me?"

He stared at her breasts, then slowly aimed his hot gaze downward, to the juncture of her thighs. "You've probably learned a few things in five years. You could be an asset to me in my business."

"I'm no longer sixteen, Arlo. You no longer

frighten me. I've learned a thing or two about men like you. I make my living capturing outlaws, or have you forgotten?"

He grabbed her before she could turn and run. She stiffened in his arms, but it didn't deter him. Pulling her roughly against him, he seized her mouth in a punishing kiss. It went on so long Meg thought she would die from lack of air. Then abruptly he released her, laughing when she scrubbed at her mouth with the back of her hand.

"You're a damn sight more woman than you were at sixteen," Arlo said in a seductive purr. "As far as I'm concerned, there was no annulment. I'm leaving town tomorrow and taking you with me."

"You're crazy. I'm not going anywhere with you."

He shook her until her head rattled.

"Aren't you? Your lover's not here to stop me. Heard tell he left town. Did old Zach Purdee tire of you?"

"I don't need Zach to protect me. I can do that on my own."

Her bravado suddenly deserted her. Where was the independence she'd fought so hard for, been so proud of? She hated Arlo for his ability to reduce her to a frightened child again after all these years.

Arlo appeared aware of her thoughts, for he smiled and tightened his grip on her. "You're frightened of me, aren't you?"

Meg searched frantically for her guns, trying to recall where she'd left them. In her bedroom, she remembered, but Zach's loaded rifle rested against the parlor wall, directly to her right. She darted a quick glance at the rifle, gauging the distance she'd have to travel and how long it would take Arlo to react if she twisted away from him.

"Don't even think about it," Arlo growled, following the direction of her gaze. "Take off your dress. I want to see what I've missed out on these past five years. Then we'll go to your bedroom, where you can show me all the little tricks your lovers have taught you."

Meg broke free and turned to flee, but Arlo was ready for her. Grasping her arm, he whirled her around to face him. She saw raw determination in the cold depths of his gray eyes and knew real fear. This man had no heart, no compassion; he was utterly merciless. When he tried to kiss her again, she bit his lip.

His hands dug into the soft flesh of her upper arms. "Bitch!"

Meg spat in his face. He raised his fist, and Meg closed her eyes, waiting for the blow.

Jess saw the horse tethered outside Meg's front door and immediately assumed the worst. Fear contorted his features as he leaped from the saddle and stormed up the front steps.

He flung open the door, and momentum carried him inside. It took but a moment for the scene before him to sink in. Howling with rage, he launched himself at the man threatening his Meg.

Arlo Skully had already let his fist fly, but Jess's timely intervention prevented it from connecting. Skully's blow ended just short of Meg's face as Jess hauled him backward, shook him like a rag doll, and tossed him to the floor. As Skully lay there shaking his head to clear it, Jess pulled Meg into his arms.

He searched her face. "Did the bastard hurt you?"

Meg shook her head, too stunned by Jess's appearance to reply.

"I came as soon as I heard."

"You knew Arlo was in town?" Meg asked, finally finding her voice.

"I treated him in my office yesterday but didn't realize he was the man who'd hurt you. I didn't know until the sheriff told me this morning that a gambler named Arlo Skully was asking questions about you. I rode out here as soon as I could."

He sent a menacing glance toward Skully, who was picking himself off the floor. "He *is* the same Arlo who hurt you, isn't he?"

"I never thought I'd see him again," Meg said shakily. "Though Zach feared he'd show up one day."

"What in the hell is he to you?" Jess demanded. "What did he do to you?"

"I believe I can answer that question," Skully said, dusting off his clothing. "Meg is my wife."

"Wife!" Skully's words sent Jess's world spinning.

"No!" Meg shouted. "Not anymore. Our marriage was annulled years ago."

"The annulment isn't legal," Skully declared. "I knew nothing about it. All I know is that I have a document in my possession that says we're husband and wife."

Meg's chin firmed. "And I have a document saying our marriage ended years ago."

"You heard the lady," Jess barked. "Get the hell out of here and don't come back."

Skully sent Meg a knowing smirk. "Is the doc another of your lovers, Meg? You do spread your favors around, don't you? That will have to stop. You're the one who needs to leave, Gentry. My wife and I have things to . . . discuss."

Jess searched Meg's face. "Is that true, Meg? Do you want to be alone with Skully?"

"Good God, no! I never want to set eyes on him again. I hate him!"

"You heard the lady, Skully. I suggest you leave before I throw you out."

Skully hesitated but a moment before reaching for his gun. Jess saw Skully's movement and with lightning speed drew his own weapon before the gambler's hand reached the butt of his gun. Skully paled, his gaze trained on Jess's six-shooter.

"How in the hell did you do that? You're a doctor, not a gunslinger."

"I can be many things when the need arises. My brothers and I perfected quick draws when we were boys down on the family farm, trying to outperform one another."

Skully stared at Jess through narrowed lids. "I know you from somewhere. One day I'll figure out where I've seen you."

"We've never met," Jess insisted. "If you're wise, you'll leave town as soon as possible. Now get out. Only a coward would bully a woman. It's obvious Meg wants nothing to do with you."

"We'll see about that," Skully growled. "Meg is my wife. Nothing will change that."

Jess had taken all he could of Arlo Skully. He started forward, intending to toss Skully bodily out the door, but Arlo didn't wait for him. He turned and fled. Jess didn't relax until he heard Skully's horse pounding down the road. Then he turned back to Meg and pulled her into his arms.

"So that's Arlo," he said tightly. "Don't you think it's time you told me about him?"

Meg nodded jerkily. "I suppose, though in truth that episode in my life is one I'd prefer to forget."

Jess lifted Meg into his arms and strode to the sofa. Then he sat down, arranging Meg on his lap. "Go ahead. I'm all ears."

Meg grew quiet, wondering how to proceed. The story was such a complicated and sordid one, she didn't know where to begin. She sucked in a deep breath and began at the beginning.

"My parents were dirt-poor farmers. I was the eldest of eight children. We lived in a soddy near Pine Bluffs, Nebraska. Arlo Skully was a professional gambler. He was passing through town one day when he saw me with my father. He started coming around to call on me. Shortly after that, Papa told me I was to marry Mr. Skully. I learned later that Arlo offered Papa money for me. No matter how much it hurts, it still boils down to the fact that my parents sold me."

"Didn't your father know the man was a gambler? That he wasn't the right kind of husband for an innocent sixteen-year-old?"

Meg shrugged. "There were too many mouths to feed and so little money. They thought Arlo would be good to me, I suppose." She shuddered. "Papa thought that insisting Arlo marry me before he took me away would make everything all right."

"But it didn't, did it, sweetheart?"

Meg shook her head. "Arlo swore to them that he'd be a good husband. Unfortunately, they didn't delve too deeply into his character. I learned the hard way."

"Did you have nothing to say about marrying a man you knew so little about?"

She gave a bitter laugh. "I had no say whatsoever. Arlo would have dragged me off if I'd refused. I hated him when I learned he'd paid Papa for me. I tried to tell myself the sacrifice was worth it, that the younger children wouldn't go hungry during the long winter, but even that wasn't enough to make up for the pain, the degradation, the utter hopelessness of my situation."

"I should have killed him," Jess gritted. "You should have been led into lovemaking gently."

Meg covered her face with her hands. Jess pulled them away and looked deep into her eyes. "You can tell me. Perhaps you need to talk about it to make it go away."

"It will never go away," Meg avowed. "The town was scarcely behind us when Arlo pulled the wagon into a stand of trees and assaulted me. Nothing about that first time, or any other time, could be called lovemaking."

A sob burst from her throat and she stood up, turning away from him. He made no move to follow.

"What happened then?"

"We came to a town and Arlo decided to stay for the night. He dragged me into a saloon offering accommodations. After booking a room, he spied a poker game and decided to join in. I wanted to go to our room, but he refused to let me go, insisting that I stay with him. I was so embarrassed I sat on a chair with my hands folded and never looked up. I had no idea Arlo was losing heavily until he pulled me forward and offered me as collateral during the play of a hand."

"He lost," Jess guessed, clenching his fists in outrage.

"He lost me to a man I'd never seen before. I was to spend the night with Mr. Dunbar to repay Arlo's debt. When I flatly refused, Arlo dragged me to our room and beat me nearly senseless."

"The bastard!"

"When Arlo left me, Mr. Dunbar came up to claim his prize. I hadn't the energy to fight him, but when he returned downstairs to purchase a bottle of whiskey, I found the strength to flee. I was hurting and sick," she recalled. "For days I wandered around in a daze, shunning travelers and towns. I don't remember much about those terrifying days, for I was delirious most of the time.

"Exhausted, dehydrated, and starving, I collapsed somewhere out on the prairie and would have died if Zach hadn't found me, brought me to his home, and nursed me back to health. I owe him my life."

"You never saw Skully again until today?" Jess probed.

"He said he looked for me after I disappeared but gave me up for dead after a few days."

"Did you really have your marriage annulled?"

"Zach saw to it. A lawyer opened an office in town about a year after I moved in with Zach. The judge granted the annulment on grounds of desertion. Skully never showed up to contest it, so I assume it's legal."

"I don't know the law, but I would be inclined to agree."

"What do you think Arlo will do now? I wish Zach were here. He's been like a father to me, a man I grew to love and trust, who offered me love in return."

"You have me, Meg. I won't let Skully hurt you."

She turned and regarded him solemnly. "Why are you still here? I thought you decided to leave Cheyenne."

"I learned Zach was called away to Philadelphia and I couldn't leave you without protection."

She gave a snort of laughter. "I'm a bounty hunter, remember? I can take care of myself."

"You aren't doing a very good job of it," Jess reminded her. "It looked to me as if Skully had the upper hand."

Meg sent him a wounded look. "He surprised me. Arlo was the last person in the world I expected to see at my door, and I didn't have my guns handy."

"What did he want?"

"He said I was still his wife, and insisted that I leave town with him. I refused, and he took exception. He wanted to . . . to . . ."

Jess's face hardened. "No need to explain. I know exactly what that bastard wanted from you. God, Meg, I would have killed him if he'd hurt you."

Meg's expression softened. She wanted to kiss him. She needed Jess, needed him to banish the memory of Arlo and the painful past she'd lived with far too long.

"Kiss me, Jess."

"Are you sure, love?"

"I've never been more sure of anything in my life."

Chapter Eleven

Jess stared at Meg as if she'd just offered him the world. "I don't think I could stop with one kiss, and I'm not sure that making love to you right now is a good idea."

Meg gave him a wounded look. "You don't want me?"

His arms tightened around her and he groaned into her ear. "I want you too much. So damn much that I'd risk anything to have you again."

Meg pulled away, searching his face as she put her fears into words. "I think Arlo recognized you."

"I've never met him, I'm sure of it."

"Then he's seen the poster," Meg said on a shaky breath. "It's not safe for you here. You have to leave, Jess. I couldn't bear to see you behind bars."

Jess's jaw firmed. "No, I won't run. Being a fugitive is not the kind of life I want for myself. The hell with Arlo. I have a good notion to return to Dodge and fight the charges. My brothers and I were wrong to flee. We should have stayed and fought for justice. We panicked, and because we did, we became fugitives from the law. I'm a doctor. I want to be free to practice my profession."

"You won't stay free if you remain here. And returning to Dodge will only land you in jail. Please, Jess, go before Arlo remembers where he saw you."

"I can't leave you, Meg. Zach is counting on me to keep you safe in his absence, and I'm not going to let him down. I'll think about leaving after he returns."

"Is there nothing I can say or do to make you understand how dangerous it is to remain?"

"No, but you can let me kiss you. That *is* what you wanted, isn't it?"

He rose and narrowed the distance between them, bringing her against him. The delicious pressure of her breasts against his chest made his breath hitch. She must have been battered by the same emotions, for her lips parted. Jess didn't wait for an invitation; he teased the lush, sensitive curve of her upper lip and nibbled gently on the full lower one. He memorized the shape of her lips with his tongue, then pressed for entry, deepening the kiss.

His hands swept up from her waist, molding her breasts. They shared a single breath as the kiss turned into a prelude to something far more intense.

He broke the kiss, his breathing ragged. He cupped her face and searched her delicate features. Her eyes were dreamy, her lips faintly swollen and damp. He grasped her bottom and pulled her into the cradle of his loins. Her eyes widened as he ground his hips against hers, letting her feel the rigid length of his erection.

"I tried to tell you what would happen if I kissed you."

She dragged in a calming breath. "I know."

"I want to make love to you, sweetheart. I need you more than the air I breathe."

"Will you leave Cheyenne afterward?" Meg pleaded.

He swept her into his arms, striding toward her bedroom. "Only if you come with me."

"You know that's impossible."

He kicked open the door and charged inside. He set her on her feet, letting her slide down the length of his body so she could feel how much he wanted her. Then he kissed her again, using his tongue to tease and torment her swollen lips, tasting her, savoring her as he would a fine wine.

"Too many clothes," he muttered against her lips as his hands found the fastenings on the front of her dress.

Meg's fingers crept under his shirt; the muscles cording his back and shoulders tensed. Her fingertips glided down his chest and dipped just inside his trousers. His flesh jerked beneath her touch. The sound he made was a mixture of pleasure and pain.

Her dress fell to the floor and he lifted her out of it. He released the ties holding her chemise together, and it soon joined the dress. She unbuckled his gun belt and it fell to the floor. She unfastened his trousers and ran her hands beneath the waistband.

With a growl of impatience, he tore off her drawers and knelt before her to roll down her stockings. He stripped them off along with her shoes. Then he stood back to admire her.

"You're so beautiful it hurts my eyes to look at you. You're mine, Meg. Someday, I don't know how, but someday, somehow, we'll be together." His hand came up to stroke the tip of one breast. "You believe that, don't you?"

Meg looked into the smoldering depths of Jess's eyes and was willing to believe anything he said. The strength of his emotion humbled her. It was bitter comfort to know it was the wrong time to tell him she loved him. He had too much on his plate; he didn't need complications.

"You're a good man, Jess Gentry. Someday you'll find a sweet, innocent woman to love." She placed a finger against his lips. "No, don't say anything. Just make love to me."

He swept her up and laid her down on the bed.

"Your trousers."

He grinned at her and skimmed them down his legs. Then he kicked them off, along with his boots. He returned to her as gloriously naked as she. She watched him hungrily. Never in her wildest dreams had she imagined herself wanting a man as desperately as she did Jess. He was broad where she was slim, hard where she was soft, every line of his powerful body a tribute to masculine beauty.

She licked her lips in anticipation as he eased his body over hers, gradually pressing his entire weight onto her. He was hard, hot, his movements wonderfully erotic.

Abruptly he rolled to his side, his hunger vividly apparent in the shining depths of his hazel eyes and the rigid length of his body. She gasped as his fingers traced the curve of her ankle, his touch light and teasing. His hand continued upward, over the swell of her calf, the sensitive indention behind her knee. He lowered his head and kissed her navel, then pressed his face against her belly. He slid lower, trailing kisses down her thighs. She trembled, waiting breathlessly for his next move.

Then he claimed her *there* and she screamed his name, winding her hands in his hair, afraid he'd go on and fearing she'd die if he stopped. He raised his head and gave her a grin that made her breath stop momentarily.

"I need to kiss you there," he murmured seductively. "Every part of you is precious to me."

One of his fingers dipped into the dewiness between her legs, using her own moistness to caress and tease her. She sucked in a breath as his head dipped down and he took another delicate taste of her honey. Meg nearly expired from the delicious pleasure of it. His hands branded her flesh, his mouth and tongue drove her to unimaginable heights.

Spreading her legs wide, she arched and writhed, unable to think coherently as he increased the pressure upon the sensitive nub he found with his tongue. She closed her eyes as his clever mouth and tongue pushed her higher and higher. He cupped her bottom and she raised her hips in invitation. She wanted to show him without words that she loved him.

Then all thought ceased as heat began to rise in her belly. It burst upon her in an agony of pleasure so intense she felt as though her soul were touching the sun.

Moments later, she felt Jess move up her body and enter her in a long, sliding stroke. Then it began again. The core of pleasure expanded as he moved inside her, thrusting hard, allowing no quarter as he stroked her to that exalted place she had visited scant moments ago. Something savage broke free inside her. It danced just out of reach, and when she finally grasped it, it inundated her with wave after wave of shimmering ecstasy.

She cried out his name but he didn't seem to hear her. His body had gone rigid, his jaw tightly clenched, his head thrown back, and his teeth bared. He plunged into her once, twice, then went still as he poured his seed into her.

Long moments passed before Meg regained her wits. When she opened her eyes, Jess was lying beside her, holding her as her trembling subsided. She smiled at him.

"I don't know why lovemaking frightened me so before. With you it's incredibly . . . wonderfully . . ." She shook her head. "Words fail me. It just feels right."

"I want it to be this way forever, love. But forever isn't possible until I'm free. All I can hope for are enough memories to last until this horrible mistake with the law is settled."

Meg didn't like the sound of that. "What are you going to do?"

"First I'm going to find Arlo Skully," Jess said tersely.

Meg swallowed a gasp. "Why?"

His jaw tautened. "I want to make damn sure my message got through to him. I won't let him bother you again."

"What if he's already gone to the sheriff

with what he knows?"

"He doesn't remember me. He might never associate me with that Wanted poster."

"The sheriff," Meg began. "He can identify you if he ever decides to glance at the Wanted posters in his drawer."

Jess glanced out the window; Meg didn't like the look on his face.

"What are you thinking?"

"I'm thinking that whatever I do will never be enough. I could get rid of Skully, but that doesn't guarantee I'll be free. There's always those blasted posters making my life a living hell. I'm not a criminal," he declared. "But who will believe me?"

"I believe you," Meg whispered.

He pulled her roughly against him. "Do you care for me, Meg?" He carefully avoided the word *love*. "Do you care for me enough to go away with me? Perhaps I *should* take your advice and leave. I can't take the suspense of waiting any longer. Every time I see the sheriff, I think he's going to arrest me."

"This is no time for declarations, Jess," Meg hedged. "Perhaps one day we can unburden our hearts, but not now. I care; let it go at that. I have an idea that just might fix things so you won't have to leave."

"Forget it," Jess said bleakly. "I don't want to involve you in my problems."

"Just give me a chance before you make

any decisions. At least listen to my plan."

"All right, I'll listen, but I'm not going to let you do anything foolish on my account."

"If it wasn't for that poster in Sheriff Bufford's desk, no one around here would know about you, right?"

"Right," Jess answered warily. "So?"

"I can get that poster and destroy it."

Jess gave her a skeptical look. "How do you propose to do that?"

"Bufford is accustomed to having me look through the newest batches of Wanted posters. He often leaves me alone in the office while I'm reading them. I'll just remove yours and destroy it. Then no one will ever know Jess Gentry is a wanted man."

"Absolutely not! What if Bufford decides to remain in his office while you're there? Too many things could go wrong. Besides, there's Skully. He might suddenly remember where he saw my face."

"Over the years, I've learned that Bufford rarely remains in his office for long periods of time. He's usually out keeping the peace. I'll just wait around until he leaves, then destroy the poster."

Jess frowned. "It sounds too easy."

"It *is* easy."

"What about Skully?"

"As long as he doesn't remember where he saw you, you're safe. He'll probably leave town before he recalls anything about you.

He's not one to stick around in one place for long."

"I'll only agree to this harebrained scheme if you move into town with me. I don't want you out here by yourself."

Meg touched his face, her caress soft and loving. "If I do that, I'll ruin your reputation. You're well liked in town, whereas I'm treated like a pariah. You could lose your patients because of me."

"My patients will be there whether or not you're with me. At least until another doctor comes to town. Right now I'm all Cheyenne has. Take it or leave it, Meg, but that's the only way I'll allow you to put your plan into motion. If you're caught, you could end up behind bars with me."

She nodded jerkily. "Very well, I'll do as you say. But you'd best be prepared to face some irate patients when they see me in your home."

"They won't remain irate long if we get married," Jess proposed, once again surprising himself. Meg had refused him once; why would she agree now? In fact, the notion was so crazy he should have retracted it at once. He didn't.

Meg stared at him. "Why —" she began.

"Marrying you is the only way to keep Skully from bothering you."

"I can take care of myself."

"I can't leave you to fend for yourself, no

matter how capable you are."

Marrying Jess would make everything right in Meg's world. But was it the right thing to do at this time? she wondered. Would it do Jess more harm than good? Would he lose his patients and the respect of the townspeople by marrying her?

"Jess, I don't think —"

"Don't think, love, just feel." He brought her hand to his groin. "Feel how much I want you?"

Her eyes widened. "Again?"

"Again and again and again."

Then he kissed her, and coherent thought fled. He kissed her until her mind spun and she melted all over him. They came together like a wild prairie storm. She opened her legs in eager surrender and he slid inside. Then abruptly he rolled with her in his arms, placing her on top.

"Ride me, sweetheart. Yes, that's right," he murmured as she gasped and bucked and squeezed her legs tightly against his sides.

Meg felt her blood thicken, her body tense. Liquid fire licked along her veins. And then she exploded. Not until she collapsed around him did Jess stop his delicious movements. She heard his labored breathing and knew he had found his own release. He held her immobile a few moments before lifting her and settling her beside him.

"I've never had with another woman what I

just experienced with you," Jess said with a hint of awe. "This could be ours forever if you marry me."

"Are you sure, Jess? Very, very sure?"

"Don't ever doubt my feelings for you, love."

"Then I'll marry you. But not until I retrieve that Wanted poster from the sheriff's office."

Idly he stroked her breast. "I'm not sure that's a good idea."

"Do you have a better one?"

"Not at the moment."

"I'd like to wait until Zach returns so he can attend our wedding. That's only another week."

"I'll wait a week, no longer," Jess said, climbing out of bed.

Meg watched with avid appreciation as Jess poured water from the pitcher into a bowl and washed himself. The play of muscles and tendons across his shoulders and chest, his taut buttocks, the long, sturdy columns of his legs — everything about him suggested strength and virility. She'd do anything to keep him from wasting away in prison.

Jess dressed quickly and walked back to the bed. "Stay here. I'll bring up some fresh water and clean towels. When you're finished, pack your belongings. You're moving to town with me immediately."

Meg didn't try to dissuade him. She knew

she'd be better off in town. Remaining out here alone now that Arlo knew where to find her was dangerous. But she meant what she'd said. She wouldn't marry Jess until that damned Wanted poster had been destroyed. She and Jess would enjoy no peace until the threat to his freedom had been eliminated.

Unfortunately, there was still Arlo Skully to contend with. Perhaps between them, she and Jess could find a way to defuse the danger Arlo represented.

Arlo Skully watched with interest as Jess and Meg rode into town. He followed at a discreet distance until they reined in at Jess's office and entered the house together. He hadn't missed the fact that Jess carried a carpetbag that obviously belonged to Meg; rage seethed through him. Meg was his. He was her first and he meant to be her last. That little piece of paper annulling their marriage meant nothing to him. In his mind, he and Meg were husband and wife, and he was already contemplating the ways in which he could capitalize on her mature beauty and sex appeal. She was much more attractive to men now than she had been as an innocent sixteen-year-old.

"You haven't been eating right," Meg scolded after she'd unpacked her clothes and went down to the kitchen to fix Jess something to eat. "There's nothing in the larder."

"I eat most of my meals out," Jess confided.

"Surely not all your patients pay with cash, do they? What do you do with the produce and livestock offered in payment for your services?"

Jess flushed. "I give everything to my poorer patients."

Her love for Jess grew by leaps and bounds. "You're a good man, Jess Gentry."

Jess sat down and pulled her into his lap. "Shall I show you how bad I can be?"

Meg's cheeks pinkened and she stood up in mock indignation. "Not now. I just heard the bell over your door jangle. You have a patient waiting for you, and I need to buy provisions at the store."

"While you're at it," Jess said, "stop in at the sheriff's office and pick up your reward. He asked me to tell you it's come in."

Jess went into his waiting room to greet his patient, and Meg put on her battered wide-brimmed hat and prepared to go shopping. No bonnet for her, she thought as she adjusted the hat on her head. At least she wasn't wearing trousers. The townspeople would just have to get used to her wearing a man's hat. Some things she was willing to forgo for society's sake, but others she was not.

A buzz of conversation followed in Meg's

wake. She knew she was grist for the gossip mill, but she was used to it. The upstanding citizens of Cheyenne treated her with contempt simply because they were jealous of her ability to excel at a man's profession. That and the fact that she lived with a man to whom she wasn't married.

Meg was so lost in her thoughts that she didn't hear Arlo Skully sidle up beside her.

"You cause quite a stir in this town," Arlo said.

Meg started violently. "Arlo, you startled me. I didn't hear you approach."

"What are you doing with Gentry? I saw you ride into town with him."

"None of your business."

He grasped her arm. "I'm making it my business. I'm still your husband."

She wrested free. "You're nothing to me. I'm going to marry Jess Gentry."

Fury contorted Arlo's features. "Over my dead body!"

"Perhaps that can be arranged," Meg hissed. "Out of my way, Arlo. You no longer frighten me. I've grown up since you bought me from my parents."

"So I see," Arlo said, leering at her breasts.

Just then two women passed by. Deliberately they pulled aside their skirts and sniffed the air as if they smelled something rank.

"Look at her," the older of the two said in a voice loud enough to carry. "Shameless hussy. Her lover hasn't been gone a week, and she's already consorting with another man."

The second woman nodded her head in vigorous agreement. "She shouldn't be allowed on the streets."

"You should consider leaving town," Arlo said after the women moved on. "I've purchased two tickets on tomorrow's train. One for you and one for me. Taking you away from here is the best thing I could do for you. You aren't right for the doctor. You'll ruin his reputation and destroy his practice if you keep company with him."

Meg knew Arlo was right. Marrying Jess was a bad idea, but, dammit, she loved him. Together they could stand united against the gossips . . . couldn't they?

"I have better things to do than stand here listening to you," Meg replied as she stepped around Arlo and continued down the street.

Arlo easily caught up to her. "Tell your new lover I'm going to remember where I've seen him one of these days. Something tells me he's not going to like it."

Meg didn't bother answering, but fear stiffened her spine. If Arlo remembered Jess from the Wanted poster, all was lost. Stealing the poster from the sheriff's office would not matter if Arlo remembered. She couldn't bear the thought of Jess going to prison.

She spun around to face Arlo. "What will

it take for you to stop trying to recall where you've seen Jess?"

"That important, is it?" Arlo asked slyly. "Well, now, we ought to talk about this in private. I've taken a room at the hotel. Come with me now."

"I . . . can't. Jess is expecting me. Do you want money? I have five hundred dollars waiting for me at the sheriff's office. You can have it if you leave town and don't come back."

Arlo stared intensely at her. "This is getting damn interesting. What could the doc have in his past that you don't want revealed?"

"Nothing! Jess is a good man. Everyone likes him."

"Like hell. I don't like him."

"Just go away, Arlo. Please."

"Not without you. Come up to my room."

"Later," Meg hedged. "Tomorrow."

"Our train leaves at three o'clock."

"I'm not going anywhere with you, Arlo."

"I'm not going anywhere *without* you."

"I'll bring the five hundred dollars. It's yours if you agree to leave Cheyenne and forget me and Jess. Think about it."

Finding herself in front of the grocery store, she hurried inside. A matron perusing the merchandise saw her, gave a snort of disgust, and quickly moved to another part of the store. She was joined by two other women, obviously mother and daughter. They made no effort to hide their disdain. Meg gave her list to the clerk, made arrangements to have the provisions delivered, and promptly left the store.

Once Meg exited, the three women hurried over to the clerk. "Where are her groceries to be delivered?" the older woman asked curiously. "Doesn't she usually take them with her?"

"She asked to have them delivered to Doc Gentry."

"Whyever for?" the second matron asked.

"You know, Kate," the older woman confided, "my husband told me Meg Lincoln and Dr. Gentry are close. You don't suppose . . . surely he wouldn't . . . it doesn't bear thinking about. Doc Gentry is too good to be taken in by a whore. Someone has to tell him."

"I'll do it, Mother," the daughter declared. "Dr. Gentry treated my sprained ankle not long ago, and we had a rather interesting conversation."

"I'm the one who should talk to him, Polly," her mother said. "You're too young to speak plainly."

"I think Polly is right," Kate argued. "Doc Gentry is a young man and Polly is an attractive girl. Let her tell him about Meg Lincoln. He's new to town and probably isn't aware of the bounty hunter's unsavory reputation."

The matter settled between them, they left the store.

Meg continued on to the sheriff's office. Bufford was just walking out the door when she arrived.

"Miss Lincoln, I was hoping you'd stop by," Bufford said. "I have your reward money. Came in on the train yesterday."

He returned to his desk and removed a bulging envelope from the middle drawer. "Here you are. Five hundred in cash."

Meg took the envelope and placed it inside her reticule. "Thanks, Sheriff, that was quick. Do you mind if I look through those Wanted posters again?"

Bufford frowned. "I was hoping Doc Gentry might have changed your mind about bounty hunting."

"I'm seriously considering retiring, but I'd still like another look at those posters. Just in case I happen to run into one of those outlaws."

"Help yourself," Bufford said. "They're still where you left them. Haven't found the time to look at them yet."

"Weren't you on the way out?" Meg asked.

"Yeah. Deputy Taylor just sent word that there's a brawl brewing at the Whistle Stop and I thought I'd go over and try to stop it before it gets out of hand."

"Don't let me stop you. I'll just look through the posters and leave when I'm finished."

"That's fine with me. Leave them on top of the desk when you're done with them. I suppose it's time I took a look at them."

Meg waited until Bufford had disappeared down the street before removing the posters from the drawer. She hadn't expected the opportunity to remove Jess's poster to arrive so soon. She had merely stopped in at the sheriff's office to collect her reward.

It took but a moment to find Jess's poster at the back of the drawer where she'd shoved it. Excitement thrummed through her as she carefully folded it and prepared to stash it in her reticule.

"What do we have here?" a harsh voice asked.

Stunned, Meg looked up and saw Arlo standing in the doorway, watching her closely.

"Where did you come from?"

"I followed you. When you remained after the sheriff left, I grew curious. What have you got in your hand?"

"Nothing that would interest you."

She stuffed the poster in her reticule and snapped it shut. "Excuse me. I must be going."

Arlo sprang at her and grabbed the reticule from her hand. Wrenching it open, he removed the poster and tossed the reticule back to her.

"Give me that!"

Arlo held the poster just out of her reach as he scanned it; then he burst out laughing. "Now I remember. Gentry is a fugitive from the law. He's wanted in Kansas for bank robbery. I recall seeing the Wanted posted when I passed through Dodge City not long ago. I would have remembered it before long. This puts a whole different face on things, doesn't it?"

"Nothing has changed," Meg ground out.

"I beg to differ with you. You were worried enough about the sheriff seeing this to steal it. Are you worried enough to save Gentry from prison?"

Meg stiffened. "What are you getting at?"

He gave her a lethal smile as he carefully folded the poster and slipped it into his jacket pocket. "Just this. You either come with me tomorrow or I give this to the sheriff. What's it going to be? How fond are you of the saintly Doc Gentry? Or is he a doctor at all?"

"Of course he's a doctor," Meg hissed. "A darn good one. For your information, the charges against him are false. He never robbed a bank. It was all a mistake."

"I'm sure it was," he returned snidely. "You never gave me your answer. Do you want me to show the sheriff the poster when he returns?"

255

"No, damn you! Putting Jess behind bars would be a travesty."

He eyed her narrowly. "You really *are* fond of him, aren't you? Enough said. Meet me at the train station at three tomorrow afternoon. We'll make a good team. You're no longer an innocent sixteen-year-old. You can do whatever it takes to bring men to my card game and I'll fleece them of their money."

"What's that supposed to mean?" Meg asked indignantly.

"It means you can use your body as long as it benefits me. But I'm the one you'll save your passion for. The rest will be only a game to us."

"You're mad!"

"Am I? I thought I was being generous. I could show this poster to the sheriff whether or not you decide to leave with me. I'm trying to please you."

Meg closed her eyes, picturing the man she loved behind bars. The vision was so distressing she knew she couldn't allow it to happen.

"Very well. What do I have to do to prevent you from showing the poster to the law?"

He gave her a smug grin. "Whatever I tell you to do. Meet me at the train station tomorrow and we'll take it from there."

Chapter Twelve

Jess was still treating patients when Meg returned home. The groceries she had ordered arrived soon afterward and she busied herself putting them away. When she finished, she peeked into Jess's waiting room to judge how long it would be before she should start supper and saw him deep in conversation with Polly, one of the women she'd seen at the store. She opened the door wider and listened to the conversation.

"It's common knowledge that you're smitten with Meg Lincoln, Doctor. Some of us feel that there are some things about her you should know."

"I have a strong suspicion you're going to give me advice I neither need nor want," Jess said with a long-suffering sigh.

"Someone has to," Polly said primly. "Meg Lincoln has a colorful past. She's not someone you should be seeing."

"I know all there is to know about Miss Lincoln," Jess said.

"Then you must be aware that she's living in sin with that crippled bounty hunter. Did you also know she's" — Polly's lips compressed — "slept with every man she's ever brought in for a reward?"

Meg flinched. How could people think that?

"You're jumping to conclusions and condemning Meg out of hand," Jess said sternly.

"I didn't just make this up," Polly maintained. "You're well thought of in town, Dr. Gentry. We'd hate to see you fall in with bad company."

"I appreciate your concern, Miss Gallagher, but I'm old enough to take care of myself."

"Very well, Doctor," Polly sniffed, "but don't say I didn't warn you. No one wants to see you taken advantage of by a . . . a fallen woman. Think of your reputation."

Meg saw Jess's jaw tighten and his fists clench and was glad she wasn't Polly just then.

"That's enough, Miss Gallagher!" Jess blasted. "I suggest that henceforth you keep your biased opinions to yourself. I find Meg Lincoln to be a forthright and admirable woman. Furthermore . . ."

Quietly Meg closed the door on the conversation. She'd heard enough. She felt like an albatross around Jess's neck. Even if he was found innocent of the robbery charge, associating with her would ruin his reputation in town. He was a doctor. He had found a place for himself and he needed patients to survive. He was so dedicated to his calling that being ostracized would be a terrible blow.

There was only one thing she could do to protect his identity and salvage his reputation. She needed to get Arlo *and* the Wanted poster out of town. Even if she had to accompany Arlo to do it.

She was resourceful, Meg reflected. It wouldn't be difficult to lose Arlo once they arrived at their destination. Or she could even jump train before they arrived. She knew Arlo. He'd be so angry at her escape that he'd forget about Jess in his eagerness to find her.

But what about Jess? her heart cried. What would he think of her if she ran out on him?

Perhaps it would be for the best, Meg tried to convince herself. He'd hate her for a while; then he'd forget her, find another woman to marry, one who would be an asset to his profession. With Arlo out of the way and the Wanted poster gone, no one would ever know Jess was a fugitive.

The door opened and Jess walked into the kitchen. "I just locked up for the day."

She gave him a distracted smile. "I'll start supper. Pork chops and mashed potatoes. I bought some late peaches, too. How does peach cobbler sound?"

"Delicious, but not as delicious as you look right now." He pulled her into his arms and kissed her soundly.

"Do you want supper tonight?" Meg asked, gently pushing him away.

"What's the alternative?" Jess teased.

"We may never eat tonight if you keep this up."

"Very well, but I'm sure that going to bed hungry won't hurt me when the rewards are so great."

"Get out of here and let me cook," Meg laughed, pushing him out the door. "I'll call you when supper is ready."

Meg leaned against the closed door and shut her eyes. Guilt stabbed her; the pain was excruciating. She felt as if she had betrayed Jess. And in a way she had. He expected her to marry him, not go off with a man she despised. What would he think when she disappeared?

A note of explanation might help, but she decided against it. Better that he hate her than pine for her. He was bound to find out she had left with Arlo and he'd probably never forgive her, or understand why it was for the best.

Briefly Meg considered Zach and what he would think about her leaving. She hated to take off with his health so precarious, but Widow Dowling could easily take her place in his life. Zach could marry Mary and live happily with the widow now that his wife was dead.

Time passed quickly as Meg cooked supper. When everything was done, she set the food on the table and called Jess to the kitchen.

"Smells good," Jess said, sniffing appreciatively. "I'm hungry as a bear." His grin told her he was hungry for more than food.

Meg's own appetite had disappeared. She pushed her fork around her plate and tried to concentrate on Jess's conversation. She failed miserably.

"Are you all right, sweetheart?" Jess asked, putting down his fork. "You haven't touched your food. Did Skully's visit upset you more than you're letting on?"

"No, it's not that," Meg quickly denied. Too quickly, obviously, for Jess slanted her a puzzled look. "By the way, I collected my reward from the sheriff."

"Did you have time to look for the Wanted poster?"

"No," she lied. "The sheriff was in his office the whole time."

"Forget it, it doesn't matter. Is that all you want to tell me?"

"That's it. I'm sorry, Jess, I guess I'm just tired."

"Go crawl in bed, sweetheart. I'll finish up here."

Another jolt of guilt smote Meg. Why did Jess have to be so good?

"Maybe I'll take you up on that," Meg

said, rising. "Just pile the dishes in the sink. Are you sure you don't mind?"

"Not at all, as long as it's my bed you crawl into. Go on, I'll be up shortly."

Meg gave him an uncertain smile and left the room. How was she going to find the courage to leave? she wondered distractedly. How would she survive without him? She made up her mind to savor him one last time tonight. Yes, she decided, tonight she'd love him as she'd never loved him before. She wanted to make enough memories to last a lifetime.

Jess finished his supper and cleared the table, his thoughts deeply disturbed as he piled the dishes in the sink. Something was troubling Meg. He knew her well enough by now to know when she was disturbed. He was fairly certain Arlo Skully was involved and decided to let her tell him in her own good time. He loved Meg too much to badger her.

Jess finished in the kitchen and slowly walked up the stairs, his lust for his beautiful Meg nearly uncontrollable. The thought of having her in his bed every night made him hard as stone. He hoped she wasn't asleep.

Jess's wish was granted. Meg had changed to her nightgown and stood by the window, staring into the darkness. Jess came up behind her, surrounding her with his arms.

"What are you thinking?"

"I wasn't thinking at all. Just enjoying the fine night."

Jess knew darn well she was lying but didn't press her.

"Come to bed, sweetheart."

Meg turned in his arms, her eyes glowing like emeralds in the lamplight. Her arms crept around his neck and she pressed her body against him. Lifting her head, she offered him her lips. Jess didn't hesitate, taking her lips in a deeply satisfying kiss. He breathed in her scent, savoring her taste, the very essence of her. His hand closed over her breast. His groan came from the deepest part of him as he swung her into his arms and carried her to bed.

He whispered sweet love words against her lips, then flicked open the front ties on her nightgown. Her hands fumbled with the buttons on his shirt. With a groan of impatience, he flung off his shirt and tossed it aside.

Meg struggled to control the guilt she felt as Jess removed her nightgown and cupped her breasts, his warm, rough palms rubbing circles over the tips. They pebbled in response. She stroked his cheek, then ran her hand down the column of his strong neck. She could feel the stubble from his day's growth of beard. Her hand moved lower until it rested over his heart. She sensed the strong beat against her palm and felt connected almost spiritually to him.

He moaned a sound of male pleasure against her mouth, a deeply moving sound that touched her to the depths of her soul. Suddenly she pushed him down and loomed over him.

"Let me love you, Jess. Let me give you the same pleasure you give me."

"That's not necessary, love."

"To me, it is. Lift your hips so I can remove your trousers."

He quickly obliged. She heard his harsh breathing and reveled in the power she had over him. The same kind of power he held over her during their intimate moments.

Then he was naked; the turgid shaft of flesh jutting out from its bush of brown hair captured her attention. He was magnificent. She climbed over him, pressing her palms flat against his hips and her face against his belly. The earthy scent of his arousal filled her nostrils, sending her senses spiraling out of control. She had to taste him or die.

She traced the column of dark hair running down from his navel, enjoying the sensation of tautening muscles against her tongue. Her hands slipped between his thighs to test the weight of the globes hanging between his legs. She squeezed gently, amazed at their softness, at the taut skin surrounding them. Then she ran her hand up his shaft, enclosing it fully in her palm. She felt his life's blood pulse strongly against her hand and lowered her head to taste him.

"Meg, no!" Jess cried on a hoarse groan. "You'll kill me."

"You'll live," Meg said moments before her tongue licked a fiery trail down the sensitive underside of his shaft. He nearly bucked her off him when she licked the pulsing head and took it into her mouth.

A cry of raw agony escaped his throat, and suddenly Meg found herself flat on her back with Jess looming over her. "I have to have you. Now," he panted into her ear. "You've driven me to the brink of madness."

He entered her. She felt his hardness, the hot, thick, rigid length of him, the pulsing fullness moving strongly inside her. Her fingers dug into his shoulders. Solid muscle bunched as she pressed her lips to his hot skin.

His lips seized hers, his tongue thrusting inside to the same rhythm as his thrusting below. He moved in deep, nudging strokes, angling himself to stimulate the hidden peak of her sex. Everything blurred as he probed deeper, harder. His hands slid under her buttocks, bringing her up to meet his pounding loins. She tensed, feeling violent contractions clutching her. She exploded. Arching, cresting; shimmering waves of ecstasy spread outward until her body was inundated with vivid sensation.

She was still lost in the throes of excitement when she felt Jess's body go rigid, heard his hoarse cry of completion echo loudly in the silence.

"I love you, Meg."

No, Meg's heart silently responded. *Don't love me. Please don't love me.*

Afterward, Meg rested in Jess's arms, tears streaming down her cheeks. Leaving the man she loved was going to be the most difficult thing she'd ever done. But she had to do it. Jess was too good a doctor to be reviled and scorned because he'd married a woman with an unsavory reputation.

Jess's soft, even breathing told her he was sleeping, and she cuddled against him. She wanted to savor every moment of her last night with him.

And Jess gave her plenty to savor. Sometime during the darkest part of the night he awakened her with kisses and made love to her again.

Meg woke before Jess. She washed and dressed quickly, then went down to the kitchen to prepare breakfast — the last she would ever cook for Jess. Jess entered the kitchen as she was setting the table.

He gave her a big hug and a kiss, then sat down. "I'm famished. Your cooking is going to make me fat."

She set a plate piled high with food on the

table. "Flapjacks and bacon. I used Zach's recipe for flapjacks."

Jess dug in with gusto. When he noted that Meg merely sipped coffee, he asked, "Aren't you hungry? You should be after last night."

Hiding her breaking heart behind a smile, Meg replied, "I couldn't wait. I ate my breakfast before you came down."

Jess had just lifted the last bite of food to his mouth when the jangling doorbell announced a patient. He glanced at his watch. "They're arriving early today." He swallowed the rest of his coffee and rose. "Looks like it's going to be a busy morning. Do you have anything planned for today?"

"I thought I'd ride out to the house and pack the rest of my clothes," Meg said, refusing to look at Jess. "I'll leave something for your lunch and see you at supper."

Jess smiled and nodded as he went out the door. Meg knew he'd soon be immersed in his work and wouldn't have a spare moment to think about her.

Meg packed her carpetbag and fixed Jess's lunch before she left. She saddled her own horse and headed out to Zach's place. Once there, she packed the clothing she'd left behind the day before. Then she donned her leather britches, vest, fringed jacket, and battered hat. With cold determination, she strapped her gun belt around her slim hips, placed her 500 dollars in a pouch, and tied it around her neck with a leather thong.

Then she rode back to town and left her horse in the lean-to behind Jess's house. The next part was more difficult. She had to slip away to the train depot without Jess seeing her. She needn't have worried on that score. When she peeked through the waiting room window, she saw that the office was crowded with patients. Jess would be far too busy to notice her absence.

Hefting her carpetbag, Meg strode down the street to the depot, ignoring the curious stares following her. The train was already in, discharging passengers. She spied Arlo standing near the platform, anxiously checking his watch. He saw her approach and met her with a scowl.

"It's about time. You nearly missed the train."

"There's plenty of time," Meg said dully. God, how she hated this man.

Arlo sent her a disparaging look. "Why are you dressed like that?"

"I wanted to be comfortable." She held out her hand. "Give me the Wanted poster."

"Not a chance."

"We had a deal. Give me the poster."

His eyes narrowed, as if he were considering her request. "When the train leaves the station and not before."

Meg gave a curt nod.

"You don't look like my Meg dressed like that."

"I'm not your Meg. You no longer frighten me. I'm perfectly capable of taking care of myself."

He opened his mouth to say something, then quickly shut it as passengers began pushing past them. "It's time to board. We'll talk about this later. I don't feel comfortable with you packing guns."

"Neither did any of the outlaws I brought to justice," Meg stated boldly. She wanted Arlo to be aware that he no longer intimidated her.

Meg smiled inwardly at Arlo's disconcerted look as they found seats midway down the car. She stared out the window until the train jerked forward and slowly rolled out of the depot. Then she held out her hand. "The poster, Arlo."

Arlo obliged. "Giving you the poster doesn't mean a damn thing," he maintained. "I know where Gentry can be found. A telegram is all it will take to put him in jail."

"But you won't do that, will you, Arlo?"

"Not if you do as I tell you."

"Of course," she lied. "Where are we going?" Meg asked, directing her gaze out the window.

"Denver," Arlo replied. "I hear the pickings are good there. Lots of silver being mined in those parts."

Meg's determined expression should have warned Arlo. She hadn't decided until just now that Arlo had to be taken care of so he'd never be a threat to Jess again. She didn't know how, but she fully intended to rid the world of a man who had beaten her so severely she'd nearly died.

Jess hadn't seen Meg all day and was eager to hold her in his arms again as he closed and locked the office door after his last patient of the afternoon had departed. The day had been long and exhausting. Word of his skill had reached outlying areas, and a stream of farm families, cowboys, and townspeople tramped in and out of his examining room. Jess considered hiring a nurse, if one could be found, to assist him.

Despite his busy schedule, Jess felt good about his work. Treating patients, diagnosing their ailments — those were the things that made his life rewarding. Medicine and Meg. They were all he needed to make his life worth living and to fulfill his destiny. He prayed that fate would allow him to enjoy his profession and the woman he loved.

Jess walked into the kitchen, expecting to see Meg working over the stove. The kitchen was empty; no delicious smells wafted from the oven. The sense of emptiness, of coldness, clutched his heart with icy fingers. He raced through the house calling her name.

The bedrooms were empty. A terrible suspicion seized him as he tore open the dresser drawers. Every last piece of clothing she'd brought was missing.

Had she moved back to Zach's place? If so, why? There was only one way to find out. He ran outside to saddle his horse and was stunned to see Meg's horse in the lean-to beside his own.

What had happened? His first thought was that Arlo Skully had hurt Meg, and that thought sent him into a towering rage. If Skully had touched one hair on her head, he'd make the bastard sorry. Returning to the lean-to, Jess saddled his horse and headed over to the sheriff's office. Perhaps Bufford knew something he didn't.

Bufford wasn't at his office, but Jess found him at the Whistle Stop, trying to subdue a rambunctious cowboy who'd had too much to drink.

"Howdy, Doc," Bufford said as he pointed the drunken cowboy in the direction of the door.

"Can I speak with you in private, Sheriff?"

"Sure thing. Let's step outside."

Jess followed Bufford out the swinging doors. Before Jess could state his business, they were joined by Deputy Taylor.

"Is it all right if my deputy stays?" Bufford asked.

Jess nodded. "Has either of you seen Meg Lincoln today? She mentioned earlier that she intended to ride out to Zach Purdee's house, but her horse is still in the lean-to. Her clothes and carpetbag are missing, and I don't know what to make of it. We were going to be married next week. I can't believe she'd up and leave without a word."

"Congratulations on your upcoming marriage," Bufford said. "Have you been out to Purdee's house yet? Maybe she hired a wagon."

"I saw Miz Lincoln today," Deputy Taylor interjected.

"When?" Jess asked eagerly.

"At the train depot. I saw her board the three-o'clock to Denver."

Jess felt as if his world had tilted. "That's impossible! Meg wouldn't leave without telling me. We were going to be married. Just last night we . . ." His words ended abruptly as he recalled the passion they had shared the night before. "It must have been someone else you saw."

"No sir, Doc, it was Miz Lincoln, all right. I remember because she was dressed in britches and packing guns. Oh, one more thing. She wasn't alone."

Jess paled, not certain he wanted to hear the rest. But of course he had to. "Who was she with?"

"That fancy gambling man," Taylor answered. "The one with the funny name."

"Arlo Skully?"

"Yeah, that's the one. Thought it strange that she was with him, but since nothing looked amiss, I didn't interfere."

"The bastard," Jess growled. "I'll kill him."

"I think it's about time you told me what's going on," Bufford said. "Shall we stroll over to my office? There's not too much you can do right now. Besides, I want to know about Arlo Skully."

Jess fumed in impotent rage as he accompanied Bufford and Tayler to the jailhouse. He paced back and forth while Bufford waited for him to begin, his fingers steepled in front of him.

"At one time Meg was married to Arlo Skully," Jess revealed. "She was sixteen. Skully savagely beat Meg a few days into their marriage. Zach Purdee found her wandering on the prairie more dead than alive and nursed her back to health. Eventually, Meg filed for and was granted an annulment.

"She never thought Skully would barge into her life again, but he did," Jess continued. "He claimed they were still married and wanted to take her away. She refused."

He turned to Taylor. "Are you sure Meg wasn't being forced by Skully? He could have had a gun in her back."

"Meg had her belongings with her,"

Bufford reminded him. "She must have planned this ahead of time."

"She hated Skully," Jess protested.

"Women change their minds."

"You saw her yesterday, Sheriff. Did she mention anything about leaving town?"

"No, our conversation was brief. She collected her reward and asked to look over the Wanted posters again. I had business elsewhere, so I left her to read the posters."

A stunned expression crossed Jess's face. Meg had told him she hadn't had a chance to remove his poster from the sheriff's drawer. What the hell was going on?

"That's the last I saw of her," Bufford continued.

"As I said before, the last time I saw her, she was boarding a train," Taylor repeated.

"I'm sorry, Doc," Bufford offered. "I didn't know you two were getting hitched. Maybe Meg just decided to go after an outlaw and didn't want to tell you. She knew you'd worry and fuss at her."

Jess shook his head. "I'm afraid it's more than that, Sheriff. I reckon I'll go back home and try to make some sense out of this."

"Do you think this Skully fellow will harm her?" Bufford asked. "Meg always struck me as a woman who could take care of herself. She wouldn't have lasted in the bounty-hunting business as long as she did if that wasn't true."

Jess had to agree, but that didn't make him feel any better.

"Good-bye, Sheriff, Deputy. I've got a heap of thinking to do."

Jess rode home in a daze. He took care of his horse and let himself in the door without any memory of doing so. His brain was muddled, his thoughts confused. He lit a lamp and carried it up to his bedroom, too upset to eat. He pulled a chair to the window and stared morosely into the darkness, trying to figure out what the hell had gone wrong.

Last night Meg was the woman of his dreams. Warm, passionate, loving. They had loved and slept and loved again, their passion unquenchable. Why had she lied about the poster? He didn't give a damn about anything as long as she loved him. And though she hadn't said the words, he knew intuitively that she *did* love him.

Love lit her eyes when she looked at him. It flowed from her heart and filled her soul. He wasn't born yesterday. She loved him. She did!

But what if he was wrong? What could have made her leave town with Arlo? What reason would she have for making a fool of him?

Nothing made sense. Obviously, Meg didn't trust him enough to confide in him. His mind grew so groggy with thoughts and suppositions that Jess's head began to nod.

Finally he rose, undressed, and crawled into bed. Sleep claimed him before he'd resolved anything.

After the worst night of his life, Jess arose early and prepared for the day. He steered clear of the kitchen, where he'd last seen Meg, and decided to forgo breakfast. His first patient arrived early. Toward noon he received a message that Mrs. Larkins was in labor and having problems. And so his day went.

Two miserable, tension-filled days passed. Jess kept waiting for a message, a telegram, anything from Meg, but nothing arrived. Another train bound for Denver was due, and Jess pondered whether he should purchase a ticket and follow Meg. His heart said yes, but his pride said no. Then he considered his chances of finding Meg if he decided to go to Denver. Meg and Arlo could have gotten off the train anywhere between Cheyenne and Denver, diminishing his chances of ever finding her.

In the end, Jess decided to remain in Cheyenne. Why should he chase after a woman who cared so little about him? She hadn't even left a note. What he'd thought was love must have simply been lust on Meg's part. The love he'd perceived had been an illusion, something he wanted to believe in and now knew didn't exist.

Jess was putting his instruments and medicines away for the day when he heard the bell over the door announce another patient. Sighing tiredly, he walked from the examining room into the reception area. He bit back a groan when he saw Zach standing just inside the door.

"Howdy, Doc. I just got off the train. I'm on my way to see Mary and decided to stop in and let you know I'm back. How's Meggie? I had the strangest feeling when I hit town. That's why I stopped here first. You didn't let her go off bounty hunting, did you?"

"Sit down, Zach," Jess invited. Shocking the man was the last thing he wanted to do. "You're looking well."

"I'm feeling good, Doc. That medicine has worked wonders. I feel like a new man. Of course, having inherited a fortune from my wife didn't hurt any. I'm rich, Doc. Now I can marry Mary and take care of Meggie. Meggie will never have to endanger her life again."

Zach searched Jess's face, his own smile dissolving as he sank into the nearest chair. "Something's wrong, ain't it? It's Meggie. Something happened to her. Tell me, Doc. I can take it."

"A lot has happened since you left," Jess began. "Arlo Skully turned up in town."

Zach shot to his feet. "The hell he did!

What happened? Did he hurt Meg?"

"As far as I know, he didn't, though he did try to convince her to leave town with him. He claimed their marriage was still valid."

"The hell it is!"

Zach's face had turned so red that Jess sought to calm him. "I brought her to town, where I could protect her. I intended for her to stay with me until you returned. Then we were going to get married."

"Now, that *is* good news."

"You're not going to like the rest. Meg left town with Skully two days ago. She was seen boarding the Denver Express. I didn't want to believe it, but there were witnesses; the facts were indisputable. I don't know why she decided to leave with Skully. What hurt the most was that she cared for me so little she didn't even bother leaving a note. She just up and left."

"Meggie would never go anywhere with Arlo Skully," Zach said with conviction. "She loved you. She couldn't hide that from me. You're a damn fool if you think Meggie left willingly with Skully."

Chapter Thirteen

Jess wanted to believe Zach; God, he wanted to believe him. If there was a logical explanation for Meg's abrupt departure, he needed desperately to hear it.

"I just don't understand. Everything was fine between us before Meg left. She said she was going to ride out to the house for the rest of her clothing, and that was the last I saw of her. It doesn't make sense."

"Arlo forced her," Zach said with conviction.

"Deputy Taylor saw them together and swore she boarded the train without any coercion from Skully. Sheriff Bufford said she'd collected her five-hundred-dollar reward the day before."

"What are you gonna do about it, Doc?" Zach challenged. "Something smells fishy to me. I don't like it one damn bit. How long did you say Meggie has been gone?"

"Four days," Jess said. "I've argued with myself about going after her, but logic prevailed. She could have gotten off the train anywhere between here and Denver. Where would I start? Besides," he stated with little warmth, "she left me. What do you think that did to my pride? I loved her, Zach, and I'm hurting."

"I gotta think about this," Zach said, dropping into a chair. "Do you think Skully knew you were wanted and threatened to expose you if Meg didn't go with him?"

"I've considered that," Jess said. "If that's the case, Meg should have trusted me to find a solution. I don't really think Skully knew about me, although he kept insisting he'd seen me before. He just couldn't remember where."

"There you have it," Zach exclaimed excitedly. "You gotta save her, Doc. Arlo Skully is one mean bastard."

Jess's expression turned mutinous. "Meg made her choice, Zach. She's too damn independent. She should have trusted me."

"Is that your last word, Doc? I thought you loved Meggie."

"I'm too tired to think straight, Zach, and you look exhausted. You're risking your health if you don't go home and get some rest."

A stubborn frown darkened Zach's worn features. "If you won't go after her, I will."

"You just returned from an exhausting trip. Rest a few days; then we'll decide together what's to be done. Go see Mrs. Dowling. She's probably eager to see you."

"You're right, Doc, I'm too tired to think properly. I'll head over to Mary's and come back tomorrow. By then I should be clear-headed and better able to think this through. But I ain't letting you off the hook. If something happens to Meggie, I'll never forgive you."

For a moment, Jess saw a glimpse of the hard, relentless man Zach had been at the height of his career.

Jess closed and locked the door behind Zach and went into the kitchen to fix himself something to eat. He hadn't the energy nor the will to buy his meal out tonight. He found biscuits left over from the day before and opened a can of beans. Then he sat down and ate without really tasting the food. He finished quickly and went up to bed, where he spent half the night being angry at Meg for disappearing without a word and the other half worrying about her.

Jess fell into a troubled sleep around dawn. He was awakened abruptly when he heard a ruckus at the front door. The room was awash in light, and he realized he had over-slept. He pulled on his shirt and trousers and raced downstairs. He opened the door and found the meat cutter from the grocery store on his doorstep. He was holding a bloody towel around his hand.

"The knife slipped, Doc," the man said. "I reckon I need a few stitches."

Jess ended up putting sixteen stitches in the fellow's palm. He promised to send over two thick steaks as payment and went on his way. Since no other patients were waiting, Jess cleaned up, donned fresh clothing, and made a pot of coffee. He scarcely had time to enjoy his first cup before the bell jangled again.

His patient was Harvey Dooley, the postmaster. He complained of a hacking cough.

"Since I was on my way here anyway, thought I'd bring this to you myself, Doc," Dooley said, handing Jess a letter. "Just arrived this morning."

Jess stared at the letter as if it were a snake about to bite him. Who would know to find him here? He wanted to tear the letter open immediately but forced himself to treat Dooley first. The moment the postmaster left, Jess ripped the letter open. Tiny bits of paper sifted out, landing at his feet.

Puzzled, he scooped the pieces up and tried to fit them together. His eyes widened in shock when he realized he was looking at pieces of the Wanted poster bearing the images of the Gentry brothers. He stared at the envelope; it bore no return address. But he knew without being told who had sent it.

Meg.

Denver

The two days it took to reach Denver had

been a lesson in perseverance for Meg. Arlo had acted as if he owned her. Once, she had dozed off and awakened abruptly to find him trying to remove her guns. She quickly put a stop to his shenanigans and insisted on getting off the train each evening so she could take a hotel room where she would be able to sleep behind a locked door. Arlo was furious at the delays, but was reluctant to cause a scene on the train. In Fort Morgan, she tore up the Wanted poster, purchased an envelope and stamp at the post office, and mailed the torn pieces to Jess. It was something she had to do.

The train pulled into the Denver station in mid-afternoon. A hired carriage took Arlo, Meg, and their baggage to the Antlers Hotel. When Arlo requested just one room for them, Meg vigorously objected, insisting on separate rooms as she had all along. When people began to stare at them, Arlo shot her a venomous look and asked for adjoining rooms. Rather than raise a ruckus, Meg agreed to adjoining rooms, vowing to keep the connecting door locked at all times. The only reason she agreed to the arrangement was because she knew Arlo would wire Sheriff Bufford and expose Jess if she didn't. Meg couldn't allow that to happen. Somehow Arlo Skully's threat to Jess would have to be dealt with.

Arlo left her at the hotel while he went out

to drum up a poker game for that evening in his room. Before he left, he ordered Meg to act as hostess during the game, serving drinks and being pleasant to his customers. Meg's refusal threw Arlo into a rage.

"Keep on defying me and I'll follow through with my threat," Arlo shouted. "One telegram will put your lover behind bars. I gave in to you during the train ride and this afternoon but don't expect me to give in to your whims again. If you're as fond of that doctor as you say, you'll put on a fetching dress and present yourself in my room to-night."

"Very well. I'll do as you say, but don't expect me to bed any of the men you intend to fleece."

"We'll see," Arlo muttered, warily eyeing her six-shooters.

Meg ordered dinner sent up to her room that evening, savoring her privacy. Two days in Arlo's company had nearly undone her. If she weren't concerned about Jess's safety, she would have run out on Arlo long ago. After she ate, Meg dressed in her best dress, a crimson silk with a snug waist and modest neckline. Zach had bought it for her on her eighteenth birthday and she'd had little occasion to wear it.

Around nine o'clock Meg heard people moving about in Arlo's room. A short time later, Arlo knocked on the connecting door and invited her inside. Dragging in a calming breath, Meg slipped a small pistol into her pocket and opened the door. She wasn't about to enter the lion's den unarmed.

Meg counted five men besides Arlo in the room. All looked like prosperous business men. Arlo always liked to go first-class. A table had been brought up to accommodate the men, and a makeshift bar and buffet was set up on the dresser across the room. All the men turned to ogle her as she entered the room.

"Well, well, who do we have here?" a stout, well-dressed man in his mid forties asked, leering at her.

"Let me introduce my wife," Arlo said, grasping Meg's arm and turning her toward the men. "Gentlemen, meet my wife. Meg is here to be of service to you. Let her know your needs and she'll be happy to accommodate you."

Meg winced but said nothing.

"Meg, the gentleman who just spoke to you is Darby Williams," Arlo continued.

Meg greeted each man coolly as Arlo introduced them. Besides Darby Williams, she met Carl Jones, Felix Menton, Bill Finney, and Larry Dodge. Six in all, including Arlo. Though the men appeared to be upstanding citizens, Meg wouldn't be surprised to learn they all were philanderers and womanizers.

"Shall we begin?" Arlo said, motioning toward the poker table. "My wife will serve drinks and food."

As the evening progressed, Meg grew excessively tired of having men look down her cleavage as she served them. It was demeaning and embarrassing. When Carl Jones groped beneath her skirt as she passed him, she upended a glass of gin on his head. Then she smiled sweetly and apologized. Arlo shot her a warning look and told her not to let it happen again.

But it did happen again. A short time later, Darby Williams got up to stretch his legs. Meg was standing at the makeshift bar with her back to him and didn't see him approach. She was shocked speechless when Williams grasped her bottom in both his hands and squeezed.

"I'll reserve a private dining room for us tomorrow night, sweetheart. You'll join me, of course. After dinner you can appease my other appetite."

Meg's temper exploded as she aimed her elbow backward into his soft gut.

"Take your hands off me! I'm a married woman," she blasted.

Williams gave a grunt of pain. "You don't expect me to believe that bullshit, do you? You're a whore, lady. Skully doesn't know any other kind of woman." His hands returned to her bottom.

Meg had had more than enough. She

whirled, at the same time pulling the small revolver from her pocket. She pointed the gun low, shoving it against his privates. Williams let out a high-pitched squeal.

"Listen, mister, and listen good," Meg hissed. "Try that again and I'll shoot off your balls and mount them on the wall."

Williams turned a sickly shade of green and backed away.

"What's going on?" Arlo asked when he saw Williams stumble backward.

"Get that whore out of here!" Williams demanded in a tone that brooked no argument. "She's a menace to society."

Arlo leaped to his feet, shoving back his chair so fast it hit the floor with a resounding thump. "What did Meg do?"

"Threatened me with that little firearm of hers."

Arlo's gaze swung around to Meg. She smiled smugly at him and said, "I refuse to be groped by scum like this. I'm not a whore. I'm not even your wife. Find someone else to service the men you intend to fleece."

Arlo raised his hand to backhand her, but Meg deftly stepped out of harm's way.

"I will *not* let you strike me. Good night, gentlemen," she said, striding through the connecting door. Before she slammed and locked it behind her, she heard one of the men ask, "What's this about being fleeced? Are you cheating, Skully?"

Meg didn't hear Arlo's answer but she knew the men would be watching him like a hawk. He'd already amassed a small fortune this evening, and she hadn't the slightest doubt that he was cheating. She earnestly prayed he got what was coming to him.

Meg was sleeping soundly when Arlo rattled the connecting door hours later.

"Meg, open up, dammit!"

Meg struggled awake, reaching beneath her pillow for her gun as she slowly regained her wits. What time was it? Late, very late, she decided; not yet morning.

"I'm sleeping. Go away," she responded grumpily.

"I'm not going away. You'd better open the door before my pounding rouses every patron in this hotel."

Meg reached over and turned up the lamp. Then she checked the chambers in her gun and pulled on a wrapper. Causing a ruckus was the last thing she wanted. Gingerly she opened the door, allowing Arlo inside. He glanced at her gun and gave a snort of disgust.

"You've ruined everything," he charged. "What would it have cost you to be nice to my clients? You're no virgin, for godsake. One more lover shouldn't make a difference to a woman like you." His gaze returned to her gun. "Put away that weapon."

"I'm not playing whore for you or anyone

else," Meg retorted.

"You'll do as I say. I'm having some important men in tomorrow night and I expect you to be nice to them — distract them, if you will. They're all silver barons. I intend to win enough money to put me on easy street. When we check out tomorrow, I may even own a silver mine or two. This is your last chance, Meg. You know what I'll do if you don't comply."

"I'll make a deal with you, Arlo," Meg offered. "I'll be as nice as I can without compromising my dignity, if you agree to let me go my own way after tomorrow night. You know I'll never be a wife to you. If you try to force me to your bed, you won't win, and you'll never know when I might take a notion to shoot you in your sleep. Furthermore, you will *not* threaten Jess's freedom."

Arlo frowned. "Are you asking me to release you from your promise and forget what I know about Gentry?"

"That's exactly what I'm asking. If I help you win a fortune, it's the least you can do. We aren't married, no matter what you say. We both know you don't really want a wife. I'll bet you were surprised to learn I was still alive and living in Cheyenne. The only reason you looked me up was out of curiosity, and maybe to punish me for running off the way I did."

She paused and sucked in a deep breath.

"If the results of the game meet your expectations, I will have fulfilled my end of the bargain. If you have any honor at all, you'll fulfill yours."

Meg's hand tightened on the butt of her gun. She had no idea what she would do if Arlo turned obstinate; shooting him to keep him quiet about Jess was an option she didn't relish.

"You're right about not needing a wife," Arlo admitted. "But stop and think about the handsome rewards for both of us if we team up. You can distract the players while I fleece them."

"One more time — that's my final offer. Do I have your promise to let Jess alone if I help you this last time?"

"I can't do that. That piece of information about Gentry is all the hold I have on you."

Meg thumbed back the gun hammer. Her finger tightened on the trigger. The metallic click was as loud as a gunshot in the silence of the room. Arlo stumbled backward, his face as pale as death.

"Don't shoot! For godsake, have mercy."

Meg didn't intend to shoot Arlo, though the thought held a certain appeal.

"It would be so easy to pull the trigger," Meg said wistfully. "You don't know me anymore, Arlo. I've changed. I've brought men tougher than you down. I'm really not the kind of woman you want to mess with."

"I can see that now," Arlo said, his gaze riveted on the gun in Meg's hand. "I've certainly misjudged you. You're too dangerous to have around. Put the gun down. Let's discuss this like civilized people."

The gun remained pointed at Arlo's middle. "I'm through talking. I'll help you win that fortune you want, but the price is Jess's freedom."

Arlo made a nervous swipe of his tongue across his lips. "I agree."

Meg gave him a stern look. "If you don't keep your word, I'll hunt you down and kill you. I can't make it any plainer than that. I'm an excellent tracker. I'm a professional bounty hunter, remember?"

Arlo swallowed convulsively. "How can I forget? Do your part and I'll keep my promise. The game begins at nine o'clock tomorrow night. Tonight, actually," he said. "It's nearly dawn."

Meg closed and locked the door behind Arlo. Though he'd given his promise, she didn't trust him. All she could do was make sure he won heavily tonight, enough to satisfy his greed.

Evening came too early for Meg's peace of mind. But a promise was a promise. After tonight she'd be free to do as she pleased. Would she return to Cheyenne? Probably not. Without Arlo's interference, Jess held a secure place in Cheyenne society. She would only hinder his career. On the other hand, perhaps she and Jess could present a united front against the gossips if she returned. Lord knows she couldn't imagine living the rest of her life without him.

Would Jess welcome her back? Meg wondered. She'd left town with Arlo, without so much as a good-bye. Perhaps he wouldn't want anything more to do with her. She wouldn't really blame him.

Later that evening, when Arlo knocked on the connecting door, Meg still hadn't decided whether she would return to Cheyenne and Jess.

"The men are here, Meg. It's time for you to join us."

Meg plastered a smile on her face and flung open the door. Arlo grasped her arms and hissed into her ear, "Remember why you're here. And keep that damn pistol I know you're carrying in your pocket."

Meg shrugged out of his grasp and walked over to meet the five men gathered around the makeshift bar. The evening went better for her than the previous one. The men seemed intent upon the game instead of her. Nevertheless, she played the part expected of her, distracting the players when the stakes were high. She didn't enjoy it one darn bit, for she knew Arlo was cheating. If she didn't think the five poker players could afford it, she would have felt more guilt than she actually did.

Meg was serving a man named Simon Pool when Arlo laid down his winning hand. A full house, aces over tens. As he raked in his winnings, including the deed to a valuable silver mine, Simon Pool leaped to his feet.

"Bastard! You cheated!" Pool charged. "I saw you deal yourself that ace from the bottom."

"You can't prove that, Pool," Arlo argued. "You're just sore because I won one of your silver mines. Cool down. You know damn well you can afford it."

"That's not the issue. A man doesn't enjoy being fleeced."

"I didn't cheat," Arlo maintained. He shoved the cards at Pool. "Your deal."

"I've had enough," Pool barked. "If I were you, Skully, I'd watch my back. Cardsharps and cheaters aren't welcome in Denver. I thought you ran a clean game."

Meg watched with trepidation, her right hand hovering near her pocket so she could reach her pistol if it came to that. It didn't. Pool left in a huff, aiming a murderous look at Arlo before he charged out the door. At that precise moment Meg was glad she wasn't Arlo Skully. It was probably a good thing he was leaving town tomorrow.

The game broke up shortly after Pool stormed out. Only one other man besides Arlo, who had won heavily, came out ahead. The rest went home with empty pockets.

"That was a rewarding evening," Arlo said after the room had cleared of all but him and Meg. "I'm going out to look at my silver mine tomorrow. Do you want to come with me?"

"Not on your life. We're quits after tonight, Arlo. You got what you wanted. We had a deal, remember? I hope I never lay eyes on you again. Good night, Arlo, and good-bye."

His eyes narrowing, Arlo grasped her arm, obviously disliking her reply. "Maybe we aren't quits. You were damn good tonight. We're a team. You distracted the men to the point that my cheating wasn't apparent."

Meg shrugged off his hands. "Pool caught you red-handed. I fulfilled my part of the bargain. If I were you, I'd take Mr. Pool seriously. I sensed a definite threat."

"He's harmless," Arlo said. "All bark and no bite. He was sore because he lost one of his mines."

Meg shrugged. "Don't say I didn't warn you." She turned to leave.

"One more thing, Meg," Arlo said in a voice that made her halt in mid step.

She turned to face him. "What?"

"I lied."

Meg froze. "About what?"

"I'm not about to break up a winning team. You'll travel with me as my partner or . . ."

"Or what?"

"Or I'll put your lover behind bars."

"Damn you! You promised."

"Not really. Good night, Meg."

He shut the connecting door in her face. Meg grasped the handle and tried to pull it open, but he had already shot the bolt. She pounded on the door a good five minutes before giving up. Things were getting out of hand. She had no choice now but to deal with Arlo in her own way.

Meg was rudely awakened from a deep sleep. She assumed it was Arlo beating on the door and told him to go away. But the pounding continued. Suddenly she was aware that someone was calling her Mrs. Skully and she remembered that Arlo had signed the hotel register as Mr. and Mrs. Arlo Skully. She dragged herself from bed, pulled a wrapper over her nightgown, and opened the door.

Her eyes widened when she saw a man sporting a badge standing on the threshold. What had Arlo done now?

"I'm Inspector Faulkner. Are you Mrs. Skully?"

Meg hesitated. She wasn't Arlo's wife. Yet something told her to skirt the issue until she learned more.

"What is this about, Inspector?"

"I regret to inform you that your husband's body was found in the alley beside the telegraph office this morning."

"He's dead?"

"That's right, ma'am. I need you to come with me to identify the body and collect his belongings. He carried a large sum of money on him."

Shock shuddered through Meg. "You found him this morning?" She glanced at the window and saw sunshine streaming through gaps in the closed drapes. "What time is it?"

"Just past noon."

"Where did you say he was found?"

"In the alley beside the telegraph office. He must have been out and about early this morning. Walter Harper said your husband was waiting for the office to open when he arrived for work. But Harper swore he didn't see or hear a thing after he sent Skully's telegram."

The telegraph office, Meg thought with alarm. "Do you know to whom he sent the telegram?"

"Yes, ma'am. He sent it to Sheriff Bufford in Cheyenne. Seems that Mr. Skully had information about an outlaw, which he passed on to the sheriff."

"I'll join you as soon as I dress, Inspector," Meg said.

"I'll wait in the hall," Faulkner said. "Take your time."

Meg couldn't move after she closed the door. Arlo was dead. It didn't seem possible.

Someone had beat her to it. Someone who wanted him dead more than she did. Over the years, Arlo had doubtless made enemies. Like Mr. Pool. Dishonest cardsharps had few friends.

If only he had died before sending that telegram.

At length Meg forced herself to wash, dress, and roll up her hair into a semblance of order. She wasn't hungry, so missing breakfast was no big thing. Some thirty minutes later she opened the door and stepped into the hall to join the inspector.

A short time later, Faulkner ushered her into the funeral parlor. The stench of death hit Meg like a fist to the gut. All she could think of was getting out of fast.

"Where is he?" Meg asked.

"This way, Mrs. Skully," the undertaker said, showing her the way into a bare room that held a table with a body laid out upon it.

The body was covered with a sheet; all that was visible were bare feet protruding out one end. Faulkner grasped her elbow as the undertaker prepared to lift the sheet. "Are you all right, Mrs. Skully?"

"Yes. Just get on with it."

The sheet was lowered, and Meg stared into the lifeless face of Arlo Skully. She couldn't recall how many times she'd wished him dead over the years, but the reality was still stunning.

"How was he killed?"

"A knife through the heart. Neat and silent. The killer was obviously skilled. Have you seen enough?"

"Yes. That's Arlo Skully. Is there anything else you need to know?"

Faulkner guided her away from the body. "I have a few questions. Did your husband have enemies?"

"He was a professional gambler. Not a particularly honest one. Does that answer your question?"

"Can you name the people who attended the card games he held in his hotel room?"

"No," Meg lied. "I wanted no part of that life. We had separate rooms. If you must know, Inspector, I was going to leave Mr. Skully today. We both had agreed upon a separation. Anything else?"

"No. You're free to go. I doubt we'll ever find his killer."

The undertaker, bearing a bundle in his arms, came bustling over to them. "Here's Mr. Skully's belongings. Inspect them if you'd like. There's a great deal of money."

Meg dutifully untied the parcel of Arlo's clothing. Inside were his watch, various pieces of jewelry, and a purse containing all the money he'd won the last two nights. The deed to the silver mine was conspicuously missing.

"I'd like to pay for the burial now," Meg said. "I'm leaving Denver as soon as I can book passage. Maybe even today. There will be no formal funeral. Mr. Skully had no friends in town."

"I reckon that can be arranged," the undertaker said. "Thirty dollars should cover the pine box and burial fees."

Meg counted out the money into his hand and bundled the rest up inside Arlo's clothing. "Am I permitted to leave town, Inspector?"

"There's no reason for you to stay," Faulkner said. "Besides, it might be a good idea. Until your husband's killer is found, you could be in danger."

That notion, though it made sense, was not comforting. "Thank you. I agree wholeheartedly."

Meg hurried back to her hotel room and locked the door behind her. Then she entered Arlo's room through the connecting door and made a thorough search of his belongings. It was just as she'd thought: the deed to the silver mine was missing. The implication was startling. Mr. Pool was behind Arlo's murder, and she could be the next victim.

Meg set the bundle of Arlo's clothing on the bed with the money intact and left the room. She wanted nothing to do with Arlo's ill-gotten gains. She packed her carpetbag, placed her guns inside, and left the hotel through the back door. She felt no guilt at skipping out without paying, for she'd left a small fortune behind to cover the bill.

The moment Meg had heard that Arlo had sent a telegram to Sheriff Bufford, she knew she had to return to Cheyenne. It didn't matter if Jess no longer wanted her; she had to be there to lend him support. It was her fault Arlo had exposed Jess, and she wasn't going to sit idly by while he was tried and convicted for a crime he hadn't committed.

Meg learned that the train to Cheyenne was due in at six-thirty the following morning. Having nowhere else to go, she settled down on a bench in the depot to wait.

Chapter Fourteen

Cheyenne

Zach barged into Jess's office with an agenda. Jess knew it the moment he saw the mutinous expression on Zach's face. Fortunately, his office was empty. Most of the men in town had joined a posse that had been formed after a recent bank robbery, and those who were left had other things on their minds besides visiting the doctor. Even the women and children seemed to be caught up in the excitement.

Jess was glad for the breather. Since Meg had left, it seemed as if the heart had gone out of him. Even his practice seemed dull, as if something vital was missing from his life. Yet he couldn't bring himself to react to Meg's disappearance with anything but anger and self-pity.

Now here was Zach again for the third time in as many days, looking fully prepared to do battle on Meg's behalf. Jess knew that Zach was going to demand once again that he go to Denver after Meg, and he was half convinced to do it. But his damn pride kept getting in the way.

"I expected to find you all packed and ready to board the next train to Denver," Zach said as he charged into the reception room.

"What good will it do? Obviously Meg wanted to leave."

"Damn fool," Zach muttered. "No help for it. I'll have to go myself. That little gal means the world to me. I won't let Skully hurt her again."

"You're not going," Jess argued. "I'll go. I don't want your death on my conscience. Stay here with Mary and plan your wedding."

"Can you be ready to leave on the train tomorrow?"

"I'll be ready, but don't expect miracles. I won't force Meg to leave if she wants to stay with Skully."

"Meg loathes Skully, trust me. Thanks, Doc. You won't regret this. I hate feeling helpless. I'm no longer the man I once was. But bad heart or not, I would have gone after Meggie if you had refused."

Meg stepped off the train and pulled the collar of her traveling jacket up over her ears to ward off the brisk wind blowing in from the north. Summer was coming to an end and there was a definite chill in the air. She paused on the platform, clutching her carpetbag and pondering her next move. She supposed she should go directly to the jail-house to learn Jess's fate. Squaring her shoulders, she silently prepared herself to view Jess behind bars.

The streets seemed unusually crowded, Meg thought as she passed knots of people engaged in conversation. Something was afoot. Was it news of Jess's arrest?

Meg hurried down the sidewalk, her heels clicking a hollow tattoo against the wooden boards. When she reached her destination, she opened the door and stepped inside. Deputy Taylor was sitting in the sheriff's chair, resting his feet on the desk. His feet came down to the floor with a bang the moment he saw her.

"Miz Lincoln! I thought you left town."

"I came back. Where's the sheriff?"

"You haven't heard? Two masked men robbed the First Union Bank. The sheriff left with the posse after it happened and hasn't returned yet. He swore he wouldn't return without the men who shot and killed Bill Towers over at the telegraph office. The poor bast . . . er, man, caught a stray bullet as he stepped outside the Western Union office to investigate the ruckus. He died instantly."

"I didn't know," Meg said, stunned by the news. "I'm sorry about Bill Towers. Did he have a family?"

"No, he was a bachelor. What are you doing here? Doc Gentry and Zach Purdee

303

have been worried sick about you."

"Zach's back?" Meg said, her face alight with pleasure.

"Returned a few days ago. Him and Widow Dowling are planning a wedding."

That was indeed good news. "How . . . how is Dr. Gentry?"

"Haven't seen him since the robbery. He's kept to himself since you took off." He sent her a quizzical look. "Doc said you two were gonna get hitched. Congratulations."

"Yes, well . . ." She dropped the uncomfortable subject, for she had no idea where she and Jess stood now. "How long has the sheriff been gone?"

She wanted to ask about the telegram but didn't dare. Had it gone astray?

"Four days now. His mail's been piling up. Some new Wanted posters came in and a couple of telegrams. Didn't read them; thought they might be personal."

"New posters, you say?" Meg asked casually. "Mind if I have a look?"

"Sheriff Bufford never objected, so I reckon it's all right. Sit here," he said, vacating the sheriff's chair. "The posters are all together in that packet. Look all you want, though I don't suppose it will make either old Zach or Doc Gentry happy to have you traipsing off after another outlaw."

Meg dropped her bag beside the door and took the chair Taylor had vacated. She pulled the posters out of the packet and made a great show of studying each one, though what she was really interested in were the two telegrams lying beside the stack of posters. At least she'd learned there were no new posters featuring the Gentry brothers.

"Find anything interesting?" Taylor asked.

"I'm not sure," Meg hedged. "I need a little more time."

As she spoke, she deliberately knocked the posters off the desk, along with the telegrams. "Oh, how clumsy of me."

Taylor sprang forward. "Here, let me help you."

Before Taylor reached her, she plucked the two telegrams from amid the scattered posters and stuck them down the top of her half boot.

"Thank you," Meg said, carefully stacking the posters she and Taylor had picked up. "I believe I have seen enough. Nothing here interest me. I appreciate your help."

"No problem, Miz Lincoln. Any time."

Meg retrieved her bag from where she'd left it beside the door and emerged from the office into the dying sun of late afternoon. She paused on the sidewalk as the tenseness left her body, breathing deeply to calm her frazzled nerves.

What if she'd been caught purloining those telegrams? What if Deputy Taylor associated her with their disappearance when it came time to give them to the sheriff? Too late for recriminations; the deed was already done.

Meg's feet carried her automatically toward Jess's office. She had to see him, even though he might want nothing to do with her. She wanted to tell him his secret was safe. That she had removed the last incriminating piece of evidence. She felt sadness for Bill Towers; his death was tragic, but she couldn't help thinking that his demise had severed the last link to Jess's past.

The reception room was empty when Meg entered Jess's office.

"I'll be out in a moment," Jess called from the examining room. "I was about to close up for the day."

A few moments later, Jess walked into the reception room, spotted Meg, and stopped dead in his tracks. He had just finished putting away his instruments when he heard the bell above the door jangle. He thought Zach had returned to badger him and he really didn't want to see Zach again. Jess had already agreed to go to Denver to find out what the hell was going on with Meg; what more did the old man want? But it wasn't Zach, it was Meg, looking as beautiful as he remembered, and his anger exploded.

"Where the hell did you come from?"

"I don't blame you for being angry," Meg

said. "I should have explained why I left the way I did."

"You don't owe me a damn thing. You didn't want to marry me. I accept that."

Meg held her hand out as if in supplication. "It wasn't like that at all. Will you listen to me?"

"No. I have no patience to listen right now. Do you have any idea how I felt when I was told you had boarded the train with Skully? I didn't want to believe it. I made all kinds of excuses, but none of them could explain away the truth. Was my proposal of marriage so abhorrent that you had to run away? Or did you want nothing to do with me because I'm wanted by the law?"

He turned around and walked away, his heart heavy. He'd never been in love before; he'd had no idea it would hurt so much to have the woman he loved abandon him.

"Wait! Don't go. Let me explain."

"Sorry, Meg, I'm not in the mood."

Jess had one foot on the bottom stair when the door opened and Zach burst in.

"I was on my way home when Deputy Taylor hailed me and said Meggie . . ." He saw her then and his face lit up. "Meggie! It's true! You did come back."

He held out his arms and Meg rushed into them.

"Why did you leave, Meggie girl? You loathe Arlo Skully. Did you tell Jess what happened?"

"I tried, Zach, but he doesn't care to listen."

Zach pinned Jess with a censuring look. "What the hell is wrong with you, Doc? Why won't you let Meggie explain?"

Jess shrugged. "It's too late. She should have explained before she left."

"You were ready to go to Denver after her," Zach charged.

Meg's eyes widened. "You were?"

"If I didn't, Zach would have, and we all know Zach isn't up to another long trip so soon after his last one to Philadelphia. That won't be necessary now, will it?"

Jess couldn't bear to look at Meg. He remembered too well their last night together. How she had clung to him, how she had loved him. Meg had driven him to the brink of madness with her hands and mouth, taking him further, higher, than he'd ever dreamed possible.

"Dammit, Jess, you're not being reasonable!" Zach chided. "Give Meggie a chance."

"Don't waste your breath, Zach," Meg said, lifting her skirt and removing from her boot the two telegrams she'd stolen from the sheriff's desk. Quickly she scanned both telegrams and handed one to Jess.

"What's this?" Jess growled.

"Just read it."

Reluctantly Jess opened the telegram and read the words Skully had sent to Sheriff

Bufford. Then he handed it to Zach.

Jess's intense gaze pierced her. "Where did you get this? It's addressed to the sheriff."

Meg's chin rose slightly. "I stole it."

Jess's jaw tautened. "From where?"

"The sheriff's desk. It arrived after he'd left with the posse."

"Who sent it?"

"Arlo."

"I told you so!" Zach crowed.

"Keep out of this, Zach," Jess warned. "I can't think straight right now. Leave, both of you. Come back in a few days. Maybe I'll be more inclined to hear Meg's explanation then."

"But the telegram —"

"I know what it says, Zach, but I need time to gather my thoughts and cool off."

"I'm not going anywhere, Jess Gentry," Meg blasted, hands on hips, eyes blistering him. "You can hate me if it will make you feel better, but you're going to listen to what I have to say. If my words don't change any-thing, I won't bother you again."

Jess couldn't listen, not now. Even as angry as he was with Meg, all he could think about was carrying her up to his bed and making love to her. In a day or two, after his temper had cooled and his need abated, he could be a more objective listener.

"You two can let yourselves out," Jess said as he started up the stairs. "I think there's a lot Zach wants to tell you, Meg."

Her shoulders sagging, Meg watched Jess disappear up the staircase.

"You ain't gonna let him get away with that, are you?" Zach asked.

"He doesn't want to talk to me, Zach. I can't force myself on him."

"The Meggie I know could and would. She ain't afraid of anything."

"Jess doesn't understand, Zach. I hurt him."

He led her to a chair. "You want to tell me about it?"

"Arlo knew about Jess," Meg began. "He caught me stealing Jess's Wanted poster from the sheriff's office and remembered where he'd seen Jess before. He'd just come from Kansas, where Jess's poster had been widely circulated."

"The bastard threatened you, didn't he?"

"Worse. He threatened Jess. I couldn't let Jess go to jail, so I agreed to accompany Arlo to Denver."

Zach paled. "He didn't . . . you didn't . . . the bastard!"

"No," Meg was quick to assure him. "We didn't . . . do anything. I insisted upon separate rooms. He held card games in his room, and I was there to distract his customers while he cheated. He threatened to expose Jess if I didn't comply."

"You told him to go to hell, and he sent

that telegram," Zach guessed.

"Something like that," Meg hedged. She wasn't about to go into detail.

"Where is Skully now? Can we expect him to show up in Cheyenne?"

"He's dead. He cheated a man out of a silver mine, and the owner took exception. Arlo was found dead the next morning in an alley. Inspector Faulkner said his killer might never be found and suggested I leave town, that my own life might be in danger since I was with Arlo at that game and might be considered an accomplice."

"Damn," Zach said, stunned to learn of Arlo's death. "The bastard got what was coming to him. What are you gonna do now? Maybe you should come home with me and get some rest. You look done in. I got a lot to tell you, honey."

Meg glanced toward the stairs. "I'm not leaving, Zach. Not until Jess agrees to listen to me. I want you to go home without me. But first, tell me quickly about your trip to Philadelphia."

Zach grinned. "I'm rich, honey. My wife's folks left her a fortune and I'm her only heir. I've asked Mary to marry me, if that's all right with you."

"Why wouldn't it be all right? I'm happy for you and Mary. You've been seeing her a long time. It's about time you two got married."

"My wife's death made it possible," Zach explained. "I ain't the kind to let my wife support me, and now I won't have to. My health ain't the best, but Mary is willing to take me as I am. I can spend the years I have left with a woman I care about. There's plenty of money for you, too, Meggie. You'll never have to take up bounty hunting for a living again."

She gave him a quick hug. "We'll see. Go on home now. I'm going upstairs to make Jess listen to me."

Zach sent her an encouraging look. "That's my girl."

"Go on, Zach, I'll be just fine."

"I wouldn't leave you if I thought Jess was a violent man. But I taught you to take care of yourself, so I reckon I'll just mosey on home."

Meg locked the door after Zach, dragged in a calming breath, and started up the stairs.

Jess paced the length of the room and back, his temper still high. He didn't know whether he was angrier at himself for letting Meg get to him or at Meg for making his life a living hell. It had taken all his considerable willpower not to turn around on the stairs and beg her not to leave.

If that telegram was meant to disarm him, it had served the purpose. She said she'd stolen it from the sheriff's desk. Had she really? Or was she lying? And where was Skully now?

Jess hated being an outlaw on the run, wondering who would recognize him next. He wasn't cut out for that kind of life. He wanted to settle down in one place and be the best doctor he could be.

He wanted a home, a family, a special woman to love, one who would love him in return. He had thought he'd found that woman in Meg. He'd disregarded logic and proposed when he had no business asking a woman to accept the kind of life he now led.

Suddenly Jess knew exactly what he had to do, what he should have done long ago. And if things worked out the way he hoped, he'd return to Cheyenne and listen to Meg's explanation, if she was still willing to give one. He dragged his bag from beneath his bed and began tossing clothing into it.

Immersed in misery, Jess failed to hear the door open.

"Jess?"

Jess whirled, stunned to see Meg standing in the doorway. "What the hell are you doing here? Didn't I make myself clear? I don't want to see you now. Go home with Zach."

She stepped into the room, her expression as fiercely determined as his. "Zach left without me. I'm not going anywhere, Jess, not until you hear what I have to say."

He dragged his hand through his rumpled

hair. "Leave me alone, Meg."

Meg's gaze settled on the bag he'd been packing. "Where are you going?"

He snapped the bag shut. "I can't live this way any longer."

"But you have nothing to worry about now. Arlo is dead. He's the only one who knew about the poster."

Jess inhaled sharply. "Did you kill him?"

She shook her head. "Someone got to him first. He was found dead in an alley."

Jess turned away. "I'm sorry your husband is dead."

"Arlo wasn't my husband anymore, and I'm not sorry he's dead. I despised him. I was planning on doing him in myself. Someone saved me the trouble."

"Tell that to someone who will believe you. You went off with your ex-husband without so much as a good-bye to me. What the hell was I supposed to think? After the night we spent together, I thought . . . I'm a damn gullible fool. I thought you and I were . . ."

"No, you were right. That night meant a great deal to me. I knew I was leaving the next day and would never see you again. You have to understand. I had to go, Jess."

"Of course you did," Jess snarled. "And now that Arlo is dead, you've decided I'm the one you want after all. Go home, Meg, I won't listen to anything you have to say. Perhaps when I return . . . *if* I return," he

314

stressed, "I'll be in the mood to listen."

Jess turned away, more disgusted with his own behavior than with Meg's. He should at least have the courtesy to listen to her. But pride was all he had left. He couldn't believe his ears when he heard the metallic click of a gun hammer. Whirling, he looked down the barrel of the Meg's revolver.

"What the hell . . . !"

"Sit down, Jess Gentry," Meg said in a voice he'd never heard before. "You're going to listen to me."

Stunned, he plopped down on the bed, but it only took a moment for him to regain his wits. "You're not going to shoot me, Meg."

"I might."

Jess's mirthless grin should have warned her. Before she had time to react, Jess wrested the gun from her hand, tossed her onto the bed, and flung himself on top of her. She arched and twisted and succeeded only in arousing more than Jess's anger.

"Dammit. Hold still," he gritted against her mouth.

"You're not going to let me explain, are you?" Meg said, glowering.

He ground his hips against her. Meg gasped, wondering how he could maintain an erection when his anger was still potent enough to sear her.

"I might listen . . . afterward."

"After . . . No, I'm not going to let you

use me. Let me go, Jess Gentry."

"You used me. Do you have any idea what your leaving with Skully did to me?"

"I had to! He was going to expose you to the sheriff."

"You could have told me and let me decide what should be done instead of traipsing off with the same man who almost caused your death."

"I heard you and Polly talking about me before I left," Meg confided. "The conversation led me to believe that the townspeople would never accept me if we married. I decided the best thing I could do for you was to leave."

"You should have let me decide that. What it all boils down to is you didn't trust me enough to tell me about Skully and your fears about us. You went haring off to God knows where with a man you professed to despise."

"I did despise him. Enough to consider killing him to keep him from exposing you."

He stared at her mouth, his eyes dark and hungry. Meg likened him to a predator stalking his prey.

Her heart contracted. "What are you going to do?"

"Since you've come to my bedroom uninvited, there is only one thing I *can* do."

His mouth bore down on hers. The heat flowing from his body to hers was incredibly arousing. But she didn't want to be aroused, not when he was still angry with her. Their loving had always been special, never born of rage. Despite her reservations, his kiss brought forth all the intense feelings Jess had always aroused in her.

Unerringly his hand slid beneath her skirts, skimming her knee, his long, knowing fingers probing between her thighs. Meg bit back a scream as he reached deep, stroking into her heated center.

"You're already hot and wet for me," he whispered hoarsely. "Do you want me, Meg?"

Fighting her own wayward body, Meg swallowed a moan and summoned the shattered remnants of her willpower. "No. Not like this. Not when you're angry with me."

He merely smiled as he teased and tantalized and caressed, then evocatively probed deeper. She couldn't find enough breath to protest as his other hand lifted her skirts high, exposing her to his heated gaze.

His hand splayed possessively over her naked stomach then shifted, fingers searching boldly through her curls. Unerringly he found the sensitive spot and rotated it gently with the pad of his thumb. Lights burst behind her eyes and she cried out. Her response seemed to satisfy him as slowly, deliberately, he lifted himself slightly and unbuttoned his fly. Then he settled between her legs.

"Don't!" Meg said, stiffening.

"Yes," Jess replied. "You want this; you know you do."

"That's beside the point," Meg managed to gasp out.

He smiled grimly and pressed the blunt head of his sex against her weeping center. Meg felt the hot, hard length of him nudge into her softness. She held her breath as he sank into her, filling her, driving himself to the hilt. Then deliberately he withdrew. Shock shuddered through her when he turned her over and propped her to her knees.

"What . . ."

Before she could protest the indignity, Jess raised her hips and thrust into her, pressing so deeply her knees would have collapsed if he hadn't had a firm grip on her hips. Again and again he filled her, his restraint shattered as he pounded into her. With one hand splayed over her belly, bracing her, and the other on her hip, holding her steady, he was driving her to the brink of madness.

Being with Jess again brought Meg nothing but joy, though she knew she shouldn't give in so easily. He thrilled her, filled her, made her aware of all the reasons she loved this impossible man.

Tucking her bottom more firmly against his jutting hips, he moved more forcefully within her, thrusting more deeply, more powerfully. Meg grasped the bedclothes in her fists and fought for coherence as Jess drove her higher and higher. The tension grew, swelled; it was all Meg could do to cling to her sanity.

Climax hovered just out of her grasp. She reached for it, tried to draw it nearer. She felt herself tighten around him, heard him groan his approval. Suddenly she was there, grasping the shimmering pleasure as it burst around her, relentless, passionate, rolling through her in iridescent waves as he sank deeper, stretched her . . .

Completed her.

Jess felt her insides quiver. Felt her contract around him and drove deeper. He was in no hurry. He wanted to savor her slippery, scalding softness, look his fill at the glowing mounds of her bottom. Slick wetness gleamed along the length of his sex. Her wetness. She fitted him as if she were made for him. He felt her tensing and squirming against him and recognized the awkwardness of her position. He held her steady and thrust his rigid length into her again and again, until he exploded and collapsed against her back.

His breath was gone and his heart was pounding as he slowly withdrew and flopped down on the bed beside her. He smiled when he saw Meg lying on her stomach, her legs sprawled in abandon. She couldn't even rouse herself enough to pull down her skirts, affording him a tempting view of her backside and long, shapely legs.

Meg turned her head to stare at him. "Why did you do that?"

"Because I couldn't wait. Did I hurt you?"

"No, not really."

"As soon as I rest, we'll undress and do it properly."

"That's not what I meant and you know it."

Her eyes were glowing with fury, her face flushed. She was lovely. Somehow, while he was pouring his passion into her, his anger had dissipated. Making love to Meg had done that to him. He'd already heard most of the story behind her leaving and understood what had motivated her, even though he deplored the abrupt way in which she had left. He wouldn't have been half as angry or upset if she had trusted him. That was what hurt the most.

"Did you think me incapable of handling Skully?" Jess challenged. "I may be a doctor, but I know how to defend myself. I grew up with two rowdy brothers and lived through a war."

Meg flopped over on her back, her pleading gaze fusing with his judgmental one.

"I couldn't bear the thought of you languishing behind bars. Or face the knowledge that I wasn't good enough for you. My reputation leaves much to be desired. I figured you'd be better off without me."

Jess's face hardened. "Did the bastard touch you?"

"No. I would have killed him if he'd tried. He realized I wasn't the same timid sixteen-year-old he had once abused. Arlo promised he wouldn't expose you if I helped him win enough money to set him up for life."

Jess's eyes narrowed. "How exactly were you to do that?"

"I made it clear from the start that I wouldn't play whore for him. I was to distract the men so Arlo could cheat during the game. He won heavily but he didn't keep his promise. He wanted us to continue the scam. He said we made a good team. That's when I contemplated killing him."

"Someone beat you to it."

"Yes. But it was too late. Arlo had already wired Sheriff Bufford."

Jess frowned. "Why wasn't I arrested?"

"The sheriff wasn't here to receive the telegram. He'd already gone after the bank robbers, and Deputy Taylor didn't think it right to open the sheriff's mail. I" — she bit her lip — "I stole the telegram."

Jess groaned. "Is there no end to your deviousness?"

Her determined gaze bored into him. "Not when your life is in jeopardy."

Jess sighed. "I suppose you think this is over? That no one will ever know I'm a fugitive?"

"It is over," Meg insisted. "The telegrapher who received Arlo's message was killed during the bank robbery. I would never have wished his death, but it does solve all your problems."

"It solves nothing, Meg. I've already made up my mind to return to Dodge City. My life will never be my own until I prove that the Gentry brothers are innocent of any crime. Perhaps Mr. Wingate will recant and tell the truth if I confront him."

"And perhaps he won't. You could end up behind bars."

"That's the chance I have to take. I'll go by stage; it's quicker than waiting for the train."

"I'm going with you."

"Like hell! You're going to stay here and attend Zach's wedding."

"Like hell!" Meg mimicked. "You might not feel the same about me as you once did, but that changes nothing. Everything I've done was for you. I went with a man I loathed to keep you out of jail. I even contemplated killing in cold blood for you. Doesn't that tell you anything?"

Jess's eyes shuttered. "It tells me you're too damn reckless for your own good, and crazy to boot." His voice lowered. "It also tells me you love me. It might be easier for both of us if you didn't."

Chapter Fifteen

Meg stared at Jess as if he'd just sprouted horns. He understood that she loved him but wished she didn't? What kind of statement was that?

"If you're trying to discourage me from going with you to Dodge City, you're not succeeding. You can't stop me, Jess. I have as much right to be on that stage as you do."

Jess pulled her on top of him and brought their lips together, effectively stopping her words. Meg struggled a moment, then kissed him back. Kissed him until her heart began to thump and blood pounded through her veins. Then, before she lost whatever good sense God gave her, she broke off the kiss.

"This isn't going to work," she said, panting.

Jess gave an exaggerated sigh, his expression pained. "I know. We need to take off our clothes this time."

"Dammit, Jess, this is no time for levity! If you carry through with your ill-advised scheme to go to Dodge City, it could mean the end of your freedom."

"It could be the beginning of my freedom," Jess insisted, turning serious. "You're not going to talk me out of this, Meg. I owe it to my brothers to see those charges dropped. If Mr. Wingate won't listen to me, I'll" — he paused, his expression bleak with determination — "marry his daughter."

Meg sucked in a startled breath. "You'd marry a woman you don't love?"

"I would if it gained my brothers' freedom. I *did* dally with Delia Wingate. Her child could be mine, though in all probability it's not. But I'm hoping it won't go that far. I'm counting on Wingate to tell the truth about the robbery."

Meg admired Jess's determination to sacrifice himself for his brothers, but deplored his reasoning. The man was utterly selfless when it came to his family. But what about her? He could deny it all he wanted, but she knew he loved her, just as she loved him. Oh, yes, she was going to Dodge. And there was no way she was going to let Jess marry another woman.

While Meg had been pondering Jess's astounding words, Jess managed to loosen the fastenings on Meg's dress and chemise. She wore no stays; she didn't believe in them and was willowy enough not to need them. It made it easier for Jess to strip her dress and chemise down over her arms and put his mouth to her breast. Meg writhed atop him as he suckled her nipples, each in turn, arousing her slowly with nipping little bites, then tenderly laving them with the rough pad of his tongue.

Heat uncoiled low in her stomach, sending spirals of sensation to the place between her legs that ached for him. She shifted restlessly, her hands gripping his shoulders.

"Jess, wait. We have to talk."

Jess lifted his head from her breasts and met her gaze. His eyes were heavy-lidded and glazed with passion. "No, Meg, I'm not going to let you talk me out of this. My mind is made up. I'm going to Dodge, and if worst comes to worst I'll marry Delia Wingate."

"What about us?"

"Things could have worked between us at one time," he said wistfully. His shrug was deliberately nonchalant. "Then again, maybe I was kidding myself. I had no business falling in love when my future was in doubt."

Meg couldn't believe her ears. "You loved me once, Jess. Do you still love me?"

He pondered his answer so long, Meg felt a terrible squeezing sensation in her heart.

"It no longer matters," Jess said dryly. "I have no right to love. I ask but one thing of you, Meg. Let me try to resolve this my own way. Then, when I return — if I return — I'll answer your question."

Meg gave him a brilliant smile, one filled

with all the love she felt for him. "You've already answered my question. Help me remove my dress so we can make love properly this time."

He kissed her mouth and returned her grin. "What do you think I've been trying to do?"

They undressed each other slowly, their hands and mouths exploring, arousing one another until the scalding passion leaping between them demanded release. Lifting her, he placed her astride him again.

Holding her eyes prisoner with his, he inserted his hand between their bodies and stroked down into her soft curls. He found the taut little button at the entrance of her sex and massaged it with his thumb. Fire spread through Meg, and with a cry of surrender, she thrust her hips down upon his engorged staff.

Meg lost all sense of time and place as Jess filled the emptiness inside her. Higher and higher she climbed, until she reached the top and tumbled down into a well of shimmering ecstasy. Jess followed close behind, grasping her hips to hold her in place as he stroked himself to a frenzied climax.

When her breathing slowed enough to allow her to move, Meg lifted herself from Jess and snuggled against his side.

"What time does the stage leave tomorrow?" she asked sleepily.

He slanted her a considering look. "Ten o'clock. Are you hungry?" he asked casually.

"A little, but I can wait until morning."

"I can't," Jess said, rising. "Lie there and rest. I'll rustle up something from the kitchen and bring it up."

"Ummm," Meg moaned, her eyes already closing.

Jess pulled on his trousers and went downstairs. Meg didn't fool him one damn bit. She thought he needed her with him, but he didn't want her involved. She was too damn hotheaded, like a loaded cannon waiting to go off. No telling what mischief she'd stir up in Dodge City. She'd placed herself in danger too many times on his account, and he feared her luck might run out the next time.

Jess went directly to his examining room and removed a bottle of laudanum from his medicine cabinet. Then he went into the kitchen to prepare something for them to eat. First he made coffee, then he sliced roast beef one of his patients had sent him and put it on a tray with slices of bread he'd purchased that morning. By the time the coffee had finished perking, the tray was assembled but for the addition of two pieces of apple pie, another gift from a patient.

Jess poured coffee into two cups and placed them on the tray with the food. Before he left the kitchen, he poured a generous dose of laudanum into the coffee meant for Meg. By the time she awakened tomorrow, the stage would be well on its way. He hated having to drug her, but it was the only way to prevent a free spirit like his Meg from following him. Should he succeed in clearing his name without having to marry Delia Wingate, he'd come back to Meg, if she'd still have him.

Meg was sleeping when Jess returned. He had to waken her and literally hand-feed her, admonishing her to chew and swallow when her eyes began to close. He got all the coffee down her, however, and after a few mouthfuls of beef and bread, he let her sleep. Then he lay down beside her and pulled her into his arms.

Jess tried to sleep, but guilt rode him. Had he done the right thing? Should he have let Meg accompany him to Dodge? He quickly discounted that notion, for there was nothing Meg could do to help him in Dodge. This was something he had to do on his own.

Jess finally slept. Meg was still sleeping peacefully when he arose at eight the next morning. He expected her to sleep at least another six hours. He went downstairs and placed a Closed sign on the door. Then he went into the kitchen and heated the leftover coffee from the night before. He drank two cups of bitter brew, ate two slices of bread, then returned to his bedroom to finish packing.

Meg hadn't stirred. She lay on her side, her hand curled beneath her cheek and her mouth slightly open. Jess finished packing and carried his bag downstairs. Then he went into his office to restock his medical bag, placing it beside the door with his carpetbag. He returned to the bedroom and pulled a chair beside the bed, staring at Meg as if he couldn't get his fill of looking at her.

Her hair was splayed over the pillow like dark silk. He reached out and carefully pushed an ebony strand away from her forehead. Unable to resist touching her, he ran the back of a callused finger down her smooth cheek. He removed his finger quickly when she sighed and flopped over on her back. The sheet covering her shifted, baring her breasts. Jess inhaled sharply and leaned forward, memorizing every sumptuous detail of her face and form.

Her throat was slim and graceful, her shoulders and arms gently curved. Her breasts were perfect in every way — creamy mounds topped by mouthwatering cherries. They were not overly large, but sufficient to fill his hands and mouth. He knew from experience that her legs were sleekly muscled, her body firm and athletic, but soft and womanly where it counted.

He also knew she was going to be madder than a wet hen when she awoke and learned he had left without her. And an irate Meg was something to be avoided at all costs. He smiled to himself, recalling the way her green eyes kindled with fire when she was angry, and how it never failed to stir him.

Finally Jess could linger no longer. He kissed Meg's lips one last time and walked away without looking back. He feared if he looked at Meg a moment longer, he wouldn't be able to leave her. Then he'd be right back where he started, wondering when someone would turn up and identify him as a fugitive.

He guessed that Meg was still slumbering when the stage pulled away from the depot. Jess could only look forward now, and pray that he wouldn't end up behind bars. Returning to Dodge was risky, but he couldn't go on living outside the law.

In the far reaches of her brain, Meg dimly heard an insistent pounding. She buried her head beneath the pillow, but the annoying noise grew louder. She groaned and opened her eyes. She looked around her and blinked, disoriented. It took several minutes of concentration to recall where she was. Almost at the same time, she realized that someone was pounding on the front door.

She rose from the bed, swayed dizzily, and wondered why she was so unsteady on her feet. She was fuzzy-brained and lethargic, not like herself at all. Usually she bounded out of bed raring to go. She didn't stop to wonder what was wrong as she quickly dressed and made her way downstairs, hanging on to the railing to steady herself. The knocking persisted until she unlocked the door and flung it open.

"Zach! What is it? Is something wrong?"

"I was just gonna ask you that," Zach said, searching her face. "Are you all right, honey? Jess didn't hurt you, did he?"

Jess! Where was he? Suddenly comprehension dawned.

"That bastard! What time is it, Zach?"

"After one, Meggie. I was worried when you didn't come home this morning, so I decided to ride into town to find out what happened."

"One!" Meg spat. "Was the stage still in town when you came through?"

"Stage? Why, no. It left hours ago."

"Damn, damn, damn. He left me. I can't believe I overslept."

"You're not making sense, Meggie. Who left you? Where is Jess?"

"There's no time to lose, Zach. I've got to change and meet the stage at the next stop." She would have dashed off if Zach hadn't grasped her arm.

"Hold on, honey. You ain't going noplace until you tell me what's going on."

"Jess boarded the stage for Dodge City this morning without me. I never sleep this long."

A sudden disturbing thought came to her.

"He drugged me! Damn him!"

"Why would Jess go to Dodge City? That's where all his trouble began. Why would he drug you?"

"Jess can't bear living the life of a fugitive. He's going to Dodge City with the intention of clearing his name."

Zach rubbed his temples. "That's crazy. How does he propose to do that?"

"He's going to confront the banker who started this whole mess and plead with him to tell the truth."

"That ain't gonna happen. Pride is a powerful emotion, honey. That banker ain't gonna admit to wrongdoing now. Jess is sure as hell gonna end up in jail."

"That's what I told him. I planned to be on that stage this morning, but he found a way to stop me. He drugged my coffee last night." She paused, gnawing on her bottom lip. "Jess said he'd marry the banker's daughter if he had to. Do you know what that means? I can't let him do it, Zach, I just can't."

"You love that boy, don't you, honey?"

"I do, even though he makes it difficult."

"He loves you, too."

She made a disgusted sound deep in her throat. "He has a damn poor way of showing it. He spurned my help. He doesn't want me."

One of Zach's shaggy eyebrows shot upward. "Where did you spend the night, Meggie? My guess is in Jess's bed. And I'd be willing to wager my fortune he'd lost his anger before he left this morning."

"Keep your fortune, Zach. I won't wager anything where Jess is concerned. He runs hot and cold. I never know where I stand with him. If he loved me, he would have let me go with him."

"What if he has to marry the banker's daughter? Jess's family means a great deal to him. I suspect the reason he doesn't want you along is because he doesn't want to see you hurt."

"Too bad," Meg gritted. "Saddle my horse, will you? I'm going to change and go after that stage. If I leave right away, I might be able to catch up with it at the next stop."

Meg didn't give Zach a chance to argue. She bolted up the stairs to don her trousers, vest, and jacket. Before she left, she piled her hair beneath her battered hat and grabbed bread and cheese from the pantry. Then she picked up the bag she'd left beside the door the day before and headed out.

"Be careful!" Zach called after her as she mounted her mare and rode hell for leather out of town.

Jess paced impatiently beside the disabled coach. Twenty miles out of Cheyenne the driver had hit a hole in the road and cracked a wheel. Fortunately, they carried a spare wheel, and the driver and the man who rode shotgun had almost finished with the repairs. They would soon be on their way again.

The other passengers were sitting in the grass beside the road, chatting among themselves. They included a matron returning home after a visit with her son, a businessman from Garden City, a cowboy going to his sister's wedding in Dodge, and an elderly woman joining her husband, an army major, at Fort Leavenworth.

"Climb aboard," the driver announced to the waiting passengers as he wiped his greasy hands on his trousers. "Don't worry, folks, we'll make up the lost time by evening."

Jess sincerely hoped so. Now that he had made up his mind, he was anxious to get this ugly business over with.

The passengers began piling inside the stage. Jess entered last and fit himself beside the cowboy, next to a window. Had they taken on one more passenger, the stage would have been filled to capacity.

When the stage didn't start forward immediately, Jess stuck his head out the window and asked what was wrong.

"Rider coming," the driver called back. "He's signaling for us to wait up. Don't know what he wants, but maybe it's important."

More delays, Jess thought irritably. What else could go wrong? In a few minutes he found out, and he didn't like it one damn bit.

Jess recognized Meg the moment she drew close. His eyes widened and a curse flew past his lips. Both the matron and the elderly lady glared at him, and he quickly apologized. Then he opened the door and stepped to the ground to confront his rebellious Meg. Did she never do anything she was supposed to?

Jess waited until Meg finished speaking with the driver and he had walked off before he lit into her.

"What the hell are you doing here?" Jess blasted.

She shot him a fulminating look. "I just bought passage to Dodge City."

His gaze drifted down her trouser-clad body. "You sure know how to draw attention to yourself."

Her eyes glared defiance. "Trousers are comfortable," she hissed. "Besides, you're the only one who knows I'm not a man."

The driver returned. "You're lucky, mister, there's room for one more passenger. I'll secure your bag with the other luggage and tie your horse to the back of the coach." He reached for her bag.

Meg slanted Jess a look that said, *I told you so.*

"Much obliged," she said gruffly, pulling the brim of her hat lower over her forehead.

"Don't you ever do anything you're told?"

Jess raged, brimming with anger. "I don't want you with me; how much plainer can I make it?"

"This isn't your decision, Jess Gentry, it's mine," Meg threw over her shoulder as she entered the stage and took the empty seat opposite Jess.

Jess followed her inside and sat down, their knees almost touching. He sent her a thunderous look, which she ignored. Then she leaned her head against the back of the seat and promptly fell asleep.

Jess fumed in impotent rage. He'd been unpleasantly surprised to see her, and he didn't like those kinds of surprises. He'd given her enough laudanum to keep most women her size sleeping well into the afternoon. He should have realized her determination was exceptionally strong. But he'd be willing to bet it had been an ordeal for her to remain in the saddle with sleep tugging at her.

He swallowed a smile, imagining her surprise when she'd awakened and found him missing. Her anger must have been stunning. The smile died abruptly as he considered how to convince her to return to Cheyenne. He didn't want her to see him behind bars. Nor did he wish her to be present if he was obliged to marry Delia Wingate. He loved Meg too much to see her hurt.

The stage hurtled over the road at breakneck speed, bouncing the passengers around like wooden pegs. Once, Meg was literally thrown into his lap. His arms tightened around her for a blissful moment before he set her back in place across from him.

They stopped at a way station for the night. The passengers piled out and stretched, then headed for the house to eat the meal the station master's wife had prepared for them. After they had eaten, the women spent the night in one room and the men in another. Meg followed the men.

Much to Jess's relief, the men hit their bunks without bothering to undress. Jess directed Meg to a bunk in the far corner of the room and took the one next to her.

The other men were already snoring when Jess hissed, "You're going back to Cheyenne tomorrow."

"I'm going to Dodge," Meg returned. "You can't stop me."

Jess had no answer to that. It galled him to think he had no control over Meg. He was still fretting and fuming over Meg's stubbornness when sleep claimed him.

The passengers boarded the stage early the following morning after a hurried breakfast. The stage lurched forward, and Jess knew intuitively that nothing he could say would convince Meg to turn back. She didn't seem to realize that her presence in Dodge wouldn't help him, that it might even make things more difficult for him.

Most of the passengers were dozing when the sound of gunshots jerked them awake. No one besides Jess and Meg seemed to realize what was happening. Jess immediately checked his guns, as did Meg and the cowboy, and moments later the stage ground to a halt. Jess searched for a target but was thwarted when someone stuck a gun through the window and ordered the passengers to toss their guns out the window or be blown to kingdom come.

"Jess," Meg whispered, "we can't give up our guns to those outlaws."

"We have to," Jess said grimly. "If we don't do as they say, there are likely to be casualties — deaths even. Innocent lives are involved. I don't want one of the victims to be you. Most likely they'll just collect our valuables and leave."

Briefly Jess considered shooting and taking his chances, but the thought of Meg being hurt in the melee quickly dissuaded him. His guns joined those being tossed out the window by the frightened passengers. Meg's were the last to go. Then the door was jerked open and the passengers were ordered out.

Jess glanced at the outlaw, and recognition slammed through him. It was Jay Calder, the man who had shot Meg. Meg must have recognized him at the same time, for Jess heard her gasp.

"This is a holdup," Calder growled. "Line up beside the coach while my partner collects your valuables. You, too," he ordered, motioning for the driver and the guard to climb down from the driver's box.

Jess caught a glimpse of the second outlaw, and his heart sank. Jay's brother Lucky was the man holding a gun on the two men in the driver's box. Jess's first thought was that the guard had fallen asleep on the job, allowing the Calders to overtake them without warning.

"Move it," Lucky barked when the men didn't move fast enough. Jess thought it regrettable that Lucky had survived his wound.

Then the guard made a tragic error. He reached for a shotgun hidden beneath the seat. He wasn't fast enough. Lucky fired, and the guard fell back, mortally wounded. The driver gaped at his dead partner and quickly clambered over the guard's body, joining the passengers standing beside the coach.

"Nice work, Lucky," Jay drawled. "Now relieve these good people of their valuables."

"Now wait a damn minute," the businessman blustered. "I'm not going to stand for this."

Without warning, Jay clubbed the businessman on the head with the butt of his pistol. "Anyone else want to object?" he growled.

The elderly woman promptly fainted.

Jess stepped in front of Meg to protect her in case the bandits recognized her as the bounty hunter who had shot Lucky. The passengers began emptying their pockets. Lucky raked in the loot, grabbing whatever jewelry they wore, while Jay kept his gun trained on them. Jess had little of value except his father's pocket watch, and he refused to part with it. While both bandits were concentrating on the businessman's full pockets, Jess surreptitiously slipped the watch from his pocket and concealed it in the waistband of his trousers.

Something must have caught Jay's eye, for he swung his gun around to Jess. "What did you just do?"

Jess lowered his head, hoping Jay wouldn't recognize him. It had been dark the night of their encounter, and there was a fair chance neither of the Calders had gotten a good look at him. His hopes were shot to hell when Jay's eyes narrowed on his face.

"Say, I know you," Jay said. "You're the pilgrim we met up with outside Cheyenne a while back, ain't ya? I see you've managed to escape the law. What did you say your name was?"

"Jess," Jess said, recalling that he hadn't mentioned a last name on the occasion of their one and only meeting.

"Oh, yeah, I remember now. My brother nearly bled to death after that damn bounty hunter shot him. I hope you sent that bastard straight to hell."

Jess merely stared at him. Jay was distracted when Lucky suddenly exclaimed, "Sonofabitch! Look what I found. That bounty hunter that shot me is a female. I thought that menace was dead!"

Jay spotted Meg standing behind Jess and grabbed her arm. He pulled her forward and yanked off her hat. Inky black hair cascaded down her back in a silken waterfall. Jess stepped forward to protect her and was promptly stopped by the barrel of Jay's gun.

"What the hell happened, pilgrim?" he blasted. "You were supposed to finish her off." He gave a snort of disgust. "Did the little whore get to you? Did she offer her body for her life?"

Jay leered at Meg and pulled her against him. "Me and Lucky could use a taste of what you gave the pilgrim."

Jess launched himself at Jay. "Take your filthy hands off her."

Jess didn't see the blow coming as Lucky came up behind him and bashed his head with the butt of his pistol. Darkness and pain closed in on him, and then he knew no more.

Meg watched helplessly as Jess made a slow spiral to the ground. She tried to go to him, but Jay's arm tightened brutally around her.

"Let me go!"

"You ain't going nowhere, bitch," Jay snarled. "You shot my brother. He nearly bled to death before I got him to a doctor."

Meg kept mum, though she badly wanted to remind Jay that he'd killed a bank guard without remorse, and had shot her and left her for dead.

"Let me go to Jess," Meg cried, trying to break free of Jay's ruthless grip.

"Is he your lover?"

"None of your business."

The barrel of his gun bit into the soft flesh of her neck. "I'm making it my business. Is the pilgrim your lover?"

"Yes. Yes!" she repeated unashamedly.

Jay sent her a grim smile. "You must be damn good. Me and Lucky are gonna find out just how good you are real soon." His smile faded. "A word of warning. We're hard to please."

"Lucky," he called, "get the other passengers into the stage, and put the pilgrim in with them."

A terrible fear seized Meg. "What about me?"

His smirk was far from comforting as he rubbed his groin in an obscene manner. "I got plans for you, lady."

Meg renewed her struggles and received a jarring blow to her head. The blow was hard enough to subdue her, but not enough to render her unconscious. She watched helplessly as Lucky and the cowboy loaded Jess into the stage. She was still reeling from the blow when she was rudely pulled away from the stage and tossed aboard Jay's horse. Jay mounted behind her while Lucky slammed the stage door shut and then leaped into his saddle.

Helplessness swamped Meg as she glanced over Jay's shoulder and prayed that Jess wasn't badly hurt. As for herself, she knew exactly what she was up against and steeled herself to fight for her survival.

Jess didn't come around until the stage pulled into the small border town of Wilson, Kansas, to report the robbery. Had he not been incoherent from the blow, he would have demanded that the stage stop and let him out to go after Meg. Unrelenting fear seized him. The Calders had a substantial head start; he worried that he couldn't catch up to them in time to save Meg from grave bodily harm.

Groggily he climbed out of the coach and arranged with the driver to leave his bag and Meg's with the station master in Dodge. Then he retrieved Meg's horse from behind the coach and joined the other passengers who had been robbed. Someone sent for the sheriff, and he appeared directly. Everyone wanted to talk at once, and Sheriff Durant was slow to sort things out.

Finally he came to Jess.

"You claim your friend was taken by the outlaws," he questioned. "Want to tell me what happened?"

"Dr. Gentry didn't see it," the cowboy interjected. "He'd been struck down. But the outlaw named Jay took her up on his horse against her will and carried her off. Funny," he said, thumbing his hat to the back of his head. "We all thought she was a man. But Jay seemed to know her. Knew Dr. Gentry, too."

"Dr. Gentry," the sheriff repeated. "A medical doctor?"

Jess nodded. "Can we get to the important issues, Sheriff? My fiancée has been kidnapped. What are you going to do about it?"

"The Calders are a menace to society. Unfortunately, they're slippery as eels. It will be a day or two before I can get a posse together. We're a small town. Might have to send down to Goodland for men."

Jess's fists clenched at his sides. "That won't do. I'm going now."

"Hold on a minute, Doc. Explain how the Calders knew you and the woman."

"Meg Lincoln is . . . was . . . a bounty hunter. Jay Calder shot her when she cornered him and his brother after they fled from a bank robbery they'd pulled off in Cheyenne."

Durant rubbed his bristly chin. "Meg Lincoln? Heard about her. What about you? Where do you fit in?"

"I saved her life, and that's all I'm going to say right now. Time's running out, Sheriff. The Calders neglected to go through my pockets after knocking me out. I'm going to buy a pair of guns and light out of here before the trail gets cold."

His face set in grim lines, Jess turned and made for the door. The sheriff made no move to stop him, though he stared thoughtfully at his departing back.

Hang on, Meg, Jess mutely pleaded as he headed for the store. *I'm coming.*

Less than an hour later, Jess was fully armed and carrying enough food to last several days as he returned to the place where the outlaws had stopped the stage and taken Meg. He fervently hoped the tracking skills he'd learned over the years would lead him to the woman he loved.

Chapter Sixteen

Meg held herself as stiffly as possible within Jay Calder's brutal embrace. Jay took outrageous liberties with his hands while they rode at breakneck speed over the rough terrain.

Once away from the stagecoach, Jay had stopped long enough to bind her wrists in front of her. He understood that she was dangerous and had bound her as a precautionary measure.

"Where are you taking me?" Meg asked over the din of pounding hooves.

"None of your business," Jay hissed into her ear.

"Jess will find you no matter where you take me."

She said it with confidence despite her misgivings. Jess was a doctor, not a skilled tracker. Even if he did eventually find her, it would be too late. She knew her time on earth was limited. The Calders wouldn't allow her to live. After they used her, they'd kill her. Her face hardened. *Not if I can help it.* She wasn't helpless; she knew how outlaws thought and intended to outsmart her captors.

At nightfall they stopped beside a creek, and Jay tied Meg to a tree. The brothers brought out their supplies and sat down to eat a cold meal of bread and cheese and drink from a bottle of whiskey. Meg was offered nothing to eat, but she didn't mind. Her stomach roiled at the very thought of food. But she did have another pressing need.

"Calder!" Meg called, catching the brothers' attention. "Untie me. I need to . . . go behind the bushes. And I'm thirsty."

Jay lurched to his feet. "I ain't untying you. I don't trust you. If we give you an inch, you'll take a mile."

"I need to go," Meg repeated.

"Damn female," Jay complained as he untied her from the tree and used the extra rope as a tether. "You can go as far as this rope will take you, but I ain't untying your hands."

Meg's legs nearly buckled when she tried to stand. Long hours in the saddle had stripped away their strength. But soon her blood began circulating again and she walked to a clump of bushes. She cast a glance at Jay and stepped behind them.

"Don't try anything funny," Jay warned, tugging the tether as a reminder.

Meg struggled with the fastenings on her

trousers, and for one of the few times in recent memory she wished she were wearing a dress.

"Hurry, I ain't got all day," Jay grumbled.

Meg reappeared from behind the bushes and walked defiantly toward the creek.

"Where are you going now?"

"I'm thirsty." She dropped to her knees beside the creek and scooped water into her mouth until she'd drunk her fill.

"You're too easy on her," Lucky complained as he watched the proceedings. "I can't forget how I suffered on her account. I damn near died."

"So did I," Meg shot back. "Jess is the finest doctor I know. He saved my life."

"You mean that pilgrim is a doctor?" Jay guffawed. "Here we thought he was an outlaw like us."

"You were wrong," Meg countered.

"Bring her over here, Jay," Lucky said, indicating his bedroll. "I want her now. I ain't never done it to a woman wearing trousers."

"You'll wait, just like me," Jay advised. "We ain't in safe territory yet and can't afford to let our guard down. Her lover could be following with a posse. Wait till we get to the hideout tomorrow; then we can both take our fill of her."

"Over my dead body," Meg hissed.

Lucky sent her a menacing glare. "That can be arranged, but I'd just soon have you alive when I poke you."

"Enough talk," Jay said, tugging Meg away from the water. "You take first watch, Lucky. Wake me at midnight to relieve you."

"What about her?" Lucky asked, glowering at Meg. "Aren't you afraid she'll escape?"

"Not if she's sleeping in my bedroll," Jay said.

"Hey, that ain't fair!"

"Simmer down, Lucky, I just want to make sure she don't escape. I told you, we'll share her when we reach the hideout. Go on, now. Climb up that rise over yonder. You should be able to see anyone approaching from there."

"Shit! Why do I have to take the first watch?"

"Because I said so," Jay retorted. "Go on, do as I say. I need to get a little shut-eye before my watch."

Grumbling, Lucky stomped off, but not before sending a hungry look in Meg's direction.

Meg listened intently to the exchange between the brothers and wondered how she could use the jealousy between them to her advantage. But first she had to survive the next few hours lying beside Jay. She trusted him no more than she trusted a snake. There wasn't a doubt in her mind that he intended to assault her the moment Lucky was out of sight.

Her fears were realized when Jay pulled her over to his bedroll and pushed her down. He stood over her a moment, then released his trousers, peeled them down to his ankles, and dropped down beside her. His hands unerringly found her breasts.

"Take your filthy hands off me!" Meg hissed. "Lucky's not going to like this."

"Lucky doesn't need to know. It's just you and me now."

"He'll know if I scream loud enough."

He pulled a knife from his belt. "Scream and I'll slit your throat. You're gonna die sooner or later anyway. We may as well have a little fun before it happens."

Meg hawked up a wad of spittle and let it fly into his face. "I'm not going to make it easy for you."

Jay wiped at the spittle running down his cheek with the back of his hand and gave her a look that promised dire retribution. He put his knife to her throat and drew a shallow crosswise slash, just deep enough to draw blood.

"Do that again and I won't be so lenient next time," he growled.

Pain exploded at the site of the wound. Meg grasped her throat and felt warm blood seeping through her fingers. But that wasn't as terrifying as watching Jay unfasten her trousers and work them down her legs. He was kneeling at her feet, knees spread apart, trying to pull her boots off so he could remove her trousers, when Meg reacted spontaneously. She drew her legs back and smashed her booted feet into Jay's groin. Satisfaction ripped through her as he let out an earth-shattering howl and fell backward onto the ground, rolling back and forth, clutching his wounded groin.

"Bitch! Bitch! Bitch!" he shrieked. "You'll pay for that."

He was still writhing in pain when Lucky came running up. "What happened? I heard you screaming clear to the top of that rise."

"Ask that . . . bitch," Jay managed to gasp out. "She practically killed me. She might have ruined my balls for good."

Moonlight provided Lucky with a pretty good picture of what had happened. "You tried to take her," he accused. "After you said we'd wait till we reached the hideout. Serves you right."

"Dammit, Lucky, kill the bitch. She's a menace."

Lucky turned mutinous as he stared at her bloodied throat. "No. Maybe later, but I want her first. She put a bullet in me and I want to make her suffer. I'll tie her to the tree so we can both get some sleep. Are you all right?"

"All right? I'm dying, dammit! I probably won't be able to sit a horse tomorrow. I'm sorry I didn't slit her throat. Get her outta my sight."

By the time Lucky returned his attention to Meg, she'd dragged her trousers back in place and managed to wind her bandana around her throat. The wound wasn't serious and had already stopped bleeding.

"Get up," Lucky said, dragging her up by the tether that was still attached to her bound wrists. "You'd better behave, 'cause I don't know if I can keep Jay from killing you if ya act up again."

Meg said nothing, deciding there were times when silence was the better part of valor. She didn't even complain when Lucky wound the rope around her so tightly she'd probably be numb by morning.

Jess picked up the trail but had to stop when darkness made it too difficult to read the signs clearly. He thanked God for the tracking games he and his brothers had played when they were children. Neither Rafe nor Sam could measure up to his skills in that department, though he wasn't as capable as they were in bagging game. He supposed it was because he didn't like killing animals unless it was absolutely necessary for survival.

Jess hobbled his horse to graze and spread his bedroll beneath a tree. He didn't dare light a fire, so he munched on dried meat and hardtack; then he stretched out and tried to sleep.

He didn't sleep. He worried. The thought of Meg in the hands of men who had reason to hate her was almost more than he could bear. She'd been with them for hours. Only one truth eased his fear. Meg was resourceful, brave, and stronger in both mind and body than any other woman he knew.

Jay kicked Meg awake at first light. She suppressed a satisfied smile when she saw him limping away. No matter how badly she'd hurt him, she felt no remorse. If he tried to touch her again, she'd give him another dose of her anger.

This time Meg was forced to ride with Lucky, whose hands were no more gentlemanly than Jay's. Though she couldn't stop him from touching her intimately, she received some consolation from watching Jay wince as he settled in the saddle.

Meg's stomach was growling. No food had been forthcoming. But she persevered, keeping track of the direction in which they traveled in case she was able to escape. When she was tracking outlaws, she had no one but herself and her instincts to depend upon. If she could escape, she knew how to survive.

The outlaws skirted around bluffs covered with coarse vegetation and a few stubborn trees that had taken root in the arid ground. They kept to the flatlands, avoiding the deep gullies sculpted from the sere earth. Meg knew real fear when Lucky reined his horse behind a bluff and she saw a rough cabin nestled against a rocky incline. It was a perfect place for a hideout, she thought. No wonder the law couldn't find them. The cabin, tucked beneath an overhanging rock, was impossible to see unless one was looking right at it. Nearby, a stream cascaded down from the bluff to form a pool of clear water at the bottom. The pool could be used for bathing, if Jay and Lucky were so inclined, and drinking water could be caught before it reached the pool.

Lucky dismounted before the cabin and yanked Meg from the saddle. "Get inside," he growled, pushing her toward the door.

Meg stumbled forward. Lucky opened the door and shoved her through. A mouse scrambled for cover and a raccoon scurried past her. The inside was a filthy mess, Meg noticed as she made a quick survey of the crude cabin. At least it had windows. Two bare cots sat against opposite walls with an untidy fireplace between them. A few cooking pots hung from hooks beside the fireplace, and the open cupboards nearby held several tins of food and cracked dishes laden with dust. A scarred table and four rickety chairs completed the cabin's furnishings.

"Well, what do ya think of it?" Lucky asked.

"I think you're both crazy. Jess will find me no matter where we are."

"He's a doctor, not a tracker," Lucky argued.

Meg feared Lucky was right but wasn't ready to sell Jess short. He had displayed talents far beyond those a doctor would ordinarily possess. Her one gnawing fear was that Jess was still angry with her for following him and didn't care what happened to her. The moment that thought was born, she quickly discarded it. Jess was too kindhearted to leave her to her own devices. Besides, in her heart she truly believed that he loved her.

Jay limped into the cabin and tossed a sack down on the table. "Fix us some grub," he ordered. "Might as well make yourself useful while you can."

Meg held out her hands. "I can't do it with my hands bound."

"I say you can," Jay barked. "Don't pull that helpless female bit on me." He rubbed his groin and winced. "I know what you're capable of."

"I'll build up the fire," Lucky said, "and open a tin of canned beef."

"I'm gonna take a look around outside," Jay said, "and make sure no one followed us. It wouldn't hurt to set up a watch for the next few nights. Not that I think anyone will find us, but you never can tell. Better to be safe than sorry."

Meg rummaged through the sack of provisions while Lucky built a fire in the hearth. Besides several tins of beef, there were flour, lard, potatoes, onions, bacon, and beans. Enough to last several days, if they were frugal. Fresh game would help round out the menu and make the staples last longer, if the men were inclined to hunt. Not that she intended to stick around that long. If she didn't escape soon, she was as good as dead and food wouldn't matter.

"I can't do this with my hands tied," Meg insisted. "Untie me. Do you think I'd be dumb enough to try anything with you and Jay keeping close watch on me? I'm only a woman."

Lucky slanted her a scathing look. "Like hell! You ain't like no female I've ever known. You'd be dead now if I wasn't hankering for a piece of you. You shot me, lady. I nearly died. You gotta pay, and killing ya is too quick. If I wanted ya dead, I'd have let Jay finish ya off when ya hurt him."

"Very well," Meg said, brazening it out. "Then cook your own dinner." She plopped down in one of the rickety chairs and glared mutinously at him.

Lucky let loose an angry growl and slapped Meg. Her head snapped back and her eyes watered, but she refused to cry.

"That felt damn good," Lucky said. "By the time I finish with you, you're gonna be damn sorry you shot Lucky Calder."

Meg didn't doubt it for an instant. She also had an ace up her sleeve, if she could get to it. She still had her small pistol concealed in her clothing. She hadn't given it up when the passengers had tossed their weapons on the ground at Jay's request. It was hidden inside her vest pocket.

"Get your ass outta that chair and fix our grub," Lucky demanded, "unless ya want more where that came from."

Meg decided not to rile Lucky further. She needed strength for the night to come, and being slapped around now was likely to weaken her. Rising stiffly, she emptied the tin of meat into a frying pan and set it over the fire. Then she chopped potatoes and onions without peeling them, dumping them into the pan with the meat. She mixed biscuit batter while the hash cooked. Though her hands were bound at the wrists, she found she could still use her fingers to hold a mixing spoon and chop vegetables.

"Food smells good," Jay said, sniffing the air as he limped back into the cabin. "At least the bitch is good for something."

"She's good for a lot of things," Lucky hinted slyly. "If she's alive after I finish with her tonight, she's all yours."

Jay bit out an oath. "I ain't gonna touch

the bitch. Kill her after you finish with her. If I were you, I'd wring her neck, it's not as messy as a bullet. Is the grub ready?"

Meg found a rag and removed the hot frying pan and biscuits from the fire, banging them on the plank table in front of the men. Jay got out a couple of chipped plates and dented spoons and set them on the table.

"Don't I get to eat?" Meg asked with a bravado she was far from feeling.

"Dead women don't need food," Jay said around his mouthful of biscuit.

Lucky frowned. "I want her strong enough to fight me. It ain't no fun poking a spiritless woman. She can have what's left."

What was left hardly filled the empty place in Meg's stomach, but it helped. She took her time, keeping a wary eye on the outlaws as she ate.

"I'll do the dishes," Meg said, hoping to delay the inevitable.

Lucky leered at her. "Leave them."

Meg stared at him. Her time was up, and she still wasn't ready to accept her fate. She'd never be prepared for rape, and God only knew what other atrocities Lucky had planned for her.

"I'll take first watch," Jay said, rising. "A word of advice. Protect your balls and keep your weapon outta her reach. I'll build up the fire so you can see what she's doing."

"Don't worry, Jay. No puny woman is

gonna get the best of me."

Jay threw two thick logs on the fire. "Call out if you need me; I'll be just outside."

"I ain't gonna need no one," Lucky muttered after Jay left the cabin. His beady gaze settled on Meg. "I want you naked."

"I can't take my clothes off," Meg said. "My wrists are tied, or have you forgotten?"

"They're gonna stay tied, lady. And so are your legs as soon as I get these damn trousers off you. Ladies are supposed to wear skirts," he complained.

Lucky must have decided he needed his weapon to control Meg, for he pulled out his gun and aimed it at her middle. "Don't move. I'm gonna unbuckle your belt and open your fly."

With one hand Lucky unbuckled Meg's belt and pulled it free. Then he unfastened her fly, cursing when the buttons offered resistance. He crowed in satisfaction when her fly finally gaped open, revealing a creamy slice of midriff. Leering at her exposed flesh, he shoved her toward the cot. She stumbled, then sprawled on her back across the unyielding surface. Lucky dropped his gun on the floor and fell on top of her.

The air left Meg's lungs and her mind went blank. This couldn't be happening to her again. Though it had been five years since Arlo had brutally raped her, she'd never forgotten how dirty and ashamed his attacks made her feel. She'd wanted to die. To crawl inside herself, to escape to another realm while Lucky practiced his obscenities on her.

Then, in some far corner of her mind she realized she was no longer a helpless sixteen-year-old, that there were things she could do, survival instincts she had honed over the years.

Meg nearly gagged when Lucky kissed her, thrusting his tongue down her throat. His hands were everywhere, but mostly they were trying to remove her trousers. She bit down hard on his tongue, his howl of pain meager comfort as he retaliated with an open-handed blow to her cheek.

"Stop that! You ain't gonna kick me in the balls and you ain't gonna get my gun."

He unbuttoned her vest, then her shirt, clamping a hard hand around her breast. She lurched beneath him when he bit down on her nipple.

Lucky grinned up at her. "Like that, did ya? Thought ya might."

Meg shook her head from side to side in vigorous denial.

"I'm gonna lift up a bit so's I can pull off your trousers. Don't try anything funny. I still have the upper hand. One hard clip to the jaw and you're out like a light." He sat on her legs and worked his fingers beneath her waistband.

Meg considered his words, an idea forming

in her head. It was tricky at best, but what did she have to lose? Her bound wrists and bent arms were pressed against her chest. While Lucky was occupied with her clothing, she threaded her fingers together, palms together, making a tight fist. She glanced up at Lucky and saw that his head was tucked down. She had to get him to lift his head.

"Lucky, wait, let me help you."

He raised his head and glared at her. "I don't need your help. You ain't gonna do to me what ya did to Jay."

"No, I'm not," Meg agreed as she gritted her teeth and slammed Lucky in the throat with her doubled fists.

Lucky made a gurgling sound deep in his throat and his eyes rolled up in his head as he clutched his neck and fell off the narrow cot. Meg leaped from the cot, her eyes blazing pure malice as her bound hands scrambled for the pistol in her vest pocket. She managed to pull it free, but it slipped from her fingers, landing at her feet.

Lucky was still on the ground, eyes bugging out, making strangling noises inside his throat. She saw him reach for his weapon and kicked it away. Lucky's mouth worked wordlessly as he tried to crawl toward it.

"Bitch," he choked out, his garbled words barely understandable. "I'll . . . kill . . . you."

"Not if I can help it," Meg hissed as she

bent to retrieve her pistol. "Don't move."

"Jay. Jay will . . . take care . . . of you."

"Go ahead and call him," Meg challenged.

Lucky opened his mouth and glared murderously at her when no sound emerged. He could hardly form coherent words, much less call for help. Meg concentrated on escaping before Lucky's wits returned along with his voice. She edged toward the door, holding Lucky at bay with her pistol. She heard the door latch rattle and whipped her head around as Jay burst through the door.

"I thought I heard . . ." His gaze found Lucky, who was writhing on the floor, grasping his throat and making unintelligible sounds. "What the hell is going on here?"

Meg whirled away from Lucky, bringing the pistol around with her. "Drop your gun belt."

"What did you do to Lucky?"

"Nothing he won't recover from. Drop your guns, I said. I'm not afraid to use this gun."

"I'll never live this down," Jay bit out. "How could one puny woman do this much damage? You won't get away with it, you know. This time I ain't gonna let Lucky talk me outta killing you."

Meg pulled back the hammer. Jay blanched, looked at his hapless brother for help, then released his gun belt. It fell to the floor. Meg kicked it out of reach.

"Your hands are still bound. How did ya do it?"

"I'm smarter than either of you. Get over there with your brother."

"Sure," Jay said amiably, "but you ain't gonna leave this room alive. There are two of us and one of you." A crafty expression flitted across his face. "I don't know why I'm standing here arguing with you. One weak woman ain't gonna bring the Calder brothers down."

The words had scarcely left his mouth when he launched himself at Meg. She pulled the trigger, but the shot went wild, lodging in the hapless Lucky. He let out a strangled gasp and collapsed. Then Meg's head hit the floor. Jay cast but a quick glance at Lucky's lifeless form and began screaming invectives at Meg. He scrambled for his gun and brought it to her head.

"Say your prayers, bitch."

Meg closed her eyes and waited for death. She'd given it her best shot and lost. She regretted leaving this life without settling things between herself and Jess; they'd had so little time together. She would have liked to look into his face and tell him she loved him one last time.

She heard the metallic click of a gun hammer and prayed for a quick death. She had no wish to linger, to suffer excruciating agony before death finally claimed her.

The loud report of the gun jarred her. She waited for pain and felt none. She wondered why death felt no different from life.

"Meg. Open your eyes, sweetheart."

Meg was stunned to hear the voice of a loved one in the afterlife. But Jess's beloved voice was clear as a bell, as if he were in the room with her.

"Come on, love, open your eyes. No one is going to hurt you now."

Meg's eyes opened slowly. How could she be alive? God must truly love her.

"Jay . . . Lucky . . ."

"Forget those two. They won't be bothering anyone again."

Jess helped her to sit up. She spied Jay lying nearby in a pool of blood and shuddered. Then she launched herself into Jess's arms, burying her head in his neck. "Is he dead?"

"Yes. Did you kill Lucky?"

"Yes, but not purposely. Jay lunged at me and the gun fired. The bullet went wild and hit Lucky."

"Good riddance. You'll have quite a reward coming for those two. I knew you were resourceful, but I think you've topped yourself this time."

She held out her hands to him. "Untie me."

Jess's shock was palpable as he cut through her bindings with the blade he carried in his boot. "How in the hell did you get the drop on them with your hands bound?"

"Can we go outside?" Meg asked shakily. "I don't want to stay in the same room with them."

She tried to stand, felt her knees wobble, and was grateful for Jess's support. "I can't believe you tracked us here. How many more surprises do you have up your sleeve, Jess Gentry?"

"Remind me to tell you about my tracking skills sometime," Jess said. "Let's get you out into the air first. You look pale as death."

"I thought I *was* dead," Meg whispered.

Jess walked Meg over to a fallen log and sat down, pulling her into his lap. He began to tremble, aware that he nearly hadn't arrived in time. His arms tightened around her.

Jess's glance slid over Meg's beloved features, his expression murderous when he saw the bruises on her face and her gaping shirt. "What did the bastards do to you? Oh, God, Meg, forgive me. I hoped I'd arrive in time to save you from this."

Meg eased his fear immediately. "I'm fine, Jess. A few bruises that will heal, nothing more." Her face hardened. "Though it wasn't for their lack of trying."

"Do you feel like telling me about it?"

Meg began to talk, revealing how she had all but crippled Jay with a well-aimed boot heel, and rendered Lucky immobile with a chop to the throat. "But in the end it didn't matter," she said bitterly. "Jay managed to get the drop on me and would have killed me if you hadn't shown up when you did."

Meg's tale left Jess nearly speechless. "You did all that with your hands bound?" he asked, his chest swelling with pride. His Meg was one helluva woman. "As soon as I settle things in Dodge, I'm going to have to marry you to keep you out of trouble."

Meg's head jerked up. "What did you say?"

"I said I intend to marry you after the charges are dropped against the Gentry brothers."

"Is that the only reason you want to marry me? To keep me out of trouble?"

Jess looked deep into her eyes. They glowed like emeralds in the moonlight; he'd never seen a more beautiful sight. "I want to marry you because I love you, sweetheart."

"Oh, Jess, you don't know how badly I wanted to hear that. You've forgiven me then for . . . for everything? Everything I've done has been for your sake."

"I know. I was a fool to fight the inevitable. I was afraid to love. I felt you deserved better than a fugitive from the law. I have nothing to offer you. I might be returning to Dodge only to end up behind bars. There's only one thing I am sure of in this life. I love you, Meg Lincoln. I can no longer deny it or push it away." He grasped her shoulders. "I love you, Meg. Do you hear me?"

"I hear you, Jess. I've loved you for a very long time. Please kiss me. Show me this isn't a dream."

"This is no dream, love. Come what may, you'll always have my love."

He kissed her then, putting his heart and soul into the kiss, showing her without words how very much she meant to him.

"You're exhausted," Jess said when he broke off the kiss. "We can share my bedroll and get an early start tomorrow."

"What about . . . them?" Meg said, motioning toward the cabin.

"We'll take the Calders back to town with us. Sheriff Durant can take care of the bodies and fill out the papers for your reward. You can stop by to pick it up on your way back to Cheyenne."

"I'm not going to leave Dodge without you, Jess Gentry. Once those false bank robbery charges are dismissed, we can return together. Do you plan on settling in Cheyenne?"

Jess didn't want to burst Meg's bubble. There was a very good chance he'd end up behind bars for a long time. "I have a good practice there."

"The citizens of Cheyenne don't like me. If it weren't for Zach, I wouldn't mind settling elsewhere."

"I'll make them like you," Jess said fiercely.

"I won't separate you from your . . . father."

"My father," Meg sighed. "Zach is all that and more."

Jess held her for a few minutes more until he felt her go limp and realized she had fallen asleep. Then he rose and carefully placed her on a bed of soft leaves while he went to prepare his bedroll.

Chapter Seventeen

Jess awakened early, intending to take care of an unpleasant task before Meg woke. After seeing to his personal needs and washing up in the stream, he returned to the cabin. The stench of death was strong, but he'd grown used to it during the war, and he went about his task with stoic determination. He returned outside and located the outlaws' bedrolls lying beside their saddles.

He slanted a glance at Meg to make sure she was sleeping and reentered the cabin when she showed no signs of awakening. Then he quickly wrapped the dead bodies in blankets and dragged them separately to where their horses were tethered. He hefted both bodies aboard one horse and tied them in place with a rope. Then he returned to the stream and washed his hands thoroughly with strong lye soap he kept in his medical bag.

Meg was just beginning to stir when he returned to his pallet. He crouched beside her so she'd see him as soon as she opened her eyes. He didn't want her to be startled or become frightened once she awakened.

She looked up at him and smiled. "Jess. I thought I was dreaming." She shuddered. "Or dead."

"You're not dreaming, sweetheart, and you're very much alive."

He cupped her chin and lifted it so he could look into her face. What he saw made his eyes darken with fury and his expression harden. "Damn! I didn't see the full extent of your injuries last night. Those bastards! Their deaths were too easy. They should have suffered for what they did to you." He rose abruptly. "Lie still. I'll get my medical bag and clean the bruises with disinfectant. There's a nasty cut on your cheek."

Then he noticed the blood-encrusted bandana around her neck and wanted to howl in outrage. Had he missed something? "Where did that blood come from?"

Meg's hand went to her throat, and a groan slipped past her lips. Jess was on his knees beside her instantly. "What is it? What did they do to you?"

Meg merely stared at him. Gently Jess removed her hands from her throat and slowly unwound the bandana. When her wound was fully revealed, he sat back on his heels, his hands clenched at his sides.

"My God! Which one of those beasts did this to you? Another quarter inch and he could have severed your jugular."

He saw Meg's throat work painfully, and red hot fury shot through him. He would have given his own life to prevent the anguish Meg had suffered. His throat was clogged with tears and he couldn't speak; he could only feel her pain as if it were his own.

Meg sent him a wobbly smile, raised her hand to his face and stroked his cheek. "It's not as bad as it looks."

Jess finally found his voice. "This needs tending. I'll be right back."

Jess returned moments later with his medical bag. "This is going to sting," he said as he poured a generous amount of disinfectant on a clean white cloth and applied it to her throat.

"I can take it," Meg said, gritting her teeth against the pain.

Though Jess was as gentle as humanly possible, he knew he was hurting Meg, but she bore it with courage, just like she faced everything else in life. His Meg was no lily-livered weakling. She was brave, courageous, and spunky as hell. And she was his.

After he tended to her cut neck and various bruises, he helped her undress so he could inspect her body for further damage. He found a livid purple bruise where Jay had kicked her, and bruises on her breasts from Lucky's heavy hand. Other than the wounds he had already treated, she had miraculously escaped serious bodily harm. And she hadn't suffered the degradation of rape. He fervently thanked God for that.

"I'd like to wash in the pool before we leave," Meg said as Jess handed her clothing to her. "Do you mind?"

"No, not at all. I'll join you. The Calders aren't going anywhere."

Meg's gaze flickered briefly to the horse carrying the bodies and returned immediately to Jess. "When did you do that?"

"While you were sleeping. Shall we find that pool?"

Jess produced a bar of soap from his bag and tenderly bathed Meg, gently laving her bruises and washing her hair. When Meg offered to reciprocate, Jess refused. He didn't think he could stand her hands on him. He wanted her too badly, and she was in no condition to make love. She needed time to heal, both in body and mind, and he intended to give her as much time as she needed. Though he ached to hold her, to love her, the sight of her bruised and battered body gave him the strength to control his raging need for the woman he loved.

Later, after Jess had fixed them a decent meal from food he found in the cabin, he and Meg prepared to leave. Meg didn't glance back once as they rode away. Jess knew she wanted to take no memories of her ordeal with her and he couldn't blame her.

"Let's get out of here," Jess said, grasping

the reins of the horse carrying the dead bodies as he fell in beside her.

"Gladly," Meg concurred. "I want to forget everything associated with this place."

They rode throughout the day, stopping often for Meg's benefit. Jess wasn't taking any chances with her health. There was no hurry to reach town.

At sundown Jess suggested they camp for the night beside a stream flanked by a few stunted trees that would provide cover from the elements. He was stunned when Meg suddenly paled and suggested they ride on a ways before stopping. Jess didn't question her as they continued on, but he vowed to learn the reason for her sudden skittishness.

Two hours later, Jess built a fire and prepared a makeshift meal from the food he'd taken from the cabin. After they ate, Meg wandered down to the stream while Jess laid out their bedroll. Then he walked to the stream to find Meg. He came up behind her and wrapped his arms around her.

He pulled aside her hair and kissed the back of her neck. "Would you care for a swim? It's a warm night, and the water will be refreshing after the dusty trail."

She shuddered. "I feel as though I'll never be clean again after being touched by Jay and Lucky."

"Why didn't you want to stop earlier?"

"I couldn't bear to sleep in the same place

the Calders used as their campsite. It brought back too many painful memories."

"I'm sorry, love. I want to erase those memories forever if you'll let me."

"Yes, oh, yes," Meg cried passionately.

Jess smiled. "Let's have our swim. I'll fetch everything we need. I won't be long."

When Jess returned, he found Meg standing at the edge of the stream, her naked body clothed in silver and gold moonlight. His admiring gaze drank in the sight of her silken black hair cascading down the elegant curve of her back. The beauty of her face and form was utterly, temptingly mesmerizing, and he quickly undressed and joined her. She heard him approach and smiled up at him. His body turned instantly hard. He wanted to hold her against his heat, kiss her senseless, and love her until they were both too exhausted to move. But he feared she was still too emotionally fragile, so he forced himself to do nothing more than hold her.

She turned in his arms, pressing her body against his. Jess froze. If she continued enticing him like this, his control would vanish like dark before the dawn. Did she realize what she was doing to him?

"You're trembling," Meg whispered against his lips.

"I want you so badly I'm shaking from the effort to control myself. My lust is the last thing you need right now."

"Are you sure?" Meg asked. "Maybe it's exactly what I need."

"Meg —"

"No, Jess, don't say anything."

She stretched on her tiptoes and pressed her lips against his. He groaned, his arms tightening around her. Breast to breast, thigh to thigh, her body branded his, making him burn to be inside her again, to possess her.

"The bath can wait," he whispered against her lips. "Don't move," he ordered as he left her for a brief moment.

He returned almost immediately with a blanket and spread it on the ground.

Meg stared at him. The sleek, masculine beauty of his body made her throat constrict. He was long and lean, his form forged in iron. His arms and legs were sculpted with muscles. A dark netting of fur covered his chest and the ridged hardness of his belly. She gazed at him in admiration, unaware that he was watching her.

Her gaze slid downward, where his staff stood boldly erect, framed by the coarse dark curls covering his groin. The breath left her throat as her gaze returned to his face. He was smiling at her, as if he knew exactly what she was thinking.

Reaching for her, he grasped her hips and brought her against him. Meg gasped. His skin was pure fire, making her burn. The eyes that bored into her were brighter than any flame. His fingers caressed her cheek, then twisted in her hair, turning her face up to his. His mouth took hers, stealing her breath and filling her throat with his own heated breath.

His kiss went on and on, his tongue dancing against hers, swirling deeper, then drawing away in teasing little strokes. She went limp in his arms. He lowered her to the blanket and followed her down, keeping the chill away with the heat of his body.

She breathed in his scent. His hand closed possessively over her breast. "Mine, all mine," he groaned into her ear. It was a deep, primal sound that sent shafts of raw pleasure clear down to the heart of her womanhood.

"Yes, yours. Always," Meg answered, cupping his cheek and caressing the length of his strong neck. His skin was warm, his jaw hard, the stubble of his beard raspy beneath her fingertips.

Her hand slid downward and stopped over his heart. It was beating hard and strong, just like hers. Then his mouth covered hers and she was lost in the thrusting rhythm of a deep kiss. She nearly lost what breath she had left when he gripped her bottom, lifted her, and rocked his hips slowly against her loins. Then a new sensation battered her as he lowered his head and suckled her breasts. That heated place between her legs throbbed; she felt her nipples harden, and the ache inside her quickened with need.

She gave a ragged cry. "Jess, please!"

"Hush." His voice was hoarse, his breathing labored as he slipped a hand between their bodies and his fingers found the core of her. He plied his magic, touching, stroking, playing with her heated center until her body wept pearly tears.

Something inside her shimmered and grew. She welcomed it, losing herself in the glowing tide of passion pushing her into the tumbling waves of pleasure. Then suddenly he removed his fingers and the building pressure subsided. She wanted to scream in frustration, but uttered a sigh of relief instead when she felt the blunt tip of his shaft penetrate the dewy lips of her pulsating center.

One hard thrust took him all the way home, filling her with his strength, his heat, the very essence of him. Then he began to move, and all coherent thought ceased as she soared beyond herself, searching for that exalted place where sensation ruled. Delicious pleasure burst upon her when she found it, and she clung to sanity with a desperation that left her hanging by a slim thread. When the thread broke, she went tumbling into an abyss of raw sensation. Jess followed her by scant seconds. His body stiffened and he poured himself into her, shouting his pleasure.

Meg was scarcely aware when Jess arose

and placed a blanket over their flushed bodies. When she regained her wits, a cozy warmth enveloped her, and she burrowed into the heat of Jess's body.

"Are you awake, sweetheart?" Jess asked when she stirred in his arms.

"Ummmm."

"Are you ready for that bath now?"

"I suppose," she muttered, preferring sleep to a bath.

"Come on," he said, pulling her to her feet. "I have the soap."

Reluctantly Meg stepped into the water. It was cool and she would have pulled back, but Jess was behind her, urging her into the shallow stream.

"Stand still," Jess said. "Let me wash your back."

Jess soaped her back first, then moved on until he'd washed every curve and crevice of her body. When he finished, he handed her the soap so she could reciprocate. By the time they had washed and dried each other, they were both eager to make love again.

This time, Jess lay down on the blanket and pulled Meg on top of him, letting her lead the way. By no means shy, she explored, kissing and teasing every inch of his body, until he was trembling and groaning uncontrollably.

"Enough!" he cried as he grasped her waist and tucked her beneath him. Then he used his hands and mouth to torment her in the same way she had tormented him. Thrusting her legs apart, he lowered his head and sipped greedily from her nectar. When he felt her body stiffen, he entered her quickly and took them both to paradise.

They rested awhile, then returned to the stream to wash away the residue of their lovemaking. They returned to their campsite sated and exhausted. Jess built up the fire and joined Meg on the bedroll she had laid out for them to share. Sleep came swiftly, and so did morning.

Meg all but ignored the two stiff bodies draped over the spare horse tagging behind them. She didn't feel the least regret over their deaths, not after what they'd tried to do to her. In fact, she'd brought in more than one dead outlaw in the same position during her bounty-hunting career.

They reached the small border town of Wilson late that afternoon. They rode directly to the sheriff's office to drop off the bodies. Sheriff Durant looked up from the newspaper he was perusing as Meg and Jess walked through the door.

"I see you've brought her back," Durant said, smiling at Meg. "Good work, Gentry." He sent Meg a sharp look. "Looks like they weren't too gentle with you. Are you hurt badly?"

"Nothing that won't heal," Meg assured him.

"Sorry I couldn't lend a hand, Gentry. Sheriff Crowley over at Goodland couldn't send the help I requested. He was getting his own posse together to hunt down a cattle rustler. Said he'd send someone up to lend a hand as soon as he returned. I just didn't have the manpower here to pursue the Calders on my own. Any idea where I can find them when help arrives?"

"A posse won't be necessary, Sheriff," Jess said. "Miss Lincoln and I brought the Calders back with us. They're both dead. The reward is to go to Miss Lincoln."

Durant let out a low whistle and tipped his hat to the back of his head. "You got them both? I'll be damned. Excuse me, ma'am," he apologized to Meg. "I reckon your reputation's not exaggerated. I'll see that you get your reward. Just tell me where to send it when it arrives."

"Send it to Cheyenne, in care of general delivery," Meg returned.

"You'll find the bodies draped over the horse outside your door," Jess said. "We'll be on our way. Got pressing business south of here."

Suddenly the sheriff's expression hardened. "Sorry, Gentry, but you're not going anywhere. I thought you looked familiar the first time we met and I finally remembered where it was I'd seen you. It was on a Wanted poster I received some weeks back. I got it out and sure enough, there you were, along with your brothers. You're under arrest for bank robbery. I've got to put you in jail."

Meg paled. "No! Jess is a doctor, not a bank robber. Those charges are false. We were on our way to Dodge to clear up the matter when our stagecoach was held up."

"I'm only doing my duty, Miss Lincoln. If the charges are false, Sheriff Diller over in Dodge will clear the matter up. I'll wire him, but I still have to put Gentry behind bars."

"You can't —"

"Meg, it's all right," Jess said in an effort to calm her. "I'll probably be sent back to Dodge, where I wanted to go in the first place. Don't worry, sweetheart."

Still not satisfied, Meg sent Durant a pleading look. "Don't put Jess in jail, Sheriff. Let him remain free while you contact Sheriff Diller. He won't go anywhere, I promise."

"Sorry, Miss Lincoln, I've got to do my duty. Hand over your guns, Gentry."

For one crazy minute, Jess considered drawing on the sheriff and fleeing. But he soon realized that following his inclination would make him the outlaw that the law proclaimed him. Accepting an unjust fate meekly, however, went against everything he believed in. But it wasn't Jess who drew his gun, it was Meg.

"Sorry, Sheriff, we can't stick around. How can Jess prove his innocence if he's rotting in jail?"

"Now see here, Miss Lincoln," the sheriff blustered. "You're breaking the law. If you don't put your weapon away, I'll have to lock you both up."

"Go on, Jess," Meg urged. "I'll hold the sheriff here until you're clear of town. I'll catch up with you."

Jess gave an exasperated sigh. "Put the gun away, Meg. You're not thinking clearly. I fled the law once and I'm not going to do it again. I told you I'm going to see my brothers freed of those trumped-up charges if it's the last thing I do, and I meant it. You're being your normal hotheaded self, and it won't get us anywhere."

Meg's chin notched upward. "It will get us out of town."

Jess took a quick step forward and grabbed the gun from her hand. "It will land us both in jail." He handed Meg's gun to the sheriff and added his gun belt. "You'll have to excuse her, Sheriff. Meg's naturally distraught after her ordeal with the Calders."

"I understand," Durant said as he placed the guns in a drawer. "You can have your gun back when you simmer down, Miss Lincoln. Come with me, Gentry. We don't have much of a jail, but it will hold you until I hear from Dodge."

The jail was little more than a hovel built as an afterthought behind the sheriff's office. One door, solid except for a small barred aperture, opened into a small windowless cell. A cot, a small table, one chair, and a slop bucket placed in a corner were the only furnishings in the malodorous room reeking of urine and rotted food.

"You can't keep him in there!" Meg charged, indignant.

"It's all we got. Step inside, Gentry," Durant prodded. "I'll wire the law in Dodge and inquire what they want done with you. Chances are they'll want you taken to Dodge. If so, I'll escort you there myself."

Jess moved inside the cell, then turned and gave Meg a bolstering smile before the door clanged shut behind him. Durant turned the lock and placed the key in the same drawer with their guns. Then he locked the drawer and pocketed the key.

"Why don't you come to the telegraph office with me, Miss Lincoln?" Durant suggested, guiding her away from the jail. "If you want my advice, you'll find yourself a room for the night."

"Very well, lead the way," Meg said, casting a glance over her shoulder at the mean little cell holding the man she loved.

"Sorry, Sheriff," the telegrapher said as he handed the sheriff's message back to him.

"Lines are down. Those red savages take a great deal of pleasure disrupting our lines of communication. It'll be a few days before repairs can be made and communication is restored."

"A few days!" Meg blasted. "You mean Jess has to stay in that pigsty more than one night?"

"Kind of looks that way, Miss Lincoln," Durant said. "I'll see that he gets plenty to eat. No need to worry on that score."

"I want to see Jess."

"Sure, you can talk through the bars. You have to come back to the office anyway to pick up your gun."

Meg accompanied Durant back to his office. Never had she seen such a poor excuse for a town. Two saloons, a general store, a feed store, barbershop, and bathhouse, and above the bathhouse, rooms that looked like a brothel. One dingy cafe and a livery stable completed the business district.

"Is there a hotel in town?" Meg asked.

"There are two boardinghouses down one of the side streets. The one run by Aggie Ronstadt is your best bet. Clean and cheap, and her cooking is as fine as you'll get anywhere."

"I'll find it," Meg said. "After I see Jess."

Meg walked back to Jess's cell. Grasping the bars, she peered inside. Jess was sitting on the lumpy cot, his head resting in his hands.

"Jess."

She must have caught him with his defenses down, for the defeated look on his face when he lifted his head made her breath hitch. A scant moment later, the despairing look was replaced by a forced smile.

"Meg, what are you doing back here? Did Durant send the telegram?"

"The lines are down. Indians. The telegrapher said it will take a few days to repair them. I'm sorry, Jess."

Jess shrugged. "Don't be. That's the way my life has been going lately. Find a room and get yourself a good night's sleep."

Meg pushed her face against the bars and whispered, "Let me bust you out of here."

"No! I won't have it. I won't let you break the law for my sake."

"You can't stay here," Meg argued. "It's not fit for human occupancy."

"I'll manage." He reached through the bars and caressed her cheek. His touch was so tender Meg wanted to cry. Was there no justice? Would she and Jess ever find the peace and happiness they deserved? "Go on, sweetheart. Come back tomorrow, after you're rested."

Unable to speak past the lump in her throat, Meg nodded mutely. As she turned away, Durant stopped her and returned her gun. "I'll be back tomorrow, Sheriff," she called over her shoulder. "Don't forget to feed Jess."

Meg found a room at Aggie's boarding-house. The room was small but neat and clean, and dinner and breakfast were included in the price. At least she didn't have to worry about money, Meg thought. She still carried the better part of the five-hundred-dollar reward she'd left Cheyenne with.

Aggie was a dear soul, though noisy beyond bearing. She clucked her tongue at Meg's masculine attire and made way too much of her still prominent bruises. Meg ended up telling her in a few terse words what had happened to her, leaving out the part about Jess being arrested.

A small, rotund woman of middle years with bright, inquisitive eyes, Aggie sent Meg a somewhat doubtful look. "I suspect there's more to it than that, my dear, but I'm glad things turned out well. You're obviously a strong woman to have suffered all you have and come away with your spirits intact. Most women would fall into a decline after being manhandled by outlaws. And you're a bounty hunter! My, my, will wonders never cease. Where is that nice man who saved you?"

"That's another story for another time," Meg said tiredly.

"Of course. How unfeeling of me to question you when you're obviously exhausted. You have time for a nap. Dinner is at eight, and it might be a good idea for you to change into a dress."

Aggie bustled out of the room, reminding Meg of a small whirlwind. Once alone, Meg's thoughts returned to Jess and his terrible circumstances. Why wouldn't Jess let her bust him out of jail? He knew she was capable. The whole situation was disheartening.

Meg was at the jailhouse bright and early the following morning. Jess was eating his breakfast, which looked fairly appetizing. It appeared that Sheriff Durant had kept his word about feeding Jess well. But Jess didn't look at all chipper. He wore a day's growth of beard and his clothing was rumpled from having slept in it.

"You don't have to stick around," Jess said when he greeted Meg at the barred door. "Go back to Cheyenne. I'm sure there's a stage coming through in a day or so."

"I'm not going anywhere without you, Jess Gentry!" Meg said stoutly. "When will you realize I love you, that I'll do anything to help you?"

"There's nothing you can do, sweetheart. Love isn't going to save me. The sooner I reach Dodge, the sooner I can try to convince the law that my brothers and I are innocent."

Meg could tell by the look in Jess's eyes that he didn't believe he'd be cleared of the charges any more than she did.

Meg's reply was forestalled when Sheriff

Durant came up to them. "I'm off to the telegraph office to try to send my telegram to Dodge again."

"Can I stay here and talk to Jess?" Meg asked.

"I reckon it's all right," Durant replied. "Don't get any ideas in your head while I'm gone. The guns and keys are locked in my drawer. And I'll take your gun, if you don't mind."

Meg minded, but she handed her gun over without complaint. She wasn't going to do anything to jeopardize her time with Jess.

They spoke of inconsequential things at first; then Jess made his wishes known concerning her future.

"If I'm convicted and sent off to prison, I want you to return to Zach. He'll take care of you. I don't know how long I'll be put away, but I won't ask you to wait for me. You're young and vital and shouldn't pine for a man who might not return to you for years. Even if Mr. Wingate tells the truth and the charges are dropped, I may be forced to marry his daughter."

"Damn you, Jess Gentry! Don't talk like that. How can you even think of giving up? Mr. Wingate has to listen to reason. I'll make him," she said determinedly.

He reached through the bars and stroked her cheek. "I don't deserve you, Meg. Yet all I can think about is returning to Cheyenne with you at my side and using my skills to heal folks. I want to raise a family with you. Is that asking too much?"

Meg sent him a watery smile. "No, that's not asking too much. It's exactly what I want, too."

He searched her face. "I haven't been as careful as I should have with you, love. Are you . . . you're not . . . dammit, how can I put this? Are you carrying my child?"

Meg pressed a hand to her stomach. It was indeed possible, but since Jess appeared upset by the prospect of a child, she shook her head. "I don't think so."

Meg realized she had given the right answer when the breath left his chest in a loud whoosh.

"I know I said I wanted children with you, but now isn't the right time. When this is behind us, we'll get married and start our family."

Meg gave him a shaky smile. Would that day ever arrive? she wondered sadly. Even if she was carrying Jess's child and he wasn't around to help raise it, she'd cherish it with all her heart.

Sheriff Durant returned, his expression thoughtful.

"Did you get through to Dodge?" Meg asked anxiously.

"No, and it doesn't look like it's going to happen any time soon. Lines are down all over the area. It's gonna take weeks to fix them."

"Weeks!" Meg all but shouted. "You can't keep Jess here for weeks."

"I've been thinking on that," Durant admitted. "The stage is due tomorrow. I'm going to put Gentry on the stage and escort him to Dodge myself."

"Not without me," Meg declared. "I'm going to be on the stage, too."

Durant shrugged. "Suit yourself."

"Meg, I beg you. Return to Cheyenne," Jess pleaded.

"No," Meg retorted, hands on hips. "You're not getting rid of me that easy, Jess Gentry. I intend to sell the horses and be on the stage when it pulls out tomorrow."

Jess didn't doubt it for a minute. How many times in the past weeks had Meg endangered herself for his sake? How often had she expressed her wish to help him, disregarding the high cost to her own safety? Too many times to count.

Soon, Jess thought. Soon he would be in Dodge again, where everything started. Unfortunately, he didn't know how it would end, and that uncertainty was eroding his confidence. All he knew was that he would do whatever it took to make Mr. Wingate repudiate his lie about the bank robbery. No sacrifice was too great for his family. For freedom.

The following day, Jess was led from the jailhouse in shackles. Sheriff Durant marched behind him, his hand resting on his gun butt in case Jess should make a break for it. Meg followed in their wake, carrying Jess's medical bag. Only one other passenger boarded the stage, an elderly gentleman traveling to Dodge to see his first grandchild. Jess hoped this stage wouldn't suffer the same fate that had befallen the last one he and Meg had boarded.

And he hoped Meg didn't take it into her head to try anything foolish.

Chapter Eighteen

Dodge City stretched before him. Jess gazed out the window at the familiar dusty rooftops poking up from the flat, parched ground and felt no nostalgia for the town he'd once called home. The town hadn't changed much during the time he'd been away. He remembered coming back from the war and proudly hanging up his shingle, and how painful it had been when the townspeople had shunned him in favor of a drunken sawbones who loved the bottle more than he did his patients.

Jess slanted a surreptitious glance at Meg and saw that she was watching him. She shouldn't be here, he thought. Hadn't she suffered enough humiliation on his account? He sighed. Knowing Meg, she'd stick around until there was no longer a reason for her to do so. God, he loved her!

The stage rumbled down the busy main street and ground to a halt before the Wells Fargo office to discharge its passengers. Jess stepped down and stretched. The ride had been long and tedious, necessitating one overnight stop. Unfortunately, he'd had scant opportunity to speak privately with Meg, for Sheriff Durant had kept them separated.

"Where's the sheriff's office?" Durant asked as he joined Jess.

"Across the street," Jess said, identifying the building with a nod.

"Let's go," Durant said, prodding Jess forward.

Jess stepped into the busy street, dodging wagons and horses. Durant followed close behind him. A glance over his shoulder revealed that Meg was trudging along behind them, her face grim with purpose.

Jess feared she was even now hatching some grand scheme to free him. He shot her a warning glance, and was rewarded with a smile that didn't bode at all well for anyone who tried to interfere with her plans.

"You first," Durant said, motioning Jess through the door.

Jess stepped into the sheriff's office. Durant was close on his heels, followed by Meg. A man Jess had never seen before sat behind the desk. Immediately he leaped to his feet.

"Are you Sheriff Diller?" Durant asked.

"No, sir, I'm Deputy Wayland. Can I help you?"

"You're new, aren't you?" Jess asked.

"I moved to town two weeks ago from Topeka and applied for this job when I learned that Sheriff Diller was looking for a second deputy to help keep the peace. I got the position because I had experience in the field."

"Where can I find the sheriff, Deputy?" Durant asked. "I've brought a prisoner for him to deal with. His name is Jess Gentry. He's wanted for bank robbery. I reckon you've heard of him."

"Can't say as I have," Wayland said. "Sheriff Diller isn't available right now. Don't know when he'll return." Wayland's curious gaze settled first on Jess, then on Meg. "I reckon I can take charge of your prisoner, Sheriff Durant."

"I'd appreciate it," Durant replied.

"What about the woman?" Wayland asked. "Is she wanted, too?"

"No. She's Gentry's woman. Insisted on tagging along and I couldn't stop her. Is there an empty cell available?"

"Yeah, follow me."

Wayland ushered them through a door into an area holding several cells. Meg was right behind them. Wayland removed a set of keys from his belt and opened the door of an unoccupied cell. Jess stepped inside without being asked. He held out his arms, and Durant removed his shackles.

"Good luck to you, Gentry," Durant said as the cell door closed in Jess's face. He turned to Wayland. "I'd like to start back right away. Can you direct me to the livery?

I'd like to rent a horse."

"Sure thing," Wayland said.

He gave Durant directions, then started to follow him out the door. Suddenly he remembered Meg, and he spun around, scowling at her.

"You'll have to leave, ma'am."

Meg's mutinous expression told him exactly what she thought of that idea. "I'm not going anywhere. Jess doesn't belong in jail. The bank robbery was a trumped-up charge."

"I don't know about that, ma'am. I can't recall hearing the sheriff mention anyone named Jess Gentry, but that don't mean he's not a dangerous outlaw."

"That's not true!" Meg protested.

"Give it up, Meg," Jess urged. "There's nothing you can do. I chose to return to Dodge — maybe not in handcuffs, but it was still my choice."

Meg's chin firmed. "I'm not going to let this happen, Jess. I'm going to pay a call on Mr. Wingate. If he's any kind of man, he'll listen to reason and clear you and your brothers."

"Wait until the sheriff returns before you go rocking the boat."

"Your man makes sense, ma'am," Wayland said. "You can't stay here; it's not allowed. Come along quietly and I'll let you visit the prisoner tomorrow."

"Go on, Meg. There's nothing you can do

here," Jess said.

Meg didn't want to leave, but it was obvious Deputy Wayland wasn't going to let her remain.

"Very well," Meg agreed with marked reluctance, "but I'll be back tomorrow."

She communicated a silent good-bye to Jess and followed Wayland out the door. The first order of business was to find a room. Then she'd consider her options.

A short time later, Meg checked into the Dodge House, the best hotel in town. She was delighted to learn the hotel had a bathing room and made use of it soon after she arrived. Clean and fresh again, and feeling more like herself after days on the road, Meg ordered dinner sent to her room. She paced until it came, pondering Jess's dilemma and the various ways in which she could help him.

During her solitary meal, Meg's thoughts led her to one conclusion. First thing tomorrow morning she would call upon Mr. Wingate and plead with him to admit that he'd fabricated the robbery charges. Other than that, there was little she could do except break Jess out of jail, and he was adamantly opposed to that.

Though the food was surprisingly good for jail fare, Jess picked at his dinner, his mind in a turmoil. Deep down in his bones he knew he was going to prison for a long, long time. A pompous man like Wingate would never admit he'd lied. He might insist that Jess marry his daughter, but Jess had recently decided that he couldn't do that, not when he loved Meg.

At first Jess had considered marrying Delia in order to save himself from prison, but that option no longer appealed to him. Nor did asking Meg to wait for him until he'd served out his prison term. It wouldn't be fair to her. He loved her too much to allow her to waste the best years of her life on a jailbird. Yet the thought of Meg giving herself to another man was like a kick in the gut.

Deputy Wayland returned for Jess's dinner tray, saw that Jess had eaten little, and asked, "Not hungry, Gentry?"

"You could say that," Jess muttered. "The prospect of a long prison term kinda takes away a man's appetite. Especially when he's innocent."

"I'm sure Sheriff Diller will straighten everything out when he returns. For now, however, there's little I can do but keep you behind bars."

Suddenly a thought occurred to Jess. It might not work but it certainly was worth pursuing. "Deputy, do you know Mr. Wingate from the bank?"

"Everyone knows Mr. Wingate. He's a mighty important person around here."

"It's imperative that I speak with him. Immediately. Can you send someone to fetch him?"

"If you robbed his bank, what makes you think he'll want to talk to you?"

"I don't know. But my future is at stake, and I'm willing to take a chance. Could you just ask him to come down here? What can it hurt?"

"Nothing, I reckon," Wayland said, sounding not at all convinced. "Except I'd hate to interrupt an important man like Wingate at his supper."

Jess gave it one last shot. "I'm not a bank robber, Deputy. I'm a doctor."

Wayland stared at Jess a long time. "You sure don't look or act like any bank robber I ever saw," he admitted. "All right, I'll fetch Wingate here myself. But there's nothing I can do if he refuses to come."

"I know, and I thank you for listening to me. I'd appreciate anything you can do to convince Wingate to see me."

Jess plopped down on the hard cot after Wayland left. He had no idea why he'd insisted on seeing Wingate when he was unlikely to change the banker's mind about the robbery. But he couldn't just sit there and do nothing.

Steeped in misery, Jess thought of Meg, the only bright spot in his otherwise dismal life. The fact that Meg loved and believed in him demanded that he restore his name and reputation. He wanted to settle down with Meg, raise their children, and use his medical skills to help people. Was that asking too much?

Minutes lengthened into a half hour. Just when Jess gave up all hope of challenging Wingate face to face, the door opened. His spirits fell when he saw Wayland enter alone; then hope was restored when Wingate appeared in the doorway. Wayland immediately unlocked the cell door and swung it open.

"You're free to go, Gentry. Mr. Wingate will explain everything to you. If the sheriff was here, this wouldn't have happened. I hope you understand that I was simply doing my duty."

Jess took a tentative step beyond the cell door and stopped, as if fearing this was all a hoax, that he'd be thrust back into the tiny cell if he tried to leave.

"It's all right, Gentry," Wingate said, motioning him forward. "I explained everything to the deputy. There was no bank robbery. I lied. Sheriff Diller is aware of the whole fiasco and how it came about."

Still unable to believe he was a free man, Jess followed Wingate from the cell area into the sheriff's office. He didn't let himself hope his release was real until Wayland unlocked the desk drawer and handed him his gun belt and guns.

"I really am a free man?" Jess asked skeptically. "What about my brothers?"

"This needs to be discussed in private," Wingate said. "Come to my house and I'll explain everything over a snifter of brandy."

Jess strapped on his guns and followed Wingate out into the cool night air. What he really wanted was to find Meg and tell her his good news, but he needed to hear Wingate's explanation before he could put this matter behind him. And he needed to know that his brothers were no longer wanted men.

Wingate's home was only a short walk away. The banker ushered him inside and led him to a room Jess assumed was a study. Wingate said nothing as he poured brandy for both of them and asked Jess to have a seat. Jess sat down in a comfortable leather chair, but he was far from relaxed. Wingate handed him a brandy and took a chair behind the desk.

Jess sipped appreciatively, letting the smooth liquid slowly roll down his throat. "Good stuff," he said. "Now about that explanation?"

"Have you seen your brother Rafe recently?" Wingate asked.

"Not since we left Dodge with the posse breathing down our necks."

"Then you don't know he turned up in Dodge a little while ago with his wife. That wife of his is some woman."

Surprised, Jess splashed brandy on his lap. "Rafe is married?"

"That's right, and she's quite a woman. Her name is Angela. She's a missionary or evangelist of some kind."

Jess gave a hoot of laughter. "Rafe married a woman with a religious calling? That's rich. Are you sure you're talking about my brother Rafe Gentry?"

"Very sure. Rafe was in jail here awaiting trial. Mrs. Gentry pleaded with me to tell the truth about the bank robbery." He gave Jess a sheepish look. "I refused, of course. But she wouldn't give up and finally enlisted the help of my daughter."

Delia had helped Rafe's wife clear up this travesty of justice?

Wingate took a long sip of brandy. "Delia didn't know I'd tried to blackmail you and your brothers into marrying her. She set me straight about her feelings on the subject. By the way, Delia is married now, to the father of her child."

"So you finally admitted the truth," Jess said bitterly. "Had you done that from the beginning, none of this would have happened. Does Sam know?"

"Not to my knowledge. Do you know where he can be reached?"

"No, and I'm sure Rafe doesn't either. What about our farm?"

"I'm sorry. The bank repossessed it, and I

gave it to Delia and her husband as a wedding gift. They love the farm and are restoring it to its former productiveness. There's no way I can return it to your family."

"What did Rafe have to say about that?"

"He didn't seem troubled over it. He and his wife own a gold mine near Canyon City, Colorado, where they intend to settle down."

"What about those Wanted posters in circulation?" Jess asked.

"Sheriff Diller took care of everything. He saw to it that they were removed from circulation, but he couldn't guarantee one-hundred-percent success. He gave Rafe a document absolving him of the crime. He'll probably do the same for you."

"If you hadn't lied, we wouldn't have been pursued by the law," Jess charged angrily. "Do you have any idea what it feels like to be a wanted man? All I wanted to do after the war was practice medicine and settle down. Because of you, I was able to do neither of those things."

"I'm not proud of what I did, but you'll better understand my motives when you're a father. The thought of Delia having a baby out of wedlock completely unstrung me."

"I can't say I'll ever forgive you, but perhaps I'll understand when I have a child of my own. At least I know Rafe is safe. Now all I have to worry about is Sam. Lord knows what trouble he's found."

"How can I make it up to you?" Wingate asked. "Do you need money or —"

Jess's lips flattened. "I don't want a damn thing from you. I left a thriving practice in Cheyenne, and I intend to return to it as soon as possible. I also have a woman I love beyond all reason. We'll be wed soon."

"Then I wish you good luck," Wingate said, holding out his hand.

Jess ignored Wingate's extended hand. "Good night, Wingate. I'm going to find my fiancée now."

"I'm sorry," Wingate repeated as he saw Jess out the door. "I nearly lost my wife and daughter because of my pride and that fabricated bank robbery. If Rafe hadn't returned to Dodge to clear his name, I might have let the lie continue."

Jess didn't respond. He was anxious to get away from Wingate. The door closed behind him and he strode out the front gate. Then he stopped, suddenly aware that he had no idea where to look for Meg. Obviously she had gotten herself a room for the night, but where? Dodge sported several boardinghouses and hotels.

Jess knew Meg wasn't hurting for money, so he figured she'd probably head for a decent hotel instead of one of the run-down boardinghouses. Using his prior knowledge of Dodge City, Jess decided to try the best hotel first and work his way down. The Dodge

House was at the top of his list.

Jess's steps were light and springy as he continued down the street. He felt as if an immense load had been lifted from his shoulders, and he supposed Rafe had felt the same. If only he knew where to find Sam. Thank God they had all agreed to meet in Denver in a few months, so they could share their experiences and assure one another of their survival.

The lobby of the Dodge House was quiet this time of the evening. Jess walked up to the desk. The haughty clerk took one look at his rumpled clothing and bristly chin and sniffed disdainfully.

"This is a high-class hotel. Our rooms aren't cheap. If you like, I can direct you to a more modestly priced establishment."

"That won't be necessary," Jess said, hanging on to his temper by a slim thread. "Did a young woman named Meg Lincoln check in here today?"

The clerk looked down his nose at Jess. "I'm sorry, we don't give out information about our guests."

"Miss Lincoln is my fiancée. I was to meet her here," Jess returned shortly.

"I'm not allowed —"

At the end of his patience, Jess grasped the clerk's lapels and pulled him over the counter until they were nose to nose. "I'm asking politely," he all but snarled. "Tell me if a Miss

Lincoln is registered here or you won't like the consequences."

The clerk's eyes widened and he swallowed, his Adam's apple moving convulsively as his arms flailed helplessly at his sides. Suddenly he spotted someone behind Jess and made a squawking sound that could have been a plea.

"What's going on here?"

Slowly Jess let the clerk slip from his grasp, then whirled to identify the intruder.

"This man is demented," the clerk complained in a voice two octaves higher than normal. "He belongs in jail, Deputy."

"Howdy, Dr. Gentry," Deputy Wayland said, touching the brim of his hat. "I was just making my rounds and happened to look in. What's the problem?"

"No problem," Jess said through clenched teeth. "When I ask a civil question, I expect a civil answer."

"I can't give out information about our guests," the clerk insisted.

"I was merely inquiring about my fiancée," Jess retorted. "She may have checked in here."

"And I said —"

"Tell Dr. Gentry what he wants to know," Wayland ordered. "I can see no harm in that."

"You know this man?" the clerk inquired, obviously surprised.

"I'm surprised *you* don't," Wayland said. "His name is Jess Gentry, and he's a doctor. He used to live in these parts."

"Gentry. Gentry," the clerk repeated. "You don't mean one of the outlaw Gentrys, do you?"

"That was all a mistake," Wayland explained. "Just tell Gentry if his woman is a guest in your hotel."

Though obviously reluctant, the clerk gave Jess what he was looking for. "A Miss Lincoln checked in here a few hours ago. She's in room 225, second floor, third door on the left."

"Much obliged," Jess muttered. "You, too, Deputy. I'm glad you happened by."

"No problem, Gentry. From what I gather, the law hasn't been good to you and your brothers. Anything I can do to help is little enough for what your family has gone through." He tipped his hat. "Good night and good luck."

Jess spared the clerk a triumphant look as he strode resolutely toward the staircase. In a few minutes he'd be with Meg, and all would be right with his world again.

Meg perched on the edge of the bed, tired of pacing but unable to sleep. She'd rehearsed at least a dozen times what she intended to say to Mr. Wingate when she called on him in the morning. Her single nagging fear was that her words would fail to move the conscienceless banker.

Weary and distraught, Meg slipped into bed, adjusted her shift, and pulled the blanket over her. Though the bed was the most comfortable she'd occupied in days, she felt a hollowness, a bone-deep loneliness that only Jess could assuage. Would they ever be together again? she wondered dismally. Would they ever have that home and those children Jess longed for?

Her hand splayed protectively over her stomach. It was entirely possible that she already carried Jess's child. The signs were all there, if she was reading them correctly. But she couldn't tell Jess. Not yet, anyway. He had enough problems to deal with without her adding to them.

Meg closed her eyes and hunkered down into the blankets, willing sleep to come. She was just starting to doze when she heard someone rapping on the door. Her eyes blinked open and she jerked upright, staring at the door with trepidation. Who would be calling on her at this time of night?

Gingerly Meg rose, turned up the lamp, and approached the door. "Who is it?" she called through the panel.

"Meg, open up. It's me — Jess."

"Jess! No, it can't be."

"I'm not a ghost, sweetheart. Open the door."

With a cry of gladness, Meg turned the key and flung open the door. Seconds later she was in Jess's arms, absorbing his strength, his warmth, savoring the closeness she'd despaired of ever having again.

"What happened? Did you break out of jail? We can leave as soon as I get dressed. We'll have to steal horses. Do you have a destination in mind?"

She heard Jess chuckle, and she frowned. She saw no reason for levity at a time like this.

"Whoa, love, there's no reason for us to steal horses or skip out of town in the dead of night."

"No reason! Are you loco?" Meg scolded. "How did you break out of jail?"

"I didn't. My brothers and I are free men, love. I can go where I please and no one will stop me."

The breath left Meg's lungs in a great rush of air. "You're free? I don't understand."

"I'll explain everything, but first let me close the door. I want to see you."

Meg didn't want to let him go for fear he'd disappear in a wisp of smoke, but she had no choice when he gently disengaged himself from her arms and firmly closed the door. He turned and stared at her. She heard Jess suck in his breath, suddenly aware that the light behind her rendered her shift transparent, and that Jess was staring at her body through the thin material.

"God, you're beautiful," he said reverently. "You're mine. All mine. Now that I'm free, I want so much, Meg. You, children, a home, a practice . . . I fear I'm asking too much."

"No, you're not," Meg assured him. Tears gathered in the corners of her eyes and she dashed them away. "I want those things, too. And we're going to have them," she said fiercely. "Nothing will stop us now. Tell me what happened."

Jess eased her down on the bed and sat beside her. Then he proceeded to tell her how Mr. Wingate came to the jailhouse and cleared him and his brothers of all charges.

"Wingate said that Rafe's new wife convinced him to tell the truth."

"Rafe is married?" Meg said. "How wonderful for him."

"I can't believe it. He married an evangelist," Jess explained. "Knowing Rafe, it's hard to imagine, but no one knows where he or she will find love. I'll find out the details when we meet in Denver in a few months. I just wish Sam knew he was no longer wanted by the law. It could change the course of his life."

Meg sat in silent contemplation. Would Jess want to settle in Dodge City now that he was a free man? she wondered. She knew he and his brothers owned a farm in the vicinity.

Perhaps he had deep feelings for the family property.

"What now, Jess? Where do we go from here?"

"Home," Jess said, grinning.

"Are you referring to your family farm?"

"The farm is gone, love. Sold to Wingate for back taxes. He gave it to his daughter for a wedding gift. From what I gather, Delia and her husband are making a go of it. That's more than my brothers and I were able to do. None of us are farmers at heart. Home is Cheyenne, where I have my practice and you have Zach."

"I was hoping you'd say that," Meg sighed happily.

"I'd never separate you from the man you consider your father. I'm going to be blunt, love. Zach isn't a well man. He should enjoy whatever time God grants him."

"My thoughts exactly. When can we leave?"

"We have to wait for the sheriff to return. He gave Rafe a document declaring him innocent of any crime, and I want the same thing."

"I love you so much, Jess Gentry," Meg whispered, snuggling against him. "Are we through talking now?" Her eyes sparkled mischievously. " 'Cause if we are, I can think of other things we can do."

"The idea of making love to you is the one thing that kept me sane while I was behind

410

bars," Jess said hoarsely. "But I need to wash the stench of jail from my body before I climb into bed with you."

"There's a bathing room down the hall. It should be empty this time of night. Hurry, love. I'll wait for you."

Jess pulled her against him, his kiss ripe with promise as he seized her mouth, stealing the breath from her. When he would have broken off the kiss, Meg clung to him, reluctant to let him go. She never wanted to let go of him again.

"I'll be back," Jess murmured against her lips.

Then he was gone, gently closing the door behind him. Meg slid into bed, anxiously awaiting Jess's return. It couldn't be soon enough for her. Despite her efforts to stay awake, Meg succumbed to the drugging pull of sleep.

Jess returned from the bathing room and quietly let himself into the room. He locked the door and turned toward the bed. A sliver of light from the lamp fell across Meg's face. A jolt of disappointment seared through him when he saw that she was sleeping. Sighing regretfully, he shed his clothing and climbed into bed beside her. He took her into his arms and cuddled her close. Scant hours ago he'd feared he would never experience the pure heaven of holding Meg in his arms again, and if all he could do tonight was hold her, it would be enough for him.

His body had other ideas.

His hand moved of its own volition to her breast. He felt the rapid beating of her heart and the warmth of her body pressing against him and became instantly erect. He groaned when he felt her body move against him and her nipple tauten against his palm. He stroked the tip, and a tiny sigh slipped from Meg's throat. The sound made the blood pound in his temples and throb low in his groin. He wanted her naked, wanted her skin against his. With slow deliberation he worked her shift up her legs and over her breasts. When he tried to pull it over her head, she opened her eyes and stared at him.

"Jess . . . I must have fallen asleep."

"I wasn't going to awaken you, love, but I couldn't help myself."

Her fingers slid into the hair at the nape of his neck. His mouth came down to meet hers, and a tiny whimper left her lips as he deepened the kiss, lashing the fragrant inside of her mouth with his tongue, savoring the taste and scent of her.

When he tugged at the shift, Meg eagerly helped him remove it. "Just the way I want you," Jess moaned. "Naked."

He kissed the side of her neck, tasted her small, shell-like ear, and took her mouth again, cupping her bottom and pulling her against his arousal. Then he nudged her legs apart and shifted his weight between them.

"Can you take me now, sweetheart? I'm sorry, I can't seem to restrain myself. Next time we'll take it slower."

Meg didn't want it slow. She was as desperate for him as he was for her, and more than ready to take him. Heat pooled between her legs, dampening her thighs with moisture.

"I'm ready," she gasped. "Please. Now."

"Thank God," Jess whispered fervently.

She felt him prodding her body's opening and pulled him to her, frantically grasping his forearms as he pushed all the way in until he filled her. She gasped and arched up, sensations spearing through her. She clamped down hard, feeling him hot and hard, buried to the hilt inside her.

Jess kissed her mouth as he began to move upon her; kissed her nipples, laved them and sucked them into his mouth as he pistoned his hips against hers. His hands moved over her body, sliding down the indentations of her spine, gliding over her hips. Meg arched upward, heat sweeping through her as unspeakable ecstasy flared and ignited.

She could feel his hardness, the hot, thick, rigid length of him, the pulsing fullness, and then pleasure, sweet and fierce, shot through her. She cried out, trembling, shuddering. His hands gripped her hips and he thrust deeper and deeper, faster and faster. It was primitive, decadent, deliciously carnal. It was more than Meg could bear as she shattered into a million pieces.

On the outer edges of her awareness, she saw Jess stiffen, heard him call out her name, and felt him collapse against her as he found the completion he sought.

Jess rested his head against hers for a moment, then lifted himself off her. His harsh breathing matched hers as they slowly regained their wits.

"That was too quick," Jess complained. "The next time we'll take it slower. I want to taste you all over, pleasure you until we're both too exhausted to move."

"And I, you," Meg whispered happily. "But perhaps you should rest first."

He laughed, wrapping an arm around her waist and dragging her atop him. "We can rest when we're old. Tonight is for us."

Chapter Nineteen

The next day, Jess and Meg retrieved their bags from the station master and boarded the stage to Cheyenne. Sheriff Diller had returned to Dodge and provided Jess with a document stating that the Gentry brothers were not outlaws, never had been, and were not wanted by the law. Diller even asked Jess to stay, citing the fact that the town needed a good doctor and assuring Jess that this time his efforts to practice medicine would not go unappreciated.

But Jess had had enough of Dodge City to last a lifetime. He politely thanked the sheriff and booked passage on the next stage to Cheyenne. Diller personally saw Jess and Meg off and wished them well.

Meg was relieved that Jess held no fondness for Dodge City. She was anxious to return to Cheyenne and check on Zach's health. She assumed Mary Dowling was taking good care of Zach, but she was still worried.

"You're awfully quiet," Jess said as he settled back against the hard seat. "Is there something you want to tell me?"

Meg frowned. She had no idea what he was talking about. Unless . . . no, how could he know?

"I was just thinking about Zach," Meg hedged. "Do you think he and Widow Dowling are married yet?"

"It's possible. I know if I were Zach I wouldn't let any grass grow under my feet."

Meg mulled over Jess's words. He hadn't mentioned a word about marrying her since the night he was released from jail. Was it just an oversight? Or had he changed his mind? Perhaps now that he was a free man he'd had second thoughts about burdening himself with a wife and family.

"I've been thinking," Jess said into the waiting silence. "Perhaps I should move my office out of the house. If my practice continues to thrive, I'll be needing more space. When we left town, I noticed a FOR RENT sign above the barbershop. What do you think about it?"

"I think you're going to have more patients than you can handle," Meg allowed. "Cheyenne is growing by leaps and bounds. Giving yourself more space for your practice sounds like a good idea."

"Then it's settled, that's what I'll do. The extra space in the house will come in handy for my wife and family."

"Your wife? You mean . . . ?"

Jess sent her a dazzling smile. "Did you think I'd changed my mind about marrying you? I'm not letting you get away from me, Meg."

Meg returned his grin. "That's all I needed to hear." She sighed happily and snuggled against him.

Suddenly a thought occurred to Meg, one that burst the bubble of her happiness. "The townspeople don't approve of me. What if they avoid you and ignore your practice because of me?"

"Let me worry about that," Jess replied. "There are other towns needing doctors, but I truly hope moving elsewhere won't be necessary."

Meg's hand stole to her stomach. She debated telling Jess her suspicions about her condition, but they weren't alone in the stagecoach. Another time, she thought, smiling inwardly, although keeping the news to herself was nearly killing her.

Three days and two uncomfortable nights later, they reached Cheyenne. The day was clear and bright, but with a definite nip in the air, heralding the return of fall and cooler temperatures. Jess arranged to have their bags delivered, then walked the short distance home.

They met many of Jess's former patients and friends on the street, and they greeted him with enthusiasm. Meg received only stares and disapproving looks. The women all but ignored her while effusively greeting Jess and inquiring about his office hours. The men gave Meg speculative glances and knowing looks, as if assessing her relationship to Jess.

This isn't going to work, Meg told herself. She was never going to be accepted into Jess's world. She'd always be that brazen women who'd taken up a shameful profession, one who used her wiles to snag the most eligible bachelor in town. She'd be a hindrance to Jess, and she loved him too much to do that.

"Pay them no heed," Jess said, obviously aware of the attention he was attracting, and of the way Meg was being ignored. "They'll soon grow accustomed to seeing us together. Everything will change once we're married."

"I wish I could believe that," Meg sighed.

"Dr. Gentry! You're back!" a feminine voice called from behind them. "You disappeared so suddenly everyone feared you'd never return. Do wait up so I can welcome you back properly."

Meg spun around, groaning in dismay when she saw Polly Gallagher hurrying up to join them.

"Don't take anything she says to heart," Jess hissed as they waited impatiently for her to reach them.

"Oh, dear me," Polly said, panting to catch her breath. "Are you back for good, Doctor?"

"I'm here to stay, Miss Gallagher," Jess returned pleasantly.

"Then let me be the first to extend an invitation to you. Please come to dinner tonight. I'm sure the whole family will want to welcome you home."

Jess slanted a quick glance at Meg before answering. "I'd be happy to accept, Miss Gallagher —"

"Please call me Polly," Polly simpered. "Shall we say seven o'clock?"

Jess's reply startled Meg. Had he forgotten her already?

"May I finish what I started to say?" Jess asked.

"Of course," Polly said, slanting Meg a superior look.

"My fiancée and I would be most happy to dine with you and your family tonight."

Polly glared at Meg. "Your . . . fiancée? Surely you don't mean . . ."

Jess placed an arm around Meg's shoulders and pulled her against him. "I'm referring to Meg. You and Miss Lincoln are acquainted, aren't you?"

"Barely," Polly sniffed.

"About that invitation," Jess prodded. "Miss Lincoln *is* welcome, isn't she?"

"Jess," Meg put in, "I don't want to go where I'm not wanted."

"I'm sure Miss . . . er . . . Polly meant to include you, Meg. That *is* correct, isn't it, Polly?"

"Of . . . of course," Polly said, stumbling over the words.

Meg nearly laughed aloud at Polly's lack of aplomb. Obviously Polly had set her cap for Jess.

"When is the wedding?" Polly asked, staring daggers at Meg.

"As soon as it can be arranged," Jess replied, smiling at Meg. "Good day, Polly. We'll see you tonight. Thanks for the invitation."

"Why did you accept?" Meg demanded once Polly had stalked off. "Are you trying to shove me down the throats of your friends?"

"I want the citizens of Cheyenne to know you the way I do. Once they do, they'll love you, too. You're a special woman, Meg Lincoln, and I can't wait to make you my wife."

"You're the only one in this town who thinks so," Meg said morosely. Her dismal thoughts continued until they reached Jess's house.

"We're home," Jess said, opening the front gate to let Meg pass through. "Soon as we settle in, we'll rent horses from the livery and ride out to see Zach."

The house was just as they had left it. They carried their bags upstairs, intending to unpack. But somewhere along the way their priorities changed, and they fell into one another's arms. They made love as if they were starved for one another, and by the time they were sated, it was too late to go anywhere.

"A bath would be wonderful," Meg said.

"I agree," Jess replied.

He carried the brass tub into the kitchen and heated water for their baths. After a good soak and some erotic play in the tub, they dressed and left for their dinner at the Gallaghers.

Polly opened the door, blatantly ignoring Meg as she greeted Jess, and invited them inside. The rest of the evening wasn't as uncomfortable as Meg had expected, except perhaps for Polly's probing questions into her past. But Jess soon put stop to unwarranted comments by making it perfectly clear they were unacceptable, and announcing that he and Meg were to be married within days. The Gallaghers seemed to take the news with equanimity, which boded well for Meg as the future Mrs. Gentry. All things considered, Meg thought the evening could have been worse.

It was even better after they returned home and Jess made love to her again.

Meg was up the following morning before Jess. She dressed and went to the store to buy food for the larder, which was completely bare. She carried home what was needed to prepare breakfast and arranged for the rest to be delivered. Then she prepared a hearty breakfast for her and Jess.

"Smells good," Jess said as he entered the kitchen and sniffed appreciatively.

"Flapjacks, eggs, and bacon," Meg said, proud of her cooking skills. "And coffee. I made a trip to the store this morning. Sit down. Everything's ready."

"So that's where you were when I woke and found you missing," Jess said around a mouthful of eggs. "For a moment . . . never mind."

"You thought I'd left," Meg teased.

"That thought did occur to me."

"You're not going to get rid of me that easy, Jess Gentry. Eat up. I'm anxious to see Zach."

An hour later they walked hand in hand to the livery, where they spied a likely gelding and mare and promptly bought them, along with saddles and tack.

They rode in silence, enjoying the fine day and each other, until the familiar house was within sight. Then Meg spurred her mare and galloped ahead.

Zach must have heard them approaching, for he stepped out of the barn and shielded his eyes against the sunlight. Meg knew the moment he recognized her, for he gave a whoop of joy and waved his arms in greeting.

Meg reached him before Jess. She slid from the saddle and ran into Zach's open arms. By the time Jess dismounted, both Meg and Zach were weeping openly.

"Praise be, you're back," Zach said, disentangling himself from Meg long enough to pump Jess's hand. "I hope this means everything went the way you wanted it to," he added meaningfully.

"The charges have been dropped," Jess explained. "The banker admitted fabricating the whole tale. My brothers and I are finally free men."

"And does your new life include Meggie?" Zach queried. "Or are you going back to Dodge to set up your practice?"

"I'm staying right here, Zach. I already have a practice in Cheyenne. And Meg has agreed to become my wife."

"That's the best news yet," Zach crowed. "We'll make it a double wedding. Me and Mary were waiting for you to return to tie the knot."

"Oh, Zach, I'm happy for you," Meg exclaimed. "You're finally going to have the life you deserve."

"And there'll be plenty of money to provide Mary with everything she needs. She won't be forced to go out and make a living for us like you did, Meggie. I don't know what I'd have done without you, honey. Half the money I inherited is yours. I already put it in the bank in your name."

"That's not necessary," Jess protested. "I can provide for Meg without your help."

"Aw, don't get hot under the collar, Doc. I ain't gonna take no for an answer. I know doctors don't get wealthy off their patients. You've probably taken more cabbages and corn for payment than hard cash." He stared pointedly at Meg's still-flat stomach. "Build yourself a big new house for all them kids you and Meggie are gonna have."

Meg said nothing as Jess placed an arm around her shoulders and gave her a hug. "We definitely want a family, don't we, love?"

"Oh, yes," Meg agreed, guarding her secret jealously.

"Good. I can't wait to bounce my grand-child on my knee. Mary's inside, Meggie. Why don't you go on in and discuss the wedding with her while I talk to Jess?"

Meg decided that was a good idea. Another minute and she'd be blurting out her secret, and she wanted Jess to know first.

"I want the wedding to be soon," Jess said after Meg entered the house.

"So do I," Zach agreed. "I know my time on earth is limited, and I want to make the most of it. How about this coming Saturday? Will you talk to Reverend Stark? He's the pastor at the Methodist church. That's all right with you, ain't it?"

"I don't care who performs the wedding as

long as it's done without delay. Meg is carrying my child," he confided.

Zach beamed. "I kinda suspected it. She's got that glow about her."

"I've been waiting for her to tell me," Jess said.

"You mean she ain't told you yet?"

Jess chuckled. "No, but I'm a doctor. Did she think I wouldn't recognize the signs? I'll let her keep her secret a while longer."

"Who you gonna invite?" Zach asked.

"The whole damn town," Jess said determinedly. "I want to make sure everyone accepts and respects my bride. I can set up my practice anywhere, but I know Meg prefers Cheyenne."

Zach gave Jess a sad-eyed look. "Meg's reputation ain't the best. The town gossips ran her name through the mud when she took up bounty hunting."

Jess's face hardened. "They'll accept her if I have anything to say about it. Let's go inside and tell the ladies to prepare for a large wedding."

"You're going to invite the whole town?" Meg asked, stunned by Jess's adamant stand on the size of the wedding.

"And I'm gonna hire the local cafe to cater the food, enough for the whole damn town," Zach added. "The wedding will be at the Methodist church, and the reception at the town hall, with fiddlers and everything. Jess is gonna make the arrangements when he returns to town."

"Zach," Mary began, "I don't think Meg is overly enthusiastic about a big wedding."

"Mary's right," Meg agreed. "I think something small —"

"No," Jess said sternly. "I want the whole town to get to know my bride. I'm sure Mary has many friends in town she'd like to invite, so why not invite the whole town? Those who don't want to come can stay home."

"The invitations," Meg protested. "We can't possibly get them all out in time."

"I'll place an announcement and open invitation in the newspapers," Jess explained. "This is only Monday. The announcement can run every day until Saturday."

"You've thought of everything, haven't you?" Meg said, not at all sure she liked the arrangements. She didn't want to be put on display before the whole town. She'd already given them enough fodder for the gossip mill.

"Zach helped," Jess said, with what Meg thought sounded like supreme satisfaction.

"It's all right with you, ain't it, Mary?" Zach asked his fiancée.

"I do have many friends in town," Mary acknowledged. "But if Meg doesn't want —"

"It's all right," Meg said. "A big wedding is fine with me. Now all I have to worry about is finding something decent to wear."

"I can help with that," Mary offered. "I have a dozen fine dresses packed away that don't fit me anymore. They're more suited to you than to my mature figure. I'm sure we can find something pretty. Come to my house tomorrow and try them on."

Meg sent Mary a grateful look. "Thank you. I'm sure I'll find something appropriate."

"Will you see Mary home for me, Jess?" Zach asked as Meg and Jess prepared to leave.

A short time later, Jess helped Meg and Mary mount their horses, then they all rode off together. Jess and Meg bade Mary goodbye at her house and continued on home.

The groceries Meg had ordered that morning had been dropped off on the front porch. Jess helped carry them inside, then left to make arrangements for the double wedding. Meg was in the midst of cooking dinner when Jess returned.

"Everything is set," he crowed excitedly. "The church is available for Saturday. The wedding will be held at ten Saturday morning, and the cafe staff agreed to provide food for the reception at the town hall. Oh, yes. The announcement and open invitation will appear in both newspapers for the next four days. And," he added, eyes glowing, "I found fiddlers to play at the reception."

Meg remained at the stove, strangely subdued. "You've thought of everything, haven't you?"

Jess came up behind her, turned her around, and drew her into his arms. "What's wrong? Any regrets?"

"About marrying you? No. About parading before people who consider me a whore? Yes."

"It will turn out fine, sweetheart, I promise. This town is going to learn to love you like I do."

"You can't shove me down their throats, Jess."

"I won't have to. Trust me."

"I've always trusted you," she whispered, turning her mouth up to his.

Groaning, Jess accepted her offering, taking her lips in a deliciously intimate kiss that made her toes curl.

"Can dinner wait?" he asked. "Suddenly I have a more pressing need."

"I'll put it in the warming oven," Meg murmured against his lips.

"Thank God."

Jess helped her put the food in the oven, then literally dragged her up the stairs to their bedroom. Clothing flew helter-skelter in their eagerness to celebrate their love. There was nothing gentle in their lovemaking as the bed became a battleground of wills. He took her swiftly once, then rolled her atop him and took her again.

Dinner was all but forgotten as they rested, arms and legs entwined, Meg's head pressed against Jess's shoulder. When Jess remained quiet an inordinate length of time, Meg asked, "Is something wrong?"

He touched her breast. "Do your breasts pain you? You cried out when I suckled them."

"I . . ." She hesitated. "They *have* been more sensitive than usual."

"When were you going to tell me, Meg?"

Meg flushed. "You know?"

His chest rumbled with laughter. "I'm a doctor, I've known for some time. The absence of menses was the first sign. Did you think I wouldn't be happy about becoming a father?"

"I didn't realize it myself until just recently. Then I thought you had too many problems to take on another responsibility. I didn't want you to worry about me. I would have told you soon, in any event. Before the wedding. Are you happy?"

His hand splayed over her stomach, his fingers caressing the place beneath her heart where his child rested. "Ecstatic. I've always wanted a home and family. I was merely waiting for the right woman to come along. I love you, Meg, and I love our child. Boy or girl, it makes no difference to me. I hope, in time, we'll have some of each. I think Zach is an anxious as I am for this child."

"He'll spoil our babe rotten."

"Let him. He deserves some happiness. He saved your life, for which I'll always be grateful."

"Are you ready for dinner? I just heard my stomach growling."

Jess laughed and rolled away from her. "Let's not keep you or that ravenous little being inside you waiting." He pulled her out of bed and helped her dress. Then they descended the stairs together.

The day of the wedding dawned cool and sunny. Meg spun before the mirror at Mary's house shortly before the ceremony, admiring the dress they had picked out together. The pale blue silk had a fitted waistline and dropped sleeves, which bared her shoulders and the upper portion of her chest without seeming vulgar or revealing. The hoops made her slim figure appear willowy and fragile, though she had never considered herself fragile. She had purchased slippers and a hat to match the dress, which set off the outfit perfectly.

Mary had chosen a violet brocade that complemented her fair coloring. The dress was slightly more demure than Meg's, befitting a woman of her maturity. Together they were a vision such as Cheyenne had rarely seen.

Jess had gotten his wish. Nearly the entire town was crowded into the church, waiting for the brides to walk down the aisle. Unbeknownst to Meg, Jess had browbeat, cajoled, and strongly urged all his acquaintances and patients to attend his wedding. He'd even threatened to refuse his services to those who absented themselves or showed disrespect to his bride.

If some of the women showed reluctance to attend, their husbands and fathers soon changed their minds. Those men were wise enough to know that Jess Gentry would eventually become a mainstay in Cheyenne society, a man in whom they could place their trust and their lives.

Meg paused in the vestibule of the church, her bouquet trembling in her hands. The church was crammed with people — the same people who in the past had crossed the street to avoid her. Mary had just started down the aisle to meet Zach, and she was to go next. Jess must have noticed her nervousness, for he smiled encouragement at her from the altar.

Mary had reached the altar. Zach stepped up to join her. Meg drew in a steadying breath and took that first step. She could feel curious eyes upon her and faltered halfway down the aisle, looking wild-eyed and frightened. She would have turned and run if Jess hadn't noticed her hesitation and sprinted up the aisle to meet her. Meg heard a buzz of voices and knew Jess had done something out of the ordinary, but he seemed not to care.

"Not getting cold feet, are you?" he whispered as he placed her arm in his and started down the aisle. Meg had no choice but to follow. Jess had broken with tradition, and the least she could do was show how much she loved him by brazening it out before the very people who despised her.

Much of the ceremony was a blur. Meg knew she said the right thing at the right time, for Jess had placed a gold ring on her finger, smiled at her, and kissed her soundly. In a daze, she let him turn her toward the congregation. Then he raised her hand and kissed it. No matter what happened in the future, Meg would always remember the cheers from the audience that followed Jess's loving gesture.

Meg recalled little of the reception, except for Mary and Zach gazing lovingly into one another's eyes. Jess was beside her constantly instilling her with the courage to greet their guests.

Meg was more than a little astonished at the number of townspeople who attended the wedding and reception, treating her as if she had never been the town pariah. Did marrying Jess make her suddenly respectable?

Food and drink flowed freely. Meg ate little

and drank nothing. The fiddlers Jess had found provided lively music, and soon dancers were forming reels and squares.

"You're not eating," Jess said.

"I'm not hungry."

Jess's eyes twinkled. "That's odd. Lately you've eaten everything in sight." He leaned closer. "Shall we go home and have our own private celebration?"

"What about Zach and Mary?"

"They've already left. Or haven't you noticed?"

"Oh, my. I haven't been very observant, have I?"

"Let's sneak out now, while the next reel is forming."

Hand and hand, they left the town hall and walked the short distance home. There was no time now for a honeymoon, but Jess had promised Meg one early next summer, when they would travel to Denver to meet his brothers. Their child would still be young, but Jess was a doctor and capable of seeing to its welfare. When they reached the house, Jess swept Meg into his arms and carried her over the threshold.

"I can't wait to show you and our baby to my brothers," Jess said as he mounted the stairs with Meg in his arms. "I'm the luckiest man alive."

Jess pushed the bedroom door open and set her on her feet.

"No, I'm the luckiest woman," Meg insisted. "I wouldn't be alive today if not for you."

They undressed one another slowly, touching and caressing as if discovering each other's bodies for the first time. They made love tenderly, gently, savoring every nuance of passion. He teased her, tormented her, his hands roaming hard and demanding over her body. Jess brought her to climax twice, once with his hands and once with his mouth, before entering her with one hard thrust. Then she came apart again beneath the potent onslaught of his unrestrained passion as he joined her still vibrating body in the ultimate of all pleasures.

When the world stopped spinning, Jess settled Meg into the curve of his body and sighed contentedly. "We're going to be happy, love. People are already beginning to accept you. The only dark cloud on the horizon is my concern for my brothers."

"You needn't worry about Rafe. From the sound of things, his life is in order. I hope we get to meet him and his wife. Do you think he'll bring her to Denver?"

"If not, we'll go down to Canyon City to visit her. It's not all that far. I hope Sam shows up. I shudder to think of the trouble he could have gotten himself into. Sam's impatient, hardheaded, and often reckless. The most difficult of the Gentry brothers. It wouldn't surprise me if Sam has stumbled into a situation that he can't get himself out of."

"Don't underestimate your brother, Jess. He's a Gentry, isn't he?"

"You're right." Jess grinned. "You do have a way of making me feel better. Now, Mrs. Gentry, go to sleep. That little one inside you needs rest."

"I love you, Jess Gentry."

"I love you, Meg Gentry. Don't ever forget it, sweetheart. Destiny brought us together. Now nothing can tear us apart."

Author's Note

Dear Reader,

I hope you enjoyed *Jess*. I believe I found a fitting heroine for him in Meg and hope you agree. The Gentry brothers are certainly unique individuals, especially Sam, as you will learn in the last book of the series. Sam has a secret not even his brothers know about.

Sam Gentry rides south to escape the posse in *The Outlaws: Sam* and finds himself in Texas. He lands in jail after throwing himself into a saloon brawl. It wasn't his intention to bring himself to the attention of the law but he couldn't let a bunch of drunks gang up on an older man.

The man turns out to be the foreman of the B&G ranch. Penniless, Sam is offered a job and quickly accepts. He is stunned when he meets the owner of the B&G. It's been six years since he'd last seen her but she is the same woman he had married during the war and abandoned after she'd betrayed him to the Yankees. For six years, Lacey believed

Sam Gentry was dead. You can imagine her shock when she comes face to face with her husband.

The story takes many twists and turns before the satisfying conclusion. Add to the mix a five-year-old boy Sam refuses to accept as his and a man determined to marry Lacey for her land. Bring in an Indian or two, and the Gentry brothers' reunion at the end, and you have a story that will keep you turning pages.

I enjoy hearing from readers. You can write to me at P.O. Box 3741, Holiday, FL 34690, or e-mail me at ConMason@aol.com. For a peek at my future releases, please visit my website at www.conniemason.com.

All My Romantic Best,
Connie Mason

The employees of Thorndike Press hope you have enjoyed this Large Print book. All our Thorndike and Wheeler Large Print titles are designed for easy reading, and all our books are made to last. Other Thorndike Press Large Print books are available at your library, through selected bookstores, or directly from us.

For information about titles, please call:

(800) 223-1244

or visit our Web site at:

www.gale.com/thorndike
www.gale.com/wheeler

To share your comments, please write:

Publisher
Thorndike Press
295 Kennedy Memorial Drive
Waterville, ME   04901